VENGEANCE
OF THE
GODS

Vengeance of the Gods
The Cursed Gods Series
Book 2

Dany Crooks

Developmental & Copy Editing: Katie Wolf

Cover: Maria Spada

Map: Ophelia Illustration

Chapter Header & Scene Break Illustration: Marta Riva

To anyone who's had to find themselves again.
This one's for you.

AUTHOR NOTE & TRIGGER WARNINGS

**Vengeance of the Gods is Book 2
in the Cursed Gods Series!**

Author's suggested reading order:
Revenge of the Forgotten (Book 1)
Heart of the Villain (Book 1.5, prequel novella)
Vengeance of the Gods (Book 2)
Book 3 — Details coming soon!

Vengeance of the Gods has themes and triggers that may not
be suitable for all audiences.

If you wish to see a list of the Trigger Warnings,
flip to page 489. If you **do not** wish to read the Trigger
Warnings, flip to the next page.

VENGEANCE OF THE GODS PLAYLIST
(Scan me with your Spotify App)

I hope ur miserable until ur dead - Nessa Barrett

Falling - Harry Styles

Alive - Spencer Sutherland

Mess It Up - Gracie Abrams

temptation - Ashley Sienna

The Elevator - Lizzy McAlpine

All I Wanted - Paramore

I want it all - Omido, Mandrazo, Rick Jansen

MATCH MADE IN HELL - Dutch Melrose, benny mayne

Every Time You Leave - I Prevail, Delaney Jane

Sucker - Arcane, Marcus King

Monster - Paramore

Broken Insides - Madeline The Person

all the good girls go to hell - Billie Eilish

Take It To My Grave - LYELL, SkyDxddy

Dear god - Tate McRae

Sparks - Coldplay

doomsday - Lizzy McAlpine

GRAVE - Avery Anna

Heroin - Jessie Murph

Everything - Alex Warren

Take Me to Church - Hozier

Shadow - Livingston

Kill Me - Hayley Williams

TOLEVARRE

VISIT WWW.DANYCROOKS.COM
FOR AN INTERACTIVE MAP

Prologue

Vega knew that voice. Their name was on the tip of her tongue. She couldn't stop the wheel of her mind from turning forward, bringing her closer to what came next.

"Come back."

The complete wipeout. The blinding pain of losing what made Vega who she was. Her memories. Without them, she wasn't whole. Without them, she was no longer the Vega she needed to be.

The curse would reset her, and she'd have to start all over. *Who will I be next?*

This was Marlena's doing—the torture of losing herself repeatedly. The agony as her memories were ripped from her mind, the pain before her heart reset.

The person who did this to Vega wasn't Marlena—it was a monster wearing her sister's skin as clothes.

I'll be gone again.

No, no. Her lightning stopped her heart. Not the dagger. *I'm not dead.*

"Come back."

Hold on.

Hold. On.

"Fuck, Vega. Why?"

The voice continued, but Vega couldn't place it to a name. Earlier it felt like it had been on the tip of her tongue.

She wasn't inside her body, couldn't feel her body. Everything was still, not a beating heart or the sound of her own breathing interrupting her thoughts. Vega floated around inside her brain through whatever current of her mind was taking the longest to reset.

"Why would you do this?"

Do what? Vega couldn't remember what she'd done. It kept slipping her mind.

And that voice. *Gods, I know that voice.*

Gods. God. Tolevarre.

Bridger.

Pain erupted in Vega's chest like a knife to the heart.

She didn't scream. She didn't move. She simply fell, allowing herself to let go. Letting the fall be the reminder she needed to know she was alive.

If only for a few more seconds...

Gone. Nothing. *I will become nothing again.*

She wasn't sure how long she was suspended in the middle of life and death. A minute? Seconds? Years?

There was nothing... nothing but pain and an itching feeling of grief.

I don't want to forget.

"You cannot escape your destiny. Death is coming." That wasn't Bridger... His voice was gone, replaced by another Vega vaguely recognized. She might have been able to place it if it weren't for the pain.

Vega shot up, gasping violently. Bright lights temporarily

blinded her. She shielded her sensitive eyes, fighting against the ache to see clearly.

She couldn't get enough air, her breathing ragged as she panted and rubbed a sore spot on her chest beside her heart.

Beep... beep... beep...

The sporadic beeping drew Vega's attention. "What the...?" She squinted, her eyes finally clear enough to see without using her hand as a visor.

"Vega?" a third voice gasped.

"Oh my God. Oh my God. You're awake. You're alive." The person was a blur, moving too quickly for Vega to see. "Nurse!"

Everything was still fuzzy. Her brain. Her voice. Her vision.

Vega blinked and blinked. After a few longer squints, her vision cleared, and a familiar blond man knelt down beside her.

Reality snapped into focus.

I'm in a hospital, and that's...

"Chase."

1

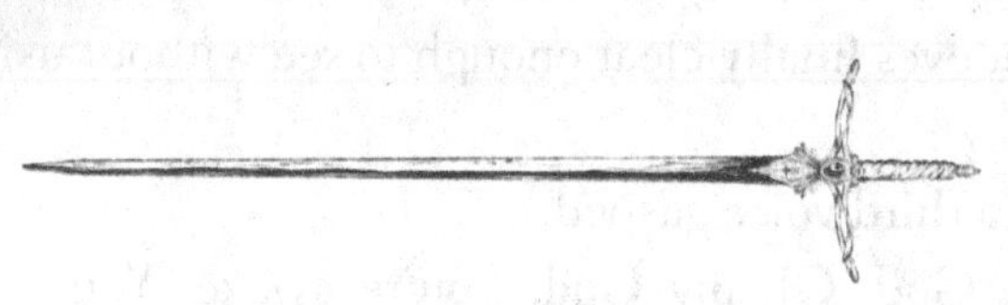

Bridger inserted keys into the lock of a door with the
number twenty-one and walked into an apartment he didn't
recognize, feeling a little lost as he stepped inside.

Where am I? His voice echoed in his head.

Bridger barely had the door shut before Vega appeared from
down a hallway, her bare feet padding across worn carpet.

If he looked confused, Vega didn't notice or care because she
threw herself in his arms.

What the fuck is going...? Bridger didn't have time to think the
whole thought before Vega's lips were on his, and she slid her hands
up his chest until they locked around the back of his neck.

Bridger hadn't realized he was touching Vega until his fingers
met bare thighs.

Her skin pebbled, lips parting to let him in. Bridger's tongue slid
inside her warm mouth. Notes of berry and smoke made Vega taste
like a delicious wine he'd like to drink to the last drop. Bridger
hoisted her up, and she instinctively wrapped her legs around him.

He couldn't stop, couldn't think of anything else but this kiss and
the way she felt against him.

"

She gasped when he pressed his growing need between her spread legs, backing her up against a wall. "Where are you?" he purred against her skin, confused why he asked that.

Bridger felt like he didn't have any control over his body, that he was only looking through his eyes while someone else made decisions for him.

Vega's eyes rolled into the back of her head, and she ground her hips as much as she could trapped between him and the wall. "With you."

Bridger kissed down Vega's jaw, inhaling the sugary scent in the crook of her neck. "And where are *we*?"

Vega whined breathlessly like the words he'd spoken were dirty. "Look around. You'll find me."

He met her lust-dazed gaze, stealing a peek at her lips, swollen and parted. He caught her next moan in his mouth.

Look around. Look around. Look around.

His eyes shot open, and it was no longer Bridger who had Vega pinned against the wall. A stranger took his place, kissing down her neck while she moaned in pleasure.

Bridger's feet felt stuck in quicksand, locking him in place.

His eyes darted to the window, the lights of the city a beacon to an unmistakable landmark in the distance.

Look around. You'll find me.

Bridger was snatched from his own mind and thrown out like a drunk bar patron. He woke to a room lit by dim moonlight, tumbling from bed and crashing into the nightstand. A lamp fell to the floor, glass shattering around his bare feet.

The commotion wasn't enough to distract him from what he'd seen.

Bridger had only been to Earth once, his overall knowledge of the world lacking, but he knew that landmark—he'd studied it as a part of Tolevarre's history.

Soaked from head to toe, Bridger wiped a bead of sweat rolling down his brow and hadn't finished buttoning his shirt before leaving the room.

The halls of Atrox bustled with early morning activity. Soldiers headed to training and lectures, while others went to or from their designated posts. Bridger liked to spend as little time as possible in Fortis's fort city, but he was suddenly glad he'd decided to stay the night instead of traveling back to Vincere after the battle in Schoenus yesterday.

Bridger spoke to no one as he passed, and everyone had the right sense to step out of his way. His footsteps were light and hurried, descending the stairs into the massive prison below the fort's foundation.

All the dreams he'd had of Vega thus far had been memories he hid away inside his mind. This one wasn't a memory... It was a sign, pointing him straight to the cell door of a face he wasn't particularly thrilled to see locked behind iron bars.

Her tight curls hid her face until she lifted her head and locked eyes with Bridger.

Unable to hold it in, Bridger admitted what he'd come all the way down here for. "I know where Vega is."

2

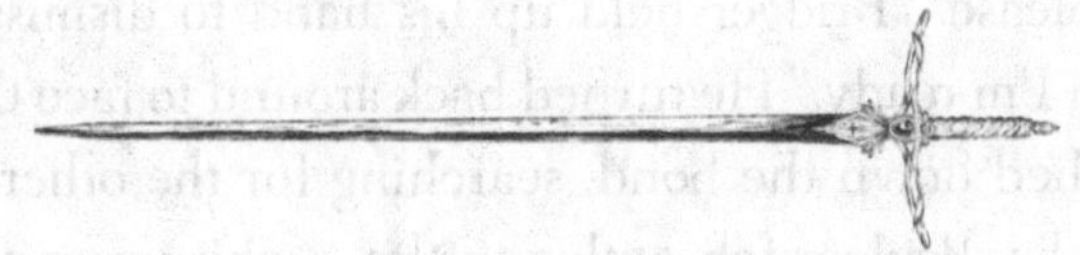

One Month Later

THE EVERGREENS RUSTLED WITH THE SOUND OF WIND BREEZING through, the lowest hanging limbs of two trees crossing together to form an arch. In between the trunks and the crossed branches, the snow from last night's storm reflected off the portal, tiny beams of light casting the space around Bridger with sparkles.

It was beautiful in the same way a destructive fire was. Dangerous and lethal. Life-changing. And in a moment, it could take everything someone loved.

The crack down the middle made Bridger shudder.

What happens if it splits in two and Vega is lost forever? What does that mean for the rest of us?

The crack appeared after Vega's body vanished from his arms. One second, he'd been holding the strongest version of Vega he'd ever known, and the next she was gone—in the blink of an eye.

"Commander." Halo's voice yanked Bridger from his daydream.

He turned to face the traveler, his eyebrow raised as if to ask, *What?*

Halo rubbed his hands together nervously. "I think we should get back." His eyes scanned the clearing. "Rebels are everywhere."

Bridger knew where the rebels were. He knew they would be looking to take whoever they could prisoner. He was aware he would be the prize of a lifetime if they got their hands on him.

If.

"Halo, please." Bridger held up his hand to dismiss him. "We will go when I'm ready." He turned back around to face the portal.

He reached down the bond, searching for the other end where Vega should be. Bridger felt nothing. Not a whisper or a breath of a response, only the tingle of the brand on his wrist and the reminder he knew where she was.

This was the first time she'd killed herself. Bridger hadn't missed the electric buzz of her body when he held her until she disappeared. If he concentrated hard enough, he could still feel his fingers tingling.

Bridger lost himself staring at the portal, slipping behind a shield to protect himself and Halo from any surprise attacks while he was distracted with everything he knew.

Arlet hadn't talked much since being taken captive, but the little she had was enough for Bridger to get some useful information.

Vega found something about her curse which pointed her back to Earth, returning her to the world that'd already stolen fifty-five years from her.

Since Vega couldn't find anyone to assist in testing her theory, she decided to take it into her own hands—pretending to kill herself to reset to a new life and search for the root of her curse, the one responsible for over twenty different deaths and for stripping her of her memories and powers.

Why she couldn't have tried walking through the portal as a starter is beyond me...

Halo's boots crunched on dry leaves, his nerves causing him to fidget.

Bridger groaned, spinning to face Halo. "We need to work on your anxiety. It's going to get you killed." He rested his hand gently on Halo's bony shoulder, squeezing lightly. "Have you been training at all?"

"We're really doing this right now?" Halo grumbled.

Halo had a lot of growing to do, mentally and physically, but Bridger wasn't ready to give up on him. He saw something inside the young boy—not just the power he possessed.

"Take me to her," Bridger said.

Halo didn't have to ask who he was talking about—it was the same person every time.

Bridger was growing accustomed to the jarring sensation of traveling, the sinking and crushing feeling of moving through space and time under someone else's control.

His feet met the stone floor of the Atrox prison. The cries of the tormented echoed through the halls, centering Bridger back to the real world. Halo deposited him and left, his black smoke floating to the low ceilings.

Standing outside her cell, Bridger tapped the hilt of his dagger against the iron bars with a reverberating ring. "Are you ready to tell me how I get to Vega?"

Arlet stared directly into his eyes from her seated position in the corner. Every bit of exposed skin covering her body was littered with bruises of varying degrees. "No."

Bridger sighed, gripping the bars with his dagger still in his hand. "You're wasting time, stealing from all of us."

"I'd rather us all die than give you another chance to hurt Vega," she spat, snarling at him like a rabid animal.

Bridger couldn't help the eye roll. "You're being very dramatic." His hand hovered over the cell door's lock. It clicked open, a tingle of power rushing up his arm from the prison's recognition. He stepped inside and closed himself in with her. "I know you didn't spend the last fifty-five years chasing Vega down to give up on her so easily."

Arlet's snarl grew larger. "You don't know me, Dimico, and you certainly don't know Vega either. She's there because she wants to be this time. She's not coming back until she breaks her curse."

It was the same answer every. Single. Time. Bridger was getting close to breaking down, to resorting to torture, but that wouldn't help. He needed to build Arlet's trust, to make her see the man he'd once been.

The man I am. He wasn't as good at convincing himself than he was others.

Bridger ran a hand through his hair, puffing a calming breath through his lips. "And what if she didn't get it right? What if she has no memories? Who's going to go get her if you're locked up? I know where she is. I saw it. All I need is for you to tell me how I get to her when the portal is on the other side of the fucking world."

Arlet's sneer started to fall as she shrugged her shoulders. "You don't. You let her die, just like you always have."

His frustration got to him, the walls of the cell trembling from the surge in his mood. "Arlet, *please*. Please. I'm begging you. Tell me what I need to do to get her back here."

Arlet meandered her gaze from Bridger's head to his toes. "You don't look like you're begging. I've seen you beg for Vega's life before, and this isn't it."

Through gritted teeth, Bridger stepped closer. Arlet had to crane her neck to look at him. "I will not get on my knees for you, Arlet Videri." He reached out and twirled a matted curl between his fingers before she swatted him away. "You might have accepted your fate, but I haven't. I will not let her be the death of me... and neither should you."

Marlena had already taken enough.

Bridger stood tall, rolled his shoulders back, and was ready to take his leave when Arlet surprised him with a question. "Do you think it worked? That Vega is still the person she was when she left?"

He didn't know how to answer that question, so he turned it around. "Do you?"

"I think Vega is going to fry everyone in her path to get the vengeance she craves, and if she doesn't remember it now, she will eventually."

Bridger closed the cell, the lock sliding into place. "And you're going to take that from her, from the people you want to save. All because you want to keep her safe. The exact reason Vega went behind your back in the first place."

Arlet chuffed a humorless laugh. "You don't know what you're talking about."

"When are you going to see she doesn't want to be protected?" Bridger cocked his head. "She's sick of people making decisions for her."

Her life had been planned out since the day she was born. Marry Khort, have dragon babies, and follow along like the perfect pawn.

He didn't need to know this version of Vega to know how sick she was of the people in her life dictating her every move.

Silence followed his question. Arlet wasn't going to budge.

Bridger took a breath and forced his shoulders to stay squared even though he felt them wanting to sag in defeat.

He would come back tomorrow, and the next day, and the next day. Bridger would come every single day for the rest of time if it meant there was a chance Arlet cracked.

He turned to leave the prison, and finally, *finally*, Arlet gave in. "Don't you think it's time Marlena helped clean up the mess she's made?"

Bridger stopped walking, peering over his shoulder at Arlet, who continued to talk.

"If the curse she created is what made the portal, what's stopping her from making another?"

3

My name is Vega Caelum.

I'm a god.

I'm from a realm called Tolevarre.

I have my memories.

I got it right. My curse is here on Earth. But where? What?

My name is Vega Caelum, and I do not have a traumatic brain injury.

I'm a god.

I'm from a realm called Tolevarre.

"Vega." A hand reached out and grazed her knee.

Vega jumped, the well-lit room around her refocusing.

Sasha startled, chuckling at herself as she settled back into her seat. "I lost you there for a second. Can you tell me what you were thinking about?" She leaned back in her chair, the tablet on her lap waiting to be used as a notebook.

"I..." Vega started, blinking through the pain in her head. "I..." She laughed, biting her lip as the ache subsided. "Sorry, I spaced out. I didn't sleep well last night."

Therapy.

It was what her doctor suggested when she awoke from a six-month coma spewing details about an impossible life, with fairy-tale-like details. According to her neurologist, traumatic brain injuries had a lot of weird side effects that sometimes didn't make any sense.

"It was all a dream," he'd said. Vega's brain created a fantasy land to live in while it healed.

Sasha smiled softly, slowly. "How have your headaches been?"

Vega shrugged. "Not as bad."

The headaches she'd been getting whenever she thought about her *real* life.

Or the headaches from the traumatic brain injury.

The traumatic brain injury she got from the night she stormed out of her apartment after an argument and got hit by a car.

She had never met a woman named Arlet.

She had never carved her initials into the dining room table.

She had never crossed into a land called Tolevarre.

It had been a dream, and when she woke up in the hospital a month ago, Chase was right there to beg her to forgive him, to take him back. And what other choice did she have?

It wasn't a dream. Or at least it hadn't felt like a dream... The scars on her face looked too close to claw marks to come from the headlight of a car.

"Good." Sasha interrupted Vega's mental landslide. "That's good." She smiled professionally. "Why don't we wrap up a little earlier today? You should go home and get some rest." Closing the case to her tablet, the therapist stood, and Vega followed. "I'll see you on Friday."

Sometimes Vega "forgot to set an alarm" and missed her sessions, so she wouldn't make any promises about showing up for her next appointment.

Vega took the long way home, but even the long way wasn't long enough. She only lived a few blocks from her therapist's office.

Her apartment building loomed in the distance. Vega stood on the corner and stared at the entrance. *This isn't my home. Tolevarre is my home.*

Vega took every opportunity to remind herself of who she really was, despite the shooting pain erupting behind her eyes at the thought. Sometimes it felt like something inside her was broken and the headaches were more pieces of herself breaking off.

But is it? There was that voice again, the one who made her doubt herself. *A dream... it'd been a dream, Vega.*

The scar on her chest, the three across her left eye, the others littered across her skin—those were from the accident.

But were they? She remembered how she got each one, and it wasn't from a car.

A car she couldn't remember hitting her, but she could remember the feel of her sister's strike across her face like it happened this morning.

Vega had spent the last month of her life questioning everything she thought she knew.

She couldn't remember entering the building of her apartment, couldn't remember walking up the stairs, and didn't realize she had put her key into the lock of apartment number twenty-one—*How ironic this is my twenty-first life, huh?*—until she opened the door and stepped inside.

Chase wasn't home, and he wouldn't be for a few more hours. Which meant she had time to snoop like she always did when she was alone.

Marlena can curse inanimate objects. So that was where she started. Looking for something, anything that called to her—made her feel like she might be on the right track. *But would it really be as easy as an object in my apartment?*

As usual, her head pounded. Vega fought through the uncomfortable pain, realizing she was becoming accustomed to it, or maybe getting better at ignoring it.

Vega shuffled through the box of keepsakes she'd found hidden on Chase's side of the closet, tucked under a pile of coats on the very top shelf.

Since waking up from her supposed coma, Vega had destroyed twenty-seven different objects of significance without Chase knowing.

Today, it was the goodbye letter from her mother—the one who'd passed away from cancer in her last life... *This life?* Vega wasn't sure she should consider this a full new life.

A small metal trash bin, lighter fluid, and a box of matches were hidden in the corner underneath the lounge chair on the balcony. Vega held a match up to the paper. The letter caught fire in seconds.

The sulfur of the match was all she could smell as she lowered what was left of the letter into the trash can.

Vega stared into the quickly dimming flames, her vision blurring while her mind wandered to the forest and Bridger—to the cliff, to the kiss. She blinked when the memory of his lips was palpable, bringing herself back to the world around her.

Her fingers fluttered over her lips, just like Bridger's lips had.

When the fire went out, all that was left were the ashes of a letter Vega had once cried over, and Vega... still stuck in a world she didn't belong.

She had no idea what she was supposed to feel or what would even happen if this worked, but it was the reason she'd come back. *It's the reason I'm alive. I got it right. I got something right.*

Another failed attempt to find the cursed object. Almost as if she weren't cursed at all.

The pain in Vega's head made her squint, but eventually, it went away like it always did when she found herself doubting her own memories.

Vega flopped down to the patio chair and watched as the sun sank behind the Colosseum in the distance.

Rome. Not Chicago. According to Chase, they'd never even lived in Chicago.

She'd never had a job at Bobby's Diner.

She'd never gotten stuck in an elevator.

She'd never gone on a cross-country road trip with a best friend and sang The Fray like it was any other car ride.

Vega felt a loneliness she'd never experienced before. At least in the other lives, she couldn't remember having loved ones. In this one, she ached for a hug from her best friend, for the zap of her electricity.

She missed home.

Vega winced at the shooting pain between her eyes.

None of that was real.

This was real. Rome, the job Chase had taken here in Italy, the affair starting only weeks after moving. The car hitting Vega because she'd been too distraught to look both ways before crossing the street after finding him between the legs of another woman. *This* was Vega's life.

Not Bridger.

Not Arlet.

Not Khort.

Not a realm with a sister who wanted her dead.

This life with Chase and the person she'd become if she let herself forget—this was real.

I don't want to forget yet.

Vega wanted to hold on to her delusion for just a little longer.

4

A BLACK PUFF OF SMOKE FOLLOWED MARLENA AS SHE STEPPED through the in-between and landed on the other side of Tolevarre.

She'd left Aeris only seconds ago and walked through to Nix, Amora's main city—it was hardly large enough to call a city but too small to call a town—the one she'd briefly called home years ago, where Bridger and his army were, tightening up restrictions on a town who'd decided to riot early this morning.

Amora had never been a problem, not in all the years Marlena ruled, but since Ivelle's death, they'd become rowdier than she could allow them to be.

Marlena didn't have friends, but Ivelle had once been the only person who stood by her side when the rest of the world turned their backs.

Finding out about Amora's riot only minutes ago, long after it'd been handled by Bridger, made the gods inside her rise with anger.

"Why would he act without you?"

"Who does he think he is?"

She shoved them down, locking the tingle of their powerful rage at bay for now.

The city's viewing center had been set up as the army's headquarters. A soldier with a level ten patch, noting her as the highest rank a member of Bridger's army could reach, stood guard at the door.

Marlena could feel the pull of her Fraus-born traveling power. The voice of Mercury, the god of Fraus's people, was almost too hard to ignore when he felt someone with an outstanding ability.

It's why he went wild around Halo...

"Halo." He drew his name out like a loving song.

A battle-trained traveler could be the deadliest in almost any fight if taught properly.

"Marlena." The woman bowed her head. "To what do we owe the pleasure?"

Formal, respectful, but not scared. It wasn't often Marlena didn't cause people to shy out of her way.

"Where's the commander?" she asked, crossing her arms and looking bored when the girl moved to open the door.

"Last room on the right." She stepped to the side, but Marlena didn't need her to. She cut the walk in half, stepping through Tolevarre's edges and landing in front of the door.

She didn't wait for it to open, allowing her control of the wind to announce her arrival.

Bridger sat at a makeshift desk in the center of the room, his attention on a monitor on the back wall playing footage of what must be last night's attack.

The shadow of a dragon darkened the snow-covered ground as it flew through the light of the moon.

"Fera's to blame for this?" she asked, standing in the center of the room with her hands clasped calmly in front.

It wasn't Bridger who answered her. "By the time my team and I arrived, he'd already had most of Nix evacuated," Meyer explained.

"How many casualties?" Marlena asked, her attention glued to Bridger, who hadn't taken his eyes off the looped video.

Bridger spoke but didn't look her way. "Fifteen across."

It wasn't a massacre.

"I don't think Khort's motivation in coming was to fight. He showed up after the riots started to get people out," Meyer added. "All my reports over the last few weeks since Vega's most recent death say he's showing up only to save the people looking to flee."

Marlena's jaw tensed the longer Meyer was in the room. "Don't you have somewhere else to be, General?"

Bridger's head snapped in Marlena's direction. "My army. My general. You do not command either while I'm alive." He rose from his chair, and the look on his stone-carved face said he meant business. His sharp jawline was taut and finally visible again after the weeks he went without shaving following Vega's second escape. His hair was freshly washed and pushed back in his normal, polished style. A few unruly pieces always fell out of place around his brow.

Marlena couldn't help but notice he wasn't wearing his commander's uniform. "Well, hello, Commander," Marlena purred. "It's nice to see you again."

Their relationship had become strained, more so than it had been at the beginning of Bridger's reign as commander. Marlena wasn't stupid. If she didn't want to run him off, she had to watch her every move.

"What do you want, Marlena?" Bridger asked, leaning against the side of the desk. He crossed his arms over his chest, and Marlena knew she'd see corded veins against his forearms had they been visible through his long sleeves.

Marlena smirked, striding across the small space to stand in front of him. "You could say hello back, you know?" She wore a long sapphire satin gown with a slit up her right leg. It hugged her curves in all the right places, accentuating Marlena's best features.

Bridger's tight chest rose and fell with a breath. "Hello, Marlena. How's your day going? Busy?" he asked, motioning to the disaster of a desk behind him. "How was your breakfast? Did you sleep well?"

Marlena interrupted his sarcastic ramblings. "Why wasn't I aware of the riot or of Khort until just now?"

A beep on Bridger's comm-device had him reaching for it on the desk. He spoke, eyes scanning over whatever message he'd received. "As I said, my army. Not yours. If I feel it's necessary for you to know, I'll tell you." His eyes shot up from the screen. "Khort had nothing to do with the attack. He was only doing what he does best." He looked over his shoulder at Meyer. "Will you handle whatever this is about?" he asked, passing the device over to him, who grumbled about incompetent children while stomping out of the room.

Bridger returned to their conversation the second the door closed. "Swooping in to play hero or whatever it is he does as the 'rebel army's leader.'" He used air quotes around the last three words and even added some flare with a quick roll of his eyes.

Marlena's blood began to boil, her fingertips longing to feel the heat of her fire. "I cannot have riots breaking out in Amora when I have no praefectus to subdue them." Her voice had an eerie similarity to the beast of the dead god of Demuto, Diana. "This needs to be taken care of. Now."

"What is it you think I'm doing here?" Bridger asked with a cocked brow. "Vacationing in paradise?" His lips held the hint of a smile at his joke.

Amora was cold and miserable all year long. She could count on two hands how many times she'd seen it get above freezing in the last decade. "Are you handling it, or should I?"

His smile spread, and it reminded her of a boy she once knew. Of the young man who fell in love with her sister... "You know you can trust me to take whatever it is that's thrown my way." He pointed to himself. "I'm here. Handling it. Making sure the rebels know there's an army presence."

"I want curfews for every city above five thousand." Marlena tightened the already short reins she allowed the people of Tolevarre.

"Done," Bridger said.

Marlena continued. "And—"

Bridger cut her off. "Ah, wait a second. Why is it you always get whatever you want, but I don't get what I want? Shouldn't there be a little balance here now? I think it's about time we share the power."

Marlena blinked away the twitch in her left eye from Bridger's tone. *Don't bite back too hard.*

"What do you want?" Her jaw burned from how hard she clenched.

Bridger leaned away from the desk, uncrossed his arms, and stood to his full height. "How did the portal appear when you cursed Vega?"

The gods inside warned to keep her mouth shut, but whatever was left of Marlena's original voice whispered of all she stood to lose if Bridger disappeared.

Reluctantly, she answered. "It started as a cursed mirror and the blood of two sisters."

Bridger didn't hesitate or pause. "You think you could build another one straight to her?"

Marlena opened her mouth, readying to tell him there wasn't anything she couldn't do, when a more important question arose. "Why would you be interested in a portal straight to Vega?"

"It took Arlet years to figure out how to navigate Earth comfortably and efficiently. We don't have years. I think it's better I get the job done quickly and come back to continue preparing for *your* war." Bridger's words were sharp enough to draw blood.

How Arlet had found Vega all those times before had been a mystery to Marlena until the responsibility fell to Bridger. It came in the shape of a dream in the location they would find Vega—nothing else. The rest had been on Arlet to figure out.

She found herself wondering how the earlier versions of Arlet even figured out how to survive in a new world. Mousy Arlet Videri, spending all her time alone in a different world, haunted by the memories she'd never escape like her best friend could.

"*Speak,*" the loudest of the gods reminded her.

Marlena shrugged like Bridger made a point. "I suppose I could try, but I'm curious." Marlena took a step closer, watching him for any movement. A flinch, a twitch, anything. Bridger didn't budge. "Why are you so insistent on finding my sister again? After losing her twice in her last life..."

The sister who'd done nothing while their parents beat her. The sister who'd chosen her friends and boyfriend over her own blood. The sister who'd once been the only person Marlena cared to save, to now become the one Marlena couldn't wait to end.

Bridger's eyes darkened, but he still didn't move. He was a statue of indifference. "Why did the portal linked to the world Vega's bound to crack if this life went the same as the rest? We all know the curse isn't going to run out, but it can be broken, and I'd say it's looking more broken than it ever has... Wouldn't you?"

One of the voices in the back of Marlena's mind waved a red flag. Could she trust Bridger anymore? He wasn't the same person he'd been at the start of this, or the same person he was a year ago, six months ago. But he also wasn't wrong. The portal had split down the middle, unlike any time before.

Bridger didn't let Marlena sit with the thoughts in her head for long. "She won't save me, and she certainly won't save you when this is all over." His words seemed to echo in her head, being repeated by the gods she'd let slither up from the depths. "But you will. You'll save me." Bridger's crooked smile slid across his lips. "If I'm gone, you won't be able to keep the order I've allowed you to have. Without me, your perfect empire crumbles."

"I don't ne—"

The raise of Bridger's eyebrow stopped her from speaking.

Heat flared at the tips of Marlena's fingers. *Down, girl.* She stopped herself from exploding.

Bridger wasn't a friend. Bridger was and would always be an asset.

One she couldn't lose.

The gods slithered around in her head, hissing in protest. The emerald fire went out. "What's your plan? I know you're not delusional enough to think Vega will come with you willingly if she remembers."

The darkness in Bridger's eyes had returned—the dead-like stare he'd subjected himself to when he used his enhanced powers from the bonded's summoning against his own mind. Shielding one's memories was a power Marlena wished to possess. Bridger had no idea how lucky he was to have it.

When Bridger started dreaming of Vega, something changed within him. Marlena noticed it the night he'd told her about them in Ardor—the night she'd come to tell him about a meeting he was to be a part of. The meeting where Bridger found out he'd be sent to Earth to retrieve the very woman who haunted his every dream.

Marlena thought it would be good for him if he was given a reminder of the girl Vega had become, only to be reminded who she'd once been while asleep. It should have been the final nail in his coffin, the one that killed the old Bridger forever, but his emotions had come back, sparks returning to the blank expression he'd worn for over three decades. The hotheaded reactions young Bridger had been known for returned, his actions becoming less calculated and more anger fueled.

Since Vega escaped the last time, the dark energy Bridger wore like a perfectly pressed suit returned.

He and the darkness are one. He likes the power, the control.

Marlena's stomach rolled with hesitancy at the twinkle in Bridger's eyes, the piece of life still left inside a god Marlena knew could do more damage than even he knew possible.

"I think I can sway her feelings towards me this time. Give her a taste of the man she once knew. Getting inside her head would be *very* easy if she trusted me again." Bridger's confidence was contagious. "If the dreams I'm having are anything other than a complete nuisance, at least they've been a good reminder as to who I was before this started." He paused for only a moment. "Weak."

Bridger's words echoed through her head like he'd spoken them into an empty room. "You're saying you want to make her fall in love with you again?" she asked with evident apprehension.

Bridger raised one shoulder, his black hair shimmering under the room's soft lighting. "It's the only option we haven't tried."

Over the last forty years, Marlena had done a lot to her sister. In the earliest years, her deaths were quick. A gentle reminder of what was waiting for her when she crossed back over. Eventually, Marlena's patience ran dry. The longer the curse kept her alive, the clearer it was that something wasn't right. It wasn't until a few years ago she realized just how much Remus had interfered with her original curse. She'd spent decades thinking Vega and the rest of her bonded bunch would wither away for good one day.

At one point she'd even considered Bridger expendable—an unfortunate loss of the curse her sister unknowingly changed. Bridger was no longer someone Marlena was willing to lose.

Once she found out how to curse her sister, how to curse a god to die, then Marlena would find a way to break Bridger's bond before killing the other three.

"Do you think you'll be able to handle that? She seems to be quite crafty herself if she outsmarted and escaped you *twice*."

Remind him of his failures—of why he needs you still.

Bridger smiled sarcastically. "She knows my moves, which just goes to show her mind is as clear as it's ever been. Whatever she's gone through in these lives created a new Vega. One who isn't afraid of you, Marlena. One who might be successfully on Earth with her memories right now... on the hunt for the end of a curse you can't afford to let her break yet." If she broke it before Marlena had her next move planned, she would no longer be on top.

"This might be the only opportunity you get to find out everything she knows, everything she's learned about the curse *you* don't understand, and I'm offering to deliver it to you on a silver platter... But for whatever reason, you're still questioning my allegiance. When will it end?"

He'd never done her wrong since joining her regime. He'd made mistakes, of course, but they all had in their growth to where they stood now.

Marlena was sick of mistakes.

"What's in it for you?" she mused, flipping her hair over her shoulder with a small gust of perfectly placed wind.

Bridger's eyes didn't wander down her exposed neck. "We find a way to remove my bond. I live. They die."

Marlena searched Bridger's face for any sign of deceit. When she found none, she asked, "How do I know you're serious?"

Bridger pulled the collar of his shirt down, revealing a scar over his heart. "Because Vega tried to kill me the day she escaped at Lake Vehemens as a way to test if you were telling the truth about being gods, and I want to return the favor one last time."

A bubble of laughter escaped through Marlena's lips, the sound giddy with excitement. "There he is. The god of wrath. I've been waiting for you to emerge."

5

Marlena's reflection stared back at her in the room of mirrors. Her image multiplied, filling the space with the powerful woman she'd become.

A room that had once been used to torture her was now a room full of tiny curses. Living, breathing memories—pieces of a sister she could barely remember loving.

A crack split the largest mirror in two, held together by only its frame. Marlena had found it broken before they discovered the portal's damage.

"She got it right."

Marlena knew the voice was right. As its creator, she could feel the curse wavering. It was hard not to wonder what fallout Marlena would face if the curse was to be broken.

How much of herself was connected to her sister by a death curse with their shared blood? A curse this big could usually only be broken by the creator... Marlena hadn't been ready to make something this large with brand new abilities she had yet to fully understand.

"We warned you." Multiple gods rattled inside her mind like a chorus.

They'd told her not to use the power in her blood—had warned her she wasn't ready. To no one's surprise, Marlena hadn't listened.

It was the only thing she'd go back and do differently. She'd give herself more time to understand the gods and how the powers worked. Marlena hadn't mastered them all at once. It had taken years to control them at the level she could now.

"She has her memories, but that doesn't mean we've—*I've* lost," she said out loud. "I still have time to fix this."

Marlena took a step forward and placed a hand over the crack in the reflective glass. She closed her eyes and inhaled until there was no room left inside her lungs. Fireflies danced across the darkness of her vision, filling her mind with a memory that wasn't hers.

Vega's head fell back in laughter as Bridger wiped his face with the palm of his hand, smearing the glow of a squished lightning bug across his cheek. "Vega, don't laugh!" he scolded, trying to be stern while fighting against a laugh of his own. "I killed the poor thing."

The bugs flickered across the night sky. Some fluttered by, others landed on the two, interrupting their midnight frolic among the Aeris mountainside.

"Bridger Dimico, future commander of Tolevarre, afraid of fireflies." She couldn't get more than a few words out at a time without laughing.

"I don't like the feel of them crawling on me." Bridger shuddered, still trying to clean the murder remnants off his face.

When Vega finally stopped laughing, she closed the distance between them. "Here." She reached her hand up to his cheek and wiped the glowing guts off with the sleeve of her sweater. She didn't pull away, allowing the tips of her fingers to gently graze against Bridger's skin.

The air around them stilled, Bridger's hand darting up to wrap around Vega's wrist. He held her touch in place, his eyes boring into hers with a look Marlena knew too well.

It was the same look he'd worn the night he met her.

Love. He loved her from the moment he laid eyes on her.

Marlena snatched her hand away from the mirror, ripping the vision from her mind.

They had been so young.

Marlena could tell by the outfit Vega wore how old she was. It was a memory from before—a memory from a life Vega never got the chance to live.

The original.

It wasn't often Marlena allowed herself to watch the memories stored inside the haunted mirrors, but when she did, they always left her feeling the same.

Hollow.

Marlena unwound the thread of invisible power inside her blood from Mercury, the god of Fraus—god of travel and trickery and the messenger of the gods.

Marlena had two abilities from him: the power to travel through their realm's invisible channels, jumping from place to place, and the power living inside her blood.

It felt like none of the others, snaking through her veins like poison. It bubbled like boiling water at the tips of her fingers, but no one would be able to tell. This was a power hidden inside her blood.

Benders, who were also coined Tolevarre's witches, were gifted Mercury's power but couldn't use it to travel. Instead, they were able to bend the power inside their blood and use it however they could. Some would help heal others with potions and tinctures, then use that same potion to kill their victim. Others could use their blood to curse another living object. Not all could, but a curse wasn't the worst thing a strong bender could do to someone.

Only a few had ever been known to use their power to create the way Marlena could. Mercury himself, a few of his earliest descendants, and an unnamed woman no one had heard from in over three centuries.

It was Marlena's least favorite power of the dead gods. The one she didn't like to use and avoided like a sickness.

How ironic it might be the strongest and deadliest power she possessed.

Marlena drew her dagger and sliced down the center of her palm, doing the same to the other. She should have felt pain, but the flow of Mercury's ichor spilling out of her open wounds numbed her.

The sensation of raw power flooding out of Marlena was euphoric.

Stronger than love. Stronger than sex.

Not letting it take over yet, Marlena focused on what she wanted, the purpose of this creation. She reached out and smeared her crimson blood down the crack in the mirror.

Her blood bubbled against the glass, fixing the crack in less than a breath. "To Vega," she whispered in Latin, waking the voice of Mercury inside her brain.

"To your sister."

It took everything inside Marlena not to lose her control over the longing in his voice. "To the place our world started. A portal for the new gods."

The wave of power in her blood made Marlena lose her breath, her lungs tender from the sudden loss of air. Pain quickly turned into a pleasure so overwhelming, Marlena was finally able to inhale a shaky breath.

Closing her eyes, Marlena let her head fall back, concentrating only on the purpose of the power making her head go fuzzy. Her lips parted, and she heard herself whimper, feeling like an unwanted guest in her own body.

The buzz in her head drowned out the Latin chants she babbled, drawing her into the broken mirror.

Power poured from Marlena, lighting her body ablaze as she lost control of her legs and sank to the floor. Her head swam with desire, and she panted through the newest wave taking over.

Her hand stayed glued to the mirror, but Marlena had lost the ability to focus, everything around her a blur.

All she knew was how badly her blood sang with need.

"Fuck," Marlena moaned, fighting to keep focus on what she'd intended to wake this power for. It made the impossible possible in most situations, but it made her lose herself to her body and mind.

It ruled her, dragging her into the undertow, where all she could do was hope to be spit out when it was done with her.

The pleasure rose to a new height, her body quivering like her muscles were begging for the release that would never come. Her desire shot to the highest peak, and before Marlena could safely crawl down the other side, she was thrown off and plummeted to the ground without a parachute.

Marlena gasped as she regained full control of her body, pulling her hand away from the mirror and blinking away the fog.

The wounds on her hands were gone, healed the second she'd finished imbuing the mirror with the power inside her. Blood still coated her hands, but when she looked up at the mirror, she no longer saw her reflection.

Instead, a vast black nothingness with swirling shadows stared back at her. The frame was no longer the dark natural wood it had been moments ago. Now it was made of iron—the same as the halo she wore atop her head.

Both made from the power in her blood, the god inside her head, and the energy of Vega's curse.

6

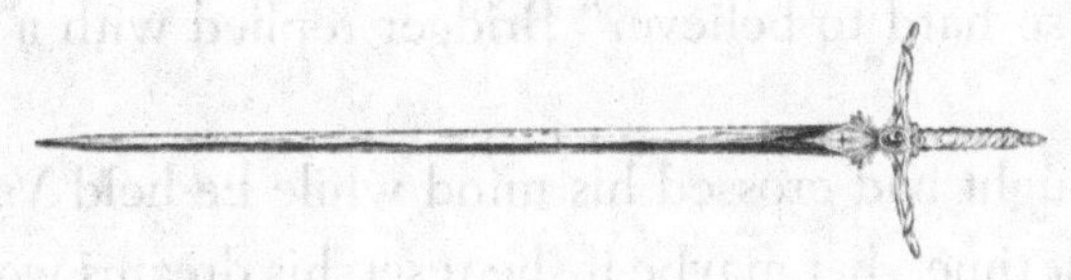

Bridger told Meyer everything.

Well, not everything.

He left out the part about the kiss but filled him in on all the other details that didn't show how torn Bridger was about the ex he should have long since been over. He'd gone through multiple stages of grief and anger over losing the girl he'd once loved.

Was Bridger ready to face those again if this didn't go the way everyone wanted?

Tossing the thought out of his mind's window and slamming it shut, Bridger laid out the plan he'd fed Marlena and then spent more time answering every single question Meyer had than Bridger on the entirety of his story.

"Do you believe Marlena can actually make a portal?"

"If she can't, no one else can."

"How do you plan on finding Vega when you get there?"

"I'm sure I'll figure it out."

"What if Vega doesn't have her memories?"

"Then I guess it'll be easier to make her trust me."

"And all of this is to what... stop dreaming?" The way Meyer asked the question made Bridger feel like he wouldn't believe him even if it were the whole truth.

Whether Meyer believed Bridger or not wasn't of any concern to him currently. He had to rid himself of the dreams.

I'll do anything to stop the fucking dreams. Bridger wasn't above begging at this point.

"Is that so hard to believe?" Bridger replied with a question of his own.

The thought had crossed his mind while he held Vega's lifeless body this last time, that maybe if she reset, his dreams would go with her. It had been clear from his first night's sleep his dreams weren't going to stop—if anything, they'd gotten worse. Moving into a part of his life Bridger never wanted to revisit.

The time he'd been not only Marlena's prisoner, but a prisoner of his own mind.

Marlena hadn't needed to do much to torture Bridger for two years—she knew if he was left alone long enough, he'd do it himself.

Maybe it was the curse causing the dreams, somehow reaching through Vega to him down their bonded connection. Hell, maybe it was their bond doing it! Bridger couldn't be certain about anything— none of this had ever been definite.

They'd been speculating what had happened to them since the first night. At this point, he was starting to question every little thing he knew.

I can't keep living this way. Afraid to go to sleep because it always led to the memories he'd voluntarily forgotten.

Here Vega was, fighting to get hers back, to keep them, and Bridger had thrown his away like they never mattered.

Words from the night Bridger visited Vega in her last life, locked in the rickety Aeris dungeon after being tortured for hours by Marlena, rang in Bridger's head like an alarm: *"And how did you escape? By lying to yourself that what we had wasn't real? You left me! You left me, and you stand here like none of it mattered to you!"*

"Are you sure that lightning strike you took on the battlefield didn't cause brain damage?" Meyer cocked his head so hard it almost touched his shoulder.

Bridger glared, shoving only the essentials into a small backpack. He had to leave tonight. He was already a month behind. "We've tried everything else."

Meyer didn't reply right away, and a sinking feeling settled into Bridger's stomach at his pause.

"You let her go, Bridger." It sounded like Meyer screamed the words, even though it was actually the guilt inside his brain amplifying the truth.

Bridger whipped around, scowling. "Yes, I did, and then she tried to kill me, so good thing I can't die!" His room inside Vincere was locked tighter than all the others combined, so he didn't mind speaking freely with Meyer.

"Do you really think this is a good idea?" Meyer sipped on a glass of gold liquor, smoked, no ice, room temperature. His signature choice.

Bridger swung his bag over his shoulder and slipped his bonded dagger from the sheath on his leg. He flipped it around, catching it by the hilt with the blade pointing towards him, and handed it to Meyer. "I don't know if I have much of a choice." Bridger knew if he still had a half-mortal soul, his bones would ache from the lack of sleep. It wasn't his body he had to worry about anymore—it was his mind.

He could still lose himself. These dreams, these *memories* coming back to haunt him still had what it would take to break Bridger. "Vega might be the answer, she might not be. All I know is the bond wants me to go to her, or it would have been Khort who had the dream instead."

Meyer eyed the dagger.

Bridger nodded for him to take it. "I don't trust this with Marlena. My sword's in the safe."

Meyer sighed, grabbing the bonded weapon from him. "You said if she dies, you die. What changed?"

"Nothing," he said. *Me,* Bridger thought and had to swallow the word to stop it from coming out. He ran a hand over his face. "I don't know, Meyer. I have no idea what I'm doing, but what I do know is I can't live like this. I can't let Vega di—" He cleared his throat, letting the word die on his tongue. "I've already crossed every line there is to cross. What's one more?"

Another long pause filled the room with silence. It pulled taut with unspoken words and white lies.

Meyer stood up abruptly, taking Bridger by surprise, and wrapped his arms around him in a tight hug.

A hug.

Bridger couldn't remember the last time someone hugged him.

"I hope you find what you're looking for on Earth." Bridger waited until Meyer pulled away from the embrace, watching as he grabbed his drink off the side table before turning for the door.

"You're in charge while I'm gone. Don't fuck anything up." Bridger ordered. "And watch after Halo, will you?"

Meyer groaned and reached for the handle. "What is it with you and that kid?" He didn't wait for Bridger to answer before making his exit.

Bridger answered out loud anyway. "He reminds me of me."

A bowl of warm stew perked Arlet up as soon as the scent hit her.

Bridger joined Arlet inside her cell, pasting on a smile. "Hungry?" He wiggled the bowl over her head, dropping a spoon into her lap.

In Arlet fashion, she threw it at his head.

Bridger caught it midair and sighed. "Arlet, please act civilized. I know you're used to acting feral after all this time in the wild, but you could at least try," he sneered.

She kicked at his feet, but Bridger took a step back, careful not to spill the stew amidst her tantrum. "I hate you."

"You don't mean that." He faked a pout. "I'm just trying to bring you some dinner and let you know I'm leaving." Bridger extended the spoon to her. "I came to ask you for advice."

Arlet snatched it out of his grasp, and it didn't come flying back at his head, which was a good sign, but Arlet did start snickering like he'd told a really funny joke. "Get fucked, Dimico," she said, but her eyes kept jumping back to the delicious smelling beef and vegetable stew.

Bridger offered the bowl to Arlet with a raised brow. "It's not poisoned, and even if it were, it wouldn't kill you." He shrugged. "The portal is ready. I'm going to Earth. I'd love to make this as easy as possible for myself and Vega's sake."

Arlet took the stew and scooted until her back met the wall. She balanced the bowl between her knees and wasted no time scooping the first bite into her mouth.

Bridger knew she fought with everything she had not to hum a contented moan.

Hunger would win every time.

"How do I know how to find Vega when I get there?" Bridger asked Arlet for probably the twentieth time this week.

Through a mouthful of still-hot stew, Arlet surprised him and said, "Wherever you saw Vega in your dream, that's where she'll be."

Pinned against the wall about to be fucked by another man? I sure hope not.

"And how will I know I'm on the right track?" he bit out.

Arlet shrugged, scarfing down another bite. "Took me a long time to figure out all the details. Guess you'll have to figure it out too."

Bridger groaned. "Will you just help me out here?"

"No," Arlet deadpanned. "I've told you all I'm willing to. I am not on your side. So what, you showed weakness and let her go a couple times? That doesn't erase everything else. If you're meant to find her, you will. Simple as that."

Bridger ground his teeth together, every muscle in his body tensing with frustration.

"If Vega was right, if she has her memories, there is nothing, not even you, that's going to get in the way of her breaking her curse. If this worked, Vega is going to be fucking *unstoppable*."

"Who said I wanted to stop her from breaking the curse?" Bridger asked, retreating from the cell. "We're bonded. Her curse is ours, right?" He locked the door, leaving Arlet alone inside again. "Have you ever thought about how much stronger we might be if Vega weren't cursed?" His brow rose. "If we're this connected now, if we've got all these new powers and abilities, what might happen if there's nothing weighing one of us down anymore?"

The look on Arlet's sullen face told him she'd thought about it—they all had.

"You're not wearing that to Earth, are you?" Arlet asked, taking her last bite.

Bridger looked down at his basic training suit. "What's wrong with what I'm wearing?"

A soft, almost genuine smile tugged at the corners of Arlet's lips. "They're going to think you're dressed up as an Avenger."

7

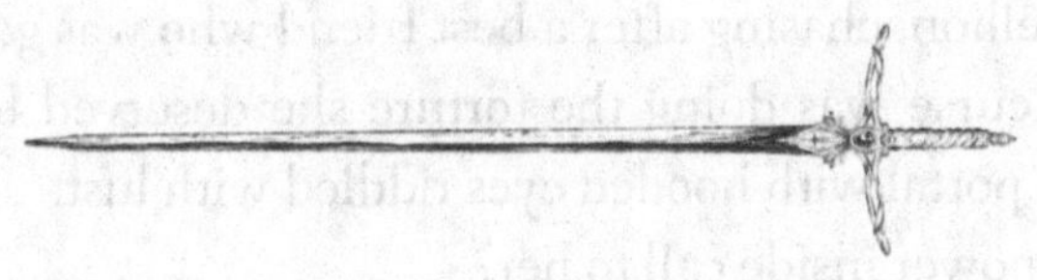

BLOOD DRIPPED TO THE FLOOR FROM THE CUT MARLENA MADE across Bridger's palm. As she'd instructed, he ran his open wound across the top of the iron frame. It looked nothing like the portal he was used to seeing in Vates.

There was no holographic sheen to it, no pull of energy. *It was so much worse.*

He stepped back after he drenched the frame with his blood. The smoke-like shadows darkened around the edge where his hand had just been. It reminded him of the remnants of travelers' powers after they jumped. Except this didn't disappear over time—it stayed put, ebbing and flowing like it had a pulse of its own.

"Are you sure this is going to work?" Bridger asked hesitantly, slipping a dagger into his waistband. After the Avengers comment, Bridger had changed into a casual outfit. He hoped a black button-down with sleeves rolled to the crook of his elbows and black slacks made to fit his body perfectly, like everything else in his wardrobe personally made for the commander of Tolevarre, would make him stand out on Earth less.

Marlena stared him down. "You doubt me?"

Bridger didn't react. "I mean, if you could make another portal this entire time, one that led right to Vega, why wouldn't you have just sent someone directly to her each time?"

Marlena's smile expanded to reveal her canines. "I never had a reason to make another portal until *you* asked, not when Arlet did the dirty work all by herself. Having her away from Khort and the brewing rebellion, chasing after a best friend who was good as dead? It's like the curse was doing the torture she deserved for me." She watched the portal with hooded eyes riddled with lust.

Did the power inside call to her?

"This curse might technically be on my sister, Bridger, but make no mistake... I designed it to fuck with everyone else's minds too. Yours. Arlet's. Khort's." Marlena smiled. "You all didn't have to endure Vega's death only once. You had to face it over, and over, and over again, slowly realizing she'd never be the person you all loved ever again."

Bridger fought off a chill.

"There's nothing I can't do," Marlena cooed.

"Except figure out how to kill your sister." Bridger clarified.

Marlena's pause made Bridger crack a smile of his own.

"So help me gods if you don't shut the fuck up."

His grin grew the longer he got under Marlena's skin. Bridger shrugged, waltzing towards the new portal. He hid the unease settling in his stomach the closer he got to the unknown. "I told you I was done doing your dirty work when it came to Vega, and yet here I am, once again, dealing with her for you. Voluntarily. I'm such a great guy. You should be nicer to me." His joking tone disappeared.

"Bridger." She practically growled his name. "I am *so* nice to you. You of all people know just how mean I can be." Marlena looked like she might implode at any second.

"Mm-hmm." He eyed the portal again. "This is going to take me right to Vega?" Bridger got serious, watching the smoke swirl.

Marlena nodded tightly. "You know where she is. This will take you wherever it is you want to go. I just hope you're sure where that is."

Gods, Marlena really pissed Bridger off.

He wouldn't let her get under his skin.

I have a job to do.

Even if that job was still a bit unclear to Bridger. All he knew was he had to find Vega—he could figure the rest out later.

He stuck a hand through the portal, keeping his body turned towards Marlena. The air inside was cold, nipping at his skin like the summer bugs on a humid night.

He pulled his arm out, bringing it back around to inspect with a quick hum, his chest vibrating. Nothing looked out of the ordinary. "I know exactly where I need to be." Bridger locked eyes with her, returning her cold stare.

"Need I remind you what happens if you cross me, Commander?" There was nothing behind her frigid eyes but malice and turmoil.

Bridger huffed a humorless laugh. "I'm well aware of what you think you can do, Your Majesty." Before Marlena could scold him for using that title, Bridger took two large steps back and plummeted into the portal.

One last time.

Except, it didn't feel the same this time. Instead of a warm tingle when his body sank through the abyss, pain and a sense of wrongness wrapped him in a tight hug and didn't let go.

He couldn't scream, couldn't break free of the suffocating anguish gripping at every piece of his being. It felt like traveling— like the in-between wanted to swallow him up.

"You can't have her. Her death belongs to me."

The chanting of a familiar voice echoed through his head and ripped the air from his lungs, leaving him starving for oxygen.

He should have trusted his gut, should have heeded the

warnings his body was trying to get him to see. But all he'd been thinking about was Vega.

Vega.

Marlena told him this portal would take him where he wanted to go.

Bridger heard his own voice shouting at him down the chasm. *Fight!*

So he did, going after the voice chanting, *"Mine. Mine. Mine. She's mine."*

He struggled through the grip on his throat, combating the urge to slip under the surface into unconsciousness. Bridger clung to the power he felt tugging him through the portal, gnawing at the chance to reach the other side.

Instead of stepping through like he'd done last time, Bridger was spat out, freefalling until he landed with shards of glass and debris raining down on him.

8

"WHAT IN THE HELL, VEGA?"

This morning Chase had pressed his lips against Vega's cheek, giving her a goodbye kiss before leaving for work. He did this every morning, and every morning Vega pretended to sleep until he was gone.

She spun around at the sound of his voice, her heartbeat pounding inside her throat. Chase shouldn't have been home for another three or four hours.

Once she got up, brushed her teeth and hair, got dressed, and made herself breakfast, there was nothing else to look forward to in the day.

"Wha-what are you doing?" he stammered, jaw sagging.

Busted.

Chase's wide eyes trailed up her arm, landing on the hammer Vega still had raised in the air.

If she went for a walk, Chase would call immediately and ask why she was out, claiming he was worried something would happen to her if she was out alone. "You'll get lost. There will be another accident." He'd used every excuse in the book.

She dropped her arm, hugging the hammer close to her chest. "I..." Vega couldn't think with Chase's gaze searing into her like he'd been the one to catch her between the legs of another woman—*no, just you on the balcony with a hammer, trash can, matches, and some lighter fluid.*

Vega searched her mind for an excuse, a lie. *Anything.* She couldn't find one. Her brain felt trapped in quicksand.

"Vega, is that...?" He trailed off, stepping forward to peer into the trash can behind her. "That's my grandmother's brooch."

A bear balancing on a ball like a circus animal. She'd found it inside one of Chase's coat pockets.

Tollybear. Bear.

She'd thought it could be a sign. She was looking for them in everything these days—hoping something would click and she'd finally stop feeling like she was living in a false reality.

Vega knew this life here wasn't right. This wasn't her home. She stared at the back of Chase's head, his sandy blond hair cut too short.

Chase's look of astonishment turned into something new. "Is this what you've been doing with the things going missing over the last month?"

She hadn't thought this through—not any of the times she'd found something inside their apartment to destroy had she planned for Chase to pop in randomly and find her.

Stupid. So fucking stupid, Vega. She scolded herself but couldn't find words to respond to Chase, her mouth clamped shut while her brain tried, *so hard,* to find an acceptable excuse.

"Don't just stand there! Answer me!" Chase screamed, his voice echoing through the courtyard and amplifying to their neighbor's balconies.

She blinked, trying to get herself together, and when Vega opened her eyes, Chase's open hand connected with her cheek.

The slap—if she could even call it that—caught her off guard, sending Vega tumbling into the glass patio door.

Somehow it didn't shatter, but Vega's head felt like it might.

The blinding pain of a bad headache made Vega put pressure on her temples as she rose.

There had once been a version of Vega who loved Chase, the sweet boy who... had always kind of treated her like a stray dog he'd graciously taken in.

This had never been love.

This was about control.

The curse's control.

Stars sprinkled her vision, fire shooting down every nerve from her head to her toes. Vega heard herself gasp, but the air caught in her throat when Chase's hands wrapped around her neck.

No, no, no. You're not weak. You will not become this person again.

Pain rained down, making Vega immobile. It was impossible for her to fight physically when she was being ravaged by something invisible on the inside.

Death.

She thought she was dead. Whether it was the pain in her head or from Chase choking the air out of her, Vega was almost completely numb, unable to feel the fire in her legs or arms anymore.

Nausea turned to bile when the oven inside her brain went from broil to slow cook. The pain dulled enough for panic to set in, black spots turning to holes in her vision.

With all the strength she had left, Vega slammed her knee in between Chase's legs.

He dropped to the patio floor, hunched over and groaning loud enough to let her neighbors know she'd handled it.

Vega gasped for air, backing away. "Don't you ever, *ever* put your fucking hands on me again! Or it'll be you burning in a bucket." Her voice was raspy, her windpipe surely taking some damage.

When he glanced up from the floor, his face was cast under the shadow of the roof's overhang. Chase's eyes looked soulless, engulfed with a blackness only a nightmare could get right.

She took a step back, and from her new angle, Vega could see it wasn't an illusion. Chase's eyes were all black—no iris, no white. All black.

Fear stole her breath.

Move.

Vega ran back inside the apartment, grabbing her coat and boots on the way to the front door. She didn't pause to put them on.

She had to get out of here.

Her chest burned with each panting breath, her inhales so loud she almost couldn't hear Chase call after her with strangled words before she slammed the apartment door.

Vega's pulse pounded in her temples, the rhythm dizzying. Steadying herself on the wall, Vega took a deep breath and fought through the ache returning to her head, darting down the three flights of stairs like she was being led by an invisible rope. Her feet told her where to go, letting her brain catch up as it went.

A familiar tug in Vega's chest and the incessant itch of the brand on her wrist made her trip over herself as she exited the building.

She knew that feeling.

Nothing, not even the pain in her head, could get Vega to forget it.

Arlet.

Vega took off running, quickly realizing she was still barefoot.

She slipped into yesterday's socks stuffed inside her boots, threw her coat on, and sprinted, finding the right track as the invisible tug drew her across the street and down the block.

People stared as she shot by, clearly not dressed for an afternoon run.

Vega dug her nails into the skin at her wrist when the crackle of the pain in her head returned. It reminded her of the time Junie, a soldier in Bridger's army, had spent in her head, twisting and turning Vega's abilities on herself.

The Colosseum stood tall as she approached, crowded with tourists excited to see one of The Seven Wonders of The World.

She caught a couple looks from a group walking by as she hopped onto an occupied bench. The older man sitting there scoffed and hopped up like Vega had jumped on his lap and not beside it.

The only words Vega could pick up from his quick Italian were "disrespect" and "youth." If dude only knew Vega probably had at least twenty years on him…

She could see over people now, ignoring everyone's curious glances.

Vega squinted through hazy vision to register anything more than a few feet away. A baby cried in the distance, a woman chatted on the phone in a foreign language, and a tour guide walked by, telling his group all about the history of the city. They'd be shocked to know a god walked among them now.

All the background noise and people faded away when a head full of curls came into view, bobbing down the path away from Vega.

"Arlet!" Vega called as she jumped off the bench and pushed her way through the crowd, earning some disgruntled responses from the tourists.

Her hand touched Arlet's shoulder, and the tug in her chest tightened.

The girl swiveled around, her eyebrows drawing together. *Not Arlet.*

Pain sliced through Vega's head again. She inhaled and stumbled back, her hands shooting to the sides of her head. "I'm so sorry," Vega bit out, ignoring the look of concern on the stranger's face. "I thought you were someone I knew." She turned away before the girl could respond, wincing at the next jolt of pain.

What is happening to me?

Vega took a breath, trying to focus on something other than the pain. Commotion of a building crowd caught her attention in the distance.

The sensation in her chest went from a tug to an all-out drag. Her feet moved without an order from her brain. Vega caught bits and pieces of the words a panicked woman spoke near the center of the crowd.

Fell. Bleeding.

Vega pushed her way through, stepping on toes to get to the front.

The portal is in California... How did Arlet make it here? Doubt crept in, but it couldn't get her to ignore the feeling that'd brought her here. She hadn't even registered the ring around her wrist burned like fire, too distracted by the dimming headache.

"Go get a medic," a man beside her called to someone outside the crowd.

"That's really not necessary," a voice cut through. A voice Vega would know anywhere...

Oh my gods.

Vega stumbled through to the front, and if her jaw could touch the ground, it would have. Standing in the middle with the woman asking for help wasn't the beautiful, curly-haired best friend she'd been accustomed to seeing on Earth.

It was Bridger... his chest covered in cuts and blood, looking disheveled and maybe even a little annoyed.

My name is Vega Caelum. I'm a god, and I'm from a world called Tolevarre.

Her life came back into focus. There was no accident, no TBI.

When Bridger's eyes locked on hers, the pain in her head, the tug of the thread in her chest, and the fire of the brand around her wrist vanished.

9

"Hey, Kitten," Bridger said with his lips pulling to one side in a lazy smile.

What the fuck—What. The. Fuck. There was no time to think about what Bridger was doing here, let alone how he got here.

The panicking woman didn't let up. "Doctor. You need hospital," she demanded in broken English.

Vega's eyes felt glued to Bridger's, and it seemed she had the same hold on him until the woman started blabbering to the new people gathering around to see what the fuss was about.

"I could use a little help here." Bridger's words broke her trance —stole the only moment of peace Vega had felt since waking up in this life.

Her body acted before her brain could catch up, still lagging from the comedown of the splitting headache.

Bridger was here.

On Earth.

In Rome.

Vega crashed into him with so much force he stumbled back a

47

few steps. Her arms snaked around his midsection, and when she inhaled, Vega smelled home. The crisp pine scent mixed with Bridger's fresh clothing. "I wasn't going crazy," she whispered, feeling tears sting behind closed eyes. She squeezed them tighter. "I knew it was real." For over a month, she'd been questioning her sanity. Day in and day out, Vega was starting to feel like she was losing her mind—creeping further into a state of psychosis.

Bridger tensed for a second before wrapping his arms around her too.

For the first time since she reset in this life, Vega felt no pain when she remembered.

I can go home. To Tolevarre.

"Hospital," the woman said again, ripping Vega back into the current world she was in.

Fuck.

He couldn't go to a hospital here. He couldn't draw the attention of authorities. He couldn't get in trouble... because he wasn't from here, and not existing in this world would cause other problems Vega couldn't deal with.

"Oh my god!" Vega exclaimed, having to remember not to add the *s* at the end. She pulled from Bridger's arms and looked up at him. "What happened? I've been looking everywhere for you." She reached up and placed her hands on Bridger's cheeks, playing the part of worried lover well. Splatters of blood had already started to dry on his neck and chest from the cut still oozing near his collarbone. Her hands warmed where they connected with Bridger's body. "Are you okay?" she asked loudly enough for everyone to hear.

Bridger's eyes flashed with recognition and something else—gratitude? *Gods, focus.*

He smiled softly, resting a hand over one of hers. Vega did her best not to flinch away. "I'm fine. I told this nice lady," he said with a sneer, "what she saw wasn't as bad as she thought. I took a wrong step and tumbled a few feet. That's all."

Vega had learned the bare minimum Italian over the last month, but she understood most of what the woman said, telling a much different story than Bridger.

She dropped her hands from Bridger's face, holding them over her heart with a gasp. "My goodness. Thank you for helping him." Vega reached for Bridger's hand.

"Medical attention!" the woman continued to yell. She was panicking, rightfully so, after seeing a man drop from the sky in front of her.

We have to get out. Bridger glanced down at her hand, then up at her quickly before his fingers slid between hers. It was as if he understood the urgency in her look without hearing the thoughts in her head.

"Is he hurt?" another voice asked.

"What happened?" Others joined in.

Vega laughed, pulling Bridger along as they barged their way through the crowd. "He's fine, really. Just a little clumsy."

A whistle from an approaching officer made a warning alarm go off in Vega's mind. A few onlookers pointed at them, drawing the police's attention.

Vega didn't hesitate. As soon as they broke through, she dropped Bridger's hand. "Run!"

Bridger kept pace beside her, hardly breaking a sweat while Vega pushed herself enough to make her lungs burn.

She hadn't gotten much exercise while here on Earth and felt it as they rounded the corner down a long roadway with lots of traffic and people; people who gawked at the two weaving between pedestrians and stopped cars.

They needed to get out of sight. Vega checked over her shoulder before slowing them to a walk and pulling Bridger by the crook of his elbow into an alleyway.

When they were deep enough to be out of sight from the road, Vega let go of Bridger's arm and spun around.

He smiled and started to say something, but Vega wasn't having it. As happy as she was to see him, it wasn't to see *him*... It was because seeing him meant she was right—it meant she wasn't going crazy, remembering a life that never happened.

It had happened. All of it. The lives. The memories. Everything.

Vega had been right.

She'd tricked the fucking curse.

And this life, the things happening in it—the headaches, the therapy for a TBI, Chase's reaction to finding her with the broken brooch, were all because of the curse.

It was still trying to take her from herself.

Vega slammed him against the alley's stone wall, pushing him back again when he tried to step forward.

Bridger threw his hands up in surrender, looking down his chest at her. "Easy, Kitten."

"What are you doing here?" she spat.

Bridger faked a gasp, acting hurt. "What happened to the girl who was so happy to see me that I got a hug?" He crowded her space, leaning forward.

Vega pushed at his chest again. He gave up quicker than she anticipated, letting his butt rest against the stone with his hands still up. "Why are you here, Bridger?"

"Isn't it obvious? I came for you." He pointed at her, letting his hands fall to his side from there. "Good to see you still have your memories. Don't you think maybe it would've been easier to, oh, I don't know, walk back through the fucking portal instead of risking yourself and your memories again?"

Vega stalled for a moment, her eyebrows drawing together. "What?" She paused to gauge his seriousness. She quickly realized he was dead fucking serious. "It doesn't work like that. I have to reset. The curse has to reset... That's the whole poi—I'm not getting into that with you right now." She shook her head, holding her hand up and wagging her finger like Bridger was a child in trouble. "How did you get here?"

Bridger reached out, grabbed her finger, and gently pushed her hand to her chest. "None of that." His voice had a deep and commanding rumble. "I came through a portal." Bridger's eyes flicked to her neck, and she watched his emotions flip as quick as a light switch. In less than a second, Bridger went from thoughtful to downright scary. "Who the fuck choked you?"

There was no stopping him from pushing off the wall now. Vega took a few steps back as he stalked her, gaining ground quicker than she could flee with his long legs. "What?" Vega asked, taken aback.

A mark must already be forming from Chase's attack.

"Your neck. There are fingerprint bruises forming on your neck." Bridger was fighting to keep his cool, but the words spoken through gritted teeth gave him away.

This time, it was Vega's back against a wall.

Bridger reached for her face, and Vega didn't flinch, didn't move. He gripped her jaw so gently she might not have known he was touching her if it weren't for the warmth of his skin and the tingles traveling through his fingertips like little tendrils of her lightning. He turned her head to the side, getting a better look. "Vega..."

Her name from his lips reminded her of the conversation they were having before, of how badly she didn't want to remember the inhuman stare of Chase's black eyes. "That's not important right now... You said portal? Like, the portal that's supposed to be in California?" Vega asked, trying to distract and pull herself away from Bridger.

He was too close. Vega couldn't think with him this close.

She hated the way he made her head feel clouded. He shouldn't make her feel anything but malice.

Her distraction didn't work. Bridger let her jaw go, though, standing his ground. "Who hurt you, Vega?"

They didn't have time to get into this right now. "Everyone! Everyone has hurt me! The curse, Chase, Marlena, this world!" Vega threw her arms up, exasperated. "You," she said on a breath.

Bridger flinched like she'd slapped him, taking a step back.

"Something is happening. Something is different in this life. We don't have time to worry about who and what is hurting me. This world is always going to try to hurt me. I don't belong here." Vega swallowed, and she could feel the tenderness in her throat now that the adrenaline was wearing off.

Bridger stood unmoving except for the rise and fall of his chest.

"How did you get here from California?" she asked, her tone direct.

A muscle in Bridger's jaw ticked, and the veins in his arms looked like they might burst from the force of his clenched fists. Vega could tell he was fighting against losing himself to rage, a natural reaction inside him as a blood-born warrior.

Bridger was trained to keep calm in situations like this—but sometimes even Tolevarre's best let their masks slip.

It took some time for him to answer. "Not that portal... a new one," he said while motioning to the cut on his chest. Blood had finally stopped dripping from the deep gash, but it smeared over his exposed skin. "Marlena made it, but apparently someone or something didn't like that because it didn't feel right. And there was a voice..." He paused, thinking about his next words. "It exploded."

"What do you mean, it exploded?" Vega asked through a rush of shock, making her sidestep to stop herself from swaying.

"I mean..." Bridger closed his fists and opened them, mimicking the sound of an explosion. He cocked his head, confusion marring his stupid-handsome face.

Vega's shock turned to fear in an instant. "Fuck, Bridger. FUCK!" Her voice echoed down the alley. Vega paced, her boots scraping against the old stone beneath her feet. "Why? Why would you come here? I was figuring it out on my own."

She definitely wasn't.

A thought hit Vega, and her feet skidded to a stop. "Where's Arlet? Why isn't Arlet here?"

Bridger's lips parted, and a sinking feeling seized control of Vega's body.

"No," she said, exhaling. "No." Vega shook her head. She already knew, even before Bridger spoke.

"Marlena has her."

Vega didn't notice her knees had buckled until Bridger was on his in front of her.

"She can't kill her." His fingers found the bottom of her chin, pulling her face up to meet his strong gaze. "She's going to be okay."

She couldn't take the physical contact. It sent her body into overdrive. It craved the simmering touch of Bridger's fingertips, but Vega's brain wasn't on the same page.

"Don't you fucking touch me." The warning imitated a snarling wildcat.

Bridger's hand shot back like he was dealing with one.

"I let Arlet down." Tears burned her eyes, but she wasn't willing to let them spill in front of him. "Death isn't the worst thing Marlena can do to us." She clenched her jaw and swallowed the lump in her throat.

"I know," he whispered.

The pain in those two words was a kick to Vega's gut. He knew... because he spent two years locked away with her.

Vega saw the man she'd fallen in love with. The softness he'd once reserved for her was back in his eyes—he looked like Bridger... not Commander Dimico.

Commander Dimico had been her enemy for forty years, had turned into a man who could stare Vega dead in the eyes and drive a dagger through her heart... but the man looking at her now wasn't the commander she'd been forced to hate.

She couldn't, *no*, she wouldn't let herself forget. Just because a piece of the old him kept breaking through didn't erase everything else.

Vega felt like she'd thrown her brain in a washing machine and turned it on Heavy Duty—she was giving herself whiplash with how fast her emotions changed.

"Does she have Khort?" Vega asked, her stomach souring more.

"No, he's with the rebels."

The word "rebels" made Vega tense.

Bridger must have noticed, adding, "He's getting people out. Towns and cities all around Tolevarre are rioting after Marlena wiped out Solum."

"Did you...?" Vega didn't know what she was even trying to ask.

He shook his head. "She acted on her own, with her own people. My army went in after. There weren't many left alive, but I ended up with a few new recruits."

He didn't kill them...

If Solum was gone, Tolevarre would starve. Or at least the people who didn't serve a purpose to her sister would.

After what felt like a lifetime, the sadness of putting Arlet in the way of Marlena turned to rage and the momentary pause between the two was over.

Vega jumped to her feet. "What game are you playing?" The wildcat was back. She felt hollow without her powers—she had the entire time she'd been back on Earth, but now more than ever she longed for the feeling of her electric current. "She sent you here, didn't she?" Vega backed up.

"No," he lied, backtracking immediately. "Well, yes, but it wasn't her idea. It was mine."

Vega's laugh was full of vitriol. "Oh, and that makes it better?" She watched as Bridger took a slow inhale, trying to control himself.

"You think we could come to a mutual agreement about something?" he asked, successfully swallowing his anger.

Vega smirked sarcastically. "Probably not, but go on."

Bridger tried and failed not to look irritated. "We're in this mess together now. I couldn't wait around, wondering if you'd gotten it right any longer. I had to know if you figured it out. I made the decision to come here on my own. You made the decision to trick the curse by yourself. Earth is obviously where we both thought we should be."

"Yeah, you decided you wanted to come to Earth and save me all of a sudden?" Vega had never been a maiden in need of saving. Not the real Vega, at least.

He didn't argue back and chose to ignore her smartass comment, which added to Vega's annoyance. *How dare he take the high road after everything he's d—*

She was just about to tell him so when he interrupted her thoughts. "I can't stop thinking about what would happen if your curse was destroyed. What would happen to the bonded if the one used as the glue to bind us was set free from a death curse?" He raised a brow, not giving her an opportunity to reply. "You're being held back, and I think we'd all benefit from releasing you." He raised a single shoulder nonchalantly. "And for some reason, I keep fucking dreaming of you." She caught the twitch of his jaw muscle. "It has to mean something."

"So what are you saying, Bridger? You chose Marlena, and now that you need something from me, you decide it's time to come crawling back?" Vega's voice was calm.

"You don't have me on my hands and knees yet." There was a tense pause hanging off the last word. "So what if that is my motive? Would you deny your cause the chance of winning because you're bitter about the choices I made?" His response wasn't remorseful. It was straight to the point—exactly how she'd expect him to be.

Vega couldn't possibly decide right this second. The sound of a slamming door made her glance over her shoulder as a man exited from the back of a business and stared at them warily before stomping off. When he was gone, Vega turned her attention back to Bridger. "I don't trust you," she admitted unabashedly.

Bridger nodded. "I'd call you crazy if you did."

Vega eyed him, rolling her gaze down his torso and back up. "It's easy to make pretty promises when you're a realm away." She crossed her arms and popped her hip. "We aren't friends, nothing you can do will change that, but we're bound together. It's time we stop ignoring that. Or..." She paused to wag her hand at Bridger. "Blocking it out, whatever it is you did to betray the girl you loved."

Bridger puffed a laugh through his lips. "Whether we like it or not, baby, we're stuck with each other." Bridger held up his wrist with the matching brand.

Vega glowered at the nickname, sending him a warning. "How did you find me?" Maybe if she asked him enough questions, she'd see the cracks in his shield—she'd be able to see through his lies.

"The same way Arlet does. I had a dream about where you were, and then somehow when I went through the new portal, it spit me out here. I found you minutes later, looking like you'd seen a ghost."

Vega knew she had to have looked crazed, coming down from the awful high of whatever the fuck had been going on in her head and frantically trying to find the end of the invisible string attached to her heart.

"We need Bridger."

Arlet's words haunted her. A reminder of what the bond was so clearly trying to tell them. If the tie from the night they summoned Remus, the night they all became bonded to each other by blood and a dead demigod, had wanted to keep Bridger out, it wouldn't have made him dream of the life he'd been trying to forget, and it definitely wouldn't have allowed him to be the one who came to get her this time... It could have chosen Khort.

"I'm sick of losing, Bridger. Sick of being considered weak because of this fucking curse. I want our world to know peace." It wasn't just about stopping Marlena—it was about Tolevarre and all the innocent lives caught up in the midst of a sisters' spat. "I'll stop at nothing to break it, to get back to the people I love. No one is going to stand in my way." She stared him down, eyes flicking to the open alleyway behind him in case she needed to make a run for it. "Not you. Not Marlena. Not in this world or our own."

Bridger sidestepped, clearing a path for her. "Lead the way."

10

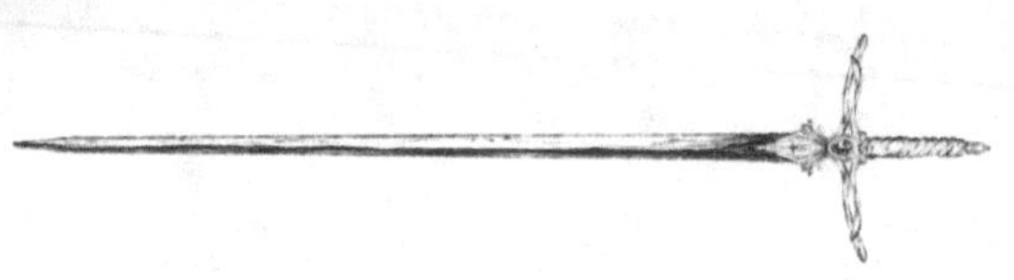

Bridger picked up a photo in a gold frame, bringing it into the stream of light filtering through the window.

It was Vega in a simple white wedding dress doing nothing to show off her natural beauty. The material looked stiff and wrinkled, like it'd been pulled out of a box moments before taking pictures. Her hair was pinned back in a tight bun, and her makeup washed out her usually bright eyes.

Vega looked nothing like he'd imagined her to on their wedding day. A vision he'd once been able to see vividly.

Next to her stood a man with neat features and an unassuming face. "Vega, this guy looks like he sleeps with a fucking nightlight." His smile looked too formal to be happy.

*Vega deserves someone who smiles at her like I used—*Bridger didn't let himself finish the thought.

Standing in the home she shared with another man wasn't something Bridger had ever expected to experience. He'd spent the first fifteen years of Vega's curse wondering what her lives were like, and now here he stood, inserted into one directly.

She poked her head around the corner and noticed the picture in his hands. "I need you to take this seriously."

Bridger could feel the frustration radiating off her skin, even from this far across the room. He scoffed. "I am taking this seriously. You told me to look to see if I noticed anything that could be cursed." He wiggled the picture in his hand. "This looks like a curse to me. You looked miserable."

Vega rolled her eyes, snatching the picture from him. Her eyes raked over it, completely unreadable. "I was. The dress was a size too small, but his mother insisted I wear the ugly family gown. She even told me it wasn't the size of the dress that was the problem."

Anger simmered low in Bridger's core, his eyes taking their sweet time up Vega's body. He started at her boots, slowly creeping up until his eyes caught on a black stone and golden band twinkling with every move of Vega's hand.

Bridger's breath caught in his chest.

She's still wearing it.

It was on the opposite hand than normal, causing Bridger's eyes to scan to her left finger. Another ring, shiny and silver with a single stone and decorative band took the spot where Bridger's sword piece should be.

The thought of Vega with another man shouldn't bother him— they'd been down that road. *It doesn't work,* he lied to himself.

Bridger moved on before thinking too hard about it.

He wanted to enjoy the view, but he couldn't look past the darkening marks around her neck. The flame of his rage grew. *So much for moving on...*

Some lives seemed to suck any life she had out of her, but this was Vega. *My Vega.* And he almost said so before being interrupted.

Vega's voice calmed the wildfire of wrath growing inside him. He didn't have time to think about what that meant. "Don't look at me like that."

"Like what?" Bridger asked, snapping out of his daze and following her into the kitchen.

"Like you're thinking of me naked," Vega quipped with a cat-like growl, slamming a drawer a bit too hard. She pulled out a hammer and whacked the frame a dozen times before she seemed content that she'd beat it enough to check it wasn't cursed. She swept the glass into the trash can and shoved the wrecked mirror under the kitchen sink, shutting the cabinet door.

Apparently, she thought he'd drop the subject and move on, but Bridger liked pushing her a little—call him a masochist, but he'd always loved being on the other side of Vega's silver tongue. If he was distracted by her sassy-ass mouth, then he wouldn't have time to think about breaking the neck of whoever had left those bruises on her.

You're here to save yourself, not cause more problems. Bridger wasn't ready to unpack the emotions of it all just yet, choosing to shove them deep, unshielded and ready to crawl to the surface at any moment.

Bridger shrugged, picking up a trinket inside a potted plant. "I hadn't gotten you completely naked in my head yet. I was distracted by the marks on your neck."

Vega chucked a cooking utensil at him—*Thank gods it wasn't the hammer*—but even without his powers, Bridger still had quick reflexes and ducked in time. "I understand you're angry with me, but you could at least pretend to be nice. We have no choice but to be around each other." He closed the distance between them and held his hand out for Vega to grab the ceramic frog from his palm.

Her eyes glanced down at it, and her frustration was palpable as she jutted a hip. "If I'm not trying to kill you, I'd say I'm being sugary sweet. Which is way more than you deserve." She plucked the frog from his palm and threw it down the drain, flipping a switch on the wall that started some kind of terrible grinding and clattering noise.

Bridger jerked away while Vega stood there, as calm as could be. "What the fuck is that?"

When the frog finally cleared through, Vega flipped the switch, and the noise came to a rattling stop. "A garbage disposal. Keep looking."

Bridger didn't move, raising a brow as if to ask, *Who are you talking to?*

"I still haven't decided if I'm going to ditch you here by yourself or not, so if I were you, I'd be on my best behavior. You're lucky you found me, and you're even luckier I have my memories, or this would have been a whole lot more complicated for you. Stop pushing your luck."

The idea of being stuck here like Vega sent a slow chill down Bridger's spine, telling him to listen. He moved throughout the apartment, positioning himself in the exact spot he'd seen in his dream. His hands fell to the table, running his fingers against the smooth wood. "Oh?" he asked, peering over his shoulder at her. "What makes you say that?"

Vega paused, standing on her tiptoes to see inside a low cabinet. "Have you stopped to think about what happens now?" She lowered herself back onto flat feet. "About how you get across the world without documentation in a place that loves to know who's going where at all times?" She came up beside him.

"I did think of that, actually. It's why I had Marlena make a new portal." He returned her attitude with a sarcastic smile. "It imploding obviously wasn't part of the plan."

"Oh yeah? And what is your plan exactly?" she inquired.

Bridger's fingers stopped meticulously trailing over the smooth table. The war waging in his mind, the torment he'd gone through once for defying Marlena, was almost enough to keep him in line. Bridger swallowed and turned around to find her scarred eyebrow raised high in question and her arms crossed over her chest.

"To get you home to Tolevarre, of course." Bridger didn't feel like he was lying, but he definitely wasn't telling the entire truth.

Vega went back to searching the apartment, checking small crevices she could only know about because she'd done it before. "I can't leave until I figure out what's holding my curse to Earth and end it, or all of this—Arlet getting taken, all my research that's led to this moment, the last fifty-five years—it will have been for nothing, and I'll be right back where I started. Cursed, useless, and better off dead."

"I mean, with the crack in the portal back home, I'd say you're on the right track." Bridger realized instantly what he'd done.

Vega's eyes grew wide. "The portal *what?*" She gaped, going pale.

Oh shit. He hadn't told her.

"It cracked. The portal cracked," he said again.

"When did it crack?" Her voice was so quiet her lips barely moved.

The entire room tensed and felt like even the shadows were waiting for Bridger's answer.

"We assume when you killed yourself," he responded, his voice lowering too.

Something clicked in her head, and he watched as it happened. "The portal."

The sound of keys clattering against a door erected Vega's spine, and her face paled a shade further. "Fuck." She practically jumped across the table, pushing her body up against Bridger's until his back was flush against the window, where they were out of view when the door opened.

"Vay?" a man's voice called through the apartment.

Bridger's nose scrunched unintentionally at the stupid nickname.

Vega caught the look with a daggered glare.

He didn't need to be inside her head to know what she was saying. *Shut up.*

Her whisper was hushed and fast. "Out the window, down the fire escape, and wait for me in the cafe down the street to the right." She reached down and unlocked the window, turning her back on him while she hurried through the kitchen. "Coming!"

Vega paused, turning one last time to find Bridger in the same spot against the wall. The look on her face was easy to read—she was terrified what might happen if he didn't leave. *Please*, her eyes begged.

Bridger, against his better judgement, ducked out the window and left Vega alone with her husband.

11

The sound of a loud bang coming from the old window falling to a close made Vega jump.

Chase tried to rush past her and investigate, but Vega grabbed his forearm gently, and it immediately stopped him, pulling his attention away from Bridger fleeing. "Sorry, I was letting in some fresh air. I forgot to close the window." Vega's voice took a mousy tone, turning into a sad, doting housewife.

His eyes softened at her touch, his body relaxing. "Hey, about earlier. I went out after you, but I lost you somewhere around the Colosseum..." He trailed off, lifting his fingers to graze the bruises forming on Vega's neck.

Vega fought against the need to back away. "It's fine. I know you're stressed," she replied with the fakest sincerity she could muster. If it weren't for Bridger, she'd break his arm for touching her. Instead, she closed her eyes and dressed her face with a somber smile. "You won't do it again."

"Never." Chase raised his hand to Vega's cheek, his touch burning like ice against her skin. "I'm so worried about you, about the damage the accident has caused. This world you've been dreaming of, I just..." He sighed dramatically, and it took everything inside Vega not to roll her eyes. "I don't want you to get stuck there, to leave me and forget about the life we have together."

Vega hummed, unsure she could say anything that wasn't *fuck you.* Keeping her mouth shut was safer and would get her out quicker.

She had to get to the cafe.

The fucking portal...

Her mind raced. *The portal. Bridger.* All of it made her heart race.

Chase eventually dropped his hand, stepping around Vega to head into the kitchen, where he discarded his wallet into the catch-all bowl on the counter. "I was thinking we could watch one of your favorite shows tonight and curl up on the couch."

Vega followed him, eyes scanning the room just in case. She let out a silent sigh of relief when Bridger was no longer taking up too much space in the compact apartment. "Did I not tell you?" she asked, cocking her head.

Chase turned around, leaning against the counter. "Tell me what?"

"Gods—shh." She slipped, trying to cover it up and move on. "I'm sorry. It must have forgotten." Vega put a strand of hair behind her ear, feigning innocence. "I have a group therapy session tonight. It starts at six." She looked up at the clock. "And I'm already running late."

Vega backed out of the kitchen, knowing Chase would follow her. "You didn't put it on the calendar."

Shrugging, Vega grabbed her coat off the back of the chair where she always left it. "It came up in this week's session. I meant to tell you about it, but I never got the chance after... well..." She locked eyes with him, batting her eyelashes sadly. She didn't have to say what he'd done.

He knows.

Chase came to stand next to Vega at the door. "No, no, this is good for you. You should definitely go." He reached out to grab Vega by the waist, pulling her in for a kiss she dodged last second.

His lips met her cheek, and before he could try again, Vega reached for the door handle and snuck out. "I'll see you in a few hours!" she called as she trotted down the hall.

The winters weren't awful in Rome, but it was a little windy out as the sun sank below the cityscape. Vega pulled the collar of her coat up, ducking out the apartment building's main door.

Vega hurried to the cafe down the block, remembering to turn off the tracking capabilities on her phone once out of view from her apartment's living room window.

She tucked inside the cafe only minutes later, the fire flickering in the corner giving the room a warm glow. It was busier than she'd hoped for at this time of night. They'd be closing in a few hours, but it seemed the chilly weather had brought everyone out for a pre-dinner warm up.

Beside the fire, staring into the flames like they had the answer to everything, sat Bridger with his thumb hooked under his chin, lips resting against his curled index finger. He leaned into the elbow on the chair's arm, and his hair was mussed, a few strands falling out of place even when he ran his hand through it.

Bridger hadn't felt Vega enter, giving her a moment to get lost in seeing him on Earth, in knowing he'd come here... to what? She wasn't sure yet, but with her memories of him and all they'd been through fresh in her mind, Vega couldn't help but fall into them—regardless of how dangerous she knew it was.

The good and the bad they'd shared could be enough to break them both.

He'd washed the blood off his chest and cleaned the wound at the apartment, buttoning his shirt one higher than he normally would to hide the slow-healing injury. He wore what might be casual in Tolevarre but was definitely leaning more business casual in this realm.

She'd dressed in an oversized T-shirt with a pair of leggings and her usual beat-up boots this morning. Vega didn't have much to choose from in her closet, and even if she did, she preferred comfort over fashion.

Marlena had always been the best dressed sister.

Bridger must have finally paid attention to the tingle of his brand, the same sensation Vega felt too, because his head shot up and his dark eyes instantly found Vega staring at him.

She walked over, slipping out of her coat and draping it over the back of the couch across from Bridger.

He watched her every move, and as soon as she sat down, he asked, "Could the portal be your curse?"

Vega let out a puff of air that might be considered a laugh. "It almost feels too obvious."

A waitress came by, and Vega ordered them a shot of espresso each. They were going to need the energy. Their lives were about to become pretty sleepless.

"It's been the only constant in all of my lives." Vega leaned back and took a second to process what Bridger had said about the crack in the portal.

"She told me the portal started as a cursed mirror and the blood of two sisters." Bridger leaned forward, resting his elbows on his knees. "The blood of two sisters who summoned gods that once called this world their home."

"If the portal is my curse, don't you think Marlena would know that? That she hasn't probably tried to destroy the portal thousands of times by now?" Vega locked her gaze on his across the coffee table. "Wouldn't she be able to feel it since she's the one who created it?"

It was weird, sitting across from Bridger, talking about this revelation like they were two friends catching up.

Marlena told Vega in her last life the mirrors were pieces of her curse, the ones holding her memories. Vega had her memories, which meant half of her curse could be broken. *And the crack in the portal is my sign.*

Bridger shook his head in small wags. "I think that's the point. Marlena created something she doesn't fully understand. This curse is more linked to you now than it is to her."

It felt right. Something inside Vega told her to trust her instinct. "When you came through the portal Marlena made, what happened?" Her eyes ticked down to where she would see the cut if it weren't hidden by his shirt.

Bridger had a far-off look to him, his expression blank. "It felt wrong immediately. There was so much pain, like something didn't want me to come here. I heard an almost familiar voice, and he kept saying you were his—that your death was his." He bit his bottom lip and let it go, his eyes finding Vega's again. "I had to fight to stay in control, reminding myself what I was coming here for." A look of unease washed over Bridger's face, his throat bobbing as he swallowed. "I followed the voice, fighting to get here. To get to you."

Vega's body went cold at the memory of the familiar voice telling her she couldn't escape her destiny. *Death is coming.* Vega had racked her brain far more times than she could count trying to match the voice to a face.

Did we hear the same voice? A million questions piled on top of each other.

"Then I was thrown out of the portal and woke up to the woman at the Colosseum. You showed up minutes later." Bridger leaned back in the chair, throwing his arm over the backrest.

The new portal had somehow set off a current of events from the moment it destroyed itself until Vega and Bridger were united at an ancient Roman graveyard. "You came through, and that's when Chase's attack started, when the pain in my head started."

Bridger straightened. "So, it was Chase." It wasn't phrased as a question.

The waitress with the pretty hair and bright smile came back, placing the drinks in front of them on the coffee table. She turned to Bridger, making a point to lean in a little closer than needed, her tits nearly spilling out of her white button-up blouse. "Is there anything else I can get for you?"

"No, we're fine. Thanks," Vega said abruptly, waiting until the waitress got the hint and left. She blew on her espresso before taking a sip. "Chase is still overall the least problematic of the men I've been stuck with." Her response wasn't a direct answer. "But these people who've been in my life are controlled by my curse, so how can I blame them for their actions when they're not the ones making them?"

A pang of something Vega knew as pity flashed across Bridger's face. "Don't you dare pity me. I'm who I am today because of what I've been put through in my lives. Just because we're stuck together for the foreseeable future doesn't mean we have to stroll down memory lane."

Bridger nodded like he understood, leaning down to grab the tiny espresso cup. It looked doll-sized in his hand. "So, what's the plan here? What's next? If it is the portal, how do we get back to it?" Bridger took his first sip and nearly choked. "What the fuck is this?" he asked with his nose scrunched.

"Espresso. Drink it. You're going to need the energy." Vega took a deep breath, collecting the multiple conspiracies bombarding her thoughts at once. "We have to get you fake travel documents." Vega rubbed her temples after setting the cup down.

"Travel documents for what? Can't we get on a ship and sail to wherever it is we need to go? I've looked at the map. There's a lot of water out there." His full attention was on Vega, like he'd saved a batch of the real him just for her.

Oh, Bridger. Clueless, handsome, stop-staring-at-me-like-that Bridger.

She didn't trust him, couldn't imagine a life where she would ever fully trust him again—not right now, at least. That didn't stop her body from playing tricks on her. "If it were that easy, do you think I'd be this stressed?" Vega asked with the roll of her eyes. "They don't really travel by sea much here. They fly."

"Fly?" he asked.

"As in these things called airplanes that go really high in the sky, and the thing about them and where you get on one is that they're very, very high security. Think Curia induction day but times ten."

Bridger's brows rose at the same time. "Fuck."

"Yeah, fuck," Vega agreed, running a hand across her face. "Once we find a way to get a passport for you, we'll have to pray to whatever gods will listen it works, and then pray some more we don't get caught anytime between now and when we land in the U.S."

It would have been much easier to do this on her own, but it was too late for that. Here Bridger was, trying to forge an alliance, if that was what Vega could even call it, in the wrong fucking realm.

I should just leave him here. But then what would happen? If she wanted to rid herself of Bridger, it would have to be in Tolevarre.

"Okay, so step one: find one Tolevarrian a passport. Step two: fly in a plane. Doesn't sound worse than anything we've done before." Bridger's words came with an ease Vega wished she could feel.

Vega downed the rest of her espresso, thankful for the temporary zing she'd get shortly. "Technically, step one is finding a place to hide you while we, two, track down a very illegal group of people who make fake passports."

The smile spreading across his face was infectious. "Good thing we know how to fight then, huh?" Bridger joked. He'd always been able to pull her out of her head, but this Bridger sitting across from her wasn't the person she remembered.

Neither am I.

So much had changed since they were two teens falling in love.

The waitress came around to check on them again, interrupting Vega's trance.

"Actually, I think we should probably get out of here." Bridger's eyes didn't leave Vega's as he answered. "She and I have a long night ahead of us."

12

Bridger stayed mostly quiet as Vega led them through the unfamiliar streets of Rome.

She hadn't gone many places without Chase by her side, but Vega had paid attention and always tried to take a new way home from therapy. She'd done enough research over the last few weeks, attempting to learn her surroundings and the layout of the city without actually being able to explore.

Rome was statistically a safe city, but anyone could find trouble if they went looking for it, and it seemed there were a few neighborhoods on the outskirts where Vega might be able to score a cheap room and a passport in the same night.

How am I gonna pull this off?

The silence between them gave her plenty of time to plan what came next. Could the portal really be the curse holding her here? Warmth spread through her chest, like her body was trying to give her a sign. Vega secretly worried it was false hope clouding her better judgement.

Bridger eyeballed everything as they descended the stairs to the metro. Vega spared a few glances at him, wondering if this is what she looked like without her memories when she got back to Tolevarre.

A little lost... but slightly amazed at all the unfamiliar and exciting surroundings.

Vega felt like she was merely a passenger in her own body, watching it go about its day. She floated onto the train when it approached the platform, chose two seats in the corner, and finally slammed back into herself when the train lurched forward. She reached out to steady herself, not paying attention to where her hand landed.

Vega's vision cleared to see her fingers digging into Bridger's thigh. Her eyes trailed up his body, catching his dark gaze.

"Ow," he said calmly.

She snatched her hand to her lap. "Sorry."

Bridger bit his lip to stifle a laugh.

Vega sank as far away from him as she could. *Why am I acting so weird? So what, you fucked him and were in a relationship for seventeen years and then he betrayed you? Get over it. You hate him now.* Touching him wasn't a big deal, and the feeling she thought she got when their skin met wasn't real.

That's what she told herself as she glanced over to find him still staring. "What?" she asked, glowering. She hated the rush of self consciousness washing over her.

"You said earlier Chase is the least problematic of all the men from these lives..." Bridger trailed off, waiting for her to respond.

Vega nodded once, unsure where he was going with this.

"You've been through a lot more than anyone knows in these lives, haven't you?" Bridger's question freed a piece of Vega, one she hadn't known was locked away.

Most people wanted to pretend these lives weren't real, that Vega hadn't lived them. It was easy to ignore the impact they had when they got written off as a product of the curse... but it wasn't. To them it might be, but to Vega? All of this, every single person she'd been, every life she'd lived, added up, making the version of herself she was today.

"So much more," Vega admitted. "It's impossible to be the girl I was from before."

The train squealed, rattling through the dark tunnels, but Bridger didn't seem to be paying attention to anything but her.

Vega felt the heat in his stare.

"Tell me something real," Bridger said softly.

Vega eyed him, his expression surprised, like the question hadn't been one he planned to ask. Bridger had caught them both off guard.

If they were going to be allies, if they were going to figure out how to work together again, she had to learn to open up—to give him what he needed to feel... needed.

That was all he'd ever wanted. *To feel needed.*

His dad had treated him like a nuisance. His mom never truly loved him. And when Vega lost herself in all this for a long time, she wasn't there to love him like she should—like she had.

Marlena made him feel like he was needed. Tolevarre needed him.

Vega's anger towards him simmered, the waters between them calm for now.

Going against what she'd told him in the cafe, she looked up at the train's ceiling, searching for the right story to tell.

"Chase's attack today was child's play compared to what other men have done to me." Vega tried to look at anything but Bridger, but the lure of his full attention on her won. "These memories, these lives, make me who I am today. During my tenth life, I was homeless almost the entire time after getting kicked out by the man I'd been dating. I couch-hopped for as long as I could, but eventually everyone got sick of me overstaying my welcome."

Vega nibbled at the inside of her lip, pausing to hold herself together. "I got really good at telling people what they wanted to hear and learned most people just needed a good sob story." She fiddled with her thumbs. Vega was unable to make eye contact with Bridger, let alone anyone, while talking about this next part. "I lied. A lot... and I got really, really good at it. Lying and crawling into beds with strangers, whether they were good or bad, was better than sleeping on the streets where even worse things happen to you."

Bridger didn't interrupt, and Vega didn't stop talking.

"I wanted to die a bunch in that life. I think it might have been my worst. Not caring whether you live or die"—those words took Vega back to Lake Vehemens, when she drove a knife through Bridger's heart—"typically means you make all the wrong decisions. Because the worst that's gonna happen is you die, right?" She finally looked at him again. "I did so many drugs." She laughed a humorless sound. Laughing in the face of her demons felt like the only way she'd ever heal from them.

"I guess what I'm getting at is these lives translated into who I was when I finally got back to Tolevarre. I'm sure you didn't keep track of them but I did. I have. All twenty-one of them." Clearing her throat, she continued on. "It was the life after you joined Marlena. I didn't get my memories back in that one, but they told me you'd left. Although I didn't know who you were, the idea that even in a life and world where I belonged, the person I loved *still* gave up on me, meant I could never stand a chance. In any life."

Bridger hadn't moved an inch since Vega started talking. Only the movement of his rising chest and blinking eyes told her he was alive and listening.

Vega hoped this truth ate at him a little.

"I could have stopped the guard who snuck into my bed and did things to me I'll never talk about before killing me..." Vega shoved the recent memory of seeing him again away, promising herself she wouldn't let the feel of his hands on her be what she remembered. "But I didn't because I didn't want to. I wanted to die. Especially when I made it to a world where I was supposed to belong and felt nothing but violated and alone." A lone tear slipped from Vega's waterline, but she quickly wiped it away with the bottom of her palm. *Do not break down now.* Bridger's words had followed her through every life, with or without him. Vega's voice didn't waver, didn't falter. "This is real. I'm real. I lived through the darkest moments of my life. Alone."

It wasn't sadness in her tone.

It was anger.

Rage.

The train's brakes started to squeak as they approached their stop.

The muscles in Bridger's jaw ticked, giving away the emotion he tried to hide.

"Everyone expects me to be the same girl I was, but I can't be. She died and so did all the others—but this new me, the one made from the lives of them... she's the one with the upper hand."

Bridger had lost most of his color when the train came to a complete stop.

"She's the one who's been tortured and stripped of everything that makes her who she is. She's the one who's stared Death in the face so many times it no longer scares her."

The train doors opened, and people began to file out.

"I won't let all those things my past selves went through be for nothing."

After pulling out as much as the ATM would allow, Vega moved to the next bullet point on her list of worries: figuring out where Bridger could crash while she worked out how to go about getting a fake passport.

Bridger couldn't stay with her, and Vega couldn't stay with him.

She'd have to go back to Chase tonight, if for nothing more than to make sure he wasn't going to become another issue for her to deal with.

Vega was starting to feel discouraged after being denied by two sketchy looking hotels. When the third sent them away, she was ready to shed some real tears... until the young woman running a hostel check-in desk fell for Vega's rehearsed sob story about their travel documents being stolen and needing a place to stay until the U.S Embassy opened on Monday morning.

Vega handed over cash in exchange for the key to a private room with one bed and access to a communal bathroom down the hall.

Once inside, Bridger plopped onto the bed, groaning as he closed his eyes and positioned his hands behind his head.

Vega sat on the edge, releasing a breath she had probably been holding since the train. "If you want to get some sleep, go for it. I'm going to head to the common room and see what information I can find about the locals in the area."

Hostels were usually full of people passing through with limited travel funds, but Vega also knew they were where some people went when they needed time to figure out what came next.

"I'd rather not sleep just yet," Bridger responded, opening his eyes and rolling to his side.

The honesty behind his words stopped Vega from getting off the bed. She could see how exhausted he looked. How long had it been since he'd gotten a full night's sleep? "The dreams?" she asked quietly.

Bridger nodded, and as much as Vega wanted to pry, she didn't. It wasn't her business.

I don't want to feel bad for him.

She forced herself to stand. If she had to remember everything he'd done, then so did he. "Okay, well, I don't know if having you come with me to make friends is going to help. No offense, you kinda give undercover cop vibes."

Vega then spent at least five minutes explaining what an undercover cop was. This had to be how her friends felt when she asked a million questions before getting her memories back... for fifty-five years.

At least they like me. I can't stand him.

The common room was abuzz with life. A few people watched the nightly world news on an old TV while a larger group sat in a circle on the floor playing cards. Some were off in their own corners, reading or playing on phones. A group of four got riled up by the pool table, laughing at someone's unfortunate loss.

A young man reading in the corner by himself caught Vega's eye. Or rather, the book did.

Alice in Wonderland. The only book she'd ever read for fun.

It was her favorite in almost every life. A girl who falls through a portal and a rabbit who always feels like he's running out of time?

She could relate.

Most wouldn't waste their time on the quiet guy in the corner, but Vega knew it was usually the people observing who knew how to find what they were looking for.

Before Vega knew it, she was outside by the hostel's back door, a joint being passed around the small circle. Everyone talked of their travels and where they were headed next.

The girl with the pink hair was headed to Prague.

The man with the pierced lip hoped to end up in Germany.

The twins said they were going to South Asia.

The boy with the book said he wasn't sure where he'd end up next.

Vega told them a half-truth about going home to California.

While everyone in the circle might be a misfit in their own right, none of them were the type of person Vega was looking for.

Vega passed the joint without taking a hit. As badly as she wanted to forget her problems, if only for a few hours, those hours weren't ones she was willing to waste.

Eventually, everyone got cold and decided to head back inside. The boy with the book held the door open. "You coming?"

She shook her head. "I think I'm gonna stay out here for a little longer, but it was really nice meeting you. Enjoy Rome." He gave her a friendly wave and dipped inside.

Vega slid down the side of the building and wrapped her arms around her knees. Resting her head on the brick wall, Vega looked up at the night sky. It was too bright to see stars, but the crisp air made the deep-blue sky shine from all the lights.

Vega closed her eyes and took a deep breath. "How the hell am I going to do this?" she asked herself out loud.

I could really use Arlet's brain right about now. She always knew how to get them home, but this time Vega hadn't been reset to a life on the same continent as the portal.

Had the curse brought her to where the gods once roamed for a reason? Was Rome a clue she was overlooking?

Rome was where Romulus wanted the capital. Romulus and Remus couldn't agree where to put it, a disagreement Romulus plotted to kill his brother over. Remus found out about the plan and couldn't stop it from happening, so instead, he bound himself to the gods. When he died, they died, their powers dispersing amongst their people to create Tolevarre. Romulus never got to see Rome rise... or fall.

Vega hadn't heard anyone approaching over the torrent of history she recited until they spoke.

"This looks like some therapy session."

13

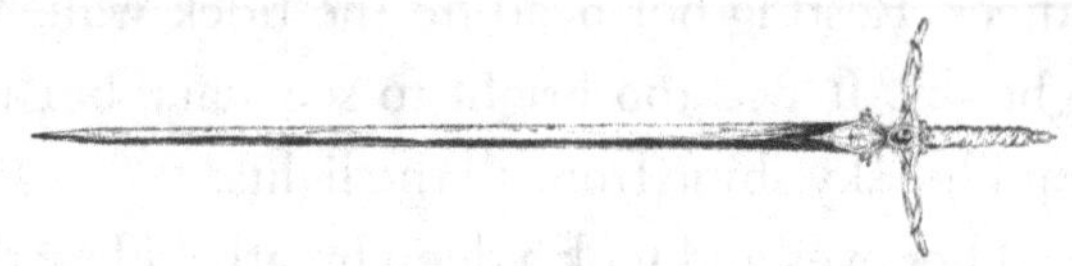

After his shower, Bridger returned to the room and waited for Vega to come back, but the longer she was gone, the more tense he became.

He was at Vega's mercy. She had every right to abandon him, letting him rot away in a realm where he didn't belong.

Just like I did to her...

Bridger distracted himself by pushing the buttons to a controller he found on the bedside table. It turned on a small wall monitor. The screen changed when he pressed the Up and Down arrows.

Nothing could stop him from spiraling about the deal he'd made with Marlena. At one point, when he was lost in the deepest part of his mind, when years passed in the blink of an eye, he would have made that deal without a second thought.

He wouldn't have felt the guilt he did right now—the turmoil he'd been trying to keep at bay since Marlena had agreed to his demands.

Bridger should want this to end. He *did* want this to end.

He just wasn't so sure he wanted it badly enough to trade Vega's life for it.

The brand on his wrist started to burn, quickly becoming too hard to ignore. A jolt of pain shot through his arm, traveling down his leg. "What the...?" he gasped, the shock returning with more power.

Bridger jumped to his feet, tossing the controller on the bed.

Something's not right.

The too familiar tug in his chest told him he was right. Bridger raced down the hall to the stairwell, following the distant hum of voices through an open door.

Heads turned as Bridger barreled in, panting not because he was out of breath, but because the pain in his arm had intensified the closer he'd gotten to the ground floor.

A bald man holding a long stick at a green table with colored balls spread around nodded at him.

A guy with a book in the corner looked over its edge.

Vega wasn't in here, but Bridger scanned the faces staring at him to make sure he hadn't somehow overlooked her.

I didn't miss her. I'd never miss her.

The tug in his chest sent Bridger sprinting for the front door, ignoring the people who approached to ask if he was okay. He expected to find Vega on the other side with how hard the invisible string yanked, but instead, a man puffed on a narrow cylinder, releasing a plume of foul-smelling smoke in Bridger's direction.

That cannot be good for you.

Bridger closed his eyes and took a quick breath, focusing on the feeling he knew would take him to Vega. His feet moved before he opened his eyes.

A voice he recognized echoed down the alley beside the hostel, followed by one he knew like his own heart beat.

"You're not fucking cursed! You have a traumatic brain injury!"

"If you take another step towards me, I'll—!"

He hadn't realized he was sprinting until he skidded to a stop behind Chase, cornering Vega at the alley's dead end. Bridger pulled out the dagger hidden in his waistband and pressed it against Chase's jugular. "I'd listen to her if I were you," he uttered in his ear.

Chase threw his hands up, tensing under Bridger's touch. "Holy shit, holy shit," he stammered.

"Bridger, don't do anything stupid." The warning was there, but he saw a gleam of pleasure in Vega watching this man fear for his life.

Bridger could feel the rapid beat of Chase's pulse vibrating through his dagger's hilt.

"If you can promise to keep your hands to yourself and be an adult about this, I'll have him lower the knife," Vega told Chase.

Chase managed to scoff with a dagger digging into his neck. "Be adults? It's a little late for that, don't you think?"

The tone he used towards Vega had Bridger digging the blade in deeper, breaking the skin. "Wrong answer, pal." He couldn't see it from his angle, but Bridger knew blood dripped down Chase's neck by the way he whimpered.

"Okay, okay. I won't touch you. I promise. I swear. We can talk. Let's talk." Chase's hands stayed up at his sides, and Vega studied his face, apparently trusting whatever look he wore.

Vega nodded at Bridger, but before he obeyed her silent command, he leaned in close again and whispered, "If you make one wrong move, I'll gut you for fun." He shoved Chase away, stepping between him and Vega. Bridger spun the dagger through his fingers, ready to flick it straight through Chase's eye socket if he didn't obey his simple order. The thought brought a smile to Bridger's face.

Chase squeaked, backing further away. "Is this you rebelling or my payback for cheating?" he asked Vega. "Because I understand what you've been through is tough, but this isn't right, Vega. Come home and we can talk about this. We can make things right." He took a step closer. Bridger tensed, ready to strike. "I'll even let you keep the money you stole from my account." His words sounded disingenuous, like he'd been given a script to follow.

"This isn't my home, Chase. It's never been my home." Vega's words were weighted with a sadness Bridger could feel in his bones.

"Not this shit again. Please, come on." He held his hand out for her to take.

Bridger watched Chase's hand until Vega's voice drew his attention.

She met Bridger's eyes. "This is what the curse does... It controls the people in my life." Vega turned back to Chase, who lowered his extended arm. "I'm sorry you got wrapped up in this. I hope you get a second chance at a normal life," Vega said with a kindness he didn't deserve.

Chase looked like he was ready to explode, his pale face turning red. "I'm not sure who you are or what she's told you, but Vega's not well. She woke from a coma only a month ago and hasn't been right since."

The back door flung open, and the girl from the front desk stepped out with a polished wooden bat, followed by the boy with the book.

"What's going on out here?" she asked, holding the bat with familiar comfort.

Vega slinked closer to Bridger. "He was just leaving."

Chase choked on a laugh. "I'm not leaving without *my wife*."

My wife. Bridger never wanted to hear that title coming from another man's mouth about Vega ever again...

If they were in Tolevarre, Chase would be nothing but a pile of remains from the deep, primal rage of a god burning through Bridger.

The building's shadow hid most of Chase's face, and when he stalked forward, the pit in Bridger's stomach turned ice cold.

His eyes were black, and not onyx colored like his own. No, all black. No pupil. No iris.

Black.

Vega went rigid at his side, a shaky breath slipping through her parted lips.

Chase extended his hand to Vega, wiggling his fingers in a slow summon. "You belong with me. Come. Let's fulfill your destiny."

For the first time in what might have been the entire time Bridger had known her, Vega purposely stepped behind him, silently asking for protection.

A sudden lust for Chase's blood coating the ground roared to life, but he never got the chance to gut him.

The loud clang of the hostel worker's bat colliding with a metal drain made everyone jump. "Get out of here. Now! Before I call the police," she yelled at Chase.

Chase's black eyes stayed transfixed on Vega peeking around Bridger's arm. "This isn't over, Vega. Not yet, and there's nowhere on Earth you can go where I won't find you." He fled and disappeared beyond the alley's shadows.

Silence held until Vega was the one to break it. "I'm so sorry," she told the employee. "I—"

"You two need to go," she interrupted. "I don't know what you've gotten yourself into, but I can't have it here."

Vega shook her head slowly. "I have nowhere else to go. I'm trying to get back home, but he has control of all my documents."

Bridger knew the tears welling in her eyes were real this time. Chase rattled her.

"That's not my problem," the girl responded and at least had the decency to sound remorseful. "I'll go get your things from your room and bring them down to you." She turned and headed back inside.

Bridger had forgotten the boy with the book was here until he spoke. "Are those bruises on your neck from him?" He paused, looking nervous. "I noticed them earlier when we were talking," he admitted with a sad smile.

Vega nodded. "Yeah, they're from him."

An emotion Bridger knew all too well washed over the young man's face. Grief. Something he saw in Vega provoked an unwanted memory. He inhaled sharply through his nose, swallowing hard enough to make his throat bob. "I think I might be able to help."

14

THE SKY FADED TO SHADES OF VIOLET AND MAGENTA, WITH shadows cast throughout the clouds by the tall mountain peaks surrounding the city.

Stella was known for nights like tonight—the chill in the air, the breathtaking sunset... but there was one big piece missing.

No one strolled down the streets, enjoying the gorgeous night. Laughter didn't echo down alleyways or filter through the opening and closing doors of the businesses downtown in the main square.

Marlena stood close to the edge of the balcony overlooking the square, glancing down at the gathered crowd. She'd demanded the most influential people in Stella be present for a realm-wide broadcast.

A livestreamed video would start in...

"Three." The woman behind the camera counted down with her fingers and mouthed the remaining numbers.

It was time Marlena made a statement. It was time she reminded the people of Tolevarre the power she had over them.

Their riots and disobedience would stop here.

"People of Tolevarre," Marlena began, her attention fixed on the crowd, giving the camera her best side.

Her long, straight blonde hair was pulled back into a sleek ponytail, not a strand out of place. She'd kept the makeup light tonight, wearing a youthful look. Appearing as young as the last time she stood above these people in an emerald gown. She would never age again—forever twenty-two.

"As you know, the rebels have continued to attack, turning cities and towns upside down." The narrative was easy. Make the rebels look like miscreants wanting to upset the balance of power Marlena had implemented.

The stronger you are, the more you have. It was simple.

The outlying territories without access to electronics of their own had been ordered into the viewing centers placed in their towns, built for when news needed to be delivered realm wide.

There wasn't a soul in Tolevarre under Marlena's control who wasn't watching her right now.

A shiver of excitement calmed her, settling into the position she was born for.

"Commander Dimico placed a curfew on the bigger cities, but I believe it's time we broaden their reach." A few murmurs from below were washed out by the sound of Marlena's voice echoing on the intercom throughout Stella. "Curfew, effective immediately, for all of Tolevarre is sundown."

The voices from below grew louder, more agitated.

"Unfair."

"Punished for their actions."

Marlena kept her cool, reeling them in for the big reveal... The real reason she'd decided to make this a live broadcast.

A way to ensure I'm still ahead of her. Of them.

Marlena tapped her fingers across the balcony's edge, her fingertips warm against the cool railing. "All businesses are to close before five, and restaurants are to cease operation indefinitely."

Marlena had wiped out most of Solum—the farmlands were part of the collateral damage.

Albeit not her most rational decision, Marlena would starve the outskirts without pause. Their food supplies would get cut off, and they'd be left to fend for themselves.

It would be of no loss to Marlena, because their lives didn't matter—they were no one worth saving. Those people would be the ones flocking to Khort the second he swooped in to save the day anyway.

Good. Let them run.

The more the rebellion had to hide, house, and feed, the better chances of failure without much effort on Marlena's end.

"Why are we being treated like the others?" someone yelled from below.

Marlena cocked her head, focusing in on the man she knew the voice had come from. It was easy to find him when she met his eyes —he looked like he might piss himself in front of the entire realm. "I'm doing this to keep you all safe," she lied through her pretty teeth. Sweeping her hand over the exposed collarbone of her dress, Marlena posed for the camera, moving gracefully. "Anyone outside after sundown will be sent directly to the mines."

The mines. Tolevarre's electric grid, fueled by the criminals too powerful to kill for their crimes.

Instead of death, they were sentenced to a fate much worse—the rest of their existence tied to the mines, becoming property of Tolevarre. Only kept alive to benefit the world Marlena had built on the ashes of their old ways.

"We shouldn't be punished alongside those people. The rebels..."

"We have never had to follow the same rules as the territories. Why would we start now?"

Marlena's nails dug into the railing. From the corner of her eye, she saw the worker behind the camera hesitate, unsure if he should keep the feed rolling or not.

"We're better than them. We're like you." The words sounded like they'd been spoken in slow motion. "Just as important."

Marlena's vision blurred at how quickly she spun to face the idiot who'd said that.

A portly man without much hair left leaned against a pillar, looking entirely too comfortable after placing himself in the same category as Marlena Caelum.

There was no hiding the look of disgust the cameras caught. She'd expected to get pushback, expected the spoiled and powerful people of Stella wouldn't like being controlled the same way the rest of Tolevarre was.

She hadn't expected such confidence from a man of his status.

The crowd below hushed, catching the shift in Marlena's mood. The air grew colder, but it stood still, not a breeze or a whistle in the distance.

Marlena hadn't realized she'd stopped the wind from moving, creating an eerie silence the longer she said nothing.

At least he had the decency to look scared. Terrified, even, when Marlena leaned against the railing and glared down at the dumbest man in Tolevarre.

Collectively, the crowd seemed to take a deep breath, and no one let it out.

No one breathed.

No one moved.

They all waited.

She felt her lips pull into a smile, and it must have looked genuine, because soft sighs of relief could be heard traveling through the crowd.

Their relief was short-lived.

"Someone's cocky." Marlena sneered, her temporary sweet-girl facade fading fast. "To think you"—she motioned at him lazily—"have ever been anything close to me is laughable." She let herself chuckle, holding her heated annoyance at bay. "But more important?"

Marlena disappeared, stepping through the balcony, into the in-between, and back out the other side. She emerged directly in front of the man within seconds, standing nearly half a foot taller than him in her heels.

Sweat dripped down his brow, his head cocked back to look at Marlena.

"Believing that isn't confidence. It's stupidity." She loved watching this grown man quiver under her stare. It filled Marlena with joy, knowing no one could or would ever hurt her again.

They can't hurt you.

With a shaky jaw, the man went to say something but gaped at Marlena instead.

"I'm feeling generous," Marlena purred. "I won't kill you for insulting me the way you did. I'll let you live and walk out of here with the reminder of your status below me." Where he'd stay forever.

He finally found his voice, but it was much meeker than it was the first time. "Oh, Marlena, thank you. You're—"

"I wasn't done speaking." The air tightened inside the square, stealing the good oxygen.

His mouth snapped shut, and Marlena could hear him attempting to swallow his fear. He didn't dare speak again.

She looked down her nose at him, chin tilted upward.

The camera was still on her. Tolevarre was still watching.

"I'll let you walk out of here alive on one condition." An actual smile pulled at the corner of her lip. "You get on your hands and knees and beg for forgiveness."

The man's eyebrows creased together in the middle, but it didn't take long for them to smooth over and for him to drop to his knees.

He pitched his head back and stared at Marlena, intertwining his fingers together. "P-pl-ease, Marlena, forgive me. I am unworthy. I-I don't know what I was thinking."

Glancing around to the other stark white faces of Stella's elite, Marlena fed off their fear, letting it propel her into the actual reason she'd called this gathering.

"I don't think you're down low enough. Bow." The gods hummed inside Marlena's head, stirring when she didn't want them to.

The man did as he was told, folding to the ground. "I have children. Please, let me get home to them."

Marlena didn't care about his children. She still hadn't decided whether she was actually going to let him live or not.

"No one..." Her eyes scanned every person she could see from where she stood, and then she stared directly into the lens of the camera. "Not a single person here will ever be as important as me." Her attention darted back down to the sobbing swine below.

His cheeks were puffy and red, eyes bulging out of their sockets as his fear found a new height. He fit the part of an animal off to slaughter almost too well.

"Because I'm not like you." She nodded towards the front row of the motionless crowd. "Or you. Or you." She fixed her stare back on the cameras, back on Tolevarre. "Or you." Her eye caught the reflection of her face in the lens. "Fifty-five years ago, I summoned the twelve original gods." It was the first time she'd spoken those words out loud to her realm. Most knew, but there had never been a confirmation from Marlena's own mouth. "The gods are gone."

They didn't like her lie, trying to claw their way out of the cage Marlena kept them trapped in. They had their own corner inside her mind, and on Marlena's best days, she could keep them locked away.

It'd been a while since Marlena had what could be considered a best day...

The gods were louder now.

"And they left me in their place."

The faces around her were a mixture of shock and disbelief. Jaws hung low, and one woman swayed on her feet.

The sky darkened, casting a deep-violet glow across Stella.

"I am your god." Marlena exhaled, the hairs on her arms sticking up from the fear rippling through the square like the aftershock of her admission. "The only living goddess our people will ever know."

Without having to move a muscle, a few people fell to their knees. Out of fear or devout loyalty, Marlena wasn't sure. She didn't care how they did it.

It was time Tolevarre recognized her as what she was.

Not just Marlena the ruler... No.

Marlena, the one true goddess.

The others were bonded by a murky demigod, and their lives were linked, souls intertwined. Vega and her friends were still half-breeds at best, and Marlena would prove she was the superior of the new gods. She didn't have a plan yet, but that had never stopped her before.

Across the sky, green lightning scattered through the low hanging clouds. The last bit of purple left in the darkening night sky was the backdrop to her neon-green light show. "It's time Tolevarre stops worshipping the old gods."

Thunder rumbled like Marlena's personal choir. She couldn't control the weather like her sister. That power was all Vega's. But the lightning came from Jupiter, the original bloodline the sisters shared through their father.

Marlena had already mastered air wielding when she summoned the gods—she didn't need Jupiter's wind, so he gave her something else instead.

She didn't use the lightning enough. It felt good, skittering across her skin like static. It was a colder heat, nothing like the inferno of her fire.

"It's time you worship me instead."

More people dropped to their knees. Unintelligible prayers from muttered lips became the soundtrack to the chorus of voices finally escaping through the iron bars of her mind.

"You wouldn't be here if it weren't for us."

"Not a lick of credit."

Marlena twitched, fighting the urge to rip her own skin off. The gods' voices and insults grated against her mind like nails on a chalkboard.

Sometimes they treated her like she was less than... like she hadn't been strong enough to withstand summoning all twelve and their powers at the same time.

Marlena reminded the gods of her strength with a zap of Vulcan's flames through her mind.

He was always the loudest, his powers the first to rise when it was time to fight.

While the gods were with Marlena, some were quieter than others, never saying much. It usually took her by surprise if a few spoke at all.

Or if they gave her a peek inside the power they somehow wouldn't let her have full control over... Apollo was the worst.

Marlena had never tasted what the Videri line was known for —she'd never experienced anything remotely close to that of a seer.

The future was unknown—more so now than it'd ever been.

She fucking hated it.

People continued to kneel until there was no one left standing but a woman dressed in an emerald-green robe.

Marlena's jaw ticked. A green robe meant she hadn't chosen a god to serve yet. "Is the robe for show?" The religious members of Oro spent a lot of time in Stella—they'd always claimed it was as close as they could get to the gods.

She couldn't be any closer to the gods right now if she tried...

The pretty young girl couldn't be more than twenty. She had an entire life ahead of her. Her deep-blue doe eyes were seconds from spilling tears. "I cannot bow when I've yet to devote my life to one god."

An older woman kneeling next to the girl made a smart move. She stood and grabbed the acolyte by the arm. "Bow," she whispered. "Before she kills you."

"I told you," Marlena droned as the girl started to fight the older woman's hand, "the old gods are gone. I am your—"

"I cannot bow to her! She isn't the only new god! She's not the only choice I have." The words were out before Marlena could react. "Her sister and the bon—"

It only took one step for her to jump from where she'd been to where she was—behind the acolyte, hands on either side of her head.

The crack of her neck sent everyone into pandemonium, scrambling to get as far away as they could.

Marlena had traveled without thinking. The only thing on her mind was shutting her up before she finished her sentence.

Calmly, Marlena turned to face the camera, noticing the small red light blinking a live signal.

One easy gust of wind sent the device crashing against the stone wall behind her. Its pieces became ricochet shrapnel with Marlena's control, whizzing through the air with a hiss before lodging into bodies.

Screams echoed through the dark sky. No one could exit the square.

They were all sealed by a shield. The one Marlena controlled because of Mars, Bridger's bloodline.

Marlena pulled a sword from the invisible sheath between her shoulders. The metal shimmered under the bright moon, appearing from thin air.

Another ability she'd had before the gods... one she'd nearly perfected before age ten.

Her eyes met the terrified gaze of a screaming woman limping on what looked to be a broken ankle.

Marlena killed her first.

Then she cleared the rest of the square.

"Marlena."

A familiar voice dragged Marlena back to the surface.

She blinked, her vision getting less blurry as life returned around her.

Arlet stood inside her cell, peering through the bars with soft hazel eyes. "Mar." Her nickname was a whisper on her lips.

She didn't have a heart to hurt, but a piece of the girl she'd once been still resided somewhere deep, deep, down, and that nickname on Arlet's lips reminded Marlena she was there.

"What happened?" Arlet took a step forward, her dirty fingers wrapping around the bars.

She didn't remember coming to the prison under Atrox. The last thing she had any memory of was the Stella square, blood and bodies piled on top of each other.

Marlena glanced down at herself, her visible skin splattered with blood. Her dress was soaked through. Not a single thread of fabric had been spared.

"Tolevarre knows I'm a god." Her voice sounded so far away and had a softness she hadn't heard in a very long time. "They know Vega's a god, and if they're smart enough, they'll know you, Bridger, and Khort are too."

Her head felt fuzzy, trapped in the in-between. She couldn't shake it.

"How?" Arlet asked with a breath.

"I broadcasted it, and then I killed them. They killed them."

Marlena floated to the bars, coming face to face with Arlet. She looked so much like the girl she used to love.

Marlena felt herself lift her hand, gently bringing her fingertips to Arlet's cheek. Blood smudged her soft skin as her fingers brushed down to her chin.

Arlet's eyelashes fluttered, and then her eyes closed. "They?"

This was a dream...

When Marlena realized it, she chuckled out loud. Gods, it almost felt so real.

Arlet feels so real.

"The gods. We couldn't let the people who witnessed the acolyte's confession live." She wrapped her hand around the same cell bar Arlet did. Their hands were less than an inch from touching.

Arlet's eyebrows drew together when she opened her eyes. "But you broadcasted it."

"I'll fix it, pet. Don't worry." Her head swam, the dream threatening to fizzle out.

Not yet.

The use of her old nickname made a muscle in Arlet's jaw twitch.

Marlena's smile grew a few inches. It felt lazy on her lips.

"I see you in there sometimes. In passing moments." Arlet's words drew Marlena's gaze from their almost-touching hands. Her eyes weren't easy to read with the tired circles under them.

This might be a dream, but dream-Arlet was identical to the real one.

Bruises lined her body, littering her pretty skin with signs of the torture she'd endured over the last five weeks.

None of them had come from Marlena directly. She'd only been the one to give the orders to try and get her to talk.

About Vega.

About the rebellion.

About everything.

About *anything*.

Arlet never said anything. She didn't even scream.

Arlet.

The only person who'd ever been able to break her heart.

Her hand dropped from her face. "No, you don't, because none of this is real," Marlena muttered, unwrapping her hand from the bar. "It's all a dream."

Before it could fall, Arlet pinned it in place with her own. "This is real. We were real."

Heat burned through to Marlena's bloodstream, and once again, she stepped through the in-between and crossed through the cell door.

Arlet retreated, taking careful steps while Marlena prowled forward. When her back hit the stone wall, there was nowhere else for her to run.

Marlena cornered her, a new fuzzy feeling overwhelming her senses. She had to blink away the black specks ready to spread across her vision. "Do you ever wonder what might have been if you would have stayed with me? What we could have become?"

She let her brain run rampant, let the dream conjure up whatever it was Marlena had been wanting to feel all these years.

She leaned into the young woman she'd once been—and she let her run wild.

If she had a heart, it might have fluttered in her chest.

Arlet's gaze didn't waver. Vega was strong, but Arlet... Arlet was something else.

For the first time since she'd been thrown down here, Arlet smiled. Slow at first, and then her lips snapped into a grin unsuited for her pretty face. It was too dark—too far from the soft girl she'd once known. "Yes." She leaned forward, surprising Marlena. Arlet's breath tickled her neck, sending goosebumps down her arms. "I think about all the things that made you tick. The way you used to kiss me when you knew no one else was around."

Arlet's fingers grazed over Marlena's, and a tingle she shouldn't have felt while dreaming made her blood run cold.

"The way you use to come when I—"

This isn't a dream.

Marlena's hand heated with anger seconds before her lit palm connected to Arlet's cheek. Her hand stung not from her fire but from the force of the slap.

Arlet's head snapped to the side, colliding with the stone wall. Her hand shot up to cup the fresh bubbling burn on her cheek. She chuckled through the pain. "It was much easier to trick you than I thought it would be. You're slipping, Mar." Arlet didn't say her old nickname like she had minutes ago—sweet, taking Marlena back to a moment in time she tried so hard to forget. This time it was a sneer and Arlet definitely wasn't the girl Marlena had once loved. "When Vega breaks her curse and brings Bridger back to slaughter, you're not going to stand a chance."

Marlena grabbed her by the throat, shutting her up. "You think you've got it all figured out, don't you?" Marlena scowled, squeezing harder. "Let me let you in on a little secret, pet," she spat, loosening her hold enough to allow Arlet a single breath. "Bridger isn't on Earth playing fetch. He's there to make sure Vega doesn't break her curse, to get inside her head. What could I learn if Bridger was allowed inside her mind?" she whispered.

Marlena dropped Arlet to the floor with a thud.

"Bridger's there making her believe he can be loved again, that he's changed." Marlena was on the other side of the cell door from Arlet in the blink of an eye. "There's nothing left of the Bridger she once loved, and with enough time, I bet I can do the same to you."

15

In less than twelve hours, Vega had somehow managed to pull off finding them each a fake fucking passport. Not to mention, someone willing to let her book a couple flights on their card for the cash in return, saving her the hassle of stealing someone's wallet and credit card information.

Unbelievable. She could barely believe it herself.

Arlet was going to be so proud.

Bridger stared blankly out the cab's window—Vega at the two forged passports in her hands.

She was right to trust her instinct. It was always the observant ones who knew where to find what they were looking for.

Jakub, the young man, no more than nineteen, sitting in the corner reading *Alice in Wonderland*, had spent a few months interning for a cyber security company contracted by the United States government—who also secretly dabbled in illegal document forgery.

Vega spent nearly every dollar she had to pay for two, and it was well worth having to pickpocket the rest of the way if it meant she didn't have to go back and see Chase with his soulless eyes.

"His eyes," Vega said softly, breaking the silence between them.

They hadn't had much time over the last few hours to talk about everything. The revelation about the cracked portal, Chase's black eyes.

"Have you seen them do that before?" Bridger asked, keeping his voice low despite the cabbie's music.

Vega swallowed the knot in her throat and nodded. "When he attacked me before I found you at the Colosseum. That's the only time I've seen it. Ever."

Bridger looked as exhausted as Vega felt. She was nearing twenty-four hours of no sleep, which meant Bridger was well past a full day by now.

Gods or not, they still had to sleep, especially with no powers to fuel them.

Silence was filled with the clueless cabbie's off-key singalong.

"You said the people in these lives are controlled by your curse..." His eyebrows drew together in question.

"Not like this. I mean..." Vega rolled her lips together while she thought about how to explain it. "The curse has basically only hijacked a person's life, forcing them into one with memories they didn't have of a life we didn't live together. It was never them going all soulless eyes, 'let's fulfill your destiny' shit."

Quiet fell between them again, their eyes staying locked.

"But now the portal's cracked. The curse might not be held to an object anymore..." Bridger mumbled like he was thinking out loud.

Vega wasn't sure about Chase, about what was going on with him or why the other portal was destroyed, but one thing felt certain now. "All signs point to the portal."

He nodded once, looking as certain as Vega was becoming. "All signs point to the portal."

Rubbing her temples, Vega slumped into the seat, sliding down until her legs couldn't go any further underneath the driver's chair. From the corner of her eye, she could see Bridger staring.

"What's next?" he asked, always needing the details.

"Airport. Security. Flight. Customs. This is the most dangerous part of the trip." Vega closed her eyes, focusing on keeping her heart rate under control. If she freaked out now, everything else would crumble around her. Vega's composure couldn't slip.

"Please tell me there's a place to eat at this plane-port because I could devour ten meals right about now," Bridger said, distracting Vega from her growing anxiety.

Vega sat upright. "Airport," she corrected. "Yes, though we might not have a ton of time for a full meal."

Bridger groaned, holding his stomach dramatically. "You're trying to starve me, aren't you? This is my payback." It was his turn to slump down, tipping towards the middle seat until his head fell into her lap.

Vega tensed, and so did Bridger.

Her body flushed, the worries of their imminent future washing away and shifting into new ones. Vega's body warmed, sending a flutter of heat through her veins. "Do you feel that?" she whispered. It was a sensation she hadn't felt in ages—one she thought she might never feel again.

Their touch had always felt electric, their own tiny current of power, like they were drawn together by an outside force.

"Yes." Bridger exhaled, not moving from her lap.

She hadn't realized she'd brought her hands to her chest. Vega slowly lowered them. "Have you felt me this entire time?" Her hand rested softly on Bridger's upper bicep.

"Every single life. I could block my brain from thinking of you, but I couldn't trick my body into forgetting you."

Fuck. Fuckfuckfuck. They were too close. Vega couldn't let them get too close... but where was she supposed to go? They were stuck inside the tiny backseat for at least another thirty minutes before they arrived at the airport, and then if they didn't get arrested trying to use false identification, they'd be stuck together on a plane. And then if—

Vega took a shaky inhale, her hand sliding up to his hair. She couldn't stop herself. It was soft between her fingers raking through the length at the top. "What do you think it means?" she asked, resting her head against the headrest and closing her eyes.

Bridger didn't answer right away, and the more time passed, she figured he wouldn't.

"That I fucked up." Bridger's words trailed off, his voice deep with sleep and a gravel Vega could feel vibrate against her lap.

Memories of his wrongdoings threatened to flood Vega's mind, but for the first time since he'd left, Vega let herself enjoy the warmth wrapping around her like a hug—the bliss of reuniting with a soul she'd been bound to deeper than the others.

No one could have predicted what time would do to two lovers destined to fall.

Vega lost track of time, focusing on the feeling of her fingers brushing through Bridger's hair and the steady breaths coming from his lips.

The calmness of the moment threatened to lull her to sleep, but before she could fall, Bridger jumped, sitting straight up, with panic flaring behind his eyes.

Vega stared at him, her lips parting to speak, but nothing came out. Bridger's eyes fell to them and then darted back up.

The cabbie slapped his hand against the front passenger seat headrest, getting their attention. "Here" was all he said.

Vega nodded, not looking at him, her focus on Bridger and the rapid rise and fall of his chest.

The dreams. He can't sleep at all without them.

Bridger snapped out of his trance and exited the cab. Vega handed the driver some money and followed Bridger into the night air without her change.

Bridger's fingers were connected behind his neck, head turned to the early morning sky.

"Are you—"

"I'm fine," he cut her off bluntly, continuing to keep his distance.

An ache filled Vega's chest... and it shouldn't. He and Vega weren't friends. They weren't even officially allies. His tone shouldn't affect her, but it did.

She was instantly mad at herself for being nice to him, for starting to feel something other than betrayal when she looked at him.

"Perfect," she sneered. "Give me your dagger." She scanned for anyone paying them too close attention.

"What?" Bridger asked, the confusion evident on his face.

"Give. Me. Your. Dagger," she said, slower this time. As if he hadn't heard her and that was why she was repeating herself.

"I'm not—"

"Yes, you are. You can't take it with you." Vega held her hand out, waiting for him to obey. She raised her scarred brow and wiggled her fingers—this wasn't up for discussion. "Why, Bridger? Why do you have to make my life so fucking difficult?" Her patience was running thin.

Bridger heaved a sigh, looked around to ensure no one saw, pulled the dagger from its spot in his waistband, and handed it over.

Vega slipped the long blade up her coat sleeve, hiding it from plain sight, and walked it over to the garbage, where she discarded it like it was nothing more than a piece of trash she was tossing before entering the airport.

"Pull yourself together," she told him when she was back by his side. "Shit could get a whole lot worse than some nightmares if this goes wrong."

She shoved everything she had, which wasn't much, into her pocket and headed towards security. Inside her coat, Vega had both their passports, a little bit of cash, her almost dead cell phone, and melted lip balm.

Bridger had a small bag from home with a change of clothes and other miscellaneous items, but he promised there was nothing inside that could be used as a weapon.

The line for security was long, people talking of delays and cancellations to flights headed to the U.S. *Great.* Vega's hands started to sweat as the line moved faster than she'd anticipated it would. "If I tell you to run, we run, understand?"

Bridger nodded, his lips set in a firm line.

"Straight to the doors we just came through."

"Vega, relax. It's going to be okay." He stepped close behind, leaning over her shoulder so no one but Vega could hear him. "The guy said they were real names and real passports with our pictures. Plus, whatever that other guy with the screen and keyboard said about the system they used being government official. Everyone seemed pretty confident about the whole thing." Bridger hooked his thumbs under the straps of his backpack and returned to scanning the airport like a museum.

Not a worry in the fucking world...

Every step closer she took to the front of the line, Vega felt like she was going to barf all over the floor.

"How are you so chill right now?" Vega spun, facing him with a bubble of annoyance churning her stomach.

A slow smile spread across Bridger's lips, and Vega wanted to smack it off. "Because one of us has to be, and since you're the anxious one currently, I have to be the anchor." His panic from whatever he'd seen in his sleep must be gone.

"You're giving me fucking hives." When she peeked over her shoulder, Bridger had the goofiest, boyish grin on his face, and it didn't help with her bubbling stomach.

"Next."

Their back and forth took Vega's focus off the moving line. She suddenly couldn't move, scared into stillness.

If this didn't work...

"Ma'am, next!" the woman called again.

"Vega," Bridger said, putting his hands on her shoulders to move her forward.

Her feet dragged like they were weighed down with cement blocks.

"Sorry, she's a little nervous," Bridger said with a laugh, earning a small smile from the woman.

"Identification, please."

Vega reached inside her pocket, fighting against the urge to run as she lifted her hand and gave the woman both their very fake, very illegal passports.

Bridger's hands were still on her shoulders, rubbing from the base of her neck down to the curve of her shoulder and back again.

Vega's body wanted to lean into his touch, but her brain acted first. She stepped back, driving the heel of her boot into Bridger's foot as inconspicuously as she could.

His hands fell from her body with the warning, and Vega immediately missed the calm his touch brought her.

The beep sounded like every other passport scanned before theirs, and the lady's eyes jumped from the picture to Vega's face twice.

Vega's esophagus tried to tighten and choke her to death.

The woman did the same to Bridger, checking the information on her screen.

Thirty. Thirty-one. Thirty-two. Vega hadn't realized she'd started counting the seconds, waiting for police to swarm them with guns drawn.

The TSA agent closed both booklets abruptly and handed them back. "Safe travels."

16

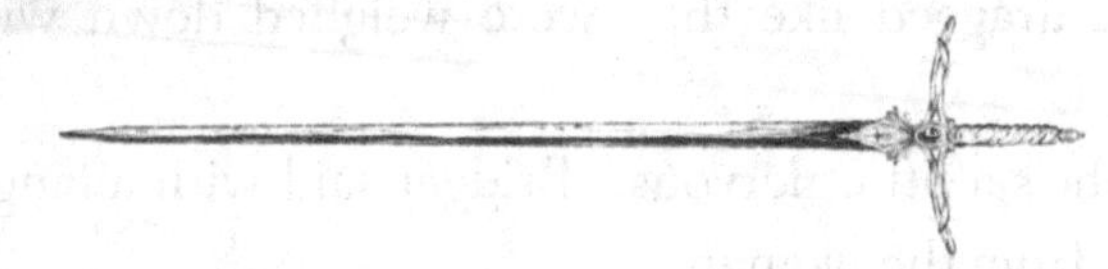

WHILE SCARFING DOWN THE BLANDEST FOOD HE'D EVER tasted, Bridger watched planes take off... and then asked Vega at least fifty follow-up questions.

But nothing could have prepared him for the feel of the plane shooting into the sky. His ears popped, and the wing visible outside the window shook like it might snap.

Gripping the armrests, Bridger felt the muscles of his throat constrict. The plane bobbed, forcing his eyes closed.

Vega was oddly quiet. The last time Bridger looked over, she looked more relaxed than he'd seen her in decades.

How the fuck is she so calm right now?

"Um, Vega." Bridger peeked over, his hands still gripping the seats as if he'd fall from the sky if he let go.

"Um, Bridger?" Vega mocked, rolling her head on the seat and opening her eyes.

"I think I'm freaking out a little," he said with another hard swallow of the saliva he was moments from choking on.

Vega's lips curved in a sleepy smile. She was enjoying this. "I see that."

Bridger squirmed in his seat, ready to crawl out of his skin. "Do you find this funny?"

Vega's heavy lids told him she had been seconds from falling asleep. "I do, actually. I was laughing all the way to my dreams."

Bridger gritted his teeth and pushed his back against the seat like he'd melt into the cushion and through it to a puddle on the floor when the plane bobbed again. "Vega, please. I've been in probably 100,000 fights in my life, and I have never been this nervous. I need..." He took a deep breath, walking himself through all the ways to calm down. "Tell me something real."

He'd said it twice now. The first time he wasn't sure what he'd meant by it, just that he wanted to hear Vega talk. This time he *needed* to hear her talk. If he sat here and thought about what would happen if this plane went down for much longer, Bridger was pretty sure his heart would explode.

Metal clinked together, and he felt the heat of her leg against his. Vega moved into the seat next to him, buckling herself in. "Something real?"

Bridger locked eyes with her, trying to feed off Vega's calm. He was her anchor earlier, but now Vega was the only thing keeping him from drowning—his life preserver.

He wasn't sure he could speak, nodding his head instead.

"In my first life on Earth, when Arlet found me, she tackled me to the ground, and I called the cops on her. She was so excited to see me, and at that point we hadn't realized my memories were gone."

Bridger homed in on Vega, doing what he could to block out the roaring of the plane's engine.

"When the cops came, I saw the sheer look of panic as they began to ask her about who she was and why she didn't have an ID. It was in that very second I knew I'd messed up. I don't know what it was, but that was the first time I *felt* her. The tingle in my wrist, the pull in my chest. Even with no memories, I trusted her."

She caught her bottom lip between her teeth, fighting a smile. Bridger's eyes fixated on the movement.

"Then I went on the first cross-country road trip with her, learned all about Tolevarre and the boy who loved me." The plane shook again, and Bridger's fingers started to go numb from his tight grip. "I didn't believe her, not just because I couldn't remember but because I had never felt worthy of love in the life I was living. My first thought was I didn't deserve to be loved. But when I met you, when we came through the portal and you were standing there, blissfully unaware that I had no idea who you were..."

His heart thudded against his chest, but as she talked about the memory, Bridger could see it.

Coming from her lips, it felt like the first time he'd remembered it in nearly forty years—even though he'd dreamed of it already.

"The look on your face." Vega paused, and when Bridger looked down to focus on her, she was staring at him. "The relief, the sparkle in your tired eyes—that's when I felt it. The love Arlet told me about."

"I remember," he croaked, clearing his throat. "I rushed to you, and the second before I wrapped you in my arms, I saw your look of apprehension. It was the moment I realized something wasn't right. Then I had to see that same look over and over again while watching the person I loved more than anything in the world turn into someone I didn't know."

Vega's smile was sad, but she still looked at him. She wasn't sinking into herself. "I never really stopped to consider what you went through, about how it would truly have felt to be in your position. I only thought of my own feelings..."

The plane shuddered, and Bridger whipped his head straight, closing his eyes again. The panic was subsiding, but he still didn't like it. "I kept losing you." He paused, the next part coming out as a whisper. "And then I lost them too."

Them... Khort and Arlet. His friends.

Opening up made him feel sick to his stomach—like somehow, by admitting this to the very girl who'd brought Marlena's torture upon him, it made him weak.

He'd spent a lot of time with unresolved anger about the whole situation, having demons only he could find a way to cope with.

With his eyes closed, Bridger couldn't see her movements, but with the next bump in their ride, Vega looped her arm under Bridger's bicep and between the seat, wrapping it back around. A long moment passed before she rested her head against his arm.

Something deep and almost primal inside Bridger hummed at her touch.

It felt as if his body was trying to tell him something...

The sound of her breathing slowed, her grip loosening as she drifted into a much-needed sleep. Bridger sat rigidly until the shaking plane calmed down some. He focused on the sound of Vega breathing, eventually succumbing to his own exhaustion.

He'd fought it for as long as he could, but it was no use. Bridger fell, tumbling into a sleep he thought he'd never see again.

A sleep with nothing but the blackness of his mind. Quiet. Peaceful. Deep.

For a while, there was nothing... Bridger slept. Dreamlessly.

So when the dream did finally creep its way in, Bridger wasn't ready for it. He'd let his guard down, and he was once again thrust into the memories he'd fought so hard to forget.

Bridger was getting used to fighting for his life, but he had a feeling he wouldn't have to for much longer as he was dragged by his hair down the hall of Fortis's prison.

Marlena's fist wound tightly at the base of his skull, his hair tangled in her fingers. "I hate to have to do this, Bridger, but you've made it clear you're not going to let me do this the easy way."

He went kicking and screaming, calling Marlena every name in the book as he tried to dig the heels of his boots into the stones underneath him.

Bridger flew through the air like a weightless sack, ribs shattering when he hit the back wall. He wasn't even sure he screamed, unable to hear over the ringing in his ears.

Through the spots in his vision, he watched Marlena turn the corner and leave him alone.

"No," Bridger squeaked, realizing he couldn't speak without pain.

He crawled across the floor until he reached the bars of the cell. He couldn't remember how he'd gotten here, and he was too far into the dungeon to recognize where he'd been taken.

Bridger spent the next few hours losing and regaining consciousness.

One of the times he came to, a hand was around his wrist, and the throbbing in his head seemed to subside the longer the touch was there.

The healer mended his big wounds, leaving the smaller ones to crack and bleed again when he moved. Bridger knew he was being healed only to be broken again. Marlena was going to keep him at the brink of death until she got her way... or got tired of him.

Bridger measured the passing of time by the light shining from a small window at the end of the hall.

He saw no one for what felt like days, and the churning in his stomach was no longer just from the pain but from hunger and guilt.

Arlet and Khort were out there by themselves, fighting a battle he should be beside them for. They'd lost Vega again... and this time so quickly.

It happened so fast.

He could still hear the crack of her neck echoing in his mind.

The click of heels echoed down the hall, amplifying the memory of Vega's snapping neck. Bridger's hands shot to cover his ears, but he could still hear the haunting crack. A scream ripped through his chest, drowning out the sound of Marlena's approach.

He didn't hear the cell door open.

Didn't smell the waft of smoke coming off Marlena's burning hands.

Couldn't feel her fingers under his chin as she forced Bridger to look at her. "I will break you down until there's nothing left of the Bridger she loves."

Those words would terrorize him for the next two fucking years... and then for the rest of his life.

Light blinded him, air rushing into his lungs from the sharp inhale he gasped. If it weren't for the restraint over his lap, Bridger would have gone flying from the seat.

He continued to pant, sucking in deep breaths until he registered the hands on his face.

Vega.

She forced him to look at her. "Relax. You're on a plane. You can't freak out right now."

Bridger's eyes scanned her face, taking in the look she was giving him. It wasn't pity. It wasn't fear. It was understanding.

She knew what it was like to remember the things you didn't want to.

"It was just a dream," she said.

But it wasn't. It wasn't just a dream.

It was his life.

It was the memories he threw away like trash while Vega fought to keep hers.

Her touch drove him mad, the buzz of their shared bond loud in his head. Bridger pulled his face out of her hands and closed his eyes, taking more deep breaths.

"Bridger—"

A happy-sounding beep played overhead, and a speaker crackled to life. "Good evening, everyone, I was hoping I wouldn't have to make this announcement, but unfortunately, due to winter storms pounding the central United States, we've been rerouted to Chicago O'Hare International Airport. We apologize to those whose final destination was LAX, but please know our first priority is always your safety. Our gate agents will get you rescheduled and home as soon as the weather clears. I anticipate we'll have some bumpy air on the way down, so I'll be turning the Seatbelt sign on for the remainder of the flight and asking your flight attendants to secure the cabin for landing as we make our final descent into Chicago. Sit tight and feel free to use your small handheld devices to make arrangements using our free in-flight WiFi."

Oh, it's about to get bad again.

"Bridger, these dreams—"

"Are mine to deal with." He unbuckled himself and stood to shuffle his way into the aisle, beelining straight to what he assumed was the bathroom with the little people on the light above the door.

Bridger fumbled with closing the door and then with the stupid fucking lock—*because what kind of lock is this?*—turning to the sink to press every single button around it until he got the water to turn on.

Fuck, this bathroom is small. Bridger had never been claustrophobic until now.

He felt larger than life trying to bend down to splash water on his face, washing the very real feel of the dream from his skin.

Water dripped down Bridger's, his dark eyes glaring back at him in the mirror. The lies and deceit, the reason he'd come to Earth, stared him right in the face.

He'd told Marlena he was here to make Vega fall in love with him... but what happened if he was the one who fell instead?

17

Welcome to Chicago, the sign above their heads read—
they were officially on the same continent as the portal.

Vega had somehow managed not to panic or pass out while going through Passport Control, even though their flight had been rerouted to Chicago. It was like this life wanted to go on one last tour of Earth.

"Holy shit, holy fucking shit. We did it," Vega muttered to herself, her heart beating so hard she could feel it in her temples. Her adrenaline plummeted, leaving behind a tight chest and a lump in her throat.

Since the plane, Vega had only spoken to Bridger if absolutely necessary, and apparently, he was done with the cold shoulder.

"I gotta know, do you plan on ignoring me for the rest of the trip or the rest of our lives?" Bridger cocked his head to the side, not looking where he was going.

"The rest of our lives if I could, but that doesn't seem possible," she grumbled.

"Is this all because I wouldn't tell you about my dream?" he asked, squinting like that was the craziest thing he'd ever heard.

"No, I'm just back to realizing I can't stand you and how you like to play by Bridger's rules. Kinda feels like Marlena's rubbed off on you." Vega dodged a man barreling towards them with his bag rolling behind.

Bridger grabbed her arm, stopping them in the middle of the busy airport. "I am nothing like her. I will never be anything like her."

If looks could kill... *I'd be a goner*.

"Then tell me, Bridger, what was the dream about?" Vega asked, knowing she wasn't going to get a straight answer.

Bridger ran a hand through his hair, frustration setting his brows. "I don't want to talk about the dreams."

"Of course you don't. You don't want to tell me anything I want to know." Vega yanked her arm from his grip, taking notice of the few people staring at them. "How convenient."

"That's not true—"

"If you don't want to tell me about the dreams, then tell me why Marlena would let you come here to get me. I know it's not out of the goodness of her heart."

Bridger said nothing.

Between his silence, her mixed feelings, and their constant back and forth, Vega was on her way to a panic attack.

Up ahead, there was a private corner behind some chairs. Vega beelined for it—she needed a minute to collect herself. She leaned against the wall, closing her eyes to focus on the rise and fall of her chest, of the breath she was using to clear the static in her head.

The hardest part was over, but Vega felt like she was finally letting everything they'd done hit her. She dug her nails into her thighs, letting the pain remind her she was alive—this wasn't a dream.

She knew Bridger loomed over her without having to open her eyes. They were connected in ways both had yet to understand—because they hadn't had time. Because Bridger betrayed her. He'd left her.

"Vega."

She hated that his voice made her open her eyes and look up, her body a traitor to what her brain wanted.

He's hiding something from you, she reminded herself. "I can't do this with you right now, Bridger. Please, I... We need to get out of here."

"You need to take a couple deep breaths," he told her, standing too close.

"I'm f—"

His fingers were on her chin, tilting her head back. "People are watching us. Stop acting like you hate me for one fucking second."

Vega couldn't look anywhere but at Bridger. "If you touch me again, I'll personally cut every finger on your hand off one by one." She took a deep breath, grabbed him by the wrist with their brand, and pulled his hand off. Vega made it look sweet, but there was nothing kind about the way she looked at Bridger. "No more planes."

Bridger was unreadable—the perfect poker face for the commander of Tolevarre. "No more fucking planes," he agreed wholeheartedly.

They walked silently side by side, doing their best to look like a totally normal, unassuming couple. News stations played on every TV they passed. Travelers watched the current weather report for the entire US, all with various looks of displeasure on their faces.

Vega skidded to a stop at the numerous thick white blobs scattered across the country.

"This is the storm of a lifetime here in Cheyenne, Wyoming. We're used to snow, but not *this* amount of snow overnight." The newscaster swept her hands behind her, dragging everyone's attention to the whiteout conditions. "We expect another two-plus feet in the next twenty-four hours."

The clip cut and moved to New York City, where another in-field reporter showed Times Square covered in a fresh blanket of snow. The next cut to Colorado, where there was so much snow, ski resorts were planning to close until the mountains were deemed safe.

"Of fucking course," Vega groaned, running a hand down her face.

The storm pushing through Wyoming was predicted to break up and scatter amongst the Midwest, barreling straight through their route to California. Screens blinked with red and yellow, announcing delayed or cancelled flights throughout the country. People stared on their phones, frantically trying to find new travel accommodations.

Every rental car booth had signs up that read No Cars Available, and their staff argued with irate customers. As if the poor girl running the counter could control the weather...

"It doesn't sound like anyone's going anywhere, so where do you think you're going?" Bridger asked, shoving his hands into the pockets of the coat he'd stolen in Rome.

They were met with the frigid winter air as the sliding doors to the airport opened. "You ask too many questions," Vega groaned but explained anyway. "Not every flight has been grounded. If someone is leaving the country, headed in the right direction, they're getting out. At least for a few more hours, and if they're leaving the country, it means their car will be left parked and unused until they return." Vega shivered when another gust of wind blew down the tunnel lined with cars, taxes, and buses.

A full bus waited by the curb, its window taped with a sign identifying it as the shuttle for parking lots C and D, but since Vega and Bridger didn't have any luggage, the driver waved them on. With the crowded bus, they were forced to stand close to each other in the corner, fighting for their lives as the driver hit every pothole from the terminal to the lot.

"Lot C!" the man called, rolling to a stop by a hut full of people waiting with their luggage.

A man on the phone dressed in a designer business suit and fancy coat caught her attention.

Vega tapped Bridger's side, nodding towards the opening bus door. "This is us." She eagerly rushed for the exit, stumbling down the last step like she had expected another one to be there.

"No, I'm in Atlanta for the week, and then I'll be in Dallas the followi—shit."

Vega flailed her arms and knocked the phone from the businessman's hand.

He reached for her, gently grabbing her forearms like he could help either of them from the situation Vega intentionally put them in.

Letting out a pathetic peep, Vega's ass hit the salted concrete below.

"Are you okay?" he asked, crouching down to help her to her feet.

Vega painted on an embarrassed expression, inhaling sharply when she put weight on her left foot. "I'm okay, I think I just twisted my ankle."

Bridger leaned down, picking up the phone Vega had knocked from his hand. He extended it out for the man to take, his glare looking less than friendly.

"I'm so sorry. I thought there was another step." Vega gave the man her best apologetic smile.

His hand struck out like a snake, snatching his phone from Bridger. His laugh was strained, nerves making his throat bob. "Oh, it's fine. Just glad you're okay." He returned her smile with one that might have made her weak in the knees in another life.

"Thank you. Sorry about your phone. Have a good day!" Grabbing Bridger by his coat pocket, Vega yanked him away from the shuttle, sporting a fake limp.

When they were out of earshot, Bridger turned to her. "You

dirty little crook." The shuttle rolled away, leaving the lot for its next destination. "Is that another trick you learned in one of your lives?"

Vega grinned, her fake limp disappearing. "No, that's from the original life." Her smile softened at the memory. "We used to make Khort so mad by cheating at cards." She hummed a short laugh. "I'd sneak them up my sleeves, and Marlena would hide them with her invisibility." It felt like someone else's life now, not her own. "I watched Arlet do it a lot in the time we spent together on Earth, but I think it's something she picked up from me and Marlena when she moved in with us."

Bridger wagged his finger at her. "I always knew you were a bad influence, Vega Caelum."

Vega flipped him off, pulling the car key out of her pocket. She pressed the lock button, hoping it would beep somewhere close by.

They wandered the aisles silently, pretending to be lost, until a beep finally drew their attention to a covered parking section and shiny, new blacked-out Cadillac Escalade.

Vega opened the backseat to make sure there wasn't anything weird or out of place. She searched everywhere she knew for an AirTag to be stored and let out a breath when she found one tucked between the third-row seats.

Bridger watched her the entire time. "What are you doing?"

Vega closed the back door and hid the AirTag under the parking curb.

"Getting rid of a tracking device. What are *you* doing?" She returned his question.

"Watching you get rid of a tracking device," he deadpanned, sliding into the passenger seat.

As soon as Vega started the car, Bridger pressed every button he saw. The overhead light turned on, shining directly into his eyes. "Ow." He squinted and turned it off. He blasted the heat, but the car hadn't fully warmed up, so it blew cold air out instead.

"Gods, stop fucking touching things." Vega slapped his hand out of the way and fixed the controls.

She hadn't expected his hand to wrap around her wrist and definitely didn't expect Bridger to pin it to the center console, not after she'd warned him to keep his hands to himself earlier. Her eyes shot up to his.

A muscle in his jaw jumped before he spoke. "You touched me first." His matter-of-fact tone made Vega try to snatch her arm from his hold.

It was no use. Bridger was stronger than her even without any powers.

"I get you're angry with me, Vega." The way he said her name while fired up made a flood of an unwanted desire drown her senses. She fought and fought, not ready to let it win. "I even agree you have every right to be mad at me, but there's one thing I must remind you of." He leaned in, bringing his face closer to hers. "I'm still the commander of Tolevarre. Watch how you talk to me."

They locked eyes and Vega couldn't ignore the growing tension between them. Her body was drawn to him, while her brain and heart tried to keep her in line.

"New rule. Let's keep our hands to ourselves. How's that sound?" He finally let her go.

Vega brought her arm to her chest, rubbing where his grip had been—not because it hurt, but because she thought she could still feel his searing touch long after it was gone. "Sounds perfect."

Every nerve ending in her body lit like a match, and Vega caught herself leaning into the warmth of the blaze Bridger had set.

18

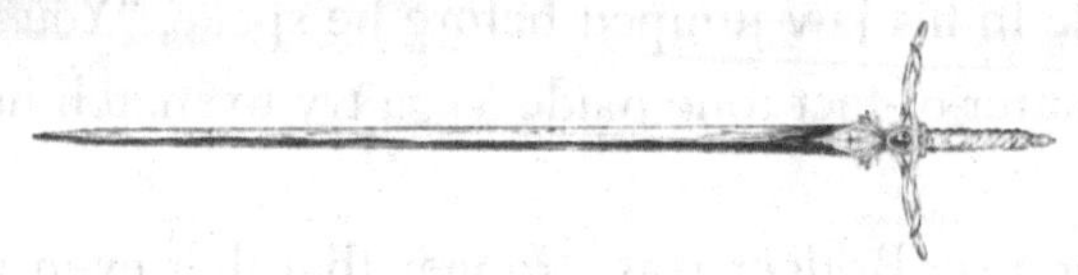

Snow covered the roads by hour seven of their drive. Bridger couldn't even see the car in front from the raging wind and white snowfall. "Okay, I've stayed quiet up until now, but I think it's time to stop for the night."

Vega's knuckles were white, her grip on the wheel tight. "We have to get to the portal," she argued—*imagine that.*

He shook his head. "Correction. We have to get to the portal *alive.*"

They'd passed car after car in ditches or in the process of losing control. Bridger didn't want to be either of those things.

Vega answered too quickly. "Last time I checked the radar, it showed we were halfway through this part of the storm."

Bridger didn't get the chance to reply as red lights came rushing towards the front of their SUV. Vega jerked the wheel to avoid crashing into the other car.

He held on to what Vega called the "oh shit" handle, realizing how accurately named it was as they slid into a ditch, whipping them both around until they came to an uncontrolled stop.

Alive. *We're alive.*

Bridger spun in his seat to inspect Vega for injuries before glancing down at himself.

I'm fucking fine. His attention had only left Vega for a second.

Her eyes were wide, and her hands still clutched the wheel, but she was unharmed. "Alright, I think it's time to pull over for the night."

Joking? At a time like this? Vega was fine.

"You think?" Bridger gestured to the ditch they were in.

Somehow, luck was on their side, and Vega was able to get out in a few tries without either having to brave the cold. She pulled into the far right lane when it was safe and got off the next exit.

They had barely said a single word to each other since Chicago, giving Bridger all the time in the world to get lost inside his head—his thoughts ranged from Marlena and his deal, and how torn he was about how to tell Vega, to the unresolved resentment he had for the girl he once loved.

What Marlena had become wasn't Vega's fault.

Falling in love with Vega had been the reason Bridger broke though... If it weren't for Vega, Bridger never would have suffered two years of torture, he never would have known what losing love felt like. He never would have—

"Hello?" Vega's voice dragged him out of his head.

"Sorry, what?" His vision refocused, and Vega's tired eyes were the first thing he saw. They were rimmed red from the strain of driving. "You almost killed me. Again. I was just spiraling a little."

Vega didn't laugh, and the sneer on her lips wasn't a smile. "And you *have* killed me, so almost is better than the alternative, don't you think?"

Snappy—just like the Vega he'd once known, but did she really have to remind him every chance she got about the whole him-killing-her thing? As if he could ever forget... *I've tried.*

"What were you saying?" he asked, batting his lashes sarcastically.

Vega's jaw tensed. "I said," she drew out, emphasizing the last word, "would you like to come in or are you planning on staying in here tonight?"

Bridger realized they were parked and the car was turned off. A bright neon sign reflected off the hood, indicating the motel had vacancy. He quickly leaned into the backseat, grabbed his bag, and followed Vega through the brittle cold and into the reception area.

"Cold out there?" the older woman behind the counter asked. "I bet you two are looking for a room to get off that nasty highway, aren'tcha?"

Bridger ruffled his hair, knocking the thick snow off. "How'd ya guess?" He gave her an endearing smile, but the undertone of his words sounded more like *duh*.

The lady wagged her finger as they approached the counter. "You're in luck. I have one room left, and it's a king size bed. Only problem is my card machine is down... so I've gotta do things a little differently than normal."

"You have nothing else?" Vega asked, her tone on the side of pleading.

The old woman's eyes darted between the two. "Uhhh, no, I'm sorry. Just the one room left."

Vega sighed. "It's fine. We'll take it." The woman held on to the card Vega gave her, completely unaware it was stolen from a woman's purse at a gas station outside Chicago.

Vega closed the curtains to their room once inside, resting her hands on her hips as she turned and took in the rather unsightly room. "Gross, but it'll do." She sighed, and with her breath, Bridger found himself relaxing a bit too.

"I really want a shower. Think you can handle grabbing some food at that diner behind here? It looked like it was still open." Vega flung her coat on the bed, not waiting for an answer as she let the braids around her face free, weaving her fingers through to untangle what she could.

"Food? Yeah. I can definitely handle food." And because watching Vega run her hands through her hair, letting it loose like she had in front of him hundreds of times before, made him want to wrap his hand—

"You're looking at me funny again." Her voice was softer than the first time she'd called him out for staring like a horny teenager.

Gods, Bridger, get yourself together. He was giving himself emotional whiplash.

Bridger huffed. "I can't help but think of the people we were the last time we were in a room alone together where we weren't trying to kill each other."

Vega pulled cash out of her pocket. "Who says I won't test another theory while we're here? We've never seen what happens if one of us dies in this realm."

Bridger couldn't help but follow the movement of her lips as they slid into a smile. He'd always been enchanted by her every move.

He called Vega's bluff, taking a step towards her. Bridger looked down at her with an impish smile of his own. "Oh, is that the theory you want to test this time?" He cocked his head. "I have a scar to prove your last test didn't go as you'd hoped."

Bridger watched as Vega's eyes trailed down his neck to his chest, like she'd be able to see through the layers of clothing he wore.

He cleared his throat, the noise lifting her gaze to his. "My eyes are up here."

Vega scowled, her pretty face twisting. "Do you think I won't try it?" She popped a hip, standing her ground.

Bridger's chuckle vibrated his chest. "Baby, the only theory we're testing is if you still make the same sounds you used to when you come." He licked his lips, letting the buzz in his body take the lead, ignoring the voice of reason telling him to stop. "Ever wonder if it's as good as we remember, or if we were just young, dumb, and in love?"

Vega's lips parted, and a puff of air released. He watched her swallow, balling her fists at her side. Bridger could tell she was fighting against the same battle he was.

She wanted him. Physically, if nothing more.

Bridger should step back... *but I can't.* It was getting harder to fight the call of their bonded souls.

Being this close to each other was dangerous.

Her pouty fucking lips were still parted, and the look in her eyes told Bridger everything he needed to know—she felt everything he did.

All of it.

When they took a break from trying to off one another, their bodies sang with a familiar need they both knew too well.

"Bridger," Vega said, exhaling softly.

"Yes, Kitten?" His voice a soft hum as he leaned in close enough to smell her damp hair from the snow, the scent of whatever shampoo she'd used last clawing inside his nose and making him lose almost every piece of control he possessed.

"Go get us some fucking food before we make a mistake we can't come back from." Vega slid the cash inside his coat pocket and disappeared behind the bathroom door.

19

VEGA RESTED HER FOREHEAD ON THE COOL BATHROOM DOOR and pressed her thumb into the lock on its handle.

She listened to the sound of her breathing, focused on the cool metal doorknob, on whatever she could to forget the way Bridger looked at her with a hunger only a god of darkness could possess.

Forty years. He'd been her enemy for forty years. He'd spent the last forty-fucking-years working for the sister who wanted her dead.

But he was haunted too.

He'd made decisions for his own reasons.

He keeps them safe. The army. Like he always wanted.

Vega shoved herself off the door, hurrying for the tub. She didn't give herself time to inspect the cleanliness and decided she didn't care anyway.

Not right now.

She needed to wash this feeling away.

Vega stripped her clothes and stepped into the frigid stream of water sputtering from the ancient showerhead. The cold sent chill bumps over her heated skin, giving Vega the shock she needed to come to her senses.

What the fuck are you thinking?

"Bridger, your ex, your ex who left you, your enemy." Saying it aloud didn't make Vega understand it anymore than she had before.

Her brain knew the facts, knew how insane it was her body was acting like a touch starved backstabber. How was she supposed to ignore their bond's instinctual physical connection?

She'd not even been with him for two days, and Vega was already ready to cave... to give in to the feeling she'd felt the last time they'd kissed.

Just one more time.

One more time would lead to nothing but complications...

Vega groaned, resting her head on the cool shower tile. "This is fucking ridiculous."

And so is talking to yourself in the shower.

Using the cheap soap in the dispenser on the wall, Vega washed her hair and body and spent a few minutes letting the conditioner sit.

The sound of the motel door slamming made Vega jump. She'd been too inside her own head to hear its creaky hinges open, and she was too hungry to yell at Bridger for rattling the entire room.

Vega quickly rinsed the conditioner out and turned the water off, the rusty handle squeaking. Vega grabbed the towel off the rack, dried herself off, and stepped out of the tub.

Slipping back into her bra and a fresh pair of the least ugly panties from a pack she'd bought with stolen money at a rest stop, Vega realized she hadn't heard anything from Bridger since the door shut. Her eyebrows knitted together as she focused harder.

Bridger would have made noise, and she should smell some kind of food. *Right?*

A creak in the floorboard had her stepping back. "Bridger?" she called, checking the bathroom for anything she could use as a weapon.

She had no idea where they'd stopped for the night or if it was safe.

When Bridger didn't answer, the hairs on the back of Vega's neck rose. *Someone else is in this room with me.*

She'd barely had time to get the thought out before the door flew open and the wooden doorframe splintered into pieces.

Her assailant's head hung low, rushing at her like a battering ram.

Vega's skull slammed against the shower tile, and the weight of a grown man landed on top of her.

Spots in her vision made it hard to see, and so did the pain in her head from the impact.

Pushing as hard as she could, Vega fought to shove him off while also bringing her knees up. "Get the fuck off me!" She was able to brace a foot against his chest and use her leg strength to kick him off.

He slammed into the pedestal sink, the force knocking the hood from his head.

Vega leapt to her feet and froze, staring into the eyes of her attacker.

Time felt like it stopped. *How?*

Chase's face broke into a smile made for a horror film, jagged at its edges, and pulling too hard at his skin. He stared through his brows, the bathroom's bad lighting casting shadows on every angle of his face.

Stunned, Vega froze in place as her brain tried to compute exactly what she was seeing.

Run! Her own voice busted through the haze.

She was able to get one foot out the bathroom before Chase's hand tangled in her wet hair and jerked her to the floor.

The air left her lungs in a whoosh. She fought to get it back as Chase straddled her waist, putting all his weight into the arm holding her down across her collarbone.

"Chase!" Vega flailed, still gasping for a full breath while trying to rotate her hips and get out from underneath him. He was too strong, pinning her with unnatural strength.

The more she fought, the harder Chase pressed into her.

"Chase, what are you doing? Let me go!" Vega screamed, hoping someone would hear her.

"One of us has to die... It's not going to be me." Chase leaned out of the shadows, and that was when Vega noticed his eyes.

The black, soulless eyes stole her breath, fear festering up her throat. "No," she gasped, clawing at his arms with her nails.

No matter how far she sank them in or how hard she fought, Chase held strong.

"Bridger!" The darkness in Chase's eyes glimmered. *What the fuck?* Chase wouldn't give her an inch. It was like he knew what her move was going to be before she made it. Almost like he was part of her...

"He can't save you." Chase's voice sounded like that of a serpent's, every *s* hissing.

He slipped his hands around Vega's neck and started to squeeze.

Vega clawed at his wrists, and he punished her by lifting her up by the neck and slamming her back against the floor.

Stars sprinkled across Vega's vision.

The voice inside her head telling her to keep fighting started to fade. *Holy shit, this is how I'm going to die. After everything I've been through, this is how it ends.*

It felt like the end. It felt *different*.

The stars in her vision faded to black at the edges.

I'm so sorry, Arlet, Khort...

Bridger.

She'd killed them all, doomed them the day she met them. Hopefully there was an afterlife for them to go to, to pass through the underworld and say goodbye before they withered into whatever happened to gods if they died.

Vega tried to keep hold of consciousness for as long as she could, and just before she lost her fight against death, Vega could have sworn she saw an angel with dark wings blending into the shadows approaching Chase from behind.

Oh, those aren't wings. Those are the shadows of—

Warm, thick blood coated Vega's chest, and the bite of air reentering her lungs burned like fire. The metallic taste made her gag as her vision came back. Even through the speckles of black taking their time to disappear, Vega saw who she'd thought was Pluto, coming to take her to the afterlife, pulling Chase's limp body off her.

But it wasn't the god of the underworld. It was Bridger.

In his hand, coated in Chase's blood, was the dagger Vega had made him leave behind in Rome.

Chase, who now lay face up with a blank stare and a six-inch gash across his throat.

Bridger grabbed her face by the cheeks, his dark eyes full of life, so unlike the black abyss Chase's had been.

"Vega, fuck. Are you okay?" His eyes bounced back and forth between hers before wandering down her exposed body. "Is any of this blood yours? Are you hurt?"

She wasn't sure.

One hand left her cheek, sliding down her body in search of wounds.

"You killed him."

Bridger didn't stop scanning every inch of her. "Of fucking course I did. He was going to kill you. I could feel it. I could feel it down the bond."

He could what?

Vega shook her head, grabbing Bridger by the wrist. "I'm fine." She was lucky he hadn't crushed her esophagus and she could still talk—despite how raspy her voice had become. "Where did you get the dagger?"

Bridger helped her up, twisting the dagger in his grasp to slide it between the waistband of his pants. "He had it."

"We have to go." Vega, although she'd almost been murdered, again, was thinking one step ahead. She looked down at Chase's dead body, blood leaking from the slash in his throat. His eyes were open and had returned to their normal color.

Vega glanced down at herself, covered in his blood. Bridger had splatters across his face and on his hands. "Clean up," she demanded, pointing to the sink as she turned the water to the shower on again.

She didn't wait for it to warm up before getting in. Vega watched the water turn red around her feet, slowly swirling down the drain.

Her ears rang, and she never heard Bridger speaking until he—fully clothed except for the boots he kicked off—got into the shower with her.

Shit, how long has he been talking?

"You're in shock," Bridger said softly, his wet pants clinging to his muscular legs. He reached out gently, pushing Vega's hair out of her face.

She wanted to be mad, pissed—wanted to throw Bridger out of this fucking shower, remind him not to touch her, but everything felt heavy.

Her body, her mind.

The color of the water faded to a light pink.

I almost died.

The searing pain around her brand made that clear.

How the fuck—*how?*

"Baby—Vega." Bridger corrected himself, his touch featherlight under her jaw. "Look at me."

Vega had a hard time focusing, but Bridger came into view, and she couldn't stop the need to be touched—to be held. She needed to feel alive. *Bridger can make me feel alive.* Taking the smallest step, Vega pressed herself against him, resting her head on his chest.

The rhythm of his heartbeat was steady against her ear.

He didn't hesitate to wrap his arms around her. "Tell me something real." Bridger's chest vibrated with his words.

Real.

This was real.

I almost died.

Chase had almost killed her.

How? What was—

"Come on, Vega. Let me inside that pretty little head of yours."

She knew he was doing it to distract her from the panic, to pull her out of the dangerous landslide of emotions that came after almost dying.

"Um," she finally said, trying to find words. "I had a cat once." Vega hadn't thought about that cute black furball in ages. "I named her Sushi." She didn't have the energy to elaborate much, but the memory gave her something else to grasp at.

"Not the pussy I thought we'd be talking about in the shower, but go on." Bridger stroked the back of her head, sending a soothing warmth shooting through her bloodstream.

"You did not just say that with a corpse less than five feet away."

She felt Bridger shrug, but she hadn't opened her eyes and certainly hadn't unwrapped herself from him yet. "Oh, a dead body? Hadn't noticed it."

Their banter worked, giving Vega the time she needed to recover. "What are we doing, Bridger?" she asked so quietly she thought he might not hear.

"We're making sure you don't crash out in this grimy tub," he answered factually.

Vega inhaled deep, breathing in the scent of his wet clothes. Pine and citrus. He'd always smelled like that. "I mean, what are *we* doing?" she asked again but this time with a different inflection.

The only sound was the water running, time standing still, until Bridger broke it with his response. "I don't know."

Dany Crooks

At least we're in this fucked-up mess together.

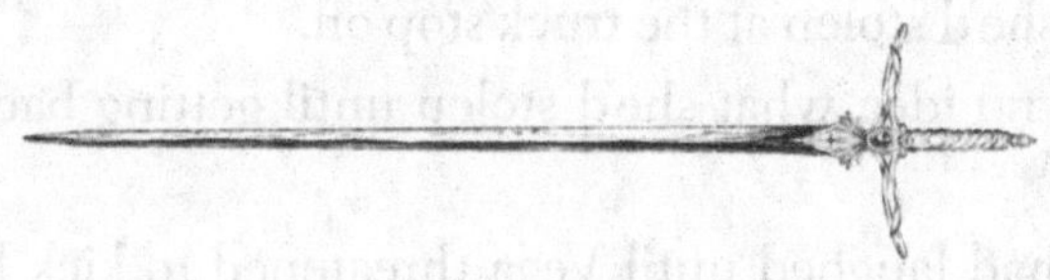

It wasn't creepy to watch someone sleep who'd nearly been choked to death.

Vega had died before, but Bridger had never felt what he had this time. Not even when he'd been the one to do it himself.

He'd been halfway back from getting them food when the tingle around his wrist started. When he got to the diner, he realized he had no idea what he was supposed to order, but at least the older woman running the place was nice enough. It took her a minute to warm up, but eventually she seemed to feel bad for him as he stared at the menu like he didn't know how to read.

She'd guessed he "wasn't from around here" and had the cooks whip up two house specials.

From one second to the next, the tingle of the brand went from normal to searing pain shooting up his arm. It felt like fingers sliding around his neck, trying to choke the life from him.

Bridger hadn't known whose throat he'd slashed until the body fell to the floor.

But it wouldn't have mattered anyway.

Actually, he might have made it slower and more painful had he known it was Chase. So if anything, he'd gotten lucky his death was quick and painless.

Vega lay curled up in the large bed, wrapped in a blanket like a cocoon. She'd hardly been able to get herself out of the shower once the adrenaline wore off. Bridger had carried her to the bed, stripped her of her wet bra and underwear—*respectfully*—and threw the large grey T-shirt she'd stolen at the truck stop on.

She had no idea what she'd stolen until getting back in the car with it.

Bridger had laughed until Vega threatened to kick him out and leave him on the side of the road.

He couldn't see the storm cloud with blue lightning because of the blanket wrapped around her, but he knew it was there. If he weren't so worried, Bridger might have chuckled about it again.

Vega had been sleeping for a few hours, and even though he knew he was going to get a fucking ear full when she woke up about how they needed to leave, he couldn't bring himself to wake her—not yet.

Bridger had no idea when the last time she'd actually slept was. She said she got a few hours while he was sleeping on the plane, but that wasn't enough for what she'd just gone through.

Across the room, Bridger sat in a chair, his elbows resting on his knees with his head in his hands. Exhaustion started to wear on him too, but he couldn't let himself sleep.

Not just because of the dreams, but because he kept telling himself he was keeping an eye on Vega, making sure she continued breathing and no one else snuck in to slit their throats in retaliation.

Bridger wasn't going to take any chances, not willing to push their luck and find out what would happen if they died on Earth.

Not when my life is linked to hers. Sometimes he tried to convince himself he acted only out of self preservation, even when he knew that wasn't the case at all. Not anymore.

So much had changed... and Bridger was ready to find out where he fit in the dawn of a new age.

Vega mumbled in her sleep, twitching, but never woke.

Bridger rose from the chair, stretching his arms over his head to release some of the pressure in his middle back. As much as he wanted to avoid the room where Vega's dead ex-husband was, he couldn't help but feel like he needed to check if the body was still there.

Of course the fucking body is still there... Where else would it be?

Bridger rolled his eyes, opening the bathroom door barely hanging on its hinges to clean floors, no blood, and a missing body.

A rush of cold paralyzed him, his veins turning to ice. This had to be a dream.

He forced himself to take a step inside, turning around like maybe he'd missed the dead body and pool of blood. "What the fuck," he whispered, running a hand over his head, holding the fallen strands of hair back.

Well, this is going to be a problem.

As much as he hated to do it, Bridger had to wake Vega. He returned to the main room and sat down on the edge of the bed. "Vega." Bridger ran a hand up and down her arm gently, trying not to startle her.

She groaned, pulling a pillow over her head.

Some things never changed.

"I need you to wake up." With his nerves spiked, Bridger's voice sounded too calm. It was how he was taught to react, to keep cool under pressure. He hadn't always been the best at it, but he'd gotten better over the years.

All he got was another groan and Vega trying to roll over and face away from him.

She didn't even know she was doing it—she'd always been hard to wake up.

"Five more minutes." That was Vega's sign she was coming to.

"Vega, please, I need you to get the fuck up." Bridger grabbed her by the arm and turned her back over, snatching the pillow off her head.

"Hey!" Vega cried, jolting up to grab it. She paused mid-move, finally realizing where she was. Her hands fell to the mattress, and she quickly looked around the room. "I fell asleep?" She pushed the covers off. "Did you undress me?"

"Yes, and yes."

Vega sneered. "Excuse y—"

"It's nothing I haven't seen before. You were crashing. What was I supposed to do? Leave you in your cold and wet underwear? No." Bridger stood, staring down at her. "But don't you worry, I was a complete gentleman," he followed with a wink.

She glared at him sleepily for a few silent seconds before moving on. "How long have I been asleep?" she asked, rubbing her eyes.

Bridger pretended to look at a watch on his wrist he wasn't wearing. "Oh, a few hours... just long enough for the body in the bathroom to disappear." The casualness of his tone jarred even himself.

"Long enough for *what*?" Vega popped off the bed, her bare feet pattering against the dingy carpet to the bathroom.

Bridger stood and watched from the side of the bed, crossing his arms and waiting for her to freak out.

In three, two, one...

"What the fuck?"

Right on time.

Vega covered her mouth with one hand and supported herself against the wall with the other. "What the fuck?" she repeated, quieter this time.

"That's exactly what I said."

Vega spun around. "How did this happen? How long ago did this happen?"

Bridger raised his shoulders. "I just noticed it."

She started to pace—a habit she'd begrudgingly picked up from Khort.

Bridger watched her bounce from one end of the room to the other.

"You didn't go in there and check on him?" she asked as she passed by.

Bridger stared at her seriously. "To do what? Ask if he was comfortable or needed a blanket?" He ignored the middle finger Vega raised. "He was dead. I didn't think I'd need to go back in there and check if he was still dead."

"Then why did you?"

Bridger's jaw tightened as she continued to pace. "Will you please stop doing that?"

Vega shook her head. "No, now answer my question."

He sighed, pinching the bridge of his nose. "I don't know. I just... felt like I needed to."

The sound of Vega's feet stopped, and when Bridger looked up, she was standing in the middle of the small bathroom. "Bodies and blood don't just disappear."

Bridger stared at her back until she turned around and he could see her face. Her eyes had that look she got when she was on to something, like she was seeing where all the answers hid. "What are you thinking?"

Vega opened her mouth and then immediately shut it, taking a second to collect her thoughts. "Chase told me only one of us could live." Chills raced down Bridger's spine when she paused, biting at the edge of her nail. "Bridger, what if the curse is inside him? The black eyes... the eerie voice and his strength. You made a good point about the broken portal."

Gods, he was starting to get a headache.

Bridger ran a hand over his tired face. "If I killed it—killed him, wouldn't that have broken it?"

Vega let out a sigh and sank into the chair Bridger had been in while he watched her sleep. "It's my curse, not yours. Death curses, blood curses, they can't be broken by anyone but the maker. I'm lucky enough to share blood with my maker, I guess. That much I've learned from my endless research. You killing him did nothing but reset him like it does to me when I die."

Vega stood from the chair and grabbed her leggings folded on top of the dresser. "I have to be the one to kill him." She stepped in one leg at a time, pulling them up her hips. "And I'm done waiting around for Death to find me."

21

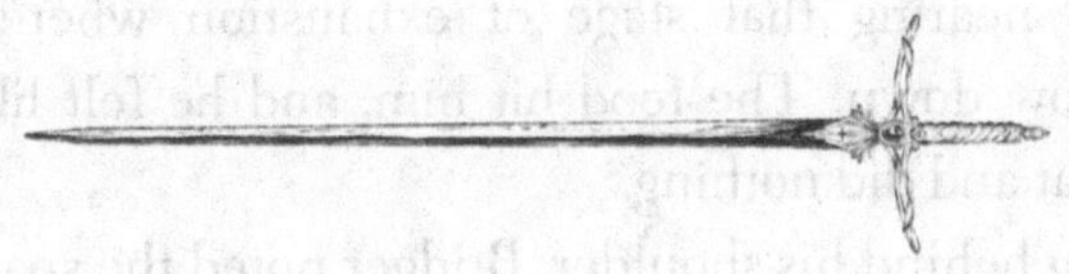

THEY WERE ON THE ROAD AGAIN IN UNDER TEN MINUTES.

The curse knew where they were going, knew they would be headed to the one spot they could finally end this.

Of course the curse wasn't an object in an apartment—it was something keeping her tied to this world... and the only object that did that was the portal.

But then what the fuck was this whole thing with Chase?

He was being controlled by the curse? But now differently than he was before the portal cracked and the other was destroyed?

Nothing about Vega's curse had ever been concrete, but it would be nice not to have so many unanswered questions.

The snow had let up enough to allow the roads to be cleared over the last several hours, so their stop hadn't been a complete waste.

The burgers he'd bought from the diner were cold, but they scarfed them down anyway. "Food kind of tastes like nothing here," Bridger admitted, wiping his hands on a thin paper napkin.

"Oh, I'm sorry. Was the burger from a crummy diner in the

middle of nowhere not up to your elite standards?" She cut him a glance as she drove.

They were still about a day out from the portal, give or take, with stopping to refuel. Vega wouldn't be able to drive twenty-four hours straight, not on what little sleep she was working with, and she'd refused to let Bridger help—not that he'd want to right now anyway.

He was nearing that stage of exhaustion where everything started to slow down. The food hit him, and he felt like he'd be a goner if he sat and did nothing.

Glancing behind his shoulder, Bridger noted the space he had to work with. "I'm assuming you're not going to want to stop at any more roadside motels?"

Vega answered with an exaggerated shake of her head. "I think one was enough for this trip. I probably won't sleep anymo—" Her head turned to glance at Bridger when the car beeped about his unbuckled seatbelt. "What are you doing?"

Bridger crawled his big ass over the center console and into the backseat. There wasn't the most room for an almost six-and-a-half-foot god, but he'd consider himself lucky after seeing some of the smaller vehicles here. "There's got to be a way to pull these seats down, right?" he asked, starting to slip his hands between the cracks, feeling for a lever or handle of some sort.

"Why?" she asked, staring at him in the rearview mirror.

"Do you always have to ask so many questions?" Bridger stopped, returning her look with one that said, *Chill the fuck out.* "We don't need the backseat for anything, so it might as well be a bed for when you're tired enough to sleep." He pointed to the road. "Focus, Caelum." Bridger saw her eyes roll before returning to the highway.

He really didn't want to end up in another ditch.

"When was the last time you slept?" she asked, passing a slow-moving car.

"The plane," Bridger told her, still trying to find a way these seats came down.

As if Vega could sense his agitation, she said, "Check behind each seat. There might be a little handle that brings the seat forward, but you need to be on the opposite side so it can fold down."

Doing exactly that, Bridger reached across the seat, found a handle, and half the backseat folded in on itself slowly.

"Wooooow," he marveled with sarcasm. "Fancyyyyy." He let the second-row seats down next.

Bridger heard a puff of air leave Vega's mouth, trying to suppress a laugh.

They used to laugh together all the time. Vega had once been his best fucking friend. At one point in their lives, Vega was the only person who'd ever shown him it was okay to want something you weren't supposed to.

Her laugh pulled him into the past, and he wanted to hear it again. And again. And again...

Leaning against the back corner of the SUV, Bridger sat diagonally and still didn't have enough room to stretch out, but at least Vega would fit comfortably. "Do you remember when we ran into each other in Demuto the week after we met?"

Vega's eyes returned to the rearview mirror. "How could I forget? It was the worst blizzard Demuto had seen in a century, and we all got stuck in the theater overnight." She hadn't mastered her control of the weather yet, and a storm that size would have been too big for her even now.

Bridger had spent the night getting to know Vega and Arlet, listening to them laugh until they cried. They had an inside joke for every day of the year.

If he hadn't fallen in love with Vega the night he met her, he would have that night.

Khort had pretended to sleep until the girls dogpiled him and forced him to join in on the conversation. It was the night he realized Khort was in love with Vega too.

A smile pulled at the corner of his mouth. It filled Bridger with a happiness he hadn't felt in a very, very long time listening to Vega recall the details of their love story. It had ended, but that didn't make it any less real.

"I wasn't supposed to be in Demuto that night. I was supposed to be at Meyer's in Ardor. Once a year, our families got together for what might have been the only normal family night, if you can call it that, we ever had. Just all of us hanging out and our parents using it as an excuse to stir up some trouble for fun." The picture in his mind of those nights was so clear—clearer than it'd been in years. He'd done too good of a job shielding out the person he'd once been. "Anyway, I didn't show, and I was supposed to go to some party with him that night. I think that's why he always kinda didn't like you." Bridger chuckled. "Because I chose to go to Demuto, where I knew you were, on the off chance I'd happen to bump into you instead of being his wingman at some party I didn't care to go to if you weren't going to be there."

The sound of Vega's laugh shot tendrils of warmth throughout his body—like she had a personal supply of endorphins to give away and she'd given them all to Bridger.

She talked through her fit of giggles. "Arlet and I always joked that we thought he might be secretly in love with you."

Bridger barked a laugh. "Meyer, in love with me? I know I speak for both of us when I say I'd rather eat a bowl of rocks." Even if either of them were attracted to men, they were practically brothers. "I chose to chase down a girl I'd just met over spending our favorite night of the year together. I hurt his feelings, so in turn, he tried to hurt mine by not liking you." It hadn't worked. "I always knew deep down he really liked you... He was just putting on an act for the sake of proving a point, and then everything happened, so he leaned into it and told himself it was real." *Just like me.* "Sometimes it's easier to play pretend."

Words Bridger hadn't been expecting poured from Vega's lips. "He came to me in my last life... offered to help me try and break my curse if it meant saving you." Vega focused on the road, both hands gripping the steering wheel. "It was the reason I was in Solum the morning of Saturnalia. I was looking for Meyer to help with my reset."

Bridger's shock made him freeze, unable to say anything at all.

Meyer had always been clear on his stance. He'd follow where his parents pointed.

Vega continued talking. "But then I ran into you instead. When the battle broke out and Meyer wouldn't help me in front of everyone, I decided it was time to do something on my own for once —it was time to be my own god."

He was truly blown away, questioning everything Meyer had said to him since Vega had come back in the last life.

His best friend had seen Bridger's walls crumbling. He knew the shields were falling and the man Bridger had once been was starting to reemerge.

He might have even pushed him to get there a little quicker.

Bridger didn't know how long it'd been since either of them said anything when Vega spoke again. "Hey, Bridger..."

When he looked up, his eyes found hers in the mirror.

"Tell me something real." Had this become their way of letting down their walls, if only for a second, to peek inside and see what was left of the person they had once loved?

Bridger took a moment, swallowing back the fear of being honest. "Deciding to come find you in Demuto was the best decision I've ever made. I wouldn't be the person I am today if I hadn't fallen in love with you. I never would have had the courage to fight against what I knew was wrong." And that was what he'd done... It's what he tried to continue to do.

It was just different now...

Bridger had never claimed to be perfect. He'd never pretended to know everything, but the one thing he was certain of was if he didn't hold the position he held, things would be worse than anyone could imagine.

The air between them felt lighter than it had in almost four decades.

From the food, and the hum of the back tires, Bridger couldn't stop the pull of sleep. He'd tried to fight it for as long as he could but lost, blackness dragging him inside the body of a memory—the one that might have been the moment everything changed.

The sharp piece of rock in his hand clipped against the stone wall.

Another day down.

422 days locked away, and no one had said a single word to him.

One year, one month, three weeks, and six days he'd been locked away with only one meal a day. One year, one month, three weeks, and six days of no contact with the outside world.

All he had was himself and the doubts in his head. The voices who told him he'd never escape—he'd never see Vega again.

Marlena hadn't come by in over sixty days, and the last time she had, all she did was stare, provoking Bridger to scream whatever obscenities he could at her.

He reminded her every chance he got that he'd kill her—slit her throat, cut off her extremities one by one. Nothing shook her.

The only noise she'd made was the *tsk* of her tongue, followed by a disappointed shake of her head.

Then she left, leaving him in silence for another sixty days.

He was allowed to shower once every three days, but when he was escorted out by a guard—who he no longer fought, because what was the point?—not even they spoke to him. Even when it was someone who knew Bridger, who had trained beside him.

It was easy to see how manipulated they'd become, how afraid they were to step out of line.

They had no one to protect them from Marlena.

With his father gone, Tolevarre's army was in limbo. The people of their world had never been in this kind of danger before.

And instead of helping, instead of protecting the people he was bound to by duty and bloodline, Bridger was locked away for one year, one month, three weeks, and six days with no end in sight.

No one is coming for you.

It got clearer every day.

Bridger had already eaten for the day, so no one else would be coming by. It would be like all the rest of the days.

Sometimes he found the energy to work out—not a real workout, but as close as he could get with the energy he had. He had to keep moving.

Other days he solved math problems in his head to keep his brain working.

A couple times, in his darkest moments, he even prayed for Death to take him.

Today? Well, today... he didn't feel like doing anything.

The silence was heavy.

Scratch.

Another mark was added on the wall.

Scratch.

And then another.

Scratch.

Four more.

Scratch.

Seven more.

The sound of footsteps echoed down the hall on day 435. The click of heels announced her arrival before she appeared.

Marlena looked as beautifully lethal as she always did with her bright lips painted in a smile. "Hello, Bridger."

The sound of her voice broke a violent need inside him. *Words.*

Do you know how fucking hard it is to go over a year without hearing a single voice outside your own?

Marlena laughed softly, stepping through the bars with her ability to travel, joining him inside the cell. She must have registered the look on Bridger's face, because he was now the mouse in whatever fucked-up game she wanted to play. "Been kind of quiet in here, hasn't it?" She knelt down to where he sat, matching his eye level. The black halo she'd started wearing after her summoning glinted in the light filtering through the cell bars.

Bridger wanted to feel his power reach inside and obliterate her to pieces... but he couldn't. His power was blocked by the mark on his forearm, leaving him hollow, and he couldn't find it in himself to stand.

"I don't have to show you how strong I am to hurt you. You know. I know you know the power I have." Marlena reached out and ran her hand over his cheek. "All I have to do is be the reminder you need." She cupped his face. "Vega will never be the girl you loved again. She's too broken now, and it's only going to get worse."

Bridger slapped her hand away, but Marlena didn't budge, only brought it to her side. Even squatted down in six-inch heels, her presence still felt too big for the meager cell.

The look behind Marlena's eyes was cold, but the fake veneer she molded to perfection could have passed for sad if Bridger didn't know any better. "I don't have to lay a hand on you. No." She shook her head slowly, her ponytail swaying. "I've shown you what I can do to you. To everyone."

"Shut up." He hadn't heard his own voice in weeks. Bridger hadn't tried to talk in *weeks.* The sound was foreign to his ears.

Marlena inhaled. "Ah, he does remember how to speak." Reaching out again, she brushed his shaggy hair from his eyes. "You're losing yourself in here. You're becoming a sad, pathetic waste of life. A waste of *power*. You're exactly what your father said you'd be... a disappointment."

Bridger reacted exactly like Marlena had wanted him to, pushing her out of his face before hopping to his feet. The quick change made his head rush, throwing him off balance.

He was wasting away in here. What good could he do from behind the bars of a prison cell?

Marlena staggered back and gained her composure in an instant. "You're holding on to a life that no longer exists for a girl who is destined to die. Vega is already dead, and she has been since the day I cursed her." She sighed. "When are you going to see I'll never let her live, Bridger? I'll let the curse kill her slowly. It will take her from you eventually. In fact, you should be thanking me. At least you got more time than you would have if I'd killed her right away like our parents." The long off stare Marlena had gotten almost made Bridger take a step back.

"It's torture for the rest of you too. It's why I haven't killed anyone off yet, because this is sweeter. Watching you fight valiantly over the years to save Vega, knowing it'll be for nothing." A single shrug of her shoulder showed how little she cared. "You're only making this harder on yourself, but I can help you. I'm *willing* to help you." She made it sound like she was about to offer him the deal of a lifetime. "But if you don't want my help, then I guess I can go ahead and kill Arlet and Khort. I was only keeping them around for the fun of it."

His voice had always been deep, but now with the gravel of unspoken words lodged in his throat, it felt like a rumble from below. "You'll never break me."

"Oh yes, I will, but I also want you to have all the success and power you deserve. The army you deserve. Imagine what you could do, imagine who you could be, if it were all yours."

"I don't want your fucking power! I want to watch you burn!" Bridger's rage made him see red, the room blurring at the edges.

Marlena materialized her way outside of his cell milliseconds before he charged. The bars shook under his grip—even with his powers cut off, this type of anger did something to him... made him someone else.

"You can want both, and one day you'll see it the way I do. Power and wrath can be combined to make something so, *so* sweet." She straightened the skirt of her long dress. "You can save them, Bridger."

He trembled watching her retreat into the hall's shadows. "And all you have to do is get over a dead girl." Marlena looked over her shoulder just before she couldn't be seen anymore. "She's back, and I've met this new version of her." A chuckle echoed off the walls. "She's so weak and pathetic she's almost unrecognizable... and she'll continue to fall further and further away from who she once was the longer this draws out."

Bridger rattled the bars, screaming at Marlena.

Her question reached him after she was already gone. "How will she ever be able to love you when she finds out you're the reason her very best friends are dead?"

Air. I need air.

The gasp rattled his entire chest, his eyes ripping open the moment he was released from the dream's confinement and allowed to regain control of his body.

It took him longer than he'd like to remember exactly where he was, fighting against a type of fear he'd never experienced before.

The car slowed, and Vega's eyes fixed on him in the mirror. They were wild with worry, the red brake lights illuminating a glow inside the backseat as the sun set behind the mountains in the distance.

Vega. I'm with Vega on Earth.

"Pull over," he wheezed, unable to calm his breaths no matter how hard he tried.

"Bridger..." she started to protest.

He crawled to the side door. "Vega, pull the fuck over before I jump out."

Marlena's words, the feeling of her mental hold, the memories flooding his mind—it was all too much.

He started to struggle to take a breath, and the walls of the vehicle grew closer and closer.

By some stroke of luck, they were passing a sign that read Rest Area, and Vega pulled them into a discreet corner of a large parking lot.

Bridger didn't let the car come to a complete stop before he stumbled into the crisp air. The snow had stopped for now, but there was a fresh dusting coating the grass crunching under his boots.

The cold air filled his lungs but hadn't begun to help calm his racing thoughts.

"Bridger." Vega's voice came from close behind, startling him to spin around on the ready. She scanned him from the ground up as the internal warfare of Marlena's torture overthrew his senses. "What did you dream of?" She asked the question gently, her tone bordering on nervous.

"I can't..."

Vega's softness turned to something Bridger couldn't place right away, her body tensing. "Of course not. You expect me to open up about the fucked-up shit I've been through, but I don't get the same in return."

The car stayed running behind them, the lights reflecting off the snow-covered trees in the distance.

Bridger's fists clenched at his side. "It's not the same."

Vega's jaw dropped, and the look on her face was one Bridger had seen hundreds of times before—the one she got before a fight broke out and she was about to explode. If they were back in Tolevarre, sparks of her lightning would light up her fingertips.

"Oh, really?" Her head cocked to the side.

"Yes, really," Bridger deadpanned, focusing on doing whatever he could to keep his mind from returning to the memory he'd been forced to relive.

"I'm trying to see how it's fair that I'm expected to spill the darkest parts of myself on command when it's what you need, but you, the one who betrayed me, gets to clam up whenever he wants? No." Vega shook her head. "No. That's not how this is going to go."

His emotions took a one-eighty, melting from the fear of being trapped alone again inside a memory he could no longer escape, to white-hot anger. "When are you going to stop fucking reminding me of my wrongdoings, Vega?" He stalked towards her, but she didn't back down—not this version of her.

It lit something in the pit of his stomach. Rage, he told himself as it warmed the rest of his body.

But it wasn't that at all. It was need.

The ache to touch Vega was stronger than ever, his control slipping faster than he could rope it back in.

"Because I know what I've done wrong. I know the choices I've made. When I close my fucking eyes, they're there to haunt me. The good, the bad, and the ugly. So excuse me for not wanting to relive them more than I already have to." He looked down, towering over her with only inches of space between their bodies.

Scoffing, Vega craned her neck, a sneer pulling her upper lip. "Welcome to the last fifty-five years of my life. If I don't get to cherry-pick my memories, then neither do you." She laughed, and it wasn't the melody he'd heard earlier.

He couldn't think straight, couldn't find his way out of the sea of anger begging him to succumb to its fury.

He wasn't but seconds from snapping.

"If you won't tell me about your dreams, then tell me how you got Marlena to agree to making a new portal. What's in it for her, Bridger? I know my sister well enough. She didn't allow you to come here without something in return."

His promise to Marlena rang in his mind, echoing beside the

threats of his latest dream. Bridger closed his eyes, trying to shut everything out without the power of his shields. "Stop," he pleaded, fighting to hold onto his last sliver of control.

"What did you tell her you'd do to me?" Vega continued to push.

"Vega, please." He muttered, resorting to begging. Bridger's forearms quivered from the tightly balled fists he had yet to loosen, his muscles straining.

"We're allies, Bridger. *Allies*. That's what you want right? You want to work together, to come back to where you were meant to be?" Well, this is how we do it. You learn to tell me the things I need to fucking hear. The things I need to trust you!"

Bridger's eyes snapped open, and the anger he felt at himself, at Marlena, at Vega, all of it, exploded.

Stalking forward, Bridger locked his focus on Vega like prey, and she must have recognised the look, because for every step Bridger took forward, she took one backwards. "You want to know what's going on in my fucked-up head? Huh? You want to know why I don't want to tell you what I'm seeing? The promises I've made?"

A breath of air escaped Vega's lips when her back collided with the car.

Bridger boxed her between his outstretched arms and instantly recognized the heavy lidded look she wore.

It was worse than the fear he'd finally expected to show.

Vega *liked* it.

Fuck. They were both so fucked.

The energy shifted, blending their anger with something neither of them could have prepared for.

Lust.

"Yes," she said on a breath, the back of her head resting against the car's window. The single word was filled with a desire Bridger felt too—no matter how much he told himself he shouldn't, it sank deeper and deeper into his skin, lighting him on fire.

"It's because you don't want to know the things I've told

Marlena I'll do to you if I get my hands on you. The things I've done to keep the people we love alive, safe... I've done enough! I've hurt you enough!" He slammed both balled fists against the Escalade's roof hard enough to leave a dent.

Vega didn't flinch. She stood still as ice, not showing a single crack. Her lips parted like she was going to say something, but her tongue flicked out, wetting them instead.

Bridger fought to drag his gaze away from her mouth. "I don't want to hurt you anymore." His voice was calmer when he spoke this time. "I don't want you to see me break over the fucking dreams that all seem to revolve around *you*. Around *us*." Bridger used his hands on the car as leverage, pushing off to put much needed space between them, but before he could run, Vega groaned a frustrated growl.

He felt the vibration in his chest before she spoke. "Fuck it."

There was no stopping what happened next.

22

THEIR LIPS COLLIDED, AND VEGA'S BODY WARMED, MELTING into the arms he wrapped around her.

Everything about this was wrong, and she knew it. She knew there were secrets Bridger was hiding, knew this wasn't going to make anything better.

But gods, she was sick of fighting it! Sick of pretending her body didn't crave his touch, his attention.

Maybe this was what needed to happen to allow them to move on with their lives—to put what they had in the past and learn what this new path looked like for them.

As good as it sounded, Vega knew it wasn't true. They were bound by ties neither would ever fully understand.

Bridger's tongue swiped over her bottom lip, begging her to open up to him.

Vega didn't hesitate a second, letting Bridger devour her with the need of their pent up desire.

They didn't need to find a rhythm, didn't need to take their time figuring out what the other liked. They already knew.

A moan slipped from Vega's throat, vibrating against Bridger's lips.

His chest rattled, a groan sounding suspiciously like a growl sending a tingle of pleasure to her core.

Bridger's hands slid down, getting a handful of her ass before he hiked her up and pinned her against the car, her legs wrapping around him. The metal might have been cold against her back, but she couldn't tell with the nearly unbearable heat of Bridger's touch.

He'd always been able to snag her up and move her to whatever position he'd wanted... and Vega had never said a single fucking word about it because why would she? What girl didn't want to be thrown around and manhandled by someone who resembled Bridger?

Vega tangled her fingers in the hair at the back of his head. He removed his lips from hers, trailing feverish kisses down her neck.

Bridger ground into Vega's spread legs with proof of his growing need pressing against her core. Pleasure burst through her like a nuclear explosion, feeding off the energy of their desire.

"Fuck me, please. I need you." She hardly recognized her voice, forgetting everything but Bridger.

At any moment, Vega felt like she might wake up from this dream—beside another man, in another life.

It's real. They were real.

It was wrong. What they were doing was wrong... but how could something she knew would send them into a spiral later feel so right in the moment?

Her words struck something inside Bridger. He grabbed her by the jaw and locked his dark stare on her, rolling his hips into her again.

Vega's body tingled, and a moan left her wet lips. "Bridger." She sighed, unable to look away from his lust-filled gaze, too afraid it would shatter the connection.

"We shouldn't," he warned, giving her the chance to back out.

Keep going.

The brand on her wrist tingled with the warmth of something she hadn't felt in a long, long time. "Stop being a gentleman and fuck me, Dimico."

Before she knew how it happened, Bridger had the door to the Escalade open, and she was on her ass, scooting across the down seats to give Bridger room to follow her in.

When he shut the door, it was as if they'd entered their own world. They didn't think about the lights beaming into the dark woods in front of the car. They didn't think about the doors being unlocked. They didn't think about getting caught.

The only thing on either of their minds was this. Them. *Us.*

Vega wasn't sure if that was her voice or someone else's. She was too distracted by the depraved hunger on Bridger's face as he crawled the short distance to her.

Gods, she might come from just the sight of him.

Bridger positioned himself over Vega, returning his lips to hers in a kiss somehow needier than the first.

His hand slid between her legs, pressing into the exact spot he was going for. No fumbling around, straight to the point.

Vega inhaled sharply as he rubbed her through her thin leggings, breaking their lips apart to lay her head back. Her eyes fluttered as pleasure pooled between her thighs.

"Soaked. Absolutely drenched," Bridger said against her skin, kissing down her neck until her stupid lightning T-shirt got in the way. He sat back, pulling her with him, only to drop her on his lap.

Vega straddled him, grinding against the rock-hard erection hidden by his pants. It had been so long since they'd been together—but some things just couldn't be forgotten.

Specifically, *his size.* She shivered as a flutter of pleasure shot through her.

Bridger ripped Vega's shirt over her head, tossing it to the side, and with an ease that shouldn't have surprised her, unclasped her bra with one hand while the other slid into the front of her leggings. Bridger's fingers slid between her slick lips and pressed into her clit. "It fucking killed me to know you weren't wearing anything under these."

When redressing in the motel, she hadn't even thought about them.

Vega moaned, rolling her hips against the fingers he massaged her with slowly—so agonizingly slow.

Bridger's free hand left goosebumps in its wake, grabbing her roughly by the back of the neck to force her to look into his eyes— and when she did, she was rewarded with two fingers slipping inside.

Eye contact. *Fuck him and his glorious eye contact.*

"That's my girl." Bridger placed a kiss on her parted lips that felt too sweet for the intensity building between them. "You have to give me one before I fuck you. You know the rules, baby." He'd always made Vega come first, sometimes multiple times, before he even considered chasing his own release.

Half the fun of sex to Bridger had always been the control part— he loved knowing he was the one delivering each wave of euphoric pleasure, getting to watch as Vega succumbed to him completely.

It was the only place she'd ever given up full control to another person—in the bedroom with Bridger, where she knew he'd take care of her.

Where she knew she was safe.

His fingers slid in and out while his thumb circled her clit at a pace not a single man after him had ever figured out. He watched every muscle in her face tick like he'd perish if he missed a single second.

"Fuck." Vega's head fell back, and she pressed into his hand for added depth and friction.

Bridger unexpectedly pulled his fingers out, and Vega whined at the loss. She threw her head forward, catching the cocky half smile on his face that shouldn't have been a turn on. He was fucking with her.

"You mother fuc—" She glared, but Bridger plunged his fingers back inside when she locked her eyes to his.

"Eyes on me." Bridger slammed his lips to hers, nipping at her bottom lip before pulling away. "I want you to come knowing who made you fall apart."

Bridger pumped his fingers again, grinding his palm against her sensitive bud.

Vega didn't stand a chance. She wanted to talk back, to tell him to get fucked, but that was what she was trying to do, and she didn't want to screw it up! So for once in her life, Vega kept her sassy-ass comments to herself and—oh, who was she kidding? She was consumed with ecstasy. There was no room left for snide remarks.

"Holy shit," she mewled, raising up on her knees to sink back down when Bridger pressed deeper.

"Gods, you're going to feel so good wrapped around my cock." Bridger gritted his teeth, leaning into her and taking a nipple in his mouth. He swirled the pebbled bud with his tongue, sucking gently before he switched to the other, using his teeth to roll it between his lips.

Vega was going to lose it. She was going to come too quickly. All she wanted was to live in this little bubble of pleasure, never letting it go.

Her nipples ached, turning cold without his warm mouth around them.

Bridger brushed over her parted lips with his thumb. "You're so fucking beautiful."

Gods. His voice was so deep she could feel it.

Vega's hands wrapped around his wrist, pulling his strong grip to her throat.

After almost being killed by asphyxiation twice in three days, most wouldn't even consider asking for it again... But Vega wasn't most, and she trusted Bridger with this. He knew what he was doing. After all, he'd been the one to discover Vega's love for rough sex in the first place.

But now more than ever, the pain accompanied with the pleasure reminded Vega she was alive.

Bridger's eyes lit with the flame she'd been hoping for. "Oh, you want to see stars?" He tightened his grip slowly, waiting for Vega to answer.

A bearable rush of pain sent a visible chill down her spine.

"Yes," Vega whimpered.

Bridger locked his massive hand under her jaw, and squeezed until she couldn't find the extra air to moan.

As expected, he was careful not to put pressure where Chase's hands had been. His hold was meant for something opposite of death.

Between the lack of oxygen, Bridger's ravenous gaze, and the third finger he'd slid inside her, Vega took a tumble.

Catching the gleam in her eye, Bridger loosened his grip, giving her the air she needed to plummet into oblivion and become one with the fucking stars.

"That's it. Come all over my fingers, baby." Bridger's voice was husky, and Vega wasn't sure what the look in his eyes meant when hers were rolling into the back of her skull.

The walls of her pussy clenched Bridger's fingers, her hips bucking as her orgasm racked through her body. "Bridger." Her moan turned his name into a version with at least ten *r*'s.

He rubbed his thumb against her clit until Vega's moans of pleasure turned into breathy pants. "Fuck, I need to be inside you." Bridger wrapped his free arm around her and slid her off his lap, pulling his fingers out and popping them into his mouth until clean. Bridger slid his tongue down them with one more long, languid lick. "You taste so much better than I remember."

When the fog of Vega's mind cleared, her fingers worked the

buttons of Bridger's shirt. He shook his shoulders, letting the shirt fall behind him. "How can someone be so gods-damned hot?"

Smooth, Vega. She hadn't meant to say that out loud.

Bridger's muscles tensed, his biceps flexing and the veins in his arms bulging as he yanked her out of her leggings. He watched Vega widen her legs, the gleam from a pole light running down her inner thigh without her knee in the way casting shadows.

Bridger trapped his bottom lip between his teeth with a famished hum vibrating deep inside his chest. "I was just wondering the same thing."

Vega fumbled with the button on his pants, not as smooth as he was after that earth-shattering orgasm. She would probably never be the same, would probably have to become celibate after this—no one was ever going to do what Bridger did to her, making her feel the way he could.

She'd had her fair share of sex to know.

Bridger didn't rush her, didn't push her to go faster. He only watched as Vega finally got her fingers to work and unbuttoned his tented pants. She trailed a hand down to the bulge of his straining cock, applying pressure with her palm.

The muscles in his stomach constricted, forming a *v* when he rolled his hips and rubbed his erection against Vega's hand. Bridger's fingers slipped into the waistband of his fitted boxers, freeing him from pants-prison.

Her mouth watered when his dick bobbed against his lower abdomen. "Holy shit." Okay, so maybe she hadn't remembered exactly how big he was.

He pumped himself once, twice, three times. Vega watched, mouth watering as his thumb slid over his tip to wipe precum across the head. "I'll go as slow as you need." Bridger shifted forward, crouching so he wouldn't hit his head, until Vega was on her back and he hovered over her.

Vega couldn't think, couldn't focus on anything but *him.*

There was no way to explain the feeling she had. The buzz inside her body with Bridger this close was intoxicating.

Her hand slid from his wrist to his forearm, her eyes fixed on the bulging veins, before trailing up to his toned bicep. Vega's other hand traveled the same length of his opposite arm, her fingernails grazing his skin lightly enough to form goosebumps.

Bridger released a breath, breaking Vega's trance with a kiss.

While their tongues danced in time together, Vega slid down his torso and wrapped as much of Bridger's girth in her hand as she could. She gave him a few slow pumps, and Bridger groaned against her mouth, biting her bottom lip when her thumb played circles around his head, smearing more of his precum across the tip.

The noises he made had always excited her, reminding her not all men were afraid to reveal their pleasures in bed.

Vega positioned Bridger at her entrance, breaking their kiss to rest her forehead against his. He rolled his hips forward, and his tip squeezed inside Vega.

Her jaw felt like it unlatched, falling open as the pressure between her legs grew. "Oh gods," she purred, digging her nails into Bridger's back.

His breath hitched as he continued to slide inside. "Fuuuuck," he shuddered. "You're so tight." Bridger pulled himself almost all the way out, only to press back in further this time.

Vega's hands fell to the small of his back, and she used all the strength she could find in the moment to bring Bridger down, taking him all the way. "I don't need slow. I need *you*."

It took only a few seconds for the words to sink into Bridger's brain, to break through whatever trance he was in. She couldn't be the only one who felt like her insides were going to burn her up. Bridger had to feel it too.

The rightness of the moment couldn't be lost on him.

With himself completely seated inside, Bridger brought one hand to her cheek, pushing back the hair that'd started to stick against her face with sweat. "I'm a fucking goner, Vega." Bridger pulled himself out and then thrust back in with more force. "You can have whatever's left of me."

He hit the spot deep inside that turned her body to mush. "Yes," she said on a breath, locking her legs behind him.

He could get deeper, and Bridger knew that. He grabbed Vega by the crook of her knee, pushing one leg into her torso to open her up. Vega's toes grazed the roof of the SUV... and then he fucked her like she'd expect a god to.

Relentless. Deep.

It took no time in this position. She came again, her hand flying out to brace herself, her skin scorching hot against the cold window as the orgasm made her quiver.

Time meant nothing. Vega lost herself inside the car. Life went on outside of it, but inside they were suspended—floating somewhere in between the worlds.

Despite the limited space they were working with, Bridger flipped her over and fucked her from behind, holding on to her hips while he hunched over and kissed the side of her neck. One hand slipped around and massaged her clit, sending her into her third fucking orgasm.

He said he was a goner, but so was she. Body, mind, and soul.

How could she ever try to get over this man, when all she'd been doing up until now was reminding herself of all the pain he'd caused, lying to herself that she could ever truly hate him?

After hitting his head a few times, Bridger moved them to the driver's seat.

Vega felt like she was floating as she lowered down, taking every inch of him until she was flush with his lap. She moaned at the fullness, locking eyes with Bridger again.

Bridger. I'm fucking Bridger. My enemy. My ex. The man who broke my heart. Her thoughts didn't stop her. They did the opposite.

Vega rode his lap, kissing Bridger with everything she wasn't ready to admit.

"Give me another," Bridger ordered. Commander Dimico came to finish her off, as she'd once expected—just not like this.

"I-I..." Vega didn't know what she was trying to say, didn't realize she was even trying to speak until the words came tumbling out. "I can't," she gasped, shaking her head.

"You can and you will." He petted the side of her face with the back of his hand, knuckles grazing over the bottom of her scar.

Vega watched his eyes brush over it, noting he didn't share the same sadness everyone else did when they fixated on her newest flaw. The softness in his eyes made Vega's heart flip in her chest.

"Come with me," she said, pushing her hips down and forward at a pace she knew would drive Bridger wild, wiggling herself at the very bottom to feel the pressure building as his swollen head pressed into her g-spot.

Bridger shivered, his eyes rolling to the back of his head for a split second. He held her hips down, pushing up with his at the same time. "Fuck, Vega, that's so good."

She didn't have to ask to be choked the second time. Bridger knew what would get her there the fastest. His grip wasn't anywhere near as tight, only applying enough pressure for her to feel her pulse thrumming against his hand.

It was as if his hold on her neck said, *Look at me*.

Vega didn't dare look away.

The other hand still held onto her hip, pushing her as deep as he could get. She was a whimpering mess. "Just like that." Her voice sounded only a little strained from his hand around her throat.

Bridger pulled her by the neck, bringing their lips together at the very moment Vega fell off the cliff and dove into the overwhelming ecstasy of her next orgasm.

He slipped his hand to the back of her neck, pulling away from their kiss to watch Vega's face as she came so hard she couldn't keep her eyes open.

Her walls tightened and stomach quivered, gripping Bridger as he thrust his hips up once more, joining her over the edge.

"Oh fuck." The gravel in his voice vibrated against Vega's lips while she felt his cock pump her full of his warm release.

She couldn't get pregnant—nothing could survive in a cursed body, so instead of spiraling about Bridger finishing inside her, Vega enjoyed the come down from her own release, watching Bridger's gaze turn into a sated and aloof stare. His lips parted as the last of his orgasm ran its course, and this time it was Vega who kissed his lips softly, letting his last groan of pleasure hum against her swollen lips.

After one more kiss, she shifted to move off Bridger's lap, but his arms wrapped around, holding her in place with his ear planted against the spot between her breasts, where her heart beat erratically in her chest. "Not yet. Give me a minute." He chuckled, the sound low. "I'm not ready to let you go back to hating me yet."

As if she'd ever truly hated him in the first place.

She smirked, pushing the sweaty hair out of his eyes while he slowed his breathing and lifted his head to look at her. "But hate-sex is so good." Vega traced her thumb down the slope of his nose.

He hummed, eyes fluttering closed for a second. "I think we proved one theory wrong." Bridger's eyes had returned to normal when he opened them.

"And what theory is that?" she asked, raising her scarred brow.

"It's definitely not as good as we remember." He licked his lips and smiled. "It's better."

23

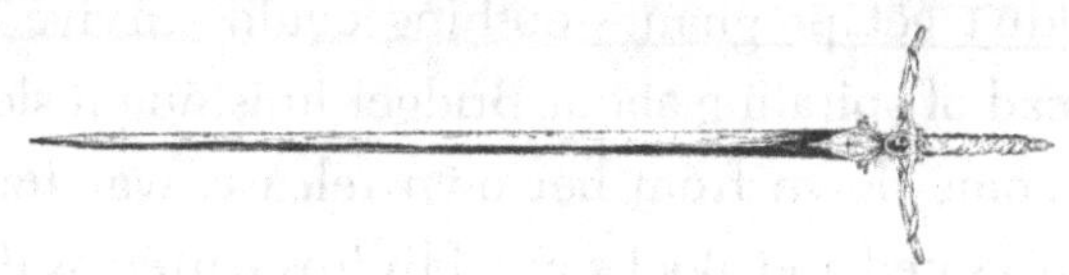

With the heat of the car keeping them warm, Vega and Bridger wrapped themselves up in the backseat, her head resting on his bare chest as her fingers delicately traced the outline of the scar he'd received when she'd stabbed him through the heart.

Even with his powers, her wound had still left a mark.

"Do you ever wonder what happened to Pluto and Romulus?" Vega asked, her voice as heavy from after-sex exhaustion as Bridger's felt.

"Mmm," he hummed lazily, opening his eyes as he twirled a piece of her hair between his fingers. "You mean god of the underworld and the twin brother who killed Remus? I mean, no, not necessarily."

"I brought it up to Marlena once, before the summoning... and now I wonder if she thinks about it like I do."

That piqued Bridger's interest, and he dropped the section of Vega's hair he'd been toying with.

"We know the gods she summoned, right? The twelve originals whose powers created our realm, and then we got Remus." Vega paused, looking at Bridger through her long lashes. "What happened to Pluto? To Romulus? And why would I get pulled back to Rome after breaking a piece of my death curse, where the tales of our bloodlines are nothing but nearly forgotten mythology?" She had always needed to talk out loud when problem solving.

"You think they're still floating around somewhere, waiting to be summoned?" he asked.

Bridger felt Vega shrug. "There's no way they're in Tolevarre or Earth. Absolutely no way or they would have answered when Marlena summoned the others."

"What if Pluto is stuck in the underworld?" When the question left his lips, Vega shot up, staring at Bridger with a look in her eyes that meant she was onto something.

Vega wore nothing but her giant gas station T-shirt, the length pooling around her waist. "When Remus bound himself to the gods and died, whatever was left of them went to create Tolevarre. Pluto would have died too, right? Or was it only the gods on Earth?" They weren't answering each other's questions, only adding more to the pile of unknowns.

"What about Romulus though? Could he be there too?" They were on the right track—Bridger could feel it, and by the way Vega looked down at her wrist, she felt it too.

"I mean, he bound all the gods together, essentially cursing them to die with him... We know that, but did he sentence his brother to something different? *Could* he have sentenced him to something different?" She sighed as she asked another question.

"Have you ever found anything about his curse? In all your years of research, there has to be *something*." Marlena hadn't found anything—that much Bridger knew or they'd probably all be dead by now.

"No. Nothing." Vega's shoulders sagged with defeat. "Not a single fucking thing. It's like he took it with him when he died."

Vega curled back up into Bridger's side, stretching her legs and shimmying herself in for warmth.

"One thing at a time, Kitten. Let's break your curse first. Then we can worry about how to deal with Marlena." Bridger went back to stroking her hair.

"You're serious about this?" she asked, and he didn't need her to elaborate to know what she meant.

Bridger lifted her chin with his index finger, forcing her to look at him and not the car's door. "I've gotten what I need out of Marlena."

"And what is it you've gotten out of her?" she asked openly.

Bridger answered with returned bluntness. "An army."

There were too many years of betrayal for her to trust him right away. They both knew that. Not even mind-blowing sex could undo the years between them.

Vega sat up again, as if she'd suddenly realized how long they'd been cuddling, and cleared her throat. "We should wash up, maybe grab some food from the vending machines."

They untangled themselves fully and got dressed, then walked across the parking lot to use the bathroom, freshen up, and find some snacks to satisfy their hunger.

They spent what they had left in cash filling their arms with as much as they could afford, and when they returned to their car, they scarfed down everything.

Bridger could have eaten the entire machine's worth of food if given the chance. He was ready for a real meal again.

Vega found a blanket stashed under a seat, offering to share it with Bridger. He shook his head. "All yours."

"Okay." She draped it over her shoulders, wrapping herself up as she found a comfortable position to sleep.

She'd told Bridger at least three times she was only going to nap for a few hours and reminded him they didn't know when Chase would pop back up again.

Bridger let her have the leg room, popping himself against the back corner like he'd done the last time he'd slept back here.

The car lights were off now, an even whir coming from the idle engine.

Bridger felt a pull in his brain, the sound of a siren trying to serenade him to sleep. He'd gotten a few hours here and there since crossing through the portal, but not enough to fight the call of exhaustion.

He didn't have it in him to fight it.

With his arms crossed over his chest and his head leaned back to rest against the vehicle's interior, Bridger sank to the depths of sleep.

It was quiet, a peaceful dark washing away his consciousness.

Not enough time passed for Bridger to enjoy the tranquility of an absent mind.

"Bridger." Vega shook his leg, dragging him out of the deepest sleep he'd—*Oh my gods*.

His eyes shot open.

There were three quick taps against the back window closest to Vega. "Hello?" A man's voice was muffled behind the closed door.

Bridger's face must have looked as confused as he felt because Vega answered without him having to ask.

"A cop," she whispered.

It wasn't only confusion he was feeling, it was shock too. *I slept... without a dream...*

It hadn't been long. He knew by the clock on the dash, but it didn't matter how long he slept—ten minutes, an hour, fifteen— Bridger hadn't gone a single sleep since the dreams started without one.

Vega's finger rested on the button to roll the window down. "Act sleepy." She pressed, sitting forward.

As the window descended, the bottom half of a man's face came into view, the rest hidden by the shadow of his large rimmed hat. "What are you two doing back here?"

Vega looked around, like she was looking for the problem he saw. "Oh, we just pulled over to sleep."

"This isn't a designated parking area, ma'am." His hand rested on the open window.

Bridger watched his every move, tracking his other hand resting on his hip.

"Sorry, I didn't realize we couldn't with the semis parked right there. It was the darkest spot in the lot. We can mo—"

"I'm going to need both of you to get out of the vehicle." He cut Vega off, his voice sounding too monotone to be normal.

Vega peeked over her shoulder. They'd caught the tone.

"For what?" Bridger asked over Vega's shoulder.

"Because I said so," the cop responded, reaching inside for the handle.

Vega beat him to it, not opening the door just yet. "We aren't trying to be a pain, but we honestly haven't done anything wrong. We're just sleeping, and I'd be happy to move the car if it's an issue."

Bridger placed his hand on the small of her back, needing to be able to touch her to determine their next move. If only they were back in Tolevarre—then he'd be able to test another theory out. One he'd been ignoring for far too long. *One I know isn't a theory at all...*

"I said get out of the vehicle," the cop ordered, his hand returning to his hip.

Vega popped the handle, putting her hands up close to her chest. "Okay, okay. We'll get out." She scooted forward, looking back to nod at Bridger.

He followed, attention fixed on the man who stood inches shorter than him.

"Backs against the car." He crowded the personal bubble Bridger would have normally gutted someone for being in. His teeth gritted so hard Vega elbowed him in the side. "Are there any weapons inside?"

Bridger shook his head. "No."

On the way out, he'd slipped his hand into the seatback pocket where he'd stashed the dagger, returning it to his waistband.

The cop ducked into the car, peering left and right, a long, skinny light illuminating wherever he pointed, with his other hand resting on what Bridger now recognized as a gun after Vega pointed the first few out on their travels. When he was deep enough inside the car where he couldn't see them, Vega mouthed, *Did you see his eyes?*

He'd never gotten a chance to see them from the shadow of his hat.

Black, she mouthed again.

Vega rested her hand on Bridger's lower back, settling at the exact place he'd stashed the dagger.

They didn't have time to speculate what would happen next. The black eyes were hint enough that this was the curse's doing.

The man backed out of the car, and the glow from the light across the lot shone in the right direction, putting a spotlight on the cop's face.

All black eyes.

His hand placement shifted, Vega and Bridger's senses connecting the moment his finger rested on his gun's grip.

In seconds, Vega stared down its chamber, in the direct line of fire.

Bridger lunged, knocking the gun from his hand. His quick reaction wasn't fast enough to stop him from pulling the trigger.

Oh, so that's what those do.

The sound it made was deafening.

The bullet blazed by Vega, narrowly missing her head. She dropped to the ground and covered her ears while the sound of the shot rang through the night air. Clutched in her hand at the side of her head was the dagger Chase had hand delivered back to them, the one she'd yanked from the back of Bridger's pants.

Thankfully, she had a skilled withdrawal and hadn't dragged the blade along his skin on the way out.

Spinning on his heels, Bridger caught the guy by his arm when he tried to rush him, the metal light crashing to the ground.

Vega recovered quickly, snatching the gun up while drawing the dagger at her stand. Bridger grabbed him by the wrist, twisted his arm, and had him on his back in less than a second.

Bridger might not have his powers, but that didn't mean he wasn't still one of the most lethal beings on this planet.

The cop's hat went flying, and the color of his eyes couldn't be clearer under the moonlight. This man wasn't acting on his own free will. He was being controlled by a curse with its own agenda.

"We can't kill a fucking cop, Bridger!" Vega said a little louder than she might have if the gun hadn't gone off next to her ear.

The man didn't stay down long, hopping to his feet with unnaturally fast reflexes.

"I don't think we have much of a choice if you want to live," Bridger reminded, dodging a right hook, acting fast to deliver a punch of his own before the cop rebounded.

His fist didn't get the chance to connect, and he was on his ass before he knew what hit him. The wind rushed out of Bridger's lungs when his back slammed into the hard concrete.

Bridger had been attacked without his powers hundreds, if not thousands of times before. Whether from his father's training or years of torture, he'd learned to fight with less inside him.

He was up, but landed a blow to his gut. Bridger groaned at the pain, hunching over to drive his shoulder into the man and flip him off balance.

The cop's strength wasn't like anything normal by Earth standards... and even by Tolevarre standards, Bridger had a good fight on his hands.

He and Bridger rolled, tumbling down the small embankment to the grass field.

Bridger grunted as they came to a stop, grabbed the cop by the shoulders, and threw him down onto the snow sodden ground. They were both covered in mud already.

"If I kill you, she goes too." His words sounded like a serpent's, every *s* slurring with a monotone. "So linked. You two are practically one, but she's my way out." The manic laugh he let out told Bridger exactly how gone this man was. "Oh, what you two could have been."

He was no longer the person he was supposed to be. This man was a cursed killing machine, completely lost inside whatever hold it had on his body.

But Bridger and Vega weren't going to be taken out so easily. Certainly not now. Not after everything.

Bridger landed a blow to the man's face, breaking his nose, the bones shifting against his fist. Blood immediately poured from his nostrils, outlining the spaces in between his teeth.

It was as if he hadn't even felt the crushing blow, using his bodyweight to overthrow Bridger's position. His hands slid towards Bridger's neck, and he laughed again, but the sound was cut short when the blade of a dagger drove through the top of his skull. Life drained from the man's eyes, and his body went limp.

Bridger rolled him off, jumping to his feet to avoid the blood, not needing to get any messier than he'd already become.

Vega stood with the gun in one hand and the dagger in the other, her chest rising and falling shallowly. Her neck bobbed when she swallowed. "We're not stopping anymore."

Bridger took the blade from Vega and wiped off the blood and brain matter from both sides on the cop's shirt.

"What did he say to you?" she asked, turning to watch Bridger slide the clean dagger into his pants again.

"He confirmed the whole 'you die, I die' thing. Said we are so linked we're basically one." Bridger couldn't take his eyes off Vega's, wondering what she was thinking, wishing he could sneak inside her brain and get a peek.

"That man had to die for no reason. The curse keeps taking innocent people and throwing them in my path." Vega shook her head, dragging her eyes from the dead man to Bridger and then over her shoulder. "We need to get out of here." She held the gun at her side still, examining it before flicking a small piece up and sliding it into her leggings at the small of her back.

"How do you know how to use one of those?" he asked as he followed her back to the car, taking in the empty parking lot with all the doors of the big trucks still closed.

No one had heard them, but it wouldn't be long before one woke up and noticed the cop car sitting at the edge of the lot or realized the sound they'd heard was a gunshot.

"I've lived a lot of lives, but there's still nothing like a dagger through the skull." Her smile didn't light up her face—it pulled the skin around her eyes taut, looking exhausted.

Vega approached the driver's seat, but Bridger put his hand out. "Let me drive. You need to sleep."

"No way are you driving. You don't even know—"

"I drive military vehicles three times this size. I think I can handle following the directions on the little screen in your pocket and pay attention to the speed signs." Bridger crossed his arms and raised his brow.

"Bridger," she scolded, looking over her shoulder. "If we get caught near this dead cop, we're fucked. We need to go."

Quickly, he slid by her and ducked into the driver's seat, already adjusting the seat to his height. "Then you better hurry up and get in." He shut the door, leaving Vega to huff and puff before stomping around to the passenger seat.

It took her a second to explain what all the buttons and gadgets did, but Bridger figured it out quickly. He just didn't realize how touchy the brakes and gas pedal were and rocked them back and forth for a bit until he got the hang of it.

Vega refused to get in the backseat, arguing she wasn't tired and was too wired to sleep, but it wasn't long before she rested her head against the window and her breaths turned shallow.

The highways stretched on for hours, and the GPS, as Vega had called it, didn't make much noise. Bridger rode in silence, the only sound being the repeated words of the last man the curse had consumed, echoing in his mind.

"Oh, what you two could have been."

24

VEGA WOKE TO THE SUN SHINING IN HER EYES, A BRIGHT GLEAM coming in from the snow on the roads.

She looked over at Bridger, who was rotating the wheel to turn into a park with a sign at the road she'd know anywhere.

Holy shit, they'd made it. Her eyes grew wide as they finally adjusted to the light. "Fuck, how long did I sleep?"

"The rest of the way." Bridger's eyes were rimmed with red. He was more tired-looking than Vega had seen him in years.

All that sex and fighting had done him in... *No, bad Vega. We aren't thinking about the sex.*

"Damn, I'm sorry. I didn't mean to—"

"It's okay." He cut her off, smiling as he followed her directions to the corner of the park where she and Arlet always abandoned the car. "You needed to sleep. After all, we're about to break a fifty-five-year-old curse. You probably needed all the rest you could get."

They had no idea what they were getting into. Vega wasn't even sure if she understood what she was supposed to do next.

All signs pointed to the portal being the curse, but what if it was more than that? What if there was something she'd missed?

"What's our plan when we get back to Tolevarre?" she spewed, staring right into Bridger's eyes. She still didn't trust him fully, and as badly as she wanted to, as annoying as it was to be close to him and feel the hum of their bodies calling to each other, Vega couldn't believe him until the decision had been made—until Bridger made it clear whose side he was on.

Of course he was on her side right now. He had to be. He had to make it back to Tolevarre—but when they got there, would this be a setup?

The worry had been floating in the back of her mind since he'd first shown up.

The days blended together. Vega couldn't even remember how long ago it'd been.

Three days? Four? What day was it?

"What do you mean?" he asked, gripping the steering wheel and tensing at her question.

"You know what I'm asking, Bridger. What's your plan when we get back and Marlena inevitably comes after me?" She was almost too nervous to ask, but she forced the words out anyway.

She had to make sure she wasn't walking into a trap—had to be prepared.

"Are you going to fight with m—with the rebellion," she corrected, not wanting this to be about her. "Or was this all a lie?" The anxiety in the pit of her stomach rolled, giving her a momentary queasiness she had to swallow like bile.

The silence between them felt deafening. Vega found herself counting the seconds before Bridger spoke.

Twenty-two. Twenty-three.

"I told her I would—" he started but never got the chance to finish because pain shot through Vega's chest, tearing a scream from her throat that pierced her own ears.

A loud crash vibrated through the redwoods, leaves and snow falling from trees as they swayed from a gust of wind.

Bridger reached out to grab Vega's hands, but as quickly as the pain came, it left, leaving Vega breathing like she'd ran a marathon. "What the..." She trailed off, wiping a bead of sweat from her forehead.

Birds squawked, soaring by the car and shooting into the sky. A bright light deep in the forest pulsed, catching their attention. It was so far away it would have been missed if that flicker of pain didn't thrum inside Vega like a pulse.

"We have to run," Bridger said with a breath, turning around to grab the dagger and gun.

Vega snatched the gun out of his hand and opened the door, abandoning everything else inside the car. There was nothing she needed to take home, nothing she cared about more than keeping herself and the bonded alive.

She knew exactly where they needed to end up—could run this path like she'd done it a hundred times before, blindfolded. Bridger kept pace with her, pushing her to go faster with his long strides and perfect control.

It usually took over an hour to walk the trail, but with Vega and Bridger booking it, they might be able to clear it in twenty minutes with the terrain and without their abilities. Another flash of light in the distance made Vega hunch over and scream, more pain radiating through her.

The portal.

The portal was going to fucking kill her.

Bridger reached under her arms and hoisted her to a standing position. "I know it hurts, but we have to keep moving. You don't get to stop now."

She'd come too far.

She'd fought too hard.

Vega wouldn't let this be the end.

This will not be the end.

They were so close—so fucking close to ending this thing.

Vega threw herself forward, fighting the fizzle of pain sitting at the back of her brain, waiting to be refired again.

They had to slow a few more times, Vega begging her own body to keep moving—to push through. To live.

The sound of maniacal laughter rang through the trees, and Vega's body reacted, goosebumps peppering her skin like jolts of electricity.

So close, Vega. You're so close.

Light flashed, dimming as they came to a skidding stop. A figure stood in front of the portal, swinging a broken piece of what looked like glass at the branches holding the portal in place.

The person froze, their voice echoing around them like it was coming from everywhere. "Ah, there you are. I've been waiting for you."

The feel of the unfamiliar male voice on her skin made Vega shudder. Bridger stepped closer as he began to turn.

Vega knew who it was the second their eyes met, his shining black against the glow of the portal.

Romulus.

Well, that answered part of their question.

Tolevarre had spent years studying how their world was built and where their powers came from. But no one ever asked about Romulus—as if he'd never existed in the first place.

Romulus was forgotten.

Erased.

He swung the piece of the portal like a sword, its tip whizzing as it caught the wind and sliced through. "I can tell you're both perplexed, so let me explain. It's the least I can do before I deliver you to your deaths."

Vega and Bridger stood side by side, ready to strike when the time came.

"For thousands of years, I was trapped in purgatory here on Earth, floating around without power, no physical form, nothing but my awareness. All because I let my selfish twin brother outsmart me." He twitched at the mention of Remus.

She soaked in his every word, waiting for him to slip and reveal something she could use against him.

Romulus stared at them like he could see through to the other side. "Remus"—he hissed the name like a snake—"trapped me here and left me to rot. Alone for the rest of eternity while he played hero and created a new world for a new people. A world he didn't think I belonged in." The anger was visible in the way Romulus's muscles tensed and his body vibrated. "But little did he know, all I had to do was wait." He gestured towards the disheveled portal. "Eventually, your curse would become my second chance at living. Marlena cursed you to a life of death, but your curse has given me life for fifty-five years... It's let me hijack the lives of others, but now, your death will give me my own back." He looked at Vega with longing, like he was saying goodbye to an old friend. "I tried to keep you here all those times before because it was what I needed to exist outside of my own consciousness."

She and Bridger were motionless, their eyes following Romulus's every move.

Romulus focused his black stare on Vega. "When Marlena cursed you, looking to banish you to another realm, her blood, your blood, my brother's blood, *our blood,* called to me. It found me, tying your curse to Earth. Tying you to me, a cursed and forgotten demigod."

He proved Marlena hadn't known exactly what she was doing when she cursed Vega, that there were things out of her control she hadn't known about.

The proud smile and truth behind Romulus's words had Vega struggling to keep a look of indifference on her face. Their abilities didn't work on Earth, but the curse did... because Romulus, the curse's connection to their world, was already here. His essence predated the fall of the original gods.

Romulus glanced down at the portal piece in his hand. "The curse should have given me the power to kill you, to take over your life, but you took that from me when you summoned him and became a bonded group of four gods."

Remus's words were starting to make sense... *I saved you. Do not waste this opportunity.* He'd made sure the curse couldn't take her life. Because Vega's life was no longer just her own—it was Bridger's, Arlet's, and Khort's too.

But how could Chase get her so close to death this time?

"I couldn't kill you, and then when you left, I had to go back to the in-between—to the purgatory my brother cursed me to." An eerie smile slid over his lips. "It's why I went easy on you in your last life with Chase... All so I could keep living, even through someone else's body."

Rage sparked to life inside her. A gust of wind picked up like it responded to Vega's growing anger. She longed for the bite of her electric heart sputtering in her chest.

Bridger's fingers grazed against Vega's wrist, reminding her she needed to breathe, to focus on what Romulus was saying. He leaned in and whispered, "He can't kill you."

Romulus's attention snapped to Bridger. "There are many things worse than death, Bridger Dimico. Have you not learned that yet?" Romulus cocked his head to the side, and a new person stood in front of them—one Vega knew, but Bridger wouldn't. "Did the dreams teach you nothing?"

Romulus turned into a chameleon, changing his appearance to all the men who'd hurt her in her lives on Earth. A mixture of different facial features, heights, hair and skin colors blended from one to another. The last one settled on Chase, his neck split open in a gaping wound while his skin looked drained of life. "Isn't that right, Vay?" When he took a step forward, Vega and Bridger both retreated, keeping distance.

Vega wasn't sure if his babbling meant anything, but something inside her screamed to *pay attention.*

She felt his breath on the back of her neck, his words so close it felt like he'd leaned over her shoulder, but he hadn't moved. He still blocked their path to the portal. "He's not going to let you cheat death forever." The portal seemed to pulse with a heartbeat of its own. "A soul has been promised at the end of this curse, and I already told you it won't be mine." He pulled the piece of portal from the ground and pointed it at Bridger, laughing maniacally. "He told you. I heard him. In the portal here, the broken one. He doesn't want you to come after what's already his."

Bridger's jaw flexed at his words, his hand tightening into a fist around the dagger.

No. No, this can't be right.

Vega felt like the blood ran from her body, going cold. "Who are you talking about?" Vega asked, flipping the safety off the gun. A piece of her was afraid to hear his answer.

He didn't answer her question. "So violent. Is that your doing, or did she come this way already?" he asked Bridger, who gripped his dagger so tightly, Vega worried it might snap in half.

"I killed you. You should already be dead," Vega said, trying to distract him while she analyzed the broken piece of portal in his grasp.

"No, you killed an innocent man," he said, turning into the cop. "He was a good guy. His wife is expecting their second child." Romulus tsked. "I'm sure she'd agree you deserve a first-class ticket to the pits of the underworld for leaving her to raise their children alone."

He kept bringing up death and the underworld. Vega shivered involuntarily.

No.

Yes, the wind seemed to hiss as it blew through the treetops above.

They all heard it. Vega knew they had by the way Bridger growled. "That's enough." He flipped his dagger over his wrist. "How about you deliver a message to the god of the underworld for me when you see him? If he wants Vega, he'll have to go through me first."

At the same time Bridger launched forward, Vega ducked to her knee, avoiding the piece of the portal Romulus threw her way.

Romulus and Pluto… the missing pieces.

Vega took aim as she stood and fired the gun, aiming directly at his heart. By no means was she a master with a firearm, but her lightning's aim had always been spot-on.

The bullet tore through his body, off to the left of where Romulus's heart should be. In the bullet's wake, was a round, perfectly circular hole where light shone through.

There was no blood, and he didn't react.

Okay, so guns don't kill him. Noted.

He looked at the hole, mesmerized for a second too long. Bridger grabbed him by the hair and pulled his head back, using his dagger to slice through the tendons of his throat with ease.

No blood poured from the wound, but his vocal cords strained when he talked. "That's not how you kill me either," he said, like he was inside Vega's head.

In the blink of an eye, Romulus bent down and grabbed another piece of the portal and pierced it through Bridger's upper pelvis. "A little lower and that could have been bad." Romulus's laugh echoed through the trees with a too-high pitch.

Bridger bent at the waist, crying out in pain while Romulus pushed the severed portal deeper.

Vega unloaded the gun into Romulus, hoping it would at least buy her time. The piercing ring in her ears drowned out the sound of anything Romulus was saying.

Holes littered his entire body.

"I hate to mark up such a perfect body." Romulus's hand was

covered in Bridger's blood, leaving a streak down his face as Romulus stroked his cheek.

Bridger's fist connected with Romulus's nose, the crunch sending Vega into action. She ran at full speed, grabbing a piece of the portal he'd launched at her earlier. It tingled in her grasp, tendrils of what felt like home sliding up her wrist, soaking into her bloodstream, reminding her of all she had to lose.

While Romulus was distracted by Bridger's hit, Vega charged after him, using a sharp piece of the portal as her own personal dagger. If it was a piece of their world, a piece of Marlena's power, she hoped it would answer her desires. She waited until the last possible second to show her move.

Romulus hooked Vega by her arm, tossing her into Bridger like she weighed nothing. They tumbled, Bridger's head smacking against the ground with concussion-like force.

Vega had no time to recover. Romulus snatched her hand and drove the piece of portal Vega had intended to use on him straight into Bridger's chest. She felt the vibrations up her arm as it tore through his tissue and shattered bones. It was inches from piercing his heart.

Romulus yanked her by her hair with such violence, Vega's neck popped, shooting pain down her leg. She screamed, drowning out most of Romulus's rambles.

Vega struggled to follow every word. "But you promised to kill your sister, and your sister has the gods with her. He gave you more time in hopes you'd deliver what he's always wanted."

She blinked away the tears, struggling to see Bridger fighting to sit up, his hands covered in blood as he tried to apply pressure to his chest.

"He's sick of waiting for you to fulfill your end of the bargain."

Vega's nails dug into Romulus's wrists, but it didn't faze him.

"It's a shame you have to go. I quite like your spunk." He sighed, bending down in front of a large sliver of the portal. "How about I give you a parting gift? I'll let you get the revenge of a god before you die." Romulus forced the long piece of portal back into Vega's hand, a sharp edge slicing her palm. Blood immediately oozed down her arm. "I'll let you kill him for all the times he's betrayed you."

Time stopped. The world stopped. Vega's vision turned to a long tunnel, the only thing on the other side being Bridger.

At one point she might have jumped at the chance to end the only man she'd ever truly loved—she would have enjoyed watching the life drain from his eyes.

No, you wouldn't have. Her inner voice surprised her.

Bridger dug the shard out of his leg, inhaling a wet breath. His lungs filled with blood. The portal's broken pieces weakened Bridger more than he already was without his powers. His normally golden color had turned pale, and the places where he'd been stabbed dripped with blood faster than average.

The piece cutting into Vega's skin right now seemed to do the complete opposite. She felt like she was feeding off it. It wasn't exactly like having her powers—didn't have the same feel as her storms or lightning—but it energized her.

My curse. My death. My hands. My blood. It's time to end this.

She didn't care who waited for her on the other side.

They'd have to wait... Vega wasn't done in this life yet.

25

Vega would be the one to save herself. She'd be the god
to save the bonded.

No one else could wield her curse better than she could.

I'm breaking this fucking curse. Vega was just as prepared to kill
a man who'd spent fifty-five years torturing her as she was to destroy
the curse that stole her life.

The Caelum sisters both made grave mistakes the night they
summoned the dead, and Vega didn't plan on making anymore when
the lives of the people she loved were hanging in the balance.

She squeezed into the sharp edges, letting her blood coat the
portal piece, feeling the release of a heavy weight the harder she
pushed.

Using what leverage she had from the ground, Vega flipped
herself over, truly catching Romulus by surprise when she broke the
shard in half with her boot and used both pieces to drive into his
sides.

The scream leaving his mouth sounded like one of multiple
people, mixing together to form a tortured howl. Blood finally

seeped from the new wounds while the others stayed hollow and grime free.

The portal is my curse. It's my weapon to wield. It's mine to break. Romulus is what ties me here...

Romulus fell to the ground, and Vega pushed into him harder, pressing her boot to his chest. She pulled one hand free, the blood from her own cut mixing with Romulus's. "For someone who's spent over half a century making sure my life was as miserable as possible, you sure fucked up underestimating me." She leaned down, lowering her boot to the left side, where about a half foot piece of portal stuck out his side. Vega stepped into it, earning another pained squeal. "You and I aren't too different though, ya know? Cursed by a sibling. Left alone to die." Proof that myth, legend, and history could all repeat themselves. "There's something very important that sets us apart. Me from you. Me from Marlena. You both fight for your own desires. I fight for the desires of others. I fight so the people I love get the happy fucking ending they deserve." The wildcat from the alley was back, and this time, it had grown in size and was ready to claw its way out.

Vega stomped on the shard protruding from Romulus's body until she felt it shatter.

His black eyes rolled to the back of his head, his body convulsing until it went limp.

It's not over. She knew it wasn't. He was going to keep coming back until the portal was gone.

Romulus wasn't her curse. He was the reason she was tied to Earth and not some other world. The portal was what held it to begin with.

She'd broken a piece and let the power seep out for Romulus to feed off.

The curse started with a mirror and the blood of two sisters.

And it would end with the death of a forgotten twin...

"Vega." Bridger's voice squeaked from behind, pulling her away from the cop's dead body.

Bridger sat on his knees about fifty feet closer to the portal, his hands wrapped around a new piece sticking through his chest from the back.

Vega's gut twisted with fear as her eyes trailed up the arm of the man standing behind Bridger, using the portal as a weapon too. She knew who it would be before reaching his face. She'd spent a lot of time memorizing the details of the man who'd done the most damage on Earth. Vega used to have nightmares of all the things he'd done to her. Then she learned what real monsters looked like again... and Antonio didn't seem so scary to her anymore.

She averted her attention back to where she'd left Romulus's last body.

Gone.

Not even blood stained the ground where he'd been. "Didn't think I'd come back that quick, huh?" The voice coming from the man's throat didn't sound like the one she'd known from a different life—this one was deeper, more animal-like.

"Bridger," Vega said, heaving, watching his jaw twitch from the pain. "No." *No!*

She hadn't come this far to get taken out so close to getting her life back.

You don't make it out of this. That's the point! A voice inside her head startled her, until she realized it was her own.

And she was only telling herself what she'd always known.

At the very beginning, Vega said she'd do this with or without anyone else. She promised to kill her sister—no matter what it took.

Vega Caelum, cursed to forget, but destined to die.

I haven't come this far to not let my friends, my world, get their lives back, she corrected.

Her eyes welled with tears, but she wouldn't let them fall.

Bridger would have healed already in Tolevarre—he would be

able to fight with her... but this wasn't Tolevarre, and she didn't need him to save her.

Bridger needed her to save him. Their relationship was complicated, but Vega realized one thing—she didn't want Bridger to die.

Vega reminded herself over and over of this as she steadily walked towards Bridger and the man still clutching the piece of portal sticking through his chest. "Not him. You don't get him." She didn't say it as a request. Vega commanded it.

"Vega, no." Blood gargled up Bridger's throat, dripping down his lips and chin.

"He won't live without you anyway. If anything, I'm doing him a favor. Now he won't endure the pain of the bond breaking when death comes for you and the others are forced to follow." Romulus took a disgusted step back, letting go of the piece of portal he held him up by when more blood splattered from Bridger's mouth.

Vega raced forward and dropped to her knees, catching Bridger under his arms before he collapsed. Her eyes met his as she held him up. Life was still there, twinkling like a star threatening to burn out. "You don't get to go anywhere, do you hear me? I'm not fucking finished with you." Vega gently rested her hand on the end of the portal sticking out of Bridger's chest. "You need to heal. I need to get you home."

"I can't leave you." Bridger gritted his teeth, the words almost too garbled to understand, but he fought to keep himself upright without Vega's help.

She rose from her kneeling position and acted on a whim, knowing this was going to do damage. She drove her foot into the large part sticking from Bridger's chest, snapping it in two.

Bridger bellowed, but his body quickly succumbed to the shock, slumping down as he fell into oblivion.

"After all he's done, you're willing to save him?" Romulus asked from a safe distance away, his black eyes darting to the jagged portal sliver in Vega's hand.

Vega stepped behind Bridger and bent to grab him by the collar of his shirt. "I'm a god. I will not explain my actions to a useless man."

He lunged for Vega, but she was done playing the victim, done being hurt. It was over. *This is over.*

"A useless man?" He barked a laugh, returning to the dead version of Chase. "He was a useless man." Romulus switched again, to a brunette who loved to pretend Vega was a punching bag. "He was a useless man." He returned back to his natural image. "I am not a useless man. I'm the son of Mars, god of war. A direct descendant of the original bloodline." His words must have given him an ego boost, because he stopped retreating and took an overly confident step towards Vega.

She squeezed tight around the shard of portal, getting her blood to flow thickly again. "You're a half-blood demigod. I'm a descendant of two bloodlines and bonded to three other original bloodlines." She swirled the makeshift blade at him, smirking when the tip clipped his cheek and blood spilled out.

He hissed, the cut bubbling around the edges of the sensitive skin.

There was something about her blood mixing with the shattered piece of her curse. Her blood acted as a poison when mixed with the power of the portal.

She had to get Romulus inside the portal. But she had to get Bridger there first.

"I should have beat you more in this life." The dead-like face of Chase stared, his head cocking to the side and bobbing with the open neck wound.

Vega gently let Bridger down and took a note out of her very first book—the one from the first life where she'd been trained by the greatest warrior in Tolevarre's history.

Strike first.

Vega rushed forward, spearing Romulus through the shoulder. He'd nearly wrapped his hands around the end of the blade as it came back through his body, but Vega ducked and rolled, taking him out by the knees.

The back of his head hit the ground first, rattling his senses long enough for Vega to drive the piece through his eye socket. It came out the back of his head and sank in the dense forest floor.

Chase stared up at her with one dead eye—it was the blue color they were supposed to be. A chill shot down Vega's spine.

Romulus would be back.

There was only one way to finish him, and she would, once Bridger was safe.

Vega would drag Romulus to his death—because hers would be waiting for her on the other side of the portal.

It was all making sense now.

By breaking a piece of her death curse, Vega had connected two realms long since left behind.

With one hand keeping hold of the blade, Vega grabbed Bridger by the collar again and pulled him the rest of the way.

He groaned, letting her know he was still alive.

Vega leaned him against the branch holding the remaining piece of portal together, squatting down to place her hands on either side of his face. "Bridger, you better fucking live or I'm going to kill you when I join you in the afterlife." Without thinking, Vega placed a soft kiss on his blood-splattered lips. Her hands slid to his shoulders, and she shoved Bridger through the portal, watching until he disappeared.

Vega grunted at the ache she felt everywhere, getting off her knees with a wobble. From Chase's attacks, the sex with Bridger, and whatever was happening with Romulus, Vega was tired. She was running on some of the worst sleep she'd ever had, and after a month of not exercising like she was used to in Tolevarre, her muscles screamed with fatigue.

But she wouldn't stop fighting. *I can't.*

"Okay, Romulus, it's just me and you." She breathed through the patter of her heartbeat, centering herself for the fight.

Vega dug her boots into the ground and rolled her neck. She had fought for her life hundreds of times, but none mattered like this one. "You want me to die so badly..." She spun slowly, her eyes raking over the wood line as far as she could see. "Then come kill me." She finished her sentence with a growl—a challenge roaring inside.

Leaves crunched from behind, and out of the darkness came the body of Antonio, who'd spent four years beating her, sending her back to Tolevarre as a version of herself no one could recognize. *Gods, I hate who I let this curse turn me into.*

Antonio looked the most like Bridger. Tall, beautiful, dark olive skin, jet-black hair, with a smile everyone fell for. But on the inside, he was rotten. "Miss me, babygirl?" The nickname sent flashes of that life fluttering through her mind.

Vega felt his phantom fist against her cheek, snapping her out of memory's hold.

Antonio might resemble an off-brand Bridger, but in all the wrong Bridger had done, he'd never let her suffer at his hands. His kills were never meant to be torture—they were meant to put her out of her misery. He deserved a second chance at the life that was stolen from him.

There was a piece inside Bridger worth saving.

Her response wasn't targeted at Bridger. It wasn't even meant for the body of Antonio. Her words were meant for the curse. "You really fucked me up. Made me question if any life was worth living. You showed me parts of myself that I'll keep locked away forever, never allowing them to see the light of day. You did that to me." A tear rolled down each cheek.

The motherfucker *smiled*.

The spilled tears weren't from a place of sadness. Where they came from was much worse.

Vega ground her teeth, her left hand squeezing into the portal shard. "But do you know what else you did to me?" She returned his sinister smile. "You showed me what it's like to be angry. Really fucking angry. You let me see what it felt like to lose myself so fully I never thought I'd find myself again... but guess what? I did. I did, and that's really fucking unfortunate for you."

Swinging the long piece around her wrist in a Bridger-like motion, she sent out a silent prayer that he was all right and took her first step towards Romulus and the body he'd chosen to die in. "I'm ready for vengeance... vengeance for the gods, and most importantly, for me."

As soon as the words left Vega's lips, she propelled herself towards him, slashing out with the shard. Romulus dodged it in time, rolling forward in a somersault, and grabbed Vega by the ankle.

Coming down, Vega caught herself with one hand and whipped the portal like a spear with the other. The piece struck its target, pinning one of Romulus's hands to the earth under his palm.

His scream rattled her eardrums.

The gun did nothing but leave holes in him. The dagger caused nothing more than surface damage. But a piece of the portal? It became death when wielded by the cursed.

The curse was hers, made for her. When it mixed with the piece of itself inside Vega already, it grabbed hold and spun a web of control she could use. "Only one of us gets to live." She ripped the spear out, freeing him for only a moment before breaking it in two over her knee. She pierced them through both hands this time.

Another screech retched from inside him.

Vega once again pulled the pieces out, spearing him through the spine. She felt bones break and his body went limp, but when she flipped him over, his black, soulless eyes weren't dead. She'd only paralyzed him. "I hope Death isn't kind to you," she said with a too genuine smile.

Pulling the pieces free, Vega grabbed him by the hair and dragged him towards the portal... and he couldn't even kick or scream. Little gargles of sound bubbled from his throat.

She fought through the burn in her muscles, ignoring the shockwaves of pain her body attempted to overload her with. *Do not break down now.*

The echo of Bridger's words from their first night as bonded souls pushed Vega to use every bit she had left inside herself to prop Romulus against what remained of the portal. She held on to his shoulders and looked him directly in the eyes. "You got it all wrong, Romulus. I was never yours, but you've always been mine. A piece of *my* curse. A piece of *my* life. And now, a piece of my death."

Vega pushed Romulus backwards, her nails sinking into his skin as they took the tumble into the portal together.

I'm falling, but I can't see anything. No matter how many times I blink, everything is clouded with a darkness I've never seen.

I will not fucking die.

My fingernails are still dug into what I know is the flesh of Romulus's skin. I can't see him, but I can feel him.

I can feel his power.

No, not his power.

The curse.

"Death," something hisses from within my mind, slipping through a door I didn't know was there. It slithers up my arm like a snake set to strike, a heat that burns like frostbite following behind in the same path... ready to take whatever is left of me.

I babble, unsure if what I'm saying or hearing is real. "I broke my curse. It's over."

A different voice, one I've heard before, speaks. "You've had enough time. Your destiny awaits."

A girl destined to die.

Cursed to forget, but destined to die.

Die.

Death.

"Death is my destiny." The words calm me, the same frosted heat extending to the edges of my mind.

"Death belongs to me," he purrs like a sated kitten by a warm fire.

The same hiss from before growls inside my head. I feel the urge to defend it. "We belong to no one."

We?

The presence in my brain vibrates gently in agreement.

"Your soul was mine before you begged for the power to kill her."

I become more aware the longer I fall through the endless portal, clinging to whatever life I have left. I'm bound to the others... If I die... "Let me save them..."

I won't let them die because of me. "I can't let them die because of me," I sob.

Orange embers spark to life, illuminating the shadows they swirl in. It's the only thing I've seen since the fall began.

The embers fall to ash, and the temperature grows cold. "And if I let you save them, what do I get in return?"

"What do you want?" I hear myself ask.

The voice echoes. "The dead gods inside your sister."

The gods are inside Marlena... Of course...

The hiss inside my head is louder this time, angrier. If it had teeth, if it existed outside my mind, it would have torn through skin in response.

What will you sacrifice to save the people you love? How far are you willing to go to kill your sister?

I feel myself nod, and the embers come back in time for me to watch the shadows peel Romulus from my grip. His body disappears inside them, and then I realize I'm no longer floating. I'm standing at the bottom of a stone well.

"If you give me the power to save Tolevarre from Marlena and keep the bonded alive, I'll personally deliver the gods along with my sister's soul as a bonus." The embers swirl around me, catching in a torrent of air.

A screech pulsates the vessels in my brain, blurring my vision. The well fades away, and the floor falls out from underneath my feet.

I'm falling again.

"Death suits you." The voice—his voice—circles my head. "I think I'll let you have her."

Venom lights my veins on fire. I scream, or at least I think I do, but I'm cracking into pieces.

There was before the curse.

Then after.

"Do not forget that Death belongs to me, Vega Caelum. You belong to me."

Now there will be before death, and then what comes after making a deal with its master.

Darkness floods my throat, stealing the breath from my lungs. I can't warn myself of the approaching collision.

Vega lost consciousness the second her body reached the bottom of her freefall.

26

The feeling came in like a rising tide. Slow and steady until it was unmistakably there. It felt like a crack inside, splintering until it was held together by will and not force.

Over the years, she'd learned not to ignore the strange sensations her body experienced, because more times than not, they were trying to tell her something.

She suddenly jerked out of the blissful state she'd been trying to distract herself in. The woman between her legs jumped, looking up at her with wide eyes.

The man who'd been kissing her neck scooted away.

People didn't follow Marlena only because they were scared. There were some who truly felt she should be worshipped—that her powers were given to her because she deserved them.

Since announcing her status as a god? More fell at her feet every day.

Saying she was a god felt almost impertinent. Marlena was more. She had *more*.

"Marlena, is—"

Marlena was already moving, grabbing her clothing from the floor. "Get out." The door flew open on her command, assisted by her wind.

Invisibility and air, her two original abilities—the strongest of them inside her only becoming enhanced when she'd taken on the gods her powers descended from.

She didn't have to repeat herself as she dressed, pulling her long, straight hair from underneath the dress she slipped over her head.

The two, who moments ago had been set on giving Marlena the pleasure she could never quite reach, sprang from the bed, grabbed the clothing they'd shed from the floor, and left without redressing.

Her door shut, and Marlena stepped through the abyss, leaving Atrox, where she'd stationed herself while Bridger was gone, and jumping into the room of mirrors.

Shattered.

Glass everywhere.

A gasp slipped through her parted lips. "No."

The gods were quiet. *Too quiet.*

The mirrors were shattered, pieces of their frames littered among the glass or hanging to the wall by nothing more than their nails and wire pieces.

"*The curse,*" a voice whispered... but Marlena was almost positive it was her own.

Shards of glass crunched under her shoes, her reflection staring up at her from jagged edges on the floor. She snapped her jaw shut when she realized it hung open.

This was exactly what Marlena had dreamed of making this room look like at one point in her life. She'd wanted to blow all the mirrors down with gale-force winds and dance on their broken corpses... but instead she'd used them to anchor Vega's memories to her curse.

Marlena had given the mirrors a new life.

Vega had ended them with hers.

The Aeris home under her feet trembled with an aftershock of a power Marlena would know anywhere... because it was hers.

After the portal she'd made for Bridger imploded, Marlena had been on edge—waiting for something to happen.

She needed to get to the portal, but Marlena was stuck staring at the remnants of a room she thought she'd be the one to destroy one day.

Vega takes everything from me.

The rasp of a maid's panic made Marlena spin, more glass crunching under her heels.

"Miss Marlena!" The round woman rested her hands on her knees, drawing in deep breaths from what Marlena assumed was a short run. Her eyes were wide, sweat glistening across her brow. "Atrox," she gasped. "A dragon is attacking the prison."

Marlena had just left. Had *just* made it to Aeris to find the mirrors shattered.

Without responding, Marlena stepped through the in-between and back to Atrox.

She wasn't prepared for the sight unfolding.

Marlena stood at the top of the stairs to the prison, and coming up from below were the faces of horrified guards and filthy-looking prisoners. Behind them was a wave of flames with the unmistakable roar of a dragon.

The shake of its vocal cords and the rumble deep in Marlena's chest had her dumbstruck.

How the fuck did Khort find his way in?

A guard with life-threatening burns crawled up the stairs, his screams shaking Marlena's eardrums. "Help! Help me!"

Marlena reached down, gripping the boy by his shoulder. His skin melted at her touch. She felt the warmth of her healing powers from the dead god Juno slither up her arm, pushing only enough to numb his pain. She didn't care if he lived or died. "Tell me what's happening."

The young boy, who probably wasn't much older than twenty, relaxed under her touch, but the fear in his eyes didn't disappear. "Your prisoner, Arlet, she—she..." he stuttered, unable to get his mind to work clearly. "That's not the normal black dragon. That's not him."

"What did Arlet do?" Marlena shook him, trying to get him to make sense.

"One second she was quiet, and the next she was screaming, convulsing." The boy sobbed in pain.

Marlena almost lost her cool waiting for him to spit it out, but everyone else was either dead or had already fled, so her options were limited.

"The dragon... it—oh gods. It came out of her. Shooting out of her, but her body stayed behind, unlike a regular shifter." The boy began to shiver, his body unable to keep up with his injuries. "The brown dragon from the battlefield returned, but it's bigger, angrier."

A rush of flames shot up the stairwell. Marlena shielded herself, dropping the boy. The sound of his scream was washed away by the crackling of the fire roaring around her bubble of safety.

Most would flee, run away from the dragon, but Marlena didn't run from fights. She walked into the flames, parting them as she descended into whatever might be left of the fort's dungeon.

The mouth of a dragon Marlena had only seen once before, on the battlefield in Solum, cut through the flames shooting from its unhinged jaw.

Ducking, she rolled out of the way in time to hear the dragon's jaws snap shut, drool splattering from the force.

Marlena jumped, moving through the dragon and its tail whacking against the cells, old stone crumbling around them. With nothing to support from underneath, this wing of the home would fall, crushing anyone left behind.

The dragon couldn't turn around quickly enough, slamming into the sides of the walls as Marlena approached the cell where Arlet had been kept. *Had.*

Arlet was gone.

"She's back." Arlet's voice startled Marlena, a small gasp leaving her lips. She hadn't heard her—it was like she appeared out of thin air.

Arlet must have seen that realization on her face, and a sickly sweet smile spread across her lips. Marlena's eyes traced the outline of them before looking back to her eyes. "You're not the only one who can hide, Mar." She held her arm up, displaying the soft and unmarked skin where a power block once was.

Confusion watered Marlena's senses.

The cell around them shifted, bringing Marlena back to a time she'd long since burned from herself. Marlena stood in the bedroom of a home she'd let crumble to ashes.

Her fingertips burned with her green flames, the taste of anger rising up her throat. "How?" she asked after turning in a circle, taking in the room she could almost believe was real if it weren't for the dragon swinging its head into the cell after her.

Arlet held up a single hand, and the mirage fell away. The angry deep brown dragon with golden eyes and a spiny tail hissed, pausing at Arlet's command. "How, what? How can I do these things?" Arlet asked, letting a fake stream of fire swirl through the air towards Marlena.

Marlena didn't move, letting the forged flame break in two against her face and disappear.

"Or how did I get my powers back?" Arlet's dragon's head swayed back and forth on its front legs, hunching to fit its head inside the cell with Arlet and Marlena. It still towered over them both.

It had been years since Marlena was stunned in the way she was now. Speechless and unable to wrap her head around exactly what was going on. She'd seen Arlet in action during the Saturnalia battle, but she hadn't been aware of the power she possessed, the secret she'd been keeping from their realm. Now, she was seeing it in action for the first time with the knowledge of just how fucking powerful Arlet had become.

"Vega set us free from the shackles your curse put on our bond." The dragon dipped its head, and Arlet's tiny hand almost got lost in the size of its massive scales as she petted the beast.

Every morsel of shock must have been pictured on Marlena's face because Arlet started laughing. The laugh was a few short chuckles at first before turning into an all-out belly laugh that rivaled even the most maniacal villains.

Marlena felt the only emotion she had left.

Fury.

Her flames shot up her arms, spreading across the already charred floor, reaching for Arlet, who was climbing up the leg of her dragon like she'd been doing this for years—*had she?*

Over the bellow of the dragon, Arlet called down, "If I were you, I'd run."

Marlena didn't wait around to get stuck in the rubble of Atrox's collapsing east wing. She stepped through the pages of their realm and landed where the portal was—where it should have been.

It was gone.

The portal's gone.

The trees' overlapping branches were just that—branches. No debris scattered the ground. It was as if this portal had imploded on itself too, leaving behind only its memory.

Vates was no longer home to the portal. It no longer sat at the end of a cobblestone road overlooking what remained of Arlet's childhood home.

Instead of the portal, Marlena was met with Vega straddling Bridger's lap, wrapped in a tight hug on top of the ivy-covered forest floor.

From her hiding spot in the trees, blending in with the shadows,

Marlena watched the relief wash over both their faces. They were covered in blood, and their clothes were dirty and tattered.

They had fought for their lives.

Marlena knew what that looked like.

"You're okay?" Vega asked, her eyes inspecting Bridger like she'd expected him to be dead.

"Yeah, yeah, I'm okay. You fucking did it." He laughed, his hands cupping Vega's face. He ran a gentle thumb over her blood-splattered cheek.

Marlena had seen this before. She'd lived this life.

"You broke the fucking curse." Bridger laughed again, a happy sound. Marlena hadn't heard that in a long time though—the lightness of Bridger's joy. "Do you *feel* that?"

"Power. Raw. Untouched. We—" Vega started but was cut off by Bridger's lips meeting hers. She was rigid at first, like she wanted to fight him off, but quickly she sank into their kiss.

And that was more than Marlena needed to see.

"Well, well, well, what do we have here?" Marlena strutted into view, the sun overhead burning off the shadows as she stepped into the clearing.

Vega jumped off Bridger, her lightning sputtering to life.

The smile lighting Vega's face was from that first zap of unbound power. The power Marlena possessed since her summoning—the power Vega would have felt earlier if Marlena hadn't cursed her.

Bridger pulled himself up slowly, too relaxed compared to her sister. He casually wiped his hands against his pants, holes indicating he'd been stabbed a few times.

"Breaking the curse wasn't part of the deal, Commander," Marlena purred, watching the cold warrior shift back into place after his interrupted kiss. "But it's good to see you're taking kissing Vega very seriously."

Bridger rolled up his sleeves, returning to the commander of Tolevarre.

<h1 style="text-align:center">27</h1>

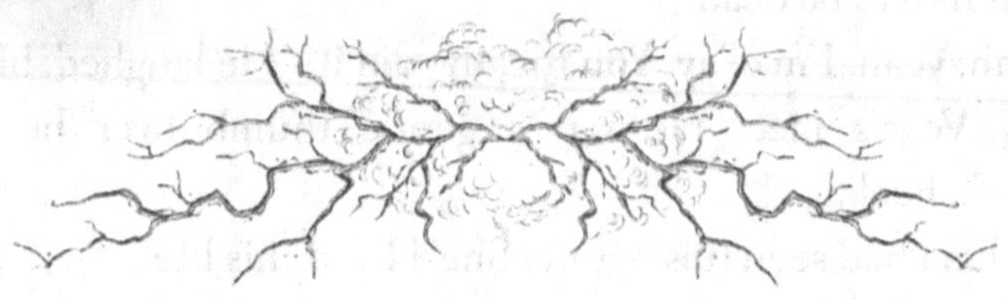

Time slowed.

Vega felt like she was watching Bridger's sleeves roll in slow motion, every flex of his hand and bulge of his forearm catching her eye.

"Do you trust me?" Bridger's voice asked... but it wasn't Bridger asking out loud, because he was standing five feet away looking like he was morphing back into the man she'd promised to kill.

Into the man with a secret.

Into the man with a *deal*.

His words caressed her brain like a feather. Like a whisper across her lips, she could feel his thoughts.

It was a feeling she'd felt a few times before but never had the whisper been so clear.

"In order for us to get home, she had to break her curse." He ran a hand through his hair, mussing it in just the right way, a small strand falling out of place and curling across his forehead.

"Trust me," Bridger said again, this time making eye contact with her when his words tickled her mind.

She saw it in his eyes this time, the scrunch of his eyebrows and the way he bit the inside of his lip. But the moment was gone, his arms crossing over his chest.

Closing himself off.

So much power sizzled in her body, so much more than she'd ever felt, but she couldn't concentrate on it, couldn't allow herself to feel the shiver of something new.

Something she'd been willing to trade her life for.

The portal had felt like a dream, and she almost told herself it was until...

A flutter of something inside her mind threatened to catch her attention, but it got lost, because Bridger took up too much space as he stepped away from Vega, settling in beside Marlena. *"Vega, I promise—"*

Her sister smirked, dragging her eyes up Vega's body, unknowingly interrupting Bridger. "You can break your curse, but you can't figure out how to break your connection to a man who's so desperate to rid himself of you that he'd—"

"Tone down the dramatics." Bridger sighed.

Vega stared at the side of his head, waiting for him to look at her. *Gods, I'd been so stupid.*

"I wasn't going to be able to stop the curse from breaking. She'd already set it in motion the moment she landed back on Earth with her memories." He picked a broken leaf off the collar of his shirt. The nonchalance of his demeanor felt like a slow, cold knife to the back. "But that didn't mean the trip had to be a total waste. I thought I could take advantage to get information we might be able to use." Bridger stole a glance at Marlena. "I have so many ideas."

His gaze finally found Vega's. Her heart was at war with her brain, which was at war with her body.

The reality of what Bridger was saying hit Vega like a freight train, and when the first laugh bubbled from her throat, it took her by surprise. The laughing didn't slow, it only grew as she began to pity her poor self.

"No way," Vega mused, finally able to get her fit of giggles under control. "You really got me."

It can't be true. It can't be. Her own voice pleaded. *That was my Bridger. He was my Bridger...*

Marlena snickered behind closed lips. "You should know better than to let your heart get in the way during a war you should be using your brain for."

Vega wiggled her fingers. The vibration of the air simply existing around her was almost overwhelming. The flap of Khort's wing beats disrupted the flow of wind enough to alert Vega of his approach.

Bridger sensed him too. She could see it in the way his head ticked to the side.

But Vega could feel the power of *everything*. From the hum of Tolevarre through her boots, to the clouds in the sky, back down to Marlena... who Vega felt magnetized to.

Vega closed her eyes and took a deep breath. When she focused on Khort, she saw a long hallway, and when she followed it, she could dip inside his head and see from his point of view, pretending she was the dragon soaring through the sky. In the middle of her mind was a door, open wide, ready for her to stick her head through and peek inside.

Vega knew Arlet was near—she could feel her too, but if she tried to dip inside her head, she saw nothing but open sky.

She could feel Bridger's breaths, count the seconds before his thoughts turned to words. "And here comes the dragon."

The ground rumbled with Khort's landing. His roar shook Vega's core, reminding her to open her eyes.

In the distance, coming out from behind crumbling cottages and overgrown yards, rebel soldiers secured the street, surrounding the entire perimeter.

The cracks of Khort's bones shifting to his human form had Vega turning at the exact moment he crashed into her, pulling her into a hug she hadn't expected. "You did it. Vega, you did it!" He placed an excited kiss on her temple as he let her go, their reunion lasting seconds before Khort's attention pinned on Bridger.

Vega had fought to save Bridger, had bargained her life for his, and look what that had gotten her—another could-have-been broken heart.

Marlena's snarl was one Vega wished she could frame on her wall.

Inside Vega was a hallway with two opposite ends. Her connection to Khort was on one side and Arlet on the other. In the middle was the circular room with the open door.

"Look at me, please," Bridger's voice pleaded, echoing through the door in her mind like he knew she was on the other side.

Her name spoken in Bridger's smooth voice and deep tone made Vega want to rub up against him like a cat in heat.

How was she supposed to forget him this time? When he was inside her fucking head! Vega slammed the door to their connection without understanding how she'd done it.

How long had he known he could do that? How long had she ignored the signs?

A sense of dread washed over Vega, and it wasn't the hallways or the door causing it. It was the gurgling pit of hunger she felt under her feet when she stood at the crossroads of her mind's pathways.

Khort studied Vega in a way she'd never seen him do before.

The time for standing around was over. Maybe Khort saw that because his eyes turned to slits, letting Vega know he was ready.

"Bridger's worth more alive," Vega said, glaring at him with a fire she knew he could feel. "And as for Marlena, well, I have something special planned for her."

Wind picked up, jostling the fallen leaves down the road. "Do you think I'm going to let you go?" Marlena asked with a hateful chuckle. "You, my dear sister, are a wanted woman. One I plan to make an example of." Her green flames sparked to life, swirling through her fingertips as they rode the gusts of Marlena's wind.

"We no longer play by your rules, Marlena," Vega told her as Arlet came into view.

A giant brown dragon landed behind Vega and Khort, seemingly out of nowhere.

Arlet only let herself be seen when she was ready, even before her powers. She'd always been happy to blend into the background.

"You fucking piece of shit!" Arlet screamed, sliding down the dragon's leg—*What the fuck, by the way.*

The dragon huffed a puff of steam, as if to say it was in on the fight too.

Arlet bounded towards Bridger, colliding with the shield he quietly slid around himself. "Arlet." He droned, playing his part well. *Too* well.

Because it's not an act.

Arlet was alive. Khort was alive. That was all that mattered. Only they mattered. Except the voice in the back of her head begged her to remember *him*.

"I held out hope for you." The way Arlet said it made Vega's chest hurt. She wasn't the only one Bridger's betrayals had hurt. "Tell her." Arlet pointed at Vega. "Look her in the eyes and tell her what you've done. I've already heard it from Marlena. Don't bother trying to lie anymore, Dimico."

She'd heard it from Marlena when she'd been locked up. Vega went cold with worry. The ichor in Arlet's veins helped her start to heal, but Vega knew the memories of what she'd gone through under Marlena's imprisonment would haunt her forever.

Arlet's words hadn't seemed to affect Bridger at all. "You want to hear it twice? Fine." He turned to Marlena, who smiled at their not-so secret. "I asked Marlena to let me go to Earth to retrieve you." His body language was unreadable, and the look in his eyes as he stared at Vega was one of a cold and calculated killer. The Bridger who'd been cracking open while on Earth hid behind the shell of a man Marlena hand crafted. "To make you fall for me again in hopes I'd get you to feed me information about your curse, your years of research..." The lifeless expression Bridger wore made Vega's stomach sink long before his words did. "Your theories."

He's going to tell her about Romulus and everything we learned.

Marlena would be preening right now if she had feathers. "And what was in it for you? What did you want in return?"

Bridger's throat bobbed as he swallowed, the clatter of him banging against their mental door almost too loud to ignore. "That we find a way to break my bond from them. I live. They die."

Stupid. Stupid. Stupid.

She hadn't felt stupid when he was between her—she stopped the thought before it crossed her mind, ignoring the taste of him still on her lips from the kiss he'd so desperately needed when they'd made it back to Tolevarre.

How could that have been fake?

Arlet and Khort flanked Vega, preparing for the fight inevitably to come.

"And it seems you did a rather fantastic job." Marlena laughed, her flames striking out again. "I hope you at least got to have a little fun with her." She winked, and then Vega felt the world shatter.

Lightning blasted from inside, grounding her to the world she belonged in—the only world she'd ever fight for again.

Her blue lightning crawled across the ground, creeping slowly to form a circle of protection around her. *That's new.* "We don't leave without Bridger." If he fell back into Marlena's hands, there's no telling what she'd do to him.

Everyone sprung into action. Khort was in the air before anyone could blink, wings creating a windstorm for Vega to play with as Arlet's dragon—or whoever or whatever it was—soared into the sky and disappeared.

It was still there, camouflaged with the clouds. "That's the craziest shit I've ever seen." Vega laughed, a newfound excitement in her tone.

We're going to be unstoppable.

How many surprises would the bonded have now that their powers and connection weren't being suffocated by a curse?

Bridger hopped over the tendrils of electricity beginning to surround him. Even without any weapons, Bridger could wipe this battlefield clean, so she let the power be his distraction. The lightning followed him, wriggling with a magnetic drawl.

Vega wanted to watch, to see how her powers reached for Bridger's touch, but Marlena started prowling around her in a tight circle, her beast-like claws tearing through her skin.

"You think because you broke your curse, you've won?" Marlena asked.

"One step closer than you are right now, and doesn't that just really, *really* piss you off?" Vega put space between them, watching her sister's every move. "I know more about the curse you created than you ever will." Her smile was big, stretching ear to ear as a taunt to Marlena.

"All you did was level the playing field for the first time since this began. I don't mind a little excitement. A little pressure," Marlena hissed, diving towards Vega with her claws.

With her powers fully restored and a new one waiting to be released, Vega couldn't waste any time, couldn't let herself think about what was next. She had to show Marlena who she'd helped create.

Marlena's claws dug into Vega's back, breaking the skin and sinking into the meat of her shoulder. Ignoring the pain, Vega wrapped her hand around her sister's wrist, and an explosion no one but Vega could feel ruptured inside her mind.

The vibration she'd felt under her feet outside the door leading to Bridger erupted, shadows shooting from an infinite pit.

A darkness unlike anything Vega had ever felt before crawled its way out, but when it emerged... it didn't come after Vega like she'd expected.

No. It's sitting at my feet, waiting for its first kill.

"*Feed me,*" it growled with a voice that sounded like it hadn't been used in thousands of years.

The world moved on around them. Vega could hear the wind clipping the wings of the dragons overhead, feel Bridger fighting with a rebellion soldier—not killing any who came after him. Saw him wielding a... *sword of lightning?* When she blinked and took a breath, everything else fell away, and all that was left was Marlena, Vega, and her hunger for death.

A piercing scream tore through Marlena's lips, her face turning red and eyes bulging as frigid heat traveled down Vega's arm. Marlena couldn't fight Vega's hold, couldn't move underneath her paralyzing touch.

Vega's veins turned black at her wrist, creeping up her arm as Marlena's claws retracted, her fingers scarred and bleeding where they'd once been. A splatter of blood peppered Marlena's face in red.

Vega lost herself to the surge of power, eyelashes fluttering from the gentle ripple of something new making itself at home inside her. Her darkened veins looked like black lightning skittering up her arms, pumping a rush of pleasure straight to her brain.

Pleasure.

Fear iced her senses, immediately washing away anything else she could have felt... The sight of death under her skin made Vega jump off Marlena, who had somehow ended up on the ground underneath her. *How did she get there?*

Vega's chest heaved, her vision spotty. Through the black spots, she could see Marlena gaping up at her like she was seeing through a new pair of eyes.

"How does it feel to be taken from? To have a piece of you ripped out?" Vega grinned, claws shooting from her hands like they once had Marlena's. "I'm going to take them all from you, Mar." She used her nickname for the first time in decades. "And then I'm going

to come for whatever's left of the scared little girl hiding inside you."
Lightning flashed behind Vega for emphasis.

The people around were frozen in place. Vega didn't know when it'd happened, only knew everyone watched the sisters now.

The fear in Marlena's eyes did something to Vega—morphed her into a person she didn't know.

It felt good.

Wicked.

And Vega *liked it.*

Vega leaned down to Marlena on the ground and asked only loud enough for her to hear, "If you became a god by inviting the gods inside your head, what would letting death inside make me?"

She didn't miss the tremble in Marlena's spine before she disappeared, smoke wafting into Vega's face as the only proof she'd been there in the first place.

This wasn't over. It had only just begun. The last fifty-five years had been child's play compared to what was coming.

Now, Vega had a direction, an idea of where they went from here. *Of how this ends...*

Everyone stared as the claws retracted, and Vega buried them deep, letting whatever was inside her now drag Diana, the goddess of Demuto, into the shiny new abyss of the circular room in Vega's mind.

When the darkness descended and Vega's mind was clear, she repelled the surge of pleasure grappling to stay alive.

A sinking feeling crashed into her like a tidal wave: *this is what it feels like when the hero decides to sacrifice themselves for the people they love.*

Vega would suck Marlena dry and send them both straight to the underworld if it meant her friends got to live.

A group of rebel soldiers surrounded Bridger, weapons drawn. Leo, the fire-wielder from Ardor who had been assigned to babysit Vega in Castra, pressed the tip of his axe against Bridger's jugular...

but he didn't back up. He stayed planted in place, slowly raising his arms in a lazy surrender. He could kill Leo without breaking a sweat, but he wasn't resisting. Bridger's stunned gaze never left Vega.

The doorway to her mind was still closed, but she could feel him banging against it, the urgency of his knocking begging her to open it. She almost did until Khort reached out and stopped her from getting too close to Bridger. Vega hadn't even realized she'd been moving, Khort's light grip on her forearm waking her from a daze. "Do I need to see if I can use this on you too or are you going easily?" she asked Bridger as Khort's hand fell away.

Bridger shook his head, ignoring the axe at his throat as he marveled at her. "Let me in, please."

"How long have you known?" she questioned, holding herself together.

"Vega—"

"How long have you known?" Vega yelled this time, the strain from her tightened throat hard to miss as she fought against the surge of betrayal.

Bridger bowed his head, looking at the axe still at his throat, and sighed before returning his eyes to Vega. "I had suspicions before Marlena's capture. We just never got the chance to test it out with my shields acting as a barrier between us." The shields their bond had taken down. "I knew for sure we could when I begged you to come back after your last death."

One nod. That was all it took. "I heard you."

Khort's touch returned, his hand cupping her elbow.

Bridger's eyes locked in on where they connected, a muscle in his jaw quivering, and a rush of irritation she shouldn't have been able to feel flooded Vega's senses.

No. Too much of us is connected.

"We should get out of the open," Khort mumbled, looking around.

"No one's going to attack you." Bridger's voice sounded far away, like he was focused on something else completely.

Leo let out a chuckle, his axe yet to leave Bridger's throat. "We're not ignorant enough to trust anything you say."

Bridger rolled his head to face Leo. "And who are you? I don't believe I was talking to you, but—"

Fire blazed through the tip of Leo's weapon, searing Bridger's skin like a tiny branding iron. With one sweep of his leg, Bridger took Leo's feet out from underneath him.

Vega wasn't the least bit surprised he'd done so with his hands still raised around his shoulder's height.

Leo jumped up, ready to retaliate, but Vega stepped in between, her eyes fixed on the fire-wielder who looked ready to detonate. "He can't die, but you can. Stop." Vega pushed Bridger back with a hand to his chest, his smug-ass grin dying the second her palm touched the skin between his open shirt.

She didn't have time to think about the way her body begged for more now that they were back in Tolevarre with their powers and a broken curse. Everything was heightened—her senses, her connections to the bonded.

And more importantly, a hunger for something more rumbled in the open pit of her mind... Vega couldn't stop staring at Bridger, the softness she'd seen coming back on Earth returning now that Marlena was gone.

"Take him to the caves." Khort ordered.

The caves.

Back to where the rebellion had first begun.

28

VEGA SQUEEZED ARLET AS HARD AS SHE COULD, SHEDDING A few tears while they continued to hug each other and not let go. "I'm sorry. I'm so sorry I put you in her path. I never expected her—"

"Stop." Arlet pulled away from their hug and stared into Vega's tear-filled eyes. A floodgate had opened when they arrived at the caves and had a moment to themselves. Bridger was locked in a cell alone—officially a prisoner of the rebels. "It's not your fault. I'm sorry I didn't trust your plan."

Khort nodded in agreement. "We should have trusted you. We let the fear of losing you blind us from what needed to happen. You were right. You did it."

I did it. But at what cost?

There were no regrets trading her life for theirs... But a prickle of sadness spread through her veins like poison. An ache for the life she thought she could have if she fought hard enough.

The peace she'd hoped for would never come.

Vega had given that up the night she begged for her sister's death and hadn't even known it.

Soon, Vega would have to face the anger she knew would be

waiting for her when she was alone—but not yet. She had plenty of time to be mad about her fate, now wasn't the time to wallow in self pity.

"How?" Arlet asked, searching her best friend's face like the answer was hidden under the smeared blood covering Vega's skin.

Vega wiped her tears, pulling her hands back to see the evidence of Romulus's death... and then she told them everything she could, skipping over anything hinting to what Vega had done, what she'd given up, or who might be the cause of it all.

"I got wrapped up in breaking the curse, in realizing how close I was to saving us. I got wrapped up in him, unable to fight the bond of our souls." Vega took a breath, wiping at her nose. "Gods, it happened so fast. It was like neither of us could tell our bodies no, and it didn't matter how many times my brain reminded my heart what he'd done to me. And now, fuck, now I can feel *everything*. I can feel his breathing again. I can see where he is if I close my eyes. He can talk to me... inside." She stopped, watching them try to school their shock at her confession. "I hate what he did to us, but I know there's a side to his story we might never understand."

Khort made a noise sounding a lot like a strained laugh. "Vega, he left us to run the army of, let's just call her what she is, our mortal enemy."

Vega stayed calm. "Enemy or not, we know what Marlena is capable of—the abuse she's capable of. Two years is a long time to be subjected to any kind of torture. Two years with Marlena?" She fought away the shudder creeping up her spine. "You were let go after seventeen days. Imagine what over seven hundred more would have done to you."

Khort narrowed his eyes. "Seventeen days, and then she killed my mom, only two years before the curse she put on my land would take my sister's life."

"She's killed everyone, Khort. Every single person we love who can die is dead, and if they aren't, they probably will be. She's left us with no one except each other. I'm not looking to fight. I don't want to fight with you two anymore. We're finally one step ahead. *Finally.* After fifty-five years we get to say we're ahead of her." Vega ran a hand through her battle worn hair, thankful for the wet cloth someone had brought her earlier to wipe her face clean.

"What did you do to her?" Arlet asked softly, keeping her voice low so no one else would hear.

Vega froze for a split second too long. Khort raised his brow, and Arlet crossed her arms.

Her friends knew her too well.

She couldn't talk about it all yet, not when she didn't understand the first thing about what she'd done. Part of her was still trying to convince herself it was all a lucid dream. But whenever she did, the darkness within surfaced, waiting to crawl its way up the pit the second Vega summoned it.

"I took Diana." Vega couldn't get around hiding everything, so she told them what she could.

Khort choked on the air he inhaled. "You what?"

Diana, the dead goddess of the hunt and wild animals. The goddess of Khort's people.

"To kill Romulus, I had to bring him through the portal. It was where Death would be waiting to collect my soul at the end of my curse." Vega could see that blackness again, the sinking feeling in her stomach returning like she was back inside the dark abyss. "It didn't matter that I'd brought Romulus in place of myself." He didn't want Romulus.

The echo of a snarl vibrated up the dark pit inside her mind.

Vega couldn't gaslight herself hard enough to believe what she'd done was a dream. Not with this *thing* inside her mind.

"I was in Death's arms, and I wasn't ready to go yet. I wasn't ready to let the people I love die because of me." She spoke with a surety she was relieved to feel. "So, I promised to deliver my sister and the gods inside her for the power to save our people." Vega bit her tongue, holding the rest inside.

For now.

She would tell them later...

Arlet stared into the shadows of the dark cave. "I saw a piece of her. The real Marlena. For just a second." Arlet's body racked with an unexpected sob, and she slid to the floor.

Vega was down with her in seconds, wrapping her in a hug as scooted back to use the cave's wall as a backrest. Arlet sank into her as Khort plopped down on the other side, smoothing her dirty hair.

"Before she told me about the deal with Bridger... she came in, covered in blood, babbling about killing everyone who'd witnessed the acolyte admit she wasn't the only god."

Khort shushed her. "Most here still don't know." They quietly filled Vega in. Her hand covered her mouth by the time they were done.

Tolevarre knew Vega was a god... But what kind had she come back as?

"You said the gods are inside her?" Arlet asked, a nervous energy coming from her shared connection making Vega tense.

That was what... he—*Gods, Vega, just say his fucking name!* She battled with herself too much to form words. Vega nodded, unable to admit how she knew.

"She told me they were. She said 'they killed' everyone when referring to the massacre in Stella. I saw her fight to keep control against them in her head. Marlena's getting messy." Arlet shook as she recalled the memory.

They sat in silence, mulling over what this all meant.

"I have to tell you both something," Arlet said against Vega's chest, still wrapped inside Vega's arms. "And I'm so sorry I kept it a secret this long, but I couldn't figure out how to approach it, not after what happened... and then the longer time went on, I didn't even know if it mattered anymore." She laughed a sad sound. "But it does matter. It does."

Khort continued to smooth her hair against her head, catching Vega's gaze over. His wide eyes mirrored the dread Vega felt.

"It matters," Arlet repeated, but this time it felt like she was saying it to herself and not her friends. "Marlena and I..."

No.

"I fell in love with Marlena before everything happened. We were in a secret relationship, sneaking around for about a year."

Vega stiffened, and Khort's hand froze in place.

Time paused while Arlet fidgeted under their touch. She didn't pull away, staying curled up against Vega's chest.

My best friend and my sister were together, and I never knew.

Vega didn't know what it was she felt. It was a mixture of complete shock, of being totally blindsided, with a hint of hurt Arlet felt she could only now come clean about this.

What if she would have told them in her first life? Where would they be today with this knowledge?

The only noises in the cave were the echoes of other conversations happening around the main room. Enough silence passed where Arlet finally decided to continue.

"I ended things the Saturnalia before her induction, after she attacked your parents. I was there that day. I saw her almost kill the guard. I saw the person she was becoming, and instead of standing by, instead of helping her through, I left her. What if I—"

"No, no, Arlet, this isn't your fault." Vega wrapped her sobbing best friend tighter, resting her hand against Arlet's head and smoothing her hair like Khort had been. His hands were in his lap, his eyes glazed over as he processed what they'd learned. "A butterfly caught in the web of a deadly spider," Vega said, using the same analogy Arlet had told her in more than one life.

"What if I could have stopped her?" Arlet's question was almost inaudible but loud enough for the two of them to hear. "What if I'm the reason she snapped?"

Arlet's sobs caused physical torment inside Vega, her body hurting alongside her best friend's. She'd been holding on to this pain all alone the entire time. "None of us could have predicted what would happen. We were basically kids. Marlena making the choices she made isn't our fault." But Vega would hold herself accountable for all eternity for not saying something to her parents, for not at the *very least* trying to save the sister she'd once loved.

The sister her best friend had once loved...

"I don't know what this new power inside me does yet," Vega admitted. She knew what she'd done to acquire it, what she'd sacrificed, but she still knew nothing about what it could do. "But I promise I'll use it to save everyone from her. I promise when this is all done, Marlena won't hurt us or anyone else ever again."

None of them moved. No one even made an attempt. They sat there for hours in complete silence after Arlet's sobs had stopped.

They were back. They were whole. And they would get their vengeance.

After they got Arlet some food and wrapped her in a blanket on a cot by the fire, Vega and Khort sat on the other side at a rickety wooden table with a mug of ale each.

"How many died?" Vega asked, needing to know who all they'd lost when Marlena found Castra.

"152 made it out," Khort answered solemnly.

Nearly 500 people called Castra home. Vega felt like she might be sick.

"Emil?" Her father's best friend and seat holder of Imber before it crumbled. He'd been their first real ally.

Khort shook his head, remorse washing over his face. "He helped get the kids out."

"Fuck." Vega closed her eyes, sending a silent prayer into the aether for the soul of a man who'd loved her like a daughter. She opened her eyes, and a lump swelled in her throat as the next name came to her mind. "Quinley?"

Khort nodded. "She's alive. She's with a small group in Amora right now."

They had allies in Amora... that was a huge deal. There had never been anyone willing to stand against Marlena there—especially while Ivelle was alive.

"Marlena wiped Solum out. Took the food supply from everyone. We're barely eating enough, we're vastly outnumbered, and everyone is exhausted." Khort rubbed his thumb against the mug in his hand, catching a falling drop of condensation. "I've spent most of my time over the last month getting people out of the outlying towns where riots and starvation have affected people the worst."

Vega sat her empty drink down and rubbed her temples. It was only a matter of time before Marlena found them here... if she didn't already know and wasn't planning her attack. "We have to get out of these caves."

Khort reached across the table and grabbed her free hand. "We'll figure it out." The touch made Vega sink into him, resting her forehead on the back of his palm.

Vega inhaled his mossy scent, and she knew she was home. It didn't matter if they were hiding in caves, outnumbered—none of it mattered if she was with them... *all of them.* "You know Bridger's a part of this, right? We don't do this without him."

Vega hated to admit it, especially after the way he'd transformed in front of her eyes when Marlena was around.

What's he so scared of?

She felt Khort stiffen beneath her, but he rolled his hand over, cupping her forehead and lifting it up, forcing Vega to look at him. "I know... and I'm sorry for everything. For the fights before you left, the stupid fucking jealousy. I..." He laughed a little, but it didn't sound like the one Vega wished she could hear right now. "I love you, and I want you to be happy. Whatever that looks like for you. But I don't fucking trust him."

Vega's lips pulled up on one side. "Me either." Khort's hand slid down to her cheek, cupping her face. She nuzzled into it and smiled.

"Glad we can agree on that."

She pulled away, taking a look around the open cave. Vega noted the makeshift cots people were doubled up on. This section of the cave smelled of the smoke wafting off the small fire keeping people warm while they slept. "You know I'm going to have to talk to Meyer."

Khort sat his mug down. "You don't *have* to."

"Meyer followed me to the Minerva Archives when I snuck away after the battle in Schoenus. He offered me help in getting back to Earth when no one else would." For Bridger. "He's going to come after Bridger. Just like you and Arlet would for me. There's nothing standing in his way. This isn't Marlena's fortress with hundreds of guards." Vega looked around the room again. "It's a cave with, what, 200 people who are starving?"

The fight wasn't over. As tired and as worn-out as they were now, it was nothing compared to what it'd be a week, a month, a year from now.

If they made it that long...

Khort's eyes were heavy with grief as he swept them over the cave and its inhabitants.

"I'm back. I'm *really* back now." Vega felt the guilt of her statement bubble until she almost choked on it.

I'm not back forever.

Her words pulled Khort's attention from the people around him. "It's time this rebellion shows Tolevarre who Marlena's up against." A real smile tugged at Vega's lips this time. "We're done hiding... We have the commander of Tolevarre."

29

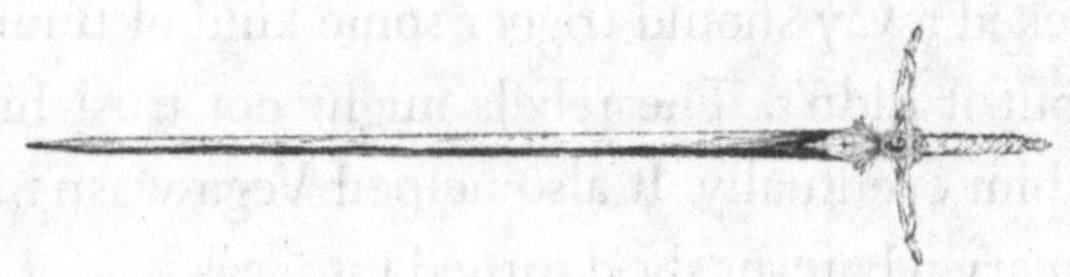

BRIDGER WOKE FROM A DREAMLESS SLEEP TO VEGA'S SCREAMS echoing through the door connecting their minds.

He knocked until the screaming stopped.

It took him a while to calm down, to stop pacing the length of his cell.

Bridger Dimico. Pacing...

If anything was going to make him go crazy, it was the pacing.

The same power that kept abilities from working in the Minerva Archives was used to disconnect Bridger from his in the cave's makeshift cell.

A fucking immortal god, and I still don't get to use my curse-free powers.

The one thing it hadn't taken away, though, was the mental connection with Vega. The only person keeping him out was her... and he wouldn't stop knocking until he heard her say she was okay.

What had her screams been about?

What scared her so badly she'd managed to wake him from his first deep sleep since before she'd returned in her last life?

Bridger could feel she was okay... but that only rested his mind enough to stop his pacing when a new guard came in with a small plate of breakfast.

Eggs scrambled with some kind of root vegetable. It wasn't much, but it was still better than anything he'd eaten on Earth.

How they'd even found enough eggs to feed people here in the middle of Vates was impressive enough.

Being locked away should trigger some kind of trauma response in Bridger, but it didn't. The rebels might not trust him, but they would need him eventually. It also helped Vega wasn't Marlena, no matter how scary whatever she'd turned into was.

Bridger had seen it, watched it all happen through Vega's eyes. While she blacked out and slipped into whatever new power she'd taken when coming back through the portal, Bridger quickly learned their uncursed bond gave them all more of a connection than they'd had before.

He'd felt her pleasure, her pull to whatever she took from Marlena... all while learning he could now wield lightning if it came from Vega's electric current.

Bridger had seen the way her veins pumped black blood from her wrist until it disappeared behind Vega's shirt.

Something wasn't right. Something dark waited in the shadows of his mind. Watching. Waiting. Bridger could feel the strain, even when he wasn't thinking about it—it was constantly nagging at him.

To top it all off, if someone didn't go talk to Meyer, he'd probably be setting the place on fire at any moment.

There was plenty for Bridger to think about while being imprisoned, but every thought kept leading back to Vega.

As if he'd willed her into existence, footsteps sounded down the tunnel, and Bridger smiled to himself—he'd know the sound of that walk anywhere. "Go get some food while it's hot." She dismissed his current guard, and when he scampered off, she turned her attention towards Bridger. "For the love of gods, please stop knocking," Vega begged.

Sitting against the wall with his legs kicked out in front of him, crossed at the ankles, Bridger let a lazy smile pull at his lips. "Ah, have you finally come to tell me why you woke me up screaming outside the door you won't open?"

Vega opened the cell door and stepped through, but she hesitated for a second, her brows pulling in long enough for Bridger to know she was about to lie.

"I had a nightmare. I have them sometimes. There's a lot my brain has to torture me with when I'm not awake to stop it... and now when I'm awake, I have to deal with your insistent knocking."

Bridger hummed, watching Vega settle on the other side of the small cell. "I'd stop knocking if you'd just let me in." He shrugged, staying seated.

"But then that means you wouldn't stop talking, and I don't want that either." Vega slid down the wall across from him, laying her head back and closing her eyes. "There's no privacy with this new connection." She inhaled, resting her palms up towards the cave's short ceiling. Her fingers emitted only a little bit of blue light.

Their powers weren't completely cut off, just dulled to basically useless. "I'm sure there's a way to learn to block it out. If my powers are mixed in, it's pretty easy once you get the hang of it." He'd done so easily for forty years until their bond decided enough was enough.

"You giving a master class?" she asked, opening one eye.

She was talking to him. That was good, but gods, she looked exhausted. "Tell me something real," he blurted out, looking to give her a distraction.

Vega blew a laugh from her nose, shaking her head, but finally opened both eyes. "I have no idea what I'm fucking doing."

"I don't think we're supposed to," he admitted. "I mean, there's never been new gods before. I think the point is to figure it out as we go."

"How do you do it?" she asked, making Bridger furrow his brow in confusion. "Talk to me. How do you send the thoughts down?"

Bridger bit his bottom lip to contain the smile. "Uh..." He paused, searching for a way to explain it. "There's a door, right? A pathway. And I can just *feel* it. Feel you."

"Does it work like that with the others?" she asked.

"No. Only you. I could see through everyone's eyes the other day though. Knew where they were and what their next strike was. But I can't feel them like I feel you." The intensity of their bond had always been there, but with no barriers... gods, Bridger had never felt anything like it in his entire life.

"They say the same thing... about the fight and being connected."

He wanted so badly to reach out and touch her, to remind her he was in this with her. To make her see he meant everything he said on Earth... but he didn't have to. Vega brought it up before he had the chance.

Vega wrapped her arms around her legs, resting her chin on top of her knees. Bridger felt her sigh in his own chest. "Why didn't you tell me about the deal with Marlena?"

Answering honestly, Bridger let himself be seen. "At first I was still so unsure of what I was supposed to want. I knew I wanted to stop my dreams, that I wanted to live. I knew I had to be the one to go to Earth. I was the one who had the dream... but then I didn't want to tell you because I was seeing the girl I loved again, and I couldn't bear the idea of losing her to some stupid scheme I'd never truly wanted." Bridger chuffed, shaking his head faintly. "I knew you'd never believe I was telling the truth about being on your side. If I would have told you what I promised Marlena, you never would have trusted me." He hadn't even trusted himself at the beginning, unsure what following Vega into another life would do to him.

"Okay, fine, but why didn't you just come clean when Marlena showed up? Why put on the act and make her believe you were the person who wanted those things? The curse is broken. You don't have to be that person anymore." The hurt finally broke through in her voice, piercing Bridger through his heart.

The stabbing of Vega's sorrows hurt almost as much as it had when she'd stabbed him through the heart with a dagger. "I'll always be the man who took an oath to protect his realm, Vega. The second Marlena finds out I'm no longer hers to control, people will suffer. She will find a way to make me pay for it. I meant everything I said to you on Earth, but I can't make rash decisions like I once did. Especially now."

Her face sank. "No matter how hard I try to hate you, I can't... I don't think I ever really could. I was mad, hurt, and it was easier to turn those feelings into rage. I can't find it in me to be mad anymore. I have too many other pressing matters to worry about now. But I don't trust you yet," Vega told him. "I know you had to do whatever was best for you, but—"

"Do what was best for me?" Bridger interrupted, cocking his head. "You think I did what was best for me?"

Vega scrunched her eyebrows like it was obvious. "Yes, I mean, sure, you lost the girl you loved, but you gained the army you always wanted in return, and it wasn't like we knew then what we know now."

"Vega, if I had done what was best for me, I would have snatched you up and found a way out of Tolevarre. I thought about it once. Forcing you back through the portal and disappearing where we could live in peace. That's what I would have done if I'd gotten my way. I did what was best for the people around me. For my best friend. For *your* best friends." He bubbled a laugh. "Marlena told me she would let Arlet and Khort live if I just fell in line where I was supposed to be. I bet she already knew none of us could die at that point, but Tolevarre was without a commander. Other bloodlines were ready to swoop in and take over." The fate of their army had been in limbo. "Could you imagine if Fraus took over the army? The madness my uncle would have unleashed alongside your sister? *No one* would have been safe."

He'd made the decision to save others instead of Vega. "When I escaped, Marlena let me stay away long enough to meet you in your next life. I left the rebels, I left you, because the you I loved was gone, and there were people, *our people,* the people you begged me to keep safe, who needed me."

Vega wasn't fuming, she wasn't ready to set anything ablaze with her ire, but the look on her face was worse than anything else he could have seen.

Pity.

"I never wanted to hurt you. You were the best thing that had ever happened to me, but I was lost—so lost without you. And then after everything Marlena said, everything I'd lived through, the people I thought were my friends didn't trust me anymore, and then you came back as the stranger Marlena told me you'd be." Bridger gripped his thigh hard enough to feel pain, letting the uncomfortable pinch keep him from cracking. "I don't know... Yes. I acted selfishly because I couldn't watch you die anymore." Joke was on him, though, because Marlena continued to make Bridger kill her. "I couldn't wait for you to become someone I didn't know—not when our people were dying. The people we promised to protect were dying... and then she was going to take Meyer. He was all I had left."

Vega kept her chin on her knees, watching him with neutrality.

"I don't expect you to understand what or why I did it, but learning to forget you was the only way I could become the commander everyone needed me to be." Bridger felt swept up in the moment, swept away in the feeling of getting all this unsaid shit he'd held in for nearly half a century off his chest. "I don't regret it, and if that means you can never learn to trust me again, then so be it. But Vega." He paused, waiting for her to look him in the eyes. When she finally did, Bridger finished. "I do regret hurting you."

They both stayed quiet for a while, emotion thick between them in the small space, when Vega decided to drop valuable information seemingly out of the blue. "Death was waiting for me when I brought Romulus back through the portal. I was forced to make a deal, promising to deliver the gods and Marlena to the underworld for the power to save Tolevarre."

Bridger held his breath until she stopped talking, breathing her name on his exhale. "Vega."

She stood, and Bridger jumped up after her, having no fucking clue what his response was supposed to be.

Vega sighed. "Stop knocking, okay?"

And then Bridger watched her lock his cell door before disappearing completely. Her absence didn't stop Bridger from speaking out loud. "It's not Death who makes deals."

Hours later, when he'd begun rolling a pebble back and forth, Bridger felt the door creak open, followed by, *"Don't make me regret this."*

Hearing Vega's words inside his head for the first time made him melt. The feeling of her inside a place that had once been only his... Gods, he could live in there forever with her. *"You found me."* Bridger's laugh echoed inside his own head. *"I promise to be on my best behavior, Kitten."*

Her groan vibrated Bridger's mind, and he laughed again... but at least she didn't shut him out.

The euphoria of Vega's first words down their bond would have lasted longer had he not decided to psychoanalyze every word Romulus had said for the fifth time through.

His conclusion: Vega hoped Bridger didn't know the difference between Death and the ruler of the underworld, or she herself didn't know the difference.

Bridger didn't believe it was the latter.

"Did you pull the short straw tonight?" Bridger asked with a sarcastic smile. It brought him joy to see how easily he got under Leo's skin.

"Shut the fuck up." The annoyance in his voice was palpable.

Fucking fire-wielders were always so grumpy. Must be the heat inside them or something—*But damn, dude.*

"Hey, can I request a guard change?" He spoke down the pathway, waiting for Vega to respond.

"What did I say about interrupting me with stupid questions?" Vega snapped back.

He relaxed at her words. *"Well, if you'd tell me anything about what's going on, what the next plan is, literally anything, I wouldn't have to be such a bother."*

Hours of silence later, and a group of footsteps came from down the hall, followed by Khort's voice. "You can take the rest of the night off, Leo."

"Hi," Vega said, opening his cell. "I think it's time the four of us talk."

They didn't let him out of the cell. Not yet. Khort and Arlet followed Vega in.

"No warning you were coming and bringing friends?" Bridger asked, raising a brow.

She answered with the roll of her pretty eyes.

The color had come back to Arlet's skin, and she looked good. Rested.

Then there was Khort, who looked like he was ready to set Bridger on fire at any moment. Typical.

Bridger smiled at him, wiggling his fingers in a sarcastic hello. "Is this my trial? To see if I'm trustworthy enough to rejoin the elite bonded?"

Vega held a hand up, keeping Khort from rushing Bridger like a bull. They could sense each other's movements, even while locked inside a cage meant to suppress even the strongest of powers.

"We're here to talk about the logistics of making this work," Arlet pointed out, always the one to step in when the three of them needed redirecting.

Vega plopped down at the other end of the cot she'd had sent to him last night. The note she'd tucked into the blanket read:

> Because the Vega I am today doesn't think you deserve to sleep
> on the cold ground. Not anymore, at least.

He'd traced Vega's quick script with his fingertip close to a hundred times.

"Do they know about your deal?" He needed to know if Vega expected him to keep it a secret.

"They know everything," Vega responded to Bridger out loud, a seamless transition into what they needed to talk about.

"Everything?" Bridger asked, cocking his brow as a crooked smirk formed across his lips.

"Everything," Khort grumbled.

Arlet stood in the middle of the room, blocking Khort and Bridger from each other while also standing in between Bridger and the only exit he had—he wouldn't take it even if he had the chance.

There was nowhere else for him to go.

Arlet sighed. "It's time you tell us your side of the story, Bridger."

His eyes bounced between Arlet and Khort, lingering on Vega the longest. She shrugged her shoulders and didn't say a word.

"You think my story is going to change the way they feel?" Bridger asked with a sneer.

"It's a start," Vega quipped.

"There's a lot I'm not ready to talk about," Bridger admitted. "And it's not because I'm hiding anything. I'm still not prepared to face every demon I locked away, and this whole *feelings* thing is kind of new to me again."

For almost forty years, Bridger had blocked out anything that could hurt him, spending nearly half a century feeling nothing but what the fearless leader of Tolevarre's army should feel.

Anger. Determination.

"Then tell us what you're willing to share." Arlet's voice was soft, but when Bridger looked up, her eyes were clouded with exactly what he'd expected. Apprehension.

Bridger had a sneaking suspicion it wasn't Arlet or Khort who'd pushed this matter.

He huffed. He didn't have a choice—it was time to open up.

Lost inside his roaring thoughts, Bridger didn't miss the caress of Vega's presence. When his eyes focused on her, she was already looking at him, her icy eyes drawing him in.

If Vega could talk about the shitty things that happened to her, Bridger could give them the peace of mind they were looking for.

"We've all fallen victim to Marlena's torture. I don't need to explain what she's able to do to someone when she has full control." Everyone nodded in unison, so Bridger continued. "When I escaped after two years, I was already a different person. I had to become someone inside that cell to keep myself from going crazy."

Bridger stared at the worn soles of Vega's boots, giving himself something to focus on while he spoke. "I spent 802 days locked away, and only three people talked to me. Marlena, when she was reminding me I had the power to save the people I loved, or when she felt it was necessary to tell me who Vega had come back as—how weak she was becoming. My mother, who never missed an opportunity to tell me what a failure I'd become, and a young level one warrior, freshly enlisted, who I manipulated and then had to kill to escape." Bridger couldn't look up—didn't want to see anyone's reactions as he continued.

"Marlena never laid a hand on me the entire time I was her prisoner. She didn't have to. She knew I could endure physical pain. I'd been raised by a man who beat me any chance he got, usually for nothing more than a reminder he could. But that didn't mean the others didn't. Guards, other leaders. My own mother." Bridger felt the breath Arlet inhaled. "Whoever felt they had a bone to pick with me." He'd been stripped of his powers the entire time, never able to fight back against the strength of those with three meals a day and unblocked abilities. "When they were done they'd all send in a healer, readying me for the next person who showed up."

Vega knew of his father's abuse, but he'd never gone into detail. Bridger had always had secrets—had been raised to keep them close to his chest. "Marlena knew what it would take to break me. She'd already taken the only person I'd ever loved... The last thing I wanted was for Vega to lose the people who loved her too."

Bridger ground his teeth together, pushing against the need to clam up.

"Keep going." Vega's words fluttered through his mind.

Having her there, in whatever capacity she was willing to give him, gave Bridger the nerve he needed to continue. "Maybe Marlena already knew the four of us couldn't die, but I didn't, and she told me she would let you both live if I joined her." A laugh actually slipped through his lips, but it didn't have any humor behind it. "Vega hadn't been the person we'd loved in a long time, and I was the one who found it hardest to deal with, but no one was in my shoes. No one was losing the only person who'd ever made them feel whole." His eyes rose to Vega. "I lost her over and over and over... I don't have to tell either of you what that felt like."

Khort rolled his eyes and started to talk, but surprisingly, Arlet cut him short. "Let him finish." She nodded Bridger on.

"So while you lost Vega too, what you didn't have, *don't have,* is the responsibility of a Dimico-born warrior. At birth, by blood, I was chosen for a specific duty." When the next commander was born, their power was already engraved in them—they didn't have to wait to come into their ability like everyone else. "I had a realm ready to tear itself apart, and no one to lead it. Do you know why the original bloodline didn't allow the commander to also be the Curia seat holder?"

None of them answered, but Bridger knew they knew.

"Because the commander's life isn't linked to one territory. It's connected to them all. A commander's obligation is to his realm, not his birthplace." Bridger's own lineage had been the ones to forget—to get greedy and want more for only themselves.

Bridger had never supported his parents' views or beliefs, but up until Vega, he'd never had the courage to act against them.

"I took an oath to our realm, was born to protect it... and Marlena was letting people die, killing them. Not just us or the people we cared about. She was letting the people who had nothing else, no one else, die. We promised to protect them. We told Remus we would." Bridger had so many conflicting feelings about Remus after everything Romulus had revealed. He hadn't even begun unpacking what he'd heard and witnessed. "I had to make a decision for them, not me. I thought I'd lost Vega for good, and I didn't have anything else to live for at that moment in my life." Bridger felt like he was being filleted open and examined for broken pieces.

Khort and Arlet's posture softened, but Bridger wasn't focused on them. He'd always said he didn't care about the others, and while that wasn't entirely true, he'd thought of Vega before everyone else.

She'd been the first and last person he'd thought of when he'd made his final decision.

"I eventually had to ask myself what Vega would have done in my situation." In the early days after his betrayal, Bridger liked to believe there was a version of Vega out there somewhere who was proud of the man he'd had to become.

Understanding wrapped around their bond. "I would have saved as many people as I could."

Hearing Vega say those words weaved a patch into the ripped fabric of Bridger's soul.

Silence stretched between the cell, no one saying anything until Bridger spoke again. "I took in who I could, saved those who would have had nowhere else to go. I changed the way the army works. I didn't choose Marlena. I chose my realm. I chose Tolevarre." A weight lifted from his shoulders. "I've made mistakes, been far more ruthless than I should have been, but without me? I promise things would have been a lot worse." He didn't know if they'd believe him, but he'd finally spoken his truth.

"So, where's your army now?" Khort asked with a smug smirk.

A rumble echoed through the cave, shrieks of terror following. *What timing!*

"Gonna go out on a limb here, but I bet that's them."

30

Khort was out of the cell in seconds, signaling an end to the conversation. Arlet was out next, disappearing before their eyes. *Where is her dragon?*

Vega jumped from her seated position, an unfamiliar swell of power bubbling in the chasm of her mind.

"Let me talk to him," Bridger pleaded.

Turned out, Vega didn't need to go to Meyer.

Meyer came to them... and it had barely been two days since Vega and Bridger had returned.

She shook her head slowly, mulling it over. "Bridger..."

"Come on. You know he'll turn this whole cave into a brick oven." Bridger urged her to make the decision quicker. "I'm the only one who's going to be able to send him away without anyone dying, and you know it."

The rebellion was close to crumbling in on itself. Without a safe place to regroup or a solid plan in motion, they were nothing more than an already failed attempt.

"We can't afford any more deaths," Vega warned, pointing at him directly and glaring down the line of her finger.

"Trust me." Bridger's voice slid into her mind, breaking a piece of the ice that had formed there. *"You have to at least try."*

Vega knew he was right. This would be the ultimate test.

What would Bridger do when faced by his best friend and the army he'd built from the shambles his father had left it in?

"I will make your life fucking miserable if you cross me, Dimico."

Vega didn't wait for Bridger but knew he would be close behind. She could feel his full power snapping back into place when he exited the dead-end cell.

As she ascended the cave, Vega paid no attention to the moon towering over the mountains in the distance, or how the reflection of light casting off it illuminated the trees and made them look as if they were covered in snow.

She didn't see Khort and Leo standing side by side with their weapons drawn, or feel the wind pick up from the power of a rebel soldier's wind.

All Vega could focus on was Meyer and the over thirty soldiers with the highest level ten rank one could get in Tolevarre's army lining their suits.

"Where's he at, Sparks?" Meyer yelled as Vega came to a stop next to Khort and Arlet.

"Hi, Meyer," Vega cooed, connecting with her powers. The sizzle of her lightning jumped behind her skin, waiting to be released, and the air turned prickly, a storm readying in the distance.

Somewhere deep inside the darkness of Vega's mind, the newest piece of her fully awakened. Its claws scraped against the stone walls of the pit.

A roar rattled overhead, distracting Vega from the fear of what she might become if she used that power when she wasn't supposed to.

Arlet's big brown dragon snapped close to Bridger's soldiers before landing on top of the cave's mouth. Her head raked back and forth slowly, wagging like she was taking in the face of every single enemy she could make a snack out of.

A few of the soldiers looked like they might flee, but just before they darted, Vega felt Bridger walk up beside her.

I'll never be able to ignore him in a room ever again. When she glanced over, his hands were in his pockets—the epitome of casual.

"Will you help defend my soldiers like you do the rebels when Marlena turns on them too?" Bridger caught Vega by surprise, stealing her breath with a single question. He stared ahead, his attention directed at Meyer, who hid his shock well.

"Is there a difference between them if they're both willing to fight against tyranny in hopes for a better world?" she asked softly.

The faintest of smiles pulled at the edges of Bridger's lips. "Hey, buddy. I was wondering when you'd show up." Bridger crossed his arms over his chest. "Two days, though? I could've been rebel food by now."

Khort glared daggers at Bridger, ready to attack if he made one wrong move.

Meyer's eyes bounced between Bridger, Vega, and then finally took in Khort's posture. "What's going on here?" he asked, pausing on Vega for a second longer—he could sense the oncoming news.

"I'm choosing," Bridger answered.

Vega froze, everyone's eyes landing on her and Bridger.

Meyer's chest fell with the release of a breath. "Her?" He nodded at Vega.

Bridger shook his head. "I'm choosing what's right for this realm. Vega's just an added bonus I'm bonded to." He sent Khort into a silent frenzy when he winked her way.

"Stop it," Vega scolded.

"But it's so fun." His reply was followed with the deep rumble of his internal laugh.

"Traitor," a guard behind Meyer hissed.

Bridger raised a dark brow. "Am I?" He took a step forward, and the man jumped back, bumping into the woman behind him. "What did you vow upon entry into my army?"

The one who'd called him a traitor didn't answer, but another down the line did. "To protect the people of Tolevarre."

Bridger turned, motioning to the people standing outside the cave, ready to take on thirty-two—Vega finished counting—of Tolevarre's greatest warriors. "Are these not the people of Tolevarre?"

"She's the enemy." A young man pointed at Vega.

Vega followed his finger straight to her chest, and then looked back up, jabbing a thumb at herself. "Me?"

"*Now look who's being snarky,*" Bridger cooed.

"Her?" Arlet asked, also pointing at Vega... but she laughed, hunching over. "Her? The girl who's been cursed and tortured for fifty-five years? *She's* the enemy?"

"Do you see how stupid that sounds when it's said out loud?" Bridger asked.

He might have saved people, changed how his soldiers were treated, but that didn't mean Bridger was soft. He hadn't earned his terrifying reputation by being gentle or kind.

That part of him had always been saved for Vega. The rest of the world knew Commander Dimico. Vega had once known Bridger. No last name, no title. *My Bridger.*

So much had changed.

"I think we all know why most of you joined... because you'd have a better chance of surviving if you got out of Marlena's warpath." Bridger locked eyes with Meyer. "You were afraid that by doing the right thing, you were sentencing yourself to death." He raised a brow again. "But does that mean you're willing to kill more innocent people? *Children?* For her? The same person who'd let you die without a second thought."

"You've worked for her for years. What changed?" another soldier asked.

"I played by Marlena's rules, sure, but I never worked *for* her. I've worked for Tolevarre, leading an army that needed to be dismantled and rebuilt." Chatter amongst his people mixed together, their words hard to tell apart as the buzz rose. "You aren't in Marlena's army. You're in mine. When an order is made, does it come from Marlena or me?" He didn't wait for the answer everyone knew. "Marlena doesn't command my forces. I do. Which means I can choose where they're needed, when they're needed—however I see fit."

Vega took a step out of line, aligning herself with Bridger. "Is Marlena who you want to go down defending?" She let her lightning crawl down her legs, spreading out against the grass. Meyer took a step back, the soldiers following his move. "Because I never said I wasn't the enemy. If you believe in the world my sister rules over, the one where innocent lives have been ripped apart... probably some of yours, your parents, siblings, friends?" She directed her question to the eyes staring her down. "Then you are my enemy, you *do* deserve to die, and I'll gladly kill you to save them." She nodded behind her to the tired rebels who'd been fighting for their lives far longer than they should have.

At the mention of killing, the darkness inside her shook itself off and eased to the top of its hole, curling around the edge in wait. It got braver as the days strung together.

"Down, Kitten," Bridger purred, taking a step into Vega's scattered lightning. It shot up his leg, split at his sides, and met again as it traveled across his right collarbone and down his arm until it extended into an electric sword.

Everyone was boggled, Vega's own lips parting in surprise even though this was the second time she'd seen it. *"How?"* she asked, reaching for the weapon.

"Your power calls to me." Bridger let her take it, the weight of the electric sword heavy in her grip until it fizzled out and became one with the power inside her again. "If Marlena's world is a world

you want to continue to live in, a world you believe is worth fighting for... then fight for her. My army is no longer a safe place for you."

Meyer eyed Bridger. "You're making us choose too?"

Vega couldn't read his expression. Meyer's features were schooled behind a mask that had certainly been taught by the best friend standing before him.

"I'm giving you a choice to make the right decision. It's not too late, Meyer." Bridger reached out and clasped a hand over his shoulder. "I know you. I know you don't believe the people of Tolevarre are less than because of the power they possess. I know the kind of leader you are." He let his hand fall from Meyer's shoulder, and Bridger stepped back. "We don't have to make the same decisions our parents made."

"I fight for you," the woman behind Meyer said, taking a step forward. "Marlena took everything from me. I won't stand by and watch her do the same to others." She unsheathed her weapons and tossed them forward, willingly surrendering them.

A few others joined her, parroting some kind of similar story.

"For Tolevarre."

"For Oliver."

"For Klara."

People named off the loved ones they'd lost to a ruler only looking out for herself.

Weapons clattered to the ground one by one.

Vega couldn't believe what was happening—what Bridger had just done. She stood shocked, and the darkness in her mind slid back inside the pit, knowing death would come...

Just not today.

Bridger turned to face Khort, nodding to the rebel soldiers who answered to him guarding the mouth of the cave. "They will not harm my soldiers who go peacefully. Understood?"

Khort lowered his chin in a single nod, making eye contact with

Leo over Bridger's shoulder. He and a few other rebels gathered up the weapons.

"We are their guests. No fighting, or I'll kill you myself," Bridger warned.

Meyer reached behind him and unsheathed a sword Vega knew wasn't his, followed by a dagger Vega would know anywhere.

Bridger's bonded weapons.

He held them out for Bridger to take. Vega felt the hum of power radiating through the palm of Bridger's hands as he took both from Meyer.

"This is where you're meant to be." Meyer's tone was soft. "I only hope you're ready for what comes next."

Meyer wasn't choosing Bridger... even after Bridger had chosen to save him over Vega. The hurt in Vega's chest was multiplied by the momentary pain Bridger found himself letting slip down their bond.

Bridger backed away from his best friend, passing his weapons to Vega. "Vincere won't be safe for anyone who stays behind once you're gone. Not until I get there. Tell them to leave."

Meyer nodded, but didn't say another word.

When he was gone, retreating back into the tree lines, Bridger turned to Vega. "More will come. I suggest we"—he motioned to the bonded—"talk about our living arrangements. I'm pretty sure I'm the only one with a viable option here."

Vega raised a brow, watching as Leo escorted Bridger's soldiers into the cave. "Your underground bunker?"

"Underground training facility," he corrected. "It fits thousands and is impenetrable from the outside. It'd be a safe place to house the rebellion."

"And how do you expect we take it?" Khort asked.

Bridger chuckled, his amusement real. "It was built for me, by me. I don't have to take what's already mine." He didn't have to act confident. He was confident. He always had been, and it was palpable standing this close to him.

"Not everyone is going to follow you," Khort pointed out.

"That much is obvious... but I know the army I've created. Most of them will. It just might take some time for them to let themselves be more afraid of dying *for* Marlena than *by* Marlena."

Like a chameleon, he morphed into whatever he needed to be in the moment, hiding what he didn't want others to see. It didn't matter how hard he tried to hide the sadness weighing him down, Vega could feel it.

I can feel everything he feels...

His best friend, despite his willingness to assist Vega in breaking her curse if it meant freeing Bridger from his dreams, would never follow Bridger to this side of the war.

"You'll make sure my people have the right accommodations. They aren't your prisoners. I'll continue to be for as long as you need, but they won't be," Bridger told Vega, not bothering to address the others. "They follow my orders. Death of any rebel at their hands before this alliance is on me. Not them."

Vega nodded, unsure what else she could say.

"*Thank you,*" he said to only her before turning and strolling back into the dark cave.

Thank you? Vega's lips parted as she watched him disappear. Arlet's dragon took off into the night sky, soaring in the direction of Meyer and the group returning with him.

Watching.

"We gotta have a conversation about this dragon thing. I have so many questions," Vega said in a monotone drawl, still staring where Bridger had disappeared long after he was gone. "But I have..." Her eyes wandered to Arlet and Khort, who were staring at her. "I have to." She had to follow Bridger.

She didn't wait for her friends to respond.

"Wait!" Vega called down the pathway, running to catch up to him.

As she approached, Bridger's shoulders sagged. It was so minuscule no one would notice the change... but Vega did. "You did it." She was still processing what those words meant.

"I did it," Bridger said on a breath, turning to let her see his face.

"I'm sorry," Vega said, unable to stop the words from tumbling out.

His eyebrows creased. "For?"

"For not fighting for you. For not seeing you. For not being there when you needed someone. For letting you walk away so easily. For giving up on you." Vega had a long list of things she felt she could apologize for. She wasn't the only victim of Marlena's abuse.

Bridger leaned against the iron cell's doorframe. "I'm the one who gave up on you."

She shook her head, taking another step towards him. Vega kept her distance, staying outside Bridger's reach. "I told you to keep our people safe. That was my exact request the first time she made you kill me." Under the rubble of what had once been her childhood home. "And then I begged you to save me instead of Meyer... because I was afraid of what *my* life would look like without you in it."

"Every time you left, I lost a little piece of myself, and I kept wondering what good I would be to our realm if I lost myself in losing you..." The hurt creasing his brow made Vega hold her breath. "But I did lose myself. I lost myself for a long time, blocking out anything that felt too real. Anything that reminded me of you. I had to erase you to become the commander of Tolevarre. The irony behind needing you now to become the god I'm meant to be isn't lost on me. There is no *me* without you. Not the real me, anyway." His dark eyes drank her in. "I'm sorry it took me forty years to figure that out. I'll wait another forty for you to forgive me if I have to."

Her heart screamed for her to move, but her feet stayed cemented in place. "Better late than never."

"I'm not the same boy I was." He said it as a warning.

"We'll never be the people we were back then." Vega retorted. "I don't want you to be. I want you to be the commander. The god."

Bridger stared at her like he could see through to the darkness making Vega's soul its home. "No secrets."

She swallowed so hard her throat bobbed, but she nodded, agreeing to it with her first lie of their fresh start. "No secrets."

They didn't need to know... not yet. Not until Vega knew how this new power saved them.

Neither moved, rooted in place by their own stubbornness.

Needing to distract herself from the sparks of desire heating her core, Vega said the first thing that popped in her head. "This doesn't mean we're back together."

Bridger's laugh was the one she remembered hearing. The one she fell in love with. "No, of course not." His lips pulled into his famous crooked grin, and Vega couldn't stop staring.

"It just means we're officially... allies."

"Allies," Bridger agreed, his lips pulling further up, up, up.

"And that you now work for Khort."

"That will never fucking happen." Bridger nudged himself off the wall with his shoulder, keeping his arms folded over his chest.

Thank the gods. Why is leaning so hot? She couldn't stop picturing him without a shirt on, which would eventually become a problem.

Vega snickered. "Just making sure you were paying attention." She stepped forward and held out her hand for him to shake.

Bridger glanced down, his eyes shooting back up to meet hers. He uncrossed his arms, and the second his hand gripped Vega's, he tugged her into his chest and snaked his arms around her back, one tangling in the hair at the base of her neck.

Vega didn't even have time to think about it before she leaned in and kissed him, leading them to what they both wanted.

Need. She was powered by the feeling of his touch, sending her into a frenzy the seconds his hands were on her.

"If allies is what you want to call it, then yes, I'm your ally." Bridger's words wrapped around her mind, making her feel safer than she'd ever felt. The warmth of his tongue against hers, him tugging her head back to kiss down her jawline, and the rumble of his sultry tone against the inside of her brain combined, sending Vega into another dimension.

She gasped for air, not finding enough to calm the roaring heat of her body.

Bridger pressed his lips delicately against the pulse at Vega's neck, slowing her breathing and the world around her. "I'm going to be the best damn ally you've ever had, baby."

His touch was gone, and Vega's body chilled a thousand degrees. When her eyes fluttered open, Bridger was shutting himself inside the cell. It took her a minute to come down from the clouds.

"What are you doing?" she asked, stepping forward to grab the closed door.

"Letting you decide when it's time to trust me." Bridger sauntered back to the corner with his cot and plopped down, crossing his calves over each other. "I do have a king-sized bed in Vincere, though. Reliable equipment, the ability to spy with all the newest tech. You know Marlena won't wait to overreact when she finds out we're not back together, but that I'm definitely your favorite ally." Bridger faked a yawn. "And I could really go for a hot shower."

31

Lining the walls of an office no one but her knew existed were Marlena's most treasured keepsakes.

Light reflected off the iron band she pulled from her head, slicing her hand with the edge. Marlena balled her fist, her blood dripping down the crack of her palm, landing on the wooden lids of the jars.

The iron ring she wore as a crown held a very important curse—a key to an object Marlena had to keep safe.

Appearing from nowhere, a jar the size of all the others slid to the front.

Marlena could feel the beating drum in her ear as she reached for it.

A knock on a door in another office echoed through to the one she was in now.

Marlena dropped her hand and put the halo back on her head, waited for the wall of jars to disappear, and stepped through the void into her proper office—the one everyone knew about. There was no sign she'd been anywhere but here. Not even her smoke dared to give her away this time.

The force of the door swinging in blew Marlena's hair over her shoulders. "Where is he?" It had been days since Meyer left on his search for Bridger.

How hard was it to find a bunch of misplaced rebels with nowhere to go?

Meyer stood on the other side of the door, stoic as always.

She hurried him in, slamming the door with a thud.

Marlena had been more on edge than usual. Vega breaking her curse was a rough blow, but the worst part of it all was what had happened to her sister when she broke the curse.

What had she turned herself into? And why couldn't Marlena reach Diana? The beast she'd been able to shift into with the god inside her was gone—and so was its voice.

As if Vega had stolen it right out of her... *How?* How had she done it?

That was what Marlena had been doing since fleeing from the fight. Research. She'd pulled apart every single book in her personal library before forcing Littera to shut down the Archives to everyone but her. There was always something to find if you knew where to look. Or at least that was what she'd always told herself, but she couldn't and hadn't found a single fucking thing about Remus and his curse in the nearly seventy years she'd been researching the gods.

Not before. Not now.

Not ever.

"Where the fuck is Bridger?" she asked again through gritted teeth.

Meyer wore his general's uniform, which was similar to Bridger's commander suit, without the billowing cape. "He stayed."

Everything sped by, crashing around without any control, until those two little words slipped from Meyer's lips.

The world halted to a stop. Ice coated Marlena's veins, rage turning her body cold. *"You lost him,"* the voices hissed.

Meyer flinched away from Marlena's rigid stance. "He what?" The question bubbled from the pit of her stomach.

"He's staying with the rebellion," Meyer repeated.

Had Marlena stepped into a time machine and walked through to the beginning of her reign? She finally moved, using her wind to send the table in the center of the room flying.

Meyer ducked away from the splintering shards of wood.

"Why? Why!" she screamed.

Meyer held his ground, and Marlena would give him credit—he didn't shake with fear like he once had. "Because he loves her."

It took everything inside Marlena not to blow this entire territory up with how hot her fury burned. "Where are they?" she asked, fearing her teeth might shatter from the force of her jaw's tightening muscles.

"Vates's caves," Meyer answered quickly. "But they're moving to Vincere."

"You left people alive?" she asked, fighting against the roar of voices in her head, only able to address one concern at a time.

He cocked his head an inch. "What would you have liked me to do, Marlena? Attack four gods, severely outnumbered, and kill children and the elderly? It would have been a blood bath, and not in the way you would have liked."

The sensible side of her knew he was right, but the piece of the real Marlena was locked in a jar and cursed to disappear. She wasn't real anymore.

"How many of the group you took stayed with Bridger?" Marlena wasn't stupid. She knew what kind of army Bridger had built after she'd killed his father—one where the majority would follow him, not her.

She'd just never thought it'd become an issue. She thought she'd had Bridger hooked for good, given him the power he wanted, the distraction he needed...

"Twenty-three out of thirty-two."

Marlena circled Meyer, doing her best to keep the anger from reaching detonation-level. She would be outnumbered as far as body count went, but not in knowledge—never in knowledge.

"Bridger told me to give the rest of the army a choice. To join him or to stay with you."

A laugh erupted from deep within Marlena. "He's got some fucking balls, doesn't he?" Marlena stopped circling and stared at Meyer. "Are you going to let him take the army you're about to inherit?"

"The army isn't yours to give away... not while Bridger is alive. It's his."

Technically, Meyer was right, but Marlena had never once cared about technicalities. Technically, she shouldn't have been able to live when she summoned twelve dead gods—but she had.

Technically, she shouldn't be alive without a heart beating in her chest! *But I am.* That was her voice, growling in her head like a rabid mutt.

Marlena lost sense of herself, disappearing to reappear with Meyer now clutched by the throat, suspended above her. "This world is mine. I am the god people will bow to when this is over. Not them."

"*We. We. We,*" the gods chanted at the same time.

Meyer kicked his feet, fighting against Marlena's crushing grip. It was no use—he'd never be able to fight her off.

"You are now in control of *my* army, General Ignis, and I don't give people choices. If you don't do as I say, you die." Marlena dropped Meyer, letting him crash to the floor. "Do I make myself clear?"

"Yes," he wheezed. "Very."

"Perfect. Get the fuck out of my office." Marlena stepped over Meyer, and the door to her office flew open as if it was getting out of her way, but the door didn't open for Marlena. It opened for Meyer as his invitation to leave.

Marlena stepped through the pages of Tolevarre, suspending in the in-between before coming through the other side and landing in a dilapidated territory she'd never had a need to visit.

It seemed the tides had turned and she was in need of more bodies. Marlena would be foolish to think no one would follow him —she had to prepare for the significant loss in numbers.

She still held power in most of the territories. Aeris bowed to her. Fraus and Ardor would follow, as would Pax, Oro, and Littera. Fortis would be a toss, and for the first time since Marlena was handed control, Amora would be too. Solum, Vates, and Imber were gone, turning into wastelands for rebels to seek shelter.

Demuto had been left to rot, with its shifters stuck inside going mad for fifty-five years thanks to the curse Marlena had put on them, binding their souls to the territory of the dead goddess, Diana.

"Diana... who you let go."

"Who was taken from us," Marlena roared back.

The gods recoiled from her explosive fit, hiding in the corners like frightened dogs.

Marlena masked her features, watching her black smoke waft above her head like a signal. The noises of Demuto hadn't changed. The crickets still chirped, and the birds sang, flying away from Marlena.

Relaying a message.

Marlena had eyes everywhere, and she knew there was a small council within the shifters who'd managed to fight off the madness, who kept their people alive.

She had just never cared enough to pay a visit. She'd never needed anything from them until now.

Until she was desperate enough to give the shifters an opportunity they'd never get again... For a price, of course.

Marlena heard them before she saw them, fast footsteps approaching from the woods behind the log cabins lining the weathered road. Leaves crunched, and then the sound of different types of feet pattered against the rickety stone. "Lay a paw on me, and I'll kill you all," Marlena warned as the mismatched pack of shifters surrounded her.

If it was done to intimidate her, it hadn't worked.

Nothing scared her anymore...

"*Nothing but Vega,*" a voice whispered.

Marlena lit a fire inside her mind, listening to the sounds of the gods scattering.

A wolf standing almost eye level bared its teeth, snapping at Marlena. The massive bear to its right pulled the mangy mutt away before Marlena could rip its teeth out.

None of the animals—*beasts*, she realized, raking her eyes across the group of shifters—could speak.

There was the wolf, the bear, a griffin flying overhead, and she could hear the chatter of a cruravis in the distance. The spider-like bird, with too many legs and razor-sharp teeth on its beak who always smelled like the rotting flesh of its prey, used to be a creature Marlena never wanted to come across alone in the forest.

Now, she was the monster waiting in the night.

"Take me to the leader of your... pack." She couldn't call them people. Marlena eyed the bear and wolf since it seemed they were the ones in charge of this band of idiots.

A bird squealed from a nearby tree, and the bear huffed low under its breath.

"*Hopefully, the leader of these mutts can actually speak.*" A hiss slid through her shields. They could always get to her if they pushed hard enough.

Marlena stunned the voice with a pop of electricity. It yelped like a scolded dog and retreated back behind the wall.

The bear dipped his head in one slow nod and turned around to lead the way. All the other shifters followed, turning their backs on Marlena.

They were either too confident or stupid. Marlena assumed the latter.

The bird from the trees swooped down like it might nip, and that was the only act of defiance she would allow to happen here today. A branch from a nearby tree shot out, wrapped its limbs around the raven, and squeezed until the pressure crushed its body. Blood rained down, splattering across Marlena's shoes.

Ceres, the dead goddess of Solum, had given Marlena control of plant life. The dense forestry of Demuto made every tree in sight a weapon.

"I warned you. Just because you've been locked behind my confines for over half a century doesn't mean I'll allow you to forget who you're dealing with." Marlena pointed to the path they were on. "Hurry. Before I get bored."

The wolf whined, and the way his body swayed as he walked had Marlena wondering if the little bird was someone important to him.

They took a turn, following a well-loved path through the middle of the forest. The soil underneath Marlena's boots squished from Demuto's dense underbrush. She could feel the moisture around her and the blossoming storm in the distance. Demuto had always been wet and muddy with a strong scent of pine.

After a short walk, the path opened to a clearing with thick tree cover. Marlena craned her neck to find a collection of tree houses hiding between the thickest branches.

Smart.

The bear nodded a lazy bob of its head to the tree at the very top of the canopy line. Marlena stepped from the ground to the patio wrapping around the home and the tree it was built around.

The relaxing breeze rustling through the home's open windows washed the strong smell of sulfur over Marlena, a distant memory bringing her back to when her family had spent a lot of time in Demuto with the Feras.

Marlena entered through the open door, and as her eyes adjusted to the dimly lit tree house, a figure in the center of the room turned to reveal the identity of Demuto's leader—someone she had never expected to see again.

The smile creeping over Marlena's lips was genuine.

"You're supposed to be dead."

32

TENSIONS WERE HIGH, AND THEY CONTINUED TO SKYROCKET the longer they sat around without a plan.

As of this morning, it had been two days since Bridger declared his stance in the war and one week since they'd returned to Tolevarre...

It was too quiet. Nothing had happened since Meyer and a large group of soldiers had been seen leaving Vincere, headed to Atrox. The fort city was locked down, as were the rest of the major cities still following her sister.

Marlena and Meyer had gone radio silent.

Vega was antsy. Now more than ever, she felt like they needed a plan. They'd wasted enough time, and the darkness inside Vega's mind grew by the day. She could no longer sleep without the whisper of a voice inside her head waking her up. It was lonely, crying out for a friend.

"Did you hear me?" Arlet asked, head cocking to the side because she knew Vega was off in La La Land.

Taking a sip of water, Vega wiped a bead of sweat from her forehead with her sleeve. "Nope, I sure didn't." The sound of voices echoing off the cave's walls rushed back, and Vega was officially out of her head. "Sorry, I haven't been sleeping well. I'm on edge waiting for the next attack."

And dealing with what might be the soul of a god screaming in my head?

A chuff mirroring the sound of a dragon's exhale echoed up from the pit, coming from the same place the screams did at night.

No, she pleaded to herself. *Not right now.*

She didn't have the energy to fight the darkness away.

It growled again, but thankfully quieted quickly and left her alone.

Bridger's soldiers were finding them here in the caves, and were mostly those stationed around Tolevarre, not anyone with knowledge of what was happening on the inside.

It was good to see their numbers grow, but it did nothing to ease the strain of mixing two sides of what used to be an opposing war.

"That's what I was saying," Arlet said, though her attention was on a rebel and soldier in the middle of a sparring session. They'd turned most of the main cave into a makeshift gym. "We can't continue to live like this. We can't house a fucking rebellion here." She shook her head. "We've tried. It doesn't work." Arlet winced when the soldier took a right hook to the jaw, blood splattering across the floor. "Losing Castra..." Vega caught Arlet's lip quiver. She'd spent so much time helping build Castra into what it'd been in its final form. "Losing Castra sucks, bad. I don't think we have any other option but to take Bridger up on his Vincere offer."

Marlena would know where they were soon, if she didn't already.

They were sitting ducks...

"Khort was in over his head without us," Vega joked. It got them both to smile for a much needed moment. "We can't fault him for always wanting to swoop in and play the hero, but without you," Vega emphasized, because she'd done nothing but add more work to their plates for fifty-five years, "he did what he knew how to do. He saved lives." They looked around the room at the proof of her words. "He let the people of Tolevarre know they don't have to suffer under Marlena's rule. There's another option."

Arlet nodded. "Yeah, but that other option is to fight, not hide. Last time we were here in these caves, we didn't have another choice. This time? We can have Vincere."

Neither of them had ever seen inside... but if it was anything like Bridger had once dreamed of making Atrox, they were in for a treat.

"Then I guess we make the decision for him. After all, who died and made him Khort 'I'm the boss' Fera?" Vega winked.

"And where is your *commander*, huh?" the rebel who'd landed the punch goaded, puffing up his chest at Bridger's soldier.

They'd taken their eyes off the fight for one fucking minute...

"Damn it, Gillan," Arlet grumbled, giving the rebel a name. Vega had been gone too long—she was still trying to learn them all!

"Oh, that's right. Locked up. A prisoner." Gillan spat a laugh, seemingly unfazed by the two large soldiers stepping up behind the one he was chest to chest with.

Bridger's soldier looked oddly familiar too, but Vega couldn't place his face.

The soldier had had enough, knocking Gillan to his ass with a punch to the nose. He should have seen it coming.

The fight went from a few thrown punches to full blown powers in seconds... and others were joining in, deciding now was the right time to pick a fight with whoever they wanted.

"*Who's your guard right now?*" Vega asked through the open door.

Bridger's soldier pulled water from pitchers and sent cupfuls down Gillan's throat. He gaped like a fish out of water, drowning from the inside.

"*My best friend, Leo,*" Bridger answered with a noticeably sarcastic drawl.

Vega threw herself in the middle. "Hey! Knock it off!" She grabbed the soldier by the shoulder.

From the depths of her own personal hell, the darkness thrust itself out of its pit with wings sprouting from its back... like a dragon. Diana's power had morphed the thing inside her to resemble a piece of what Vega stole.

Panic surged, making the shadow creature cower its head and sniff the air. Vega released her grip on the soldier's shoulder and stumbled back.

The soldier stared at her with horror-filled eyes, retreating like he couldn't disappear fast enough into the crowd of brawling bodies.

"*Vega? Is everything okay?*" Bridger slipped inside her head, spying on what was happening in the common room.

"*Tell him the princess said to let you out.*" It sounded so stupid even thinking it, but it was the only way Leo would actually know it was Vega telling Bridger to relay a message.

"*Do I want to know why he would know you as 'princess?'*" The hesitation in his response caused flutters of excitement to bubble inside, and the dragon-like shadow to strut around the pit like Bridger would be able to see it preening for him.

"*Just do it, and get here right now.*"

When one fight broke up, another started beside it. For the first few, Vega and Arlet used little force, and Vega was able to hold the darkness off, begging it to stay put.

This isn't what I need you for.

She had no idea if she could talk to it, and if she could, would it listen?

Eventually, there were too many fighting and not enough trying to break it up that Arlet was forced to use her illusions to regain control.

The room went completely black, no light coming through even the smallest of cracks.

It was eerie, the way Arlet's visions felt so real. People gasped, a few screamed, but they all stopped moving. After a few moments of silence, Arlet let the apparition fall apart. It spread to the corners of the room before disappearing.

Looks of bewilderment, shock, and fear were the common themes among the soldiers as they focused on Arlet and Vega.

"The fighting is getting ridiculous," Arlet scolded and then laid into the group. A few of their heads dipped like they were being grounded by their mothers.

The water-wielder Vega tried so hard to place wiped his lip, smearing blood across his cheek. "Well, for starters, the rebels think—"

"Consider your next words wisely, Jak." Bridger's voice ricocheted off the cave walls, commanding attention without having to try. "I promised to kill for fighting."

The name made a connection. Jak was Junie's twin... Junie, the soldier who'd been used as one of Vega's personal torture devices by Marlena.

Junie's power wasn't one Vega would be forgetting anytime soon.

Bridger strode through the room like he owned the place. He cut her a look, smiling like Vega was the only person in the room, and then returned to the asshole army commander everyone else knew. "You are now a rebel." He stopped beside Arlet, who nodded at his words. "The second you decided to join me, you became one."

Leo came up on Vega's other side, leaning in to whisper, "I knew the princess nickname would stick."

She flicked her wrist, popping him on the arm hard enough to sting. "He *will* kill you."

Leo's bright smile had Vega wondering if the fire-wielder had a secret death wish.

"They don't even want us here," another one of Bridger's soldiers added, with a few mumbling their agreements in unison.

Arlet huffed a laugh. "Well, that sucks because we lose this war otherwise." Straightforward—Vega breathed a sigh of relief at the realistic approach.

They were out of time, unable to waste what little they had left babying their people.

"I understand this is probably hard. I mean, look, I've been tasked with spending all my time with Commander Dickhe— Dimico, sorry." Leo corrected himself under Vega's stern glare.

She'd called Bridger that one gods-damned time in front of Leo while they were running together at Castra, and now the man couldn't let it go!

"You two are closer than I originally thought..." Bridger's agitation burned white-hot, embers of his jealousy warming Vega's blood.

"Why do they have you locked up like a prisoner? That's what this really boils down to!" A young girl with a scar from the corner of her jaw to the tip of her nose spoke up. "If they can't trust you, then how are we supposed to trust them?" Her stare fell on Vega.

Bridger's mouth opened, but he was interrupted by another one of his men.

"We're here because of you, and yet we haven't even seen you at all until now, when we cause a huge scene."

"Doesn't seem fair," another added.

The room buzzed with conversation, and it wasn't good chatter. They got louder the longer their leaders stayed quiet.

Leo leaned towards Vega again, whispering out the side of his mouth, "Feel free to jump in anytime, Princess."

In an instant, Bridger was in between them, towering over Leo. "Call her that one more fucking time, and I'll mount your head in my cell like a trophy." His anger shook the cave walls, small pebbles falling from the ceiling. Bridger's soldiers froze, and the others soon followed. "Enough." A whisper was all it took to quiet the room.

Leo's Adam's apple bobbed when he swallowed, nodding tightly to show he understood his threat.

Bridger shifted his attention from Leo to the group of pale-faced soldiers. "My whereabouts and the reason I'm choosing to stay in a cell are not up for debate. The in-fighting stops now, or we've already lost this war, and we might as well surrender."

"Sir, what's the plan here?" the girl with the scar asked. "We can't hide in the caves forever. We won't..."

Bridger let the question fall on Vega's shoulders, shifting the room's focus with his gaze.

Everyone stared, waiting. Vega felt the weight of every life in this room, knew what she'd traded her soul for.

Because that's what I did... I traded my soul for the darkness inside me. For death.

Her dark pet fluttered its wings, reminding her it hadn't retreated back to the depths where it disappeared to sometimes, doing gods knows what while gone. It rested itself on the edge, a hind leg hanging down lazily.

"C'mon, Kitten. Don't be shy now."

Bridger's words sparked something inside her—she'd never felt like a leader. Not when most of her life had been spent trying to find herself... but Vega was the reason the four were bonded at all.

Vega shared a look with Arlet, and it didn't matter they couldn't talk internally—she could feel her answer.

Taking a deep breath, Vega made the decision they should have made days ago. "Vincere." Bridger's soldiers perked at the mention of their home. "We move to Vincere," Vega declared.

"When?" someone asked through growing excitement.

"As soon as possible." Vega would deal with Khort later.

She had to get their people to safety. Vega didn't know what kind of time limit she had. How long would it take for the darkness—

"Death." The shadow shifter sat up, stretching like a cat waking from its nap. It shook its shadowy wings, their shape reforming once settled.

Vega felt like she was in two places at once. Physically in the real world, fighting to remain calm, and stuck inside her head with the dark—*No, wait.*

It corrected her... Death. Not darkness.

"Death," Vega repeated.

The shadow dragon nodded. *"Us."* It leapt down the pit, leaving Vega to feel hollow in a way that made her sick to her stomach.

Bridger's fingers stroked over Vega's pulse at her wrist, bringing attention to the rapid beat of her heart. *"Are you okay?"*

She couldn't hide from Bridger...

Vega wanted to be annoyed that his touch was the distraction she needed, but she was too grateful to escape the alternate reality in her mind to spend a moment griping. *"Better now,"* she replied honestly, even if she wasn't telling the whole truth.

"We don't have time for division." His eyes trailed over the group. Bridger's fingertips grazed Vega's delicately before returning to his side. "Learn to work together or find a way to accept your imminent death." His words left the group silent, their two unfavorable options staring them in the face. "Get back to training."

Bridger made his order, and then turned to leave without saying goodbye.

"I hope you're prepared for the fit Khort's going to throw when he finds out we made this decision without him," Arlet said, grabbing her belongings from the floor.

"I'd rather he throw a fit than lose more lives because he's letting his ego get in the way." Vega hugged Arlet tight. "Stay safe tonight. I love you."

Arlet was taking the overnight sky shift, letting Khort have the night off.

"I love you too," Arlet told her before Vega jogged after Bridger.

She caught up to Leo first, reaching out to grab his arm. A flash of Jak's horrified face running from Vega made her hand fall to her side. "New assignment. Go make sure they don't kill each other in there, please."

"What about Bridger?" he asked hesitantly.

"I can handle Bridger," Vega answered. "Plus, it's probably not safe to leave you two in a room alone together for a while." She spun and walked backwards, still facing him. "Since Loose Lips Leo can't keep a gods-damned secret." She smiled smugly and popped her shoulders, turning her back to him.

"You know what, Vega Caelum? I hope he handles you real good. Maybe it'll make you nicer to your friends!" Leo's infectious laugh broke the tension forming in Vega's muscles.

"Where are you going?" she asked, catching up to Bridger who moseyed at a much slower pace than he normally did.

"Back to my cell until you summon me again. I'm like your own personal god you pray to when you're bored or need backup." He ticked his head and raised a brow, ready for Vega to argue.

She tingled all over from the playful look in his eyes.

"You caught me..." Vega sighed, toying along. "I didn't even get to start praying for the good stuff yet. I had so much to ask for." She pouted, jutting her bottom lip out. She watched Bridger's eyes dart to it and linger until they pulled into a smile. "How does a frigid cold shower sound?" Vega asked, quickly adding, "Not with me." Bridger mimicked her pouting. Vega ignored it. "But I'm headed to the houses outside the cave and just figured—"

"You wanted to spend a little time with me," Bridger cooed. His husky voice inside Vega's head might not ever be something she got used to.

"No." She shook her head and rolled her eyes. "That you'd want a real shower for the first time in gods knows how long. Sponge baths aren't cutting it." She scrunched her nose and waved her hand in front. "It's why no one wants to let you out of there yet." Vega nodded to the cell.

He didn't stink, but she couldn't let him know it was actually because she wanted to be alone with him outside his cell for more than a few minutes.

Bridger chuckled, shaking his head. "Fine, but know I'm only coming because I don't think you should venture out by yourself and not because I think I actually stink." He sniffed his shirt's collar anyway.

On the way out, Vega grabbed their weapons from the bonded's private arsenal. When Bridger hummed his approval for being reunited with his bonded blades, Vega imagined that vibration somewhere else... *No!* Scolding herself didn't actually seem to work, but she did it anyway.

Vega knew they didn't need to complicate things more than they already had, but it also didn't mean she'd stopped thinking about what they'd done in the back of that Escalade on Earth.

Vega cleared her throat and sheathed her daggers at her thigh.

Bridger's nimble fingers slid over the chip in his sword, his eyes wandering to the ring Vega hadn't taken off since her last life.

"Why did you start wearing it again?" He finally asked the question he'd been wondering since he'd noticed it on Earth the first time.

Vega didn't answer right away. She wasn't sure why she felt an attachment to the ring again. Maybe it was as simple as the ring being one of the most gorgeous pieces of jewelry Vega had ever seen... or because throwing it in the Sea of Ros hadn't made her stop loving him like she'd hoped it would.

They sank into the tree line unnoticed before Vega spoke. "It feels right." There was no other way to describe it.

"Why do you still use a broken sword? You can rebond to something new." Vega was genuinely curious to hear his answer. A ring made from the chip in a sword was one thing, but a chipped sword was against the army's regulations.

Fortis-born warriors had special connections to weapons forged by a metallurgist in Ardor, bonding their powers and increasing their strength when using them.

Khort had a sword.

Arlet had a double edged blade known as a swallow.

And Vega had her dagger.

It was all thanks to their bond with Bridger.

"It's chipped, not broken." He defended the sword in his grasp, the blackness of the blade twinkling in the low evening sun like her ring did. "Getting rid of the sword would have felt like officially going back on the promise I made when I gave you the ring."

We are so fucked.

When they reached the small village a few minutes later, they both naturally quieted to focus on their surroundings.

At the end of the row of small homes, there was a cottage with a broken window and a front door hanging on for dear life by a single hinge—but it at least had two working showers. The rest of the homes in the neighborhood had been checked through, ravaged for whatever could be used inside the caves.

Vega wiggled her boot under the crack in the door and yanked it open.

Bridger had to duck under a corner of the ceiling that had caved in since the last time Vega was here a few days ago.

"There's no way this place still has running water," Bridger commented, looking around at the remains.

"Amazing, I know. The water pressure sucks, and it's painfully cold before you get used to it, but at least you get clean. No one's willing to be out in the open at the river, so this is what everyone's been using." The showers wouldn't hold up for much longer.

A patchwork couch sat against the back wall, making the place smell of damp mildew. The home sat in an alcove of trees off the main road, and despite the broken windows letting fresh air in, it got little to no breeze tucked in this tight.

"I've been so spoiled." Bridger looked out of place. Even in his donated clothing, he looked like he belonged somewhere else. Like a handsome actor playing a part in a movie he only got because of his good looks.

"Yeah, some have been living like this for a really, really long time." Vega followed his gaze to the children's toys in the corner—dolls, a fake tea set, some dried-up coloring markers.

Bridger looked away, but Vega could feel his heartache like it was her own.

"One of the bathrooms is this way." She changed the subject, directing him to the larger of the two. "It's kinda dark in this one. I think there's a..." She trailed off, checking under the sink for the old lamp with the rusted handle. It didn't have a wick or bulb—it was meant to be used by fire and light-wielders, using their abilities to create their own light source.

Vega learned pretty early on she could pop a small spark of lightning inside, and a glow of blue electricity would bounce around in there for a while before it flickered out.

The blue light danced against the glass, casting a new shadow every second from its constant movement.

She smiled at it, happy to see the simplest of things sometimes. Being stripped of all the menial things she'd once done without thinking stacked up.

"Remember the time we knocked over a lamp in a bathroom?" Bridger asked, sliding inside Vega's mind. *"It really ruined the moment."*

Vega looked up from the dancing lightning, and Bridger was leaning against the doorframe, watching her.

Ugh, if he doesn't stop with the leaning...

"You mean, when you got electrocuted for the first time and acted like a total baby about it?" Vega asked, batting her eyelashes a few extra times while feigning innocence. The whole time her mind wandered to what they'd been *doing* in that bathroom.

Or trying to do...

Bridger placed a hand over his heart. "Not all of us are a live wire with our own personal electric grid."

Vega's lips quirked to the side. "Wimp."

She felt boxed in the skinny bathroom with Bridger blocking the door. Something inside her flared with excitement while nerves fluttered her stomach.

The shadow chuffed happily from the pit like Vega had heard Khort do a million times.

Death. Us.

If Vega had paid closer attention...

Death suits you.

She would have understood sooner...

I think I'll let you have her.

He wasn't talking to Vega when he'd said that last part. He was talking to Death because it was already inside her.

It finally clicked.

I became my destiny. I became Death.

And Death belonged to him—he'd told Vega so.

A growl shook Vega's chest like it was her own. She heard her voice in her head like she'd thought the words again.

We belong to no one.

Vega saw her face pale in the mirror's reflection. *I'm never going to be alone inside my head again.*

Bridger read her like a book, pushing himself off the frame. "What's going on with you?" Vega felt the heat from his body as he slowly crossed the room to her.

Vega slid past, turning to face him on the other side of the open door. She ignored his question. "I'll be on the other end of the house. Take your time." Her boots squeaked against the damp linoleum as she fled Bridger's hungry stare.

She felt it too. The *need*. The *want*. The *ache*.

It felt as if she couldn't control it. Like if she didn't act on it while in the same room, she might combust.

Not being alone inside her mind started to wear on Vega. She couldn't escape Death's presence... It lived inside her now. There was no Vega without Death.

She closed the bathroom door—a little too hard—locked it, and fled to grip the sides of the pedestal sink. She stared at herself in the mirror, gulping down a few deep breaths while focusing on the other abilities inside her.

Her electric pulse sizzled against her skin, and the wind outside the broken window acted as her own personal breeze.

Vega allowed her original powers the opportunity to ground her, lowering her pulse. *"How do I block them out?"* she asked Bridger.

The idea of anyone accidentally seeing her naked because she couldn't keep them out had Vega reaching to Bridger for help.

His chuckle made her shiver. *"It's the same idea as shutting the door connecting us, but it's from the shield around your mind instead. You get that from me, by the way."* His voice sounded proud, and she could hear the smile on his face.

Vega closed her eyes, standing in the middle of the room—listening, feeling.

"Can you feel the shield's veil? It's usually on the outside of your actual power."

She breathed through her layers, bypassing the hum of her electricity, the thunder of her storms, and skipped over the pit like it didn't exist... and on the very outside was a thin sheet fluttering against it all. *"Got it,"* she told Bridger.

"Good." The word felt like a purr. *"Now grab the edges and wrap it around your mind."*

Vega thought of it like making a bed, struggling to find all the corners before it shot back one way and she was left trapped in the middle.

She got frustrated and stomped her foot like a toddler—no, she wasn't proud of it, but Vega had never liked when she couldn't immediately perfect something.

"I heard that." Bridger reminded her she wasn't actually alone in the small house.

"Fuck off." Vega snagged the edges again and wrapped them

around each other, tying them together like a sack. When she opened her eyes, she felt the veil of privacy.

She was alone.

Not even Death could reach her.

Vega slid down the wall and sat in silence for a while before turning the shower on.

33

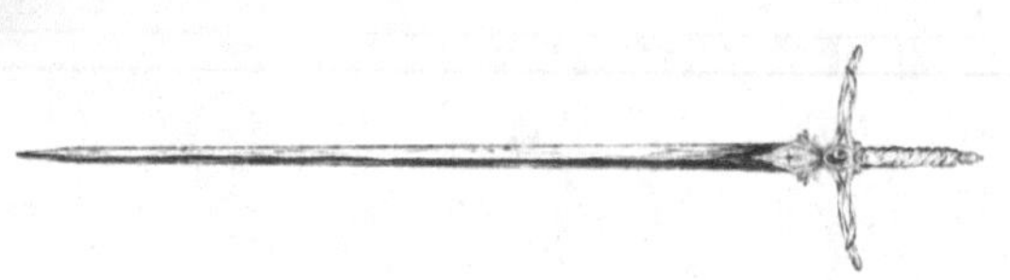

THE PATHWAY WAS BLOCKED, AND BRIDGER SMILED TO HIMSELF, knowing Vega was enjoying the peace of having a mind and body to herself for the first time since being back home.

He wished he could enjoy a moment of peace, but he hadn't been able to rest for a single moment since Vega told him about the deal she'd made.

She wasn't telling the whole story.

He could tell in the way she avoided his questions, could see the fear in her eyes when she thought about getting everyone to Vincere as quickly as possible. He could feel the panic in her voice as she screamed down their bond when she was supposed to be sleeping.

Vega told him she promised to deliver her sister and the gods to Death for the power to save Tolevarre, and Romulus revealed who'd spoken to Bridger in the portal to Earth.

The people of Tolevarre might not be well versed in the intricacies of death, but Bridger, before he was the commander of their realm, was the son of a commander, and the Dimicos knew more about it than any other bloodline.

Bridger's life had revolved around death.

Learning about death.

Avoiding death.

Protecting from death.

Causing death.

Falling in love with a girl destined for death.

Bridger knew Death.

He'd prayed to her, begged her to take him on his darkest days when the loneliness got to be too much.

Somehow, over time, Death became synonymous with the god of the underworld and the dead. Before Tolevarre existed, when the gods walked among men, Mors was the personification of death, and she wasn't considered a goddess—but a servant to the god of the underworld.

The two weren't one being. It wasn't Death who made deals. It wasn't Pluto who controlled deaths.

Bridger would bet almost anything Pluto had chosen Vega as his modern-day Mors—his bringer of death.

It was the only way she could deliver souls to the underworld.

Vega could lie and tell half-truths to the others, but she couldn't lie to Bridger. He'd been there with her. He'd heard everything Romulus revealed... and even some of what he hadn't.

Pluto was alive, and for whatever reason, he wanted Vega.

Bridger stripped out of his shirt, folding it neatly on the counter. He propped his foot on the edge of the tub and began undoing the laces of his boots.

A loud *pop* rattled the walls, followed by Vega's scream.

Bridger was across the small house with his sword in seconds. He couldn't reach her internally or see what was happening thanks to his fucking shielding lesson!

The locked door didn't stop him. Bridger pulled it off its hinges to get to Vega.

Vega... who stood in the middle of the room in nothing but her underwear, covered in rust-colored water, her hands protecting her face as she fumbled with the now busted pipe exposed in the wall.

She made the tiniest yelps of protest as she fought with the faucet. "Fuck, fuck, fuck." Vega couldn't get it to turn off.

Bridger reached over her shoulder and twisted the handle. The water eventually stopped shooting out like a missile, trickling down the wall in a slow stream.

Her shoulders sagged, and she took a loud breath. "Vincere is sounding sweeter by the second."

Bridger leaned against the wall, letting the panic subside, knowing Vega was fine and he'd freaked out over nothing.

She finally turned around to look at him, and he didn't miss the heavy-lidded stare she raked down his body, taking her time over the cut of muscle between his hips. Her eyes landed on his sword in a death grip, focusing on the veins popping in his forearm.

The tip of his sword scraped against the old flooring. "I couldn't see. I couldn't get to you. I didn't know what was happening." He chuckled at himself for overreacting. Scanning her for any real injuries, Bridger watched water droplets smear stains down her skin. Her lacy white underwear was speckled orange, but the set was mismatched, and the black bra would survive the incident.

Vega licked her lips and locked eyes with Bridger.

His skin felt like it was on fire.

"Don't look at me like that," he told her with little to no conviction. Her heavy stare burned him, making it hard to concentrate on anything other than the craving he had for her—he'd never be able to rid himself of Vega again.

"Like what?" she asked breathily.

"Like you want me to stop being a gentleman and fucking devour you already." Even to his own ears, Bridger's voice had a low gravel anyone would recognize as lust.

Vega squeezed her thighs together, immediately catching

Bridger's attention. His mouth watered at the dirty thoughts filling his head.

Vega's legs spread open. My head between them.

He swallowed the saliva pooling in his mouth, forcing his stubborn eyes to pull away from the spot between Vega's thighs. She fucking whimpered when their eyes met again, trembling under nothing but his gaze.

It was over.

Bridger closed the gap between them, the sound of his sword clattering to the floor second to the pounding heartbeat in his ears.

They crashed together in a kiss that made everything around them vanish.

Vega breathed a faint sigh as Bridger hoisted her up, her bare legs wrapping around his waist. Her arms rested on his shoulders as her hands instinctively fingered through the hair at the nape of his neck, sending a violent chill down his spine.

"*Vega…*" he moaned, never removing his mouth from hers.

The whisper of her name down the bond turned Vega into putty in Bridger's hands. Her head fell back, and she writhed like she might come right that very second. Vega's nails dug into his shoulders, eyes fluttering closed. "*Do it again.*"

Bridger grabbed the back of her neck and yanked her forward, pulling her back to his lips while he stalked out of the tiny bathroom. "*My Vega,*" he whispered.

"Oh my gods," she moaned hard against his lips.

He dropped one arm to the worn dining room table, clearing the odds and ends off in one quick sweep and rested Vega on its edge. Vega's legs stayed wrapped around his body, keeping Bridger close.

He gripped her neck underneath the chin, tipping her head back to return his undivided attention to kissing Vega like they had forty years to make up for in one day.

Vega's hands flew to the button on his pants.

Bridger grabbed both wrists with his free hand and pulled his lips from hers.

Vega's eyes shot open.

With his hand around her throat and wrists wrapped in a strong grip, Vega was at his mercy. A smile tugged at the corners of his mouth a second before he snatched her arms over her head and pinned her against the table. Bridger leaned over, crowding her space as he let go of her throat and slid to cup her jaw.

Vega rolled her hips, legs still open wide, and rubbed her pussy against the erection Bridger had become increasingly aware of. Her need for him was visible in her bleary, lust-ridden gaze.

Bridger got drunk off her reaction.

He'd always lost his mind and every bit of control he had watching Vega in bed. Bridger did feel sorry for the rest of the universe and all the others in between, because they'd never get to see Vega look at them the way she looked at him now.

Pinned down and not fighting his hold, Bridger watched her hips roll without breaking the eye contact she knew he wanted.

"You fucking gorgeous, *gorgeous* goddess." He cooed, watching her quiver with need.

"Bridger, please. Please. Fuck m—"

He slammed his shield in place, not allowing her to finish that sentence.

No. He'd give in if he heard her beg. Bridger wanted to stay in control. He wanted to watch Vega sink into the euphoria of her pleasure. "You don't get to fuck me this time, baby." His deep voice vibrated against his chest. "But I promise to make you come until you can't think straight."

The noise that erupted from her lips was a mixture of disappointment and need. "Let me in," she begged, wiggling against Bridger's hold.

Their pathway had once been foggy and hard to find. It'd felt like Bridger was searching for a door in a room full of other doors—

guessing until he found the right one, but now there was only one left. It was open, inviting Bridger inside. *"You want back in?"* Bridger gripped her wrists tighter, his fingers digging into her pulse point. Vega could get him off if she really wanted with a single zap of her lightning. She had electricity at her core—and everyone knew she would use it.

She was happy right where she was.

"Yes," Vega whimpered, popping her bottom lip out. "How are you doing that?" she groaned through gritted teeth.

If the door was open, Vega should be able to reach him, but not if he had a shield in place. Nothing could reach him then, and if she hadn't let hers slip somewhere in between the bathroom and now, Bridger wouldn't be able to get in either. *"You don't feel whole, do you?"* he asked, leaning down to run his palm up her torso, leaving warm kisses in its wake. He pulled the cups of her bra down, her nipples already hard from excitement.

"No." Her words were breathier every time she spoke. Her blatant need for him was enough to keep him on his current path.

He brought his teeth down on Vega's nipple, his tongue flicking out to roll around the bud. Vega stared down her body at him as best she could with her arms still pinned. *"I'll let you in under one condition."*

"Fuck, Bridger, what?" Her voice had grown desperate.

"Put that shield back in place. We don't need the others seeing what I'm about to do to you." Bridger snuck behind her eyes and watched himself sink lower and lower down her torso, the taste of rust not enough of a deterrent to stop him from sucking on the delicate skin around her hips until he left his mark.

Inside Vega's head was a dangerous place to be when she wanted him so desperately.

"Shit," she cursed, tying her shield back together and tossing Bridger out of her head on the first try.

One day she'd know how to tell each individual shield apart, picking and choosing who she let in and when. Shielding was hard work—it took the best warriors years to perfect, but Vega caught on quick.

"Good girl." Bridger cupped the other breast in his free hand, pinching her nipple lightly between his fingers. He finally let go of her hands above her head, but only to grab her by the hips and drag her ass to the end of the table. He sank down on one knee between her spread legs.

It wasn't a tall table, and on his knee, Bridger had the perfect vantage point to dive into what would undeniably be the best meal of his life.

Vega stared down at him, resting on her elbows when Bridger slid his shield up and let only her in.

"I hate how much I need you," she admitted immediately.

"Hate all you want. You're still begging me to fuck you." Bridger nipped the inside of her thigh, slipping two fingers underneath the band of her rust-speckled panties. "But I won't. Not until you tell me what you gave him."

The look on Vega's face made Bridger chuckle. The confusion, the anger, the deception. "I... I don't know what you're talking about..." Her body fought against the opposing emotions trying to pull her in different directions. It didn't know whether to tremble under Bridger's touch or go stiff at his words.

Did she really think he couldn't tell when she was lying?

"Liar." Bridger rumbled. "But don't worry. I'll figure it out." He was afraid he already knew...

Vega leaned her hips to the side as he stripped her bare and discarded the thin lace material to the floor like trash. The new position covered the view Bridger had been dying to see, her hips and legs resting to one side.

Bridger grabbed Vega by her bent knees. "Don't be shy now, baby. Let me see that pretty pussy." He pulled her legs apart, and his head literally rolled back at the sight. *"Fuck."* He hardly recognized what the lust had turned his voice into.

He raised his head, both his hands trailing down the inside of Vega's thighs at the same goosebump-raising speed. He wanted to savor this, to enjoy his time between the legs of the most beautiful woman he'd ever known.

"My mouth is watering at the memory of how good you taste." Bridger pressed a kiss on each side of Vega's very inner thighs, his thumbs meeting between her lips, parting her open. He blew a short breath over her clit.

Vega bucked her hips. *"Bridger."* The moan was like music inside Bridger's head—his very own symphony.

His name in that tone did him in.

Bridger had never needed her more—had never needed *anyone* more.

He ran his tongue from hole to clit, lapping up the sweet taste of her arousal. He hummed low in his throat, listening to every little peep and moan Vega made.

Bridger circled her clit with his tongue, pressing his index finger inside her tight entrance. While he worked his tongue in perfected flicks, Bridger pushed in as far as he could, rotating his hand up to reach the soft spot he knew would instantly make Vega shake.

Vega gasped, the muscles of her stomach clenching as he gently massaged her g-spot and wrapped his mouth around her clit and sucked.

Bridger had always loved pleasuring women. Before Vega had come along, he'd had a reputation as a bit of a ladies man... and everyone expected him to go back to who he'd been when he returned from the rebels. But he never had, and while he hadn't been celibate, the sex had always felt like it was missing something —someone.

Vega.

He'd been missing Vega.

The sounds she made. The way her body rolled when a wave of pleasure rushed through. The heat from her lightning simmering beneath her skin. All of it.

Vega got squirmy the closer she got to her climax, forcing Bridger to loop his free arm through her leg and around her hip—he held her down and slipped another finger inside.

Two fingers was already a tight fit. His cock bobbed with the memory of her pussy pulsing around him. *"Gods, you're gripping me so tight."*

"Imagine what your cock would feel like wrapped up inside my sopping wet cu—"

Bridger replaced his mouth with his thumb over Vega's clit, pressing tight circles as he crashed his mouth against hers, trapping the rest of her sentence inside.

His fingers pressing in with more force stopped Vega from forming a coherent thought, allowing Bridger to refocus on the point he was trying to make here. He pulled away from their kiss, continuing to work Vega's clit with his thumb, fingers pumping in and out.

He locked his eyes on her brilliant blues and felt his smile crook to one side. "I'll fuck you if you tell me the truth about what you did."

Vega's eyes fluttered to the back of her head. "I..." Bridger could tell she was trying to keep her eye contact, fighting against the high of her approaching orgasm to form the right words.

"Exactly. Now shut up and let me hear you scream my name." Bridger kissed his way back down Vega's torso and put his mouth around her clit again, savoring the taste of her on his tongue.

Her hips bucked, but Bridger kept his hold, smiling against her when he knew she wasn't going to last much longer. He'd once taken pride in how fast he'd been able to make Vega come... and it seemed

Bridger still had what it took to send her over the edge without having to try.

"That's it, baby." He kept his fingers buried deep, rolling his tongue over her clit.

Vega's walls clasped around his fingers, and Bridger watched from between her thighs as she tumbled into oblivion.

Her eyes rolled back, and the fucking noise that came out of her mouth—*Gods, please let that be the last thing I ever hear.*

"Bridg..." Vega wiggled, unable to finish his name, trying to free herself from the steadfast hold he had on her as he continued to work her through the tremors of an aftershock.

"I'm not done," he mumbled against her oversensitive bud. "Give me another."

Beads of sweat formed on Vega's forehead, her eyebrows pulling together. "I-I can-can't."

Bridger's throaty chuckle against her mound earned him another melodious whimper. He backed away from her long enough to pull his fingers out and swirl his tongue around them. "You say that a lot for someone who's been known to give me what, eight, nine in one night?" Bridger kissed her inner thigh. "One more is all I'm asking for. I know you won't be content without another. One's never enough for you, baby. We both know it."

Bridger didn't wait for her to argue because there was nothing to argue about. Vega was going to come again.

End of story.

He lowered onto his other knee and spread her legs open as wide as they'd go, butterflying her on the table like she was a buffet for one.

He groaned a tortured sound, sliding two fingers inside just to watch her pussy clamp around them. Bridger fingered her slowly, taking his time like he'd wanted.

She panted by the time he removed his fingers and sank back

between her legs again, using nothing but his mouth to bring her to the next release Bridger planned on lapping up like a starved fucking animal.

Vega dragged Bridger's hand up her torso, popping the two fingers he'd just pulled out of her inside her warm mouth. Her tongue slid in between his index and middle finger, cleaning her own mess off Bridger's fingers.

He felt like he was fighting for his fucking life, pushing away the thought of her tongue on his rock-hard cock pressing uncomfortably against his zipper.

She deep throated his fingers, gagging.

Fuck, I'm done for. He took his gaze off Vega's mouth, sliding his fingers out. They trailed down her chin, neck, chest, between the valley of her perky tits...

He watched his fingers instead of Vega. It was no secret Bridger loved eye contact. In fact, he demanded it most of the time, because there was nothing better than seeing the woman he was worshipping come undone for him—but this wasn't just any woman.

There wasn't anyone on this planet, in their realm or any other for that matter, who could wind Bridger up this tight.

"Look at me." It was Vega who demanded eye contact this time, earning a low growl of approval from Bridger.

He locked eyes with her, and that was when Bridger saw it.

His future.

He'd spend the rest of his immortal existence making up for his wrongdoings if it meant she'd look at him like that forever. It reminded him of the night he'd promised to follow her to the underworld.

Love.

It had been so long since Bridger had felt loved.

"Yes, yes. Fuck." Her mouth opened, soft moans caressing the inside of Bridger's brain, and her direct eye contact almost brought him to the edge.

Vega reaching her second orgasm was the distraction he needed. Her body shuddered underneath him as she threw her head back and broke the connection that had him thinking of a future for the first time since... well, since he'd met her.

Bridger licked her slit from opening to clit again, taking as much of her release as he could. "Fuck, Vega." She jerked as he wiped the cum dripping towards the table with an open palm, leaning back on his heels as his hand glistened with her latest orgasm. "You're a mess." He licked from the inside of his wrist to the tip of the fingers that had pressed against the back of Vega's throat moments ago.

She didn't sit up immediately, and Bridger was a-okay with that, because it meant he got to watch her tits bounce while she slowed her breathing. Her dark brown hair cascaded over her shoulders, no braids to hold the different layers back.

"That was..." Vega rasped. "Jesus Christ, Bridger."

"Who?" he asked in confusion.

Her laugh was light and breathy. It sent goosebumps down Bridger's arms. She sat up, thighs meeting in the middle as she leaned forward and situated her breasts back inside her bra.

Bridger was smitten, staring at her from the floor.

"You look good on your knees," Vega teased, winking as she slid off the edge of the table.

He watched every single fucking move she made, eyes drinking her in. It only took her a single step to stand directly in front of him. Bridger's hands were like a magnet to Vega. He ran them up her soft legs, her skin so much smoother than his war-trained hands. His eyes hadn't met hers yet—he was too distracted by Vega's glistening inner thighs. He licked his lower lip, biting down hard enough to remind him she'd spoken.

"The view's really great down here too." He finally flicked his gaze to Vega's. She cupped her hand under his chin, guiding him to his feet.

Bridger stood, towering over her again, and placed his hands on either side of Vega's face, trying to get inside her head and see every thought.

"We're so fucked," she said what Bridger was thinking.

Bridger couldn't help himself. As if under a spell, he brought his face down to Vega's and pressed his lips to hers in a delicate kiss, his hands still cupping the sides of her face.

It wasn't a kiss with the underlying expectation of wanting more. It was a kiss that made the air around them feel scalding hot, like warmth was seeping back into Bridger's life after years locked outside in the cold.

He could stay here forever, in this moment with Vega until the rest of the world fell away.

And she seemed content to stay with him too.

For now. It felt like someone else's voice warning him.

The patter of a set of light footsteps triggered Bridger's senses. He pulled away from their kiss, and Vega groaned in protest, blissfully unaware of the company who'd slipped in without them noticing.

He blocked Vega's nearly naked body from the red-and-black fox frozen in the middle of the room with Bridger's bonded dagger gripped between its teeth. It garbled a growl and fled for the front door.

"Hey!" Bridger yelled, scooping Vega's underwear off the floor and passing it to her.

She tugged them on quickly, and as soon as she was no longer naked, he took off after the fox. Bridger's bonded sword flew through the home, finding his outstretched hand by its bond to his power.

He checked over his shoulder before he blew through the front door to find Vega already stepping into her pants.

The fox didn't look back, flinging dirt once it was out in the open. It did its best to get away, but Bridger was too fast, snatching it up by the scruff of its neck.

His bonded blade clattered to the cobblestone below as the red fox screamed for help—he didn't have to speak to animals to recognize the cry.

Bridger held the too large sword against the animal's throat, but Vega came out ready to defend—as usual. "Bridger, no! It's a bonded animal!"

Bonded animals were similar to Bridger's bonded weapons, only alive. And depending on how deep the soul connection was, if a bonded animal died, so would their person.

"No, please! Don't kill her." A woman who could be anywhere from twenty to over a hundred, with hair the same color as the fox's deep red chest, came crashing out of the shadows with her hands up, approaching slowly. "Please."

"Grab your blade and put her down," Vega told him.

The fox wriggled in Bridger's unrelenting grasp, doing what it could to sink its claws or teeth in him.

"Tilie, calm down. It's okay," the girl ensured her bonded pet, taking small steps towards Vega and Bridger.

Bridger extended his sword to Vega. She took it, and as if she'd lost no time at all with weaponry too big for her body, Vega sliced through the air, holding the girl at the tip of the blade. "Don't come any closer."

Bridger watched her throat bob. "I promise we mean no harm." Her hands stayed up, and she let her eyes rove from the sword at her neck. "I didn't know it was you two. Only that two people were in there, distracted, and they might have food or weapons." She shrugged her shoulders apologetically.

The fox continued to thrash. Bridger scooped his dagger up and plopped the feral animal on the ground—maybe a little harder than he should have.

She snapped at Bridger once but scurried quickly to hide behind the redhead. She weaved through her ankles before sitting between her parted feet like she'd done it a million times before. Her thick tail flicked as she watched Bridger. "Tilie says she's sorry."

With the way the fox hissed, Bridger knew she was lying.

"Who are you?" Vega asked.

"I'm Octavia. Tav. This is Ottilie. Tilie." She nodded down to the red fox. "And I was sent by the leader of Demuto. I need to talk to Khort."

34

"WHO THE FUCK IS SHE?" BRIDGER ASKED AS THEY WATCHED Octavia and her fox's hips sway in sync.

Vega carried the bow and arrows Octavia had strapped to her back. They looked well-loved, and so did her dark leather clothing. She reminded Vega of Robin Hood, if Robin Hood were a girl and Little John were a ten-pound fox.

"I don't know, but the leader of Demuto? She's obviously Solum-born. What do you know about Demuto?" Vega braided a few pieces of her hair as they walked, doing what she could to make it seem like she'd actually showered and hadn't spent the last half-hour letting Bridger eat her out on a kitchen table.

"That it's basically No Man's Land. Shifters can go in, but they can't come out... and anyone else stupid enough to enter is usually never seen again." Bridger raised a brow. *"Except for you."*

She'd spent an entire night alone in Demuto after she stabbed Bridger through the heart, traveling for hours to get to the Vates border where she knew Khort would be waiting. Vega shivered at the memory of the cruravis hunting her through the early morning until it got bored.

Bridger made Octavia lead the way, giving her instructions only when necessary.

"I can't believe it's true you're back with the rebels." Octavia kept talking, even though Bridger had made it clear he wasn't answering any questions.

Anytime she talked, Bridger would poke her in the back with his sword—which earned a stern look from Vega and an internal scolding.

"What part of 'walk silently' do you not understand?" Bridger asked, his aggravation hard to miss.

Vega elbowed Bridger in the side, hardly fazing him.

"How long have you been in Demuto?" Vega decided to try to get any piece of information out of her before they got back to the caves.

"We don't even know if anything she says is true," Bridger pointed out.

"Oh, so you're the one deciding who to trust now?" Vega snapped, slamming her door closed. She wasn't going to deal with him right now—not when someone was potentially willing to talk about what was going on in Demuto.

They'd lost contact with them too long ago to fuck this up.

"No offense, but I'm not ready to spill all my secrets yet. I'll explain when we get to Khort." Tilie climbed up a tree ahead, scampering down the limb to land gracefully on Octavia's shoulder. Her beady black eyes glowered whenever they caught Bridger's.

Vega could relate.

As if Arlet had been waiting for their return, she came sprinting from the cave's mouth when they approached nearly ten minutes later. "Hi. Khort found out about your Vincere announcement. Incoming in three, two..." Arlet never made it to one.

"Since when are you the one to have the final say in what goes on around here?" Khort stormed out of the cave, headed straight for Vega.

"Watch yourself, Fera." Bridger's voice boomed like thunder as he blocked Khort's path.

His eyes turned to slits when they landed on Bridger. "I bet it was you, huh? Getting inside Vega's head, telling her everything she's wanted to hear for the last forty years."

Arlet and Vega shared a look that didn't need words. *Oh boy.*

Bridger chuckled as Khort crowded his personal space. "Ah yes, my evil plan is working. Fuck Vega one last time just to see how she tas—"

Khort swung, but his fist never made contact with Bridger's nose like intended. Bridger shielded himself, and Khort's fist slammed into the impenetrable force field.

Vega heard a couple bones crack, but Khort didn't seem to notice.

Bridger continued, apparently hell-bent on finishing his thought. "Tastes. To see how she tastes before screwing you all over."

Vega flung the door open between their minds.

"Is that all it took to get you to let me back in? Too easy, Kitten," Bridger purred, sending an inappropriately timed shiver down her spine.

Khort huffed a breath of steam. "You fucking—"

"Stop." Vega growled the word, her anger scattering down the bond to the others. "Enough of this shit." She slipped her way in between the two angry gods.

Vega's hands pressed into both Bridger and Khort's chests, shoving them away from each other with an encouraging zap from her lightning—not enough to hurt, just enough to warn them. "How do we expect people, *our people*, to fight for us when we act like this in front of them?"

Khort's eyes returned to normal, no longer seconds from shifting, but his chest rose and fell heavily as he swallowed down his anger.

Bridger breathed like nothing had even happened. Slow,

controlled. It was what made him a great warrior—he was calm under pressure.

Khort wasn't built for control.

"We cannot trust him, Vega," Khort said through clenched teeth.

Arlet sighed, grabbing Khort by the wrist and tugging him back. She must have seen the same glimmer of excitement in Bridger's eyes Vega saw.

They didn't need to fight, and Bridger was always ready for one.

"Listen to yourself." Vega let her hand fall off Bridger's chest. "Look who's watching." She nodded to the gathering crowd growing, more bodies emerging from the cave. "Innocent people are suffering. His soldiers have chosen to fight for what's right." Vega locked eyes with Bridger the same moment a sliver of something sweet slipped down their bond. Vega turned back to Khort. "Beside us."

"And how do you know he's not playing you? That this isn't exactly what his plan has been from the start?" Khort eyed Vega. "To get you to feed him information, just like he told Marlena he was going to. What if this is a trap?"

Of course Vega had wondered about all of those things too. She'd be stupid not to. But one thing she did see that Khort couldn't was the hurt inside Bridger—the emptiness he felt by being away from the very duty he was born for.

Bridger wouldn't sit around in limbo for much longer. Vega could feel his patience wearing thin, no matter how well he hid it.

"This has nothing to do with my and Bridger's relationship. Past, present, or future. Don't you see that? I'm not making decisions based on whether a man loves me or not. I'm making decisions, *hard decisions,* to forgive, to move forward, to do what's best for our world." Vega wished he could see that. "You don't have to forget everything he's done to agree that having him here, with us, is our best chance of saving as many lives as we can. Khort, he's built the strongest, most lethal army this world has ever seen. These people..." Vega motioned to the men and women still in their nice training suits. "They trust him. They might not be here because they want the same things as us—she pointed to herself, Arlet, and Khort—"but they trust Bridger. They trust their commander to make those decisions for them."

She could sense a wave of calmness wash over Khort as he inhaled and exhaled large, shaky breaths. "Going to Vincere means being outnumbered if this goes badly."

If this goes badly... meaning if Bridger does backstab us.

"I'd like to point out that while yes, you would be outnumbered, you'd also have a place for your people to live as humans, not animals."

Tilie gabbled, and Bridger, to Vega's surprise, responded to her. "No offense... to the animals." Bridger had never been a wildlife kind of guy. He barely liked riding horses when forced. "Successful wars are won when you're prepared. When your people are rested and fed, not hiding and waiting for the next fucked-up thing to happen." He shrugged, unbothered by his brashness. "Our odds of losing are still high if we don't level up this blended army, even with Vega's new ability."

The shield around the pit rattled with a muffled roar, like Death heard Bridger talking about it. Its screeching was unlike anything she'd ever heard, making her vision shake.

Death sliced its razor claws into the fabric of her shield, tearing a shred into ribbons. It went back for another slash, but Vega acted quickly.

She shot a zap of lightning through her mind. A bolt collided with Death's shadow, losing its dragon shape as it skittered back, diving for the safety of the dark pit.

Death. Us.

Was Vega really Death? Or was she just filled with it?

It felt like a separate entity and a new piece of her soul at the same time. It wasn't wholly Vega, and yet she couldn't hide anything from it.

"We were doing fine until you and your army destroyed Castra." Khort's eyes turned to slits again.

This could get ugly very fast.

Bridger shook his head. "That wasn't my army. That was Marlena. All by herself. She killed those people, and she will continue to kill people until she's stopped. She knows she can't kill us."

Arlet shushed him, but Bridger rolled his eyes. "Has keeping secrets gotten us anywhere? Tolevarre already knows. The army knows. What are you trying to accomplish by hiding the truth from the rebellion? They're going to find out one way or another we're gods. They might as well hear it from us."

Murmurs of surprise and disbelief washed over the gathered crowd.

"Gods?" a voice gasped.

"How long have they known?" another echoed from behind.

"How are any of you surprised?"

"Is it true?"

The questions got louder and more aggravated the longer they went unanswered.

Vega turned to them, her face serious as she streamlined all the questions together. "Yes, gods. We survived a successful summoning too. We confirmed it's true in my last life. This changes nothing for our cause." Her rapid-fire answers calmed the crowd... for now.

"She can't kill us, but she will kill our people. Do not forget who we're dealing with here." Bridger spoke directly to Arlet—as if she could ever forget. Bridger returned his attention to Khort. "I don't care if you don't trust me, and I certainly don't care if you like me or not, Khort. I never will, but I do care about winning this war."

Khort, despite his statue-like posture, nodded once at Bridger. He didn't need to speak for everyone to know he agreed.

"And that is how a rebellion becomes a revolution."

Fuck. Octavia. Vega had completely forgotten about her.

Everyone's attention drew to her, and Khort finally took notice of the newcomer. "Who the fuck are you?"

Octavia didn't shy away, earning some respect from Vega. It wasn't every day someone stared into the eyes of a man on the verge of transforming into an angry, fire-breathing dragon and didn't take a step back. "Sorry, I didn't want to interrupt. I've been trapped in Demuto with shifters for too long. What have we missed?"

Khort went fucking *white* at the mention of Demuto. "What did you say?"

Octavia cocked her head. "Did she mention anything about him being hard of hearing?" she whispered to Tilie, balancing across her shoulders.

Khort rushed Octavia, and Tilie went flying off in defense. She somehow caught the fox midair, nearly toppling out of her arms before she pulled Tilie against her chest.

"Demuto. You said you've been trapped in Demuto."

Octavia took a step back, putting enough space between her and Khort so Tilie couldn't grab a chunk of his arm. "Oh yeah, well. As you can see." She struggled to keep hold of the wiggling fox. "Not a shifter, so..." She chuckled as Tilie broke free and took guard behind her, making sounds Vega didn't even know how to describe. "I get to come and go as I please."

Everyone gawked. When was the last time any of them had heard of someone coming and going from Demuto?

Octavia's eyes trailed over the long row of ogling faces. "Oof, tough crowd. Okay, let's start over. Since these two stole my thunder." She shot her thumb in Vega and Bridger's direction. Octavia's shit-eating grin reminded her of someone... but who?

Who the fuck is this girl?

Vega watched as Arlet sized her up from head to toe, doing an awful job hiding the smile pulling the corners of her lips.

She cleared her throat, and Tilie sat in between her feet like she'd done earlier. "I'm Octavia. This is Ottilie. Tav and Tilie." It wasn't common for bonded animals to allow their full name to be spoken to others, and Tilie had allowed Octavia to do it twice now. It was a huge sign of Tilie's trust in her. "I came here for Khort because the leader of Demuto, or rather, what's left of Demuto, would like to talk to you."

Everything went eerily silent, and a rumble from the south shook the trees, birds scattering from their branches. A bright light lit up the dark sky, and something similar to thunder rolled their way.

It looked exactly like the light shining through the redwoods from the portal. The birds scattering added to the vision in Vega's mind—at least this time she wasn't bent over in pain.

"*A storm?*" Bridger asked, eyes fixed on the horizon until the very last bird disappeared.

The hair on Vega's arm stood like it would if a natural storm approached. But she knew immediately it wasn't the welcome sensation of a brewing storm by the cold tendrils of a silent warning creeping through her veins. "*No...*" she replied with unease.

Octavia's sigh shook with nerves, her shoulders rolling forward. "It wasn't supposed to happen yet. I should have had more time..."

The bonded stared at her, sharing the same hesitancy to speak—afraid of what she was going to say next.

Octavia's face gave away how nervous she actually was. "I was sent to warn you. Demuto is accepting a deal with Marlena to break the curse on the land and its people. In return they have to vow a blood oath to Marlena, pledging their loyalty to her during the upcoming war." Octavia nodded to Bridger. "Seems she's worried about her numbers. More worried than she made herself seem if she's days ahead of schedule. On my way here, I heard whispers that a large number of your soldiers were seen returning to Vincere after Meyer left for Fortis."

Vega's brow furrowed, and Bridger didn't let Octavia finish.

"If Marlena knows people stayed behind at Vincere..." Bridger's words died in his throat as Arlet's dragon swooped overhead.

Dread washed over Bridger, and his complexion noticeably paled. *"She's going to kill them."* Bridger's realization rolled Vega's stomach. *"Marlena's adding the shifters to her ranks to get ahead, not even."* His voice trailed off. *"I need... I have to be there to defend Vincere. I should already be there."*

Vega tasted bile as she swallowed. The look in Bridger's eyes was one she'd only seen from him once before. The last time Vega had seen it, Marlena was driving a dagger through her heart for the first time. "You're with us?" she asked Bridger out loud, losing her connection to him through the fogginess of her mind.

"I'm with you." He placed a hard emphasis on the "you."

People burst into action, soldiers from both sides running into the caves to grab weapons and reemerging to wait for their orders. Arlet's dragon landed on top of the cave's mouth and bellowed, her claws digging into the rock.

It didn't matter what was happening around them. For a split second, it felt like just the two of them again. Vega dipped her head in a quick nod, finding the fuzzy pathway again. *"Go."*

Trust me, he'd begged her when they'd returned home. She had a million reasons not to, but at one time she could have given two million reasons why he was the only person she *could* trust.

Bridger took a step forward, grabbing Vega's chin between his thumb and forefinger, cocking her head back to search her face with his dark eyes—for what? Vega wasn't sure, but he wet his lips, and the most unexpected thing happened. Her six-foot-five ex-boyfriend turned enemy to ally to... whatever the fuck he was now leaned down and placed a gentle kiss on her lips for everyone to see.

Bridger pulled away slowly, treating Vega like a wild animal who might spook. "Be careful. I'll see you soon." His fingers fell from her chin, and by the time Vega blinked, Bridger was already halfway to the tree line.

"Stop him!" Khort roared, his voice a mixture of beast and man.

"He needs to get to Vincere!" Lightning erupted from a low-hanging cloud, stopping two rebels from chasing after Bridger. "He has people—*we* have people there who need protection. It's not just the rebels anymore." She couldn't believe she was about to say this, but... "We have to trust him. He deserves to be trusted."

"Do you? Trust him?" Arlet asked, glancing at her massive brown dragon tracking Bridger from above.

What a loaded fucking question.

It wasn't one Vega felt she could answer with a "yes" or "no" response.

She never got the chance to answer anyway.

"I hate to break this up... Seems important, but we really, really need to go. We need to meet my—" Octavia cleared her throat over the start of someone's name, slipping up.

No one else seemed to notice the mistake. Vega had, and now she was more eager than ever to return to Demuto.

"I was told if something happened early to get to the meeting spot as soon as I could." Octavia looked at the bow and arrows still slung over Vega's shoulder. "I have a twenty-year-old sister who's been sheltered by the elders her entire life. She doesn't need to see whatever's about to happen to our people."

A sister's love...

Vega pulled Octavia's weapon over her head and offered it back. "You lead. We'll follow."

35

AFTER VEGA'S SUGGESTION TO LOAD THE FEW PEOPLE THEY were taking up onto the backs of Khort's and Arlet's dragons got shot down in a sea of resounding no's, they tacked up the few horses people from Solum brought when they'd been chased out of their home, and doubled up.

Vega and Arlet cozied up together while Khort flew overhead, keeping watch from the skies.

Vega finally got all her questions answered about Arlet's dragon, Speravi, known to others as Avi. Her full name was Latin for "I have hoped." A fitting name Arlet picked when she was nothing more than a mirage.

"I learned about halfway through your last life I could manifest her. At first, Khort and I thought it was just an illusion like everything else. It didn't take long to realize she was so much more." Their horse slowed to a lazy walk through some thick brush, following close behind Octavia, who refused to ride with anyone for the sake of Tilie.

"She's had a personality and a voice of her own from the

moment she first appeared inside my mind, like I created her separately from myself, but I could still control if she was there or not. It was like projecting her, but her home was nestled inside my power somewhere... but when you broke the curse, that piece of me broke and I'd been in so much pain, all I could think about was dying and taking her life too. So I pushed her out, giving her whatever chance to live she might have without me." Avi swooped down from the clouds, flying level with Khort.

"Can you and Khort talk through her?" Vega asked as they ducked under a low hanging branch.

"Only when Khort's in dragon form. Avi channels his voice to me and then sends my thoughts back. It's so weird." Arlet laughed, leaning back in the surprisingly large saddle when they cleared through the thick brush.

"Is it like a doorway? That's what it feels like with me and Bridger."

She felt Arlet's body bob with a shrug against her back. "Ours is more like a long tunnel. I'm on one end, Khort at the other, and Avi relays the messages." Their different bonds were intricate in ways Vega hated not understanding. "How is that, by the way? Not getting a break from Bridger seems like... a lot."

Vega focused on that bond, on the connection to Bridger cemented inside her in a way she never thought she'd be comfortable with... and she fucking sighed in contentment at the feel of him on the other end.

Thankfully, their horse followed Octavia's, giving Vega nothing else to focus on other than her response. "It kinda feels like coming home." She chuckled at how silly it sounded out loud. "I can't believe I didn't realize it sooner. There were a couple times where I remember thinking, 'Hmm, that's weird. I didn't say that out loud,' And then when I heard him begging me to come back after I'd stopped my heart."

Arlet chuckled like Vega had told a funny joke. "He definitely wasn't begging for you to come back. The second your body disappeared he—oh." It hit Arlet then. "He was begging you to come back *inside*."

Vega nodded, letting silence wash over them. Without the sound of their voices, the horses crunching fallen leaves beneath their hooves became the soundtrack to the start of Vega's spiral.

"You and Bridger then?" Arlet asked, pulling Vega up from the whirlpool of what-ifs threatening to drag her under.

"I'm not sure yet," she replied. She wasn't ready to answer that question.

Arlet wrapped her arms around Vega's midsection and squeezed. "I trust you know what you're doing even if it doesn't feel easy."

Vega let one hand go from the reins, holding on to Arlet's wrist in a backwards hug. "I don't deserve you." The girls held the hug for longer than normal, their breaths syncing and hearts thudding in time. "I won't forget what he's done. I know better than to let myself lose pieces of what we've gone through... but he had to do it. There's no telling what would have happened had he not taken control of the army." She squeezed Arlet's hand, three quick pumps, and let her hand fall back to the loose reins. "I don't expect you to trust him. I mean, I'm learning to do it all over again. All I'm asking is that you give him a chance."

"For you? Anything." There was a pause, and then Vega practically felt the twisted grin Arlet wore. "But you better make that motherfucker grovel."

Vega laughed, liking the happy sound. "Oh, don't you worry. He's not off the hook yet."

The rest of the ride went by fast, their horses happy for a break when they reached the edge of Demuto. Lake Vehemens roared angrily, bringing back the memory of the last time Vega had been on the edge of this lake—she'd told Bridger she didn't care if he died.

Guilt made her reach out. *"Made it to the border of Demuto and Pax. You getting close?"* Vega asked, sliding off the saddle after Arlet.

"I stole a military vehicle when I crossed into Ardor. It's a quiet night here," he shot back immediately.

"Is it really stealing if it's a vehicle from your own army?"

Bridger had gone alone, leaving his soldiers to assist in returning to Demuto and behind in the caves to watch over the children and elderly who couldn't defend themselves if something happened.

She didn't expect him to respond, so when he did... Vega actually choked on nothing but the saliva in her mouth.

"The quiet has given me plenty of time to play around in everyone's head. Khort hasn't been doing anything fun, which I guess is good since he's keeping watch..."

Playing around in everyone's head? No.

Vega was going to kill him.

"But Arlet? Well, Arlet Videri has been in a position most men, myself included, would love to find themselves in. Riding you from behind, having conversations about the future. Me and you." He drew out the last word. *"You and me."*

Vega slammed the door shut, rattling the walls of her own mind as Khort landed on human feet, shifting from his dragon to the perfect landing.

She didn't keep the door closed for long, afraid of what might happen if he couldn't get to her if he needed. Vega grumbled under her breath at the sound of Bridger's belly laugh cutting through the closed door.

It was slightly unsettling how her need to have access to him at all times had become somewhat of a lifeline.

Vega had spent a lot of time feeling alone.

It was nice to know she wasn't anymore.

"Why are we stopping outside Demuto?" Khort asked, coming up on Octavia with urgency.

Tilie went for his ankles.

Khort made the right decision, stopping to give them both their space.

"This is where I was told to meet," Octavia answered matter-of-factly. "Tilie will make contact and let them know we're here."

Khort huffed. "That's a waste of time when I can get there faster in the skies."

Octavia rolled her eyes, landing on Arlet and Vega. "Is he always like this?"

"Yes," the girls answered in unison.

The look on Khort's face made Vega feel like a bit of a traitor. She shrugged, smiled, and said, "It's the truth."

Octavia rolled her shoulders with a triumphant smile. "I know you're eager. Demuto was once your home, but no offense... you currently have no connection to it, nor have you stepped foot inside its boundaries for what, fifty-five years? Fifty-four? It was before I was born, and that's all one big history lesson the children of Demuto missed out on." Octavia fluttered her fingers toward the direction of Demuto. "Ya know, cause no schools. Everyone is killing themselves or going crazy." She grimaced.

Vega wondered what all she'd seen in her lifetime.

"Our leader doesn't want anyone crossing over, especially not when no one has any idea what this curse being broken is going to look like. It's their job to protect the shifters. It's my job to adhere to their orders." She motioned to her fox already disappearing into the trees of Demuto. "Tilie knows what she's doing."

After Vega and Arlet got Khort to relax, as much as Khort could relax, at least... Vega figured a good distraction would be teaching him and Arlet how to shield their minds for privacy.

Leo and Octavia sat next to each other on the other end of the fire he'd started with the three level ten soldiers standing in a group of their own, not allowing their guards down.

They'd definitely been trained by Bridger.

"Okay, so you feel that sheet, cover, whatever thin fabric you wanna call it?" Vega asked.

Khort and Arlet held their eyes shut tight. Arlet scrunched so hard the creases of her face wrinkled like she was a hundred years older than she actually was.

But they'd never age again.

Arlet nodded.

Khort concentrated too hard to do anything more than grunt.

"Good, now grab it." Vega wasn't as good as Bridger was in explaining this.

"Grab it, how?" Arlet asked, letting her concentration go when she popped her eyes open.

Khort followed suit, throwing his arm over the log he sat in front of. Octavia used it as a bench, thoroughly engrossed in what the three were doing. Her mouth opened and then closed. She tapped her lips with her finger and then opened her mouth again. "Fuck, I don't even know where to start. It's not often I'm at a loss for words." She laughed, her eyes bouncing over them. "You three—four being gods is going to rattle the shifters. Especially you." Octavia nodded to Khort.

Khort looked up from the flames and stared into Octavia's green eyes for a few silent heartbeats before cocking his head and asking, "Who are you?" He shook his head, correcting his question. "I mean, who's the shifter bloodline you descend from?"

Khort was meant to rule Demuto one day. He had once known everything there was to know about his home territory.

Octavia looked like she had been put under a spotlight, tensing at his question. "Um." She paused. "I'm not really sure. My mom doesn't talk about the past much, and she doesn't shift either. I've never even seen her in her shifter form, and I'm fifty-one." Another pause. "Sometimes they don't know if they'll come back out if they do."

She was lying... at least about part of it.

Vega glowered, wishing she could see through to exactly what she was hiding.

"While I'm not a shifter, my mom and sister are... or Nora will be. She's showing signs and can't leave Demuto but hasn't manifested anything yet. The few children who've been born over the last half-century aren't encouraged to shift or lean into their power like they once were. The longer they can avoid it, the better."

Khort took on a pale shade of green, and his throat bobbed like he was fighting off spewing the contents of his stomach in front of the group.

Keeping a shifter from its true form had once been use as a torture tactic against the people of Demuto—it was the fastest way to make someone go crazy.

"You're the fox saved rebels talk about, aren't you?" Leo interjected, cocking his head to the side.

"The fox?" Vega asked, her eyebrows pinning together.

Octavia stiffened, shaking her head slowly.

"Oh, come on, "Leo huffed. "I knew it the second I saw you. About twelve years ago, shortly after I escaped from the mines, I joined a group of rebels outside the border of Demuto in Pax. We lived in the woods. One night, a group of soldiers found us while we were sleeping. By the time I woke up, the others had been killed. I was weak and hadn't built my strength back yet." Leo paused, clearing his throat. His eyes were fixed on the fire before shooting over to the redhead.

She was beautiful in a way that felt effortless. Her dark brown cloak made the warm tone of her skin stand out in the fire's light. Freckles splattered her face, thicker around her cheeks and the bridge of her nose. Her complexion didn't look as if she'd spent years hiding inside the dense forests of Demuto.

"You and Tilie saved me that night." Leo paused, giving Octavia the opportunity to explain.

She didn't.

"If you hadn't killed them, I'd be dead." It seemed Octavia might argue against his claim until he raised a brow and challenged her. "I might have been beaten senseless and back on the verge of death, but I could never forget your face... or that fox."

Everyone stared at her, no longer concerned with anything else they'd been doing or talking about prior.

Leo held up an index finger. "And before you say you're not the only person with a fox as a companion, I'm over 100 years old and I've never seen a fox like yours."

Tilie stood out with her deep red and midnight black coat. She wasn't the standard red fox people were accustomed to seeing.

Octavia groaned. "Ugh, okay, fine." She sat up from her relaxed position and criss-crossed her legs. "The shifters obviously haven't been able to leave, but I can. You get bored, growing up in a place without many other kids."

Vega could feel the tightness in Khort's chest. She wanted to give him a big hug—but what once felt normal didn't anymore.

Boundaries. How had it taken her so long to realize what she'd been doing to Khort?

Gods, too many emotions right now.

Arlet grabbed his hand instead, scooting closer to him. She winked at Vega, who smiled knowingly.

"I did what any kid looking to escape would do. I snuck out and then eventually bugged my father until he caved and let me go with him on his trips to Solum. It became routine for me to be his sidekick. My dad was a rebel. From day one." She smiled to herself, a glassiness coating her eyes.

Vega knew that look... Her dad was dead.

"When he got killed, I kept contact with his people in Solum. Sometimes it's the only way my family and our group have any food. The winters in Demuto are rough, as you all know, and food is scarce when shifters are stuck in their forms and ravaging anything they can get their paws on." Octavia didn't have trouble looking people in the eyes when she talked. The confidence she had in herself and the words she spoke could be a dangerous combination. "I find myself in many situations where I want to jump in and join the fight, but I can't. I have a family and people I care about to keep alive. I do what I can."

The sun began to rise, slowly brightening the sky. "When I'm on trips, I come across fights where rebels are outnumbered and they'll surely die if someone doesn't step in. I attack from the shadows where Tilie and I like to stay. If I don't get too close, don't let myself be seen, even by those I save, then I can keep doing it." Octavia bit her lip. "I guess I haven't been as discreet as I thought." She puffed a faint laugh, but her face fell in the blink of an eye, and she whipped her head to the tree line.

Her connection to Tilie...

Octavia jumped to her feet at the sound of ruffling leaves, abandoning her bow when a man with no clothes wandered out. Everyone stared, not because the man was naked, but because he trembled with wide eyes, looking lost—like he was seeing the world for the first time.

She stripped from her cloak and wrapped it around his shoulders at the same moment he stepped out of Demuto and into Pax. He crumpled to the ground and cried out, tears smearing the dirt on his cheeks.

"Poe," Arlet said, voice fading into a wisp. "He was one of Marlena's guards in Amora."

Before.

Everyone stood, making sure not to crowd. Poe must have been back in his human form for the first time in what surely felt like an eternity for him.

"I almost forgot what you looked like under all that fur." She smiled so wide, tears welled in her eyes.

Khort pulled a pack off the back of a horse and rummaged

through to find a blanket Poe could wrap around his waist. "Let's get you warm."

Poe nodded a thanks, his hands shaking too much to take the blanket from Khort's extended hand.

Octavia slipped it around his waist, tucking the corner in tight before she helped him to a seated position by the fire.

Distracted by Poe, no one noticed the second figure step out of Demuto's confines. The movement of her long coat caught Vega's attention, eyes landing on a young woman with dark curly hair and eyes the same color as Octavia's... the same color as Khort's. The same as...

No.

Dots connected.

Tilie trotted beside the girl, looking comfortable in her presence.

Octavia followed Vega's gaze before anyone else noticed her staring. "Oh gods, Nora." Vega could feel her relief as she ran to her sister and wrapped her arms around her. "You're okay," she stated instead of asking.

Vega glanced at her friends, who both wore the same uneasy expression.

"She came in the middle of the night. Got Mom out of bed and said it was time," Nora said, looking up with her big green eyes the few inches Octavia had on her.

"Did she see you? Gods, tell me she didn't see you." Octavia shared the same wide-eyed look as Poe.

Nora shook her head. "No, no. She didn't. Marlena told Mom she only had a few hours to get her shifters up to speed on the newest plans. The kids are hiding in the basement of the old school."

When Vega glanced at Khort, he seemed to be fitting puzzle pieces together as he stared at the girls.

"Octavia, who's Demuto's lea—" he started to ask, but the words caught in his throat, and he went white like he'd seen a ghost.

"Mom." Octavia sighed with relief.

Vega followed Khort's stunned stare to the newest person crossing the Demuto border. She felt like she was floating. Her neck snapped to what—no, *who* had stunned Khort into silence.

There's no fucking way.

The ghost smiled, her pretty deep red hair the same color as Octavia's. Or rather, Octavia's hair was the same color as hers...

Not a ghost.

"That would be me."

36

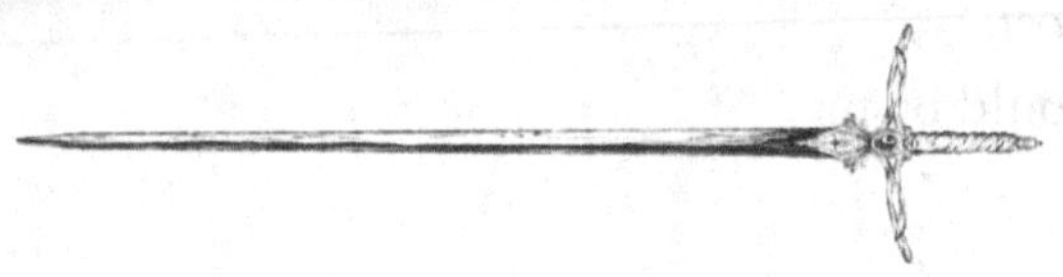

Ardor had been quiet.

Silent.

Bridger should have known something was wrong. The territory known for its fire had always been the rowdy type.

Smeared across the wall in blood at the entrance of Vincere was a message for Bridger.

> Their blood is on your hands.
> Welcome back to the rebellion, Commander.

Marlena signed with a heart.

Bridger's knees buckled, collapsing to the floor as silent grief seized his body. Blood seeped through the thin material of his pants to the skin at his knees—it was still warm.

Lifting his hands, Bridger rubbed his fingers over his thumbs. The blood wasn't tacky yet.

He'd almost made it in time.

He'd done this.

He'd sentenced them to death.

He could have saved them.

He should have been here to save them.

Why would they come back? I should have been here. I should have been here to protect them.

Not between Vega's legs...

Bridger let out a pained cry that rocked all of Vincere.

The what-ifs ran rampant. He'd been tasked by the gods to keep his people safe. It was the oath he'd taken as the commander of Tolevarre... and look at what he'd let happen.

At the sake of doing what he knew was right, he had sentenced nearly a thousand of Tolevarre's best soldiers to their untimely death.

Whose body was he going to find when he looked through the carnage?

Bridger stood on wobbly legs, feeling like his body wasn't his own.

Bodies of his soldiers littered the common room, the mess hall, and training pits. People lay in their beds, with varying stages of awareness on their faces.

Some must have tried to flee, lying on the floor close to their beds. Many's eyes were wide open, probably waking just before their slaughter.

The bodies were still warm. Bridger had missed the massacre by no more than a half hour.

Trailing down the hall to his room, Bridger swung the door open and peeked inside. Nothing was out of place.

When he reached Meyer's door, Bridger had to pause, fighting against the roll of his stomach. He swallowed down the bile crawling up his throat and twisted the knob, toeing it open.

Meyer's room was untouched.

Bridger dropped to the chair by the door, hiding his head in his hands. "Meyer's alive," he said out loud, even though he knew it might not be true.

Meyer was in danger, regardless. Hopefully he knew it and had time to get out of Marlena's warpath.

She would stop at nothing and no one. Killing the bonded wasn't possible—but she'd kill everyone else to prove a point, leaving no one but the five gods alive.

Bridger checked every room, searching for anyone who might have survived.

Marlena left no one. She probably did it one by one, making the others watch.

Bridger was the only heartbeat left in Vincere.

He physically hurt, aching for the lives lost. These were the feelings he'd learned to block out when he first left Vega—the pain he felt every single day knowing what he'd done to the only girl he'd ever loved...

He would never be able to hide behind the man he'd pretended to be again. His shield would never be strong enough to push her out twice.

Bridger's heightened senses caught the sound of boot steps coming from overhead. He jumped from the seat in Meyer's room and sprinted down the hall to the stairwell. He took the steps two at a time and flung the door leading to the next level open.

The door stopped short, slamming into someone, followed by an unmistakable deep groan of pain.

"Owww," Halo whined, rubbing the fast forming bump on his forehead.

Seeing a living person felt like he'd been pulled from the undertow of furious waters.

"Halo, thank fucking gods." Bridger let out a breath and pulled the young man into an unexpected hug. He stood only a few inches shorter than Bridger but was significantly smaller in stature.

Halo went rigid, patting Bridger on the back awkwardly.

Bridger tensed and backed away. "Did you just pat me on the back?"

Halo nodded, swallowing hard. "Yes. I-you caught me off guard. You don't *hug* people!"

Bridger cleared his throat and flexed his fists at his side. "I've had a hand in training every single soldier who calls Vincere home, and now they're all dead. Excuse me for being relieved to find someone I care about alive."

"Who's all dead?" He asked softly, peeking around Bridger's shoulder like he'd be able to see through the walls.

Bridger's relief didn't last long, suspicion taking its place at Halo's response. "What are you doing here, Halo?" He gripped the hilt of the dagger sheathed on his thigh.

Halo noted Bridger's hand placement, having the sense to look nervous. "I was one of the many who stayed behind when Meyer gave us the option. He said Vincere was yours and anyone who didn't want to fight beside you was to leave and head to Fortis with him. They've been gone for a few days now..."

All of Vincere was Bridger's. Every single slaughtered soldier had chosen to fight with Bridger and had been killed for it.

Marlena eliminated the rebellion's forces—all by herself.

"Why weren't you here during the attack?" Bridger pressed.

He liked Halo, saw a piece of himself—the unwanted kid he'd once been—inside him, but that didn't mean he couldn't betray Bridger.

Betrayal could come from anyone. Bridger knew that better than most.

Halo didn't hesitate to answer. "I've been out looking for you. When Meyer said you'd decided to stay with the rebels, he wouldn't tell me where you were. Everyone thought it was okay to return since it'd been a few days..." He wasn't stumbling over his words like he did when he was nervous or lying. "Is it true? You're with the rebels?" he asked, his eyes void of any distinct emotion.

"I'm with Vega."

Vega.

"Fuck!" He finally realized his shields were up. They'd been up this whole time.

Halo jumped, reaching for a dagger strapped to his side. "What?!"

Bridger ignored him, opening his shields. *"Vega..."* He stood locked in place, waiting to hear her reply. *"I..."* He started to apologize. *"They're all dead."*

He started to panic as the seconds ticked by without a response. *"Vega,"* he said with an urgent plea.

The door was open and unlocked. She should be able to hear him, should be able to respond.

"Are you okay?" Halo asked, taking a step towards Bridger.

"Yes, no. I don't know. Vega and I can talk to each other... *internally*." Because what other way was he supposed to explain it? "She's not responding."

He reached for her again, this time attempting to slip behind her eyes to see where she was—to see if she was okay.

The door was open, but her mental shields were locked tight. Why? What was she trying to keep out? "Shit. She's at the border of Demuto and Pax right now, meeting with their leader."

"Demuto has a... leader?" Halo asked, stunned.

Before he could get Halo up to speed, Bridger felt the shift in the room's temperature, his spine going stiff in warning.

He spun around to find Marlena leaning against the wall only a few feet away, inspecting her nails. She was covered in blood, dressed like Bridger hadn't seen her in years. Her curves were hugged by the well-fitting material of Tolevarre's best fighting gear, daggers lining every holster on her chest and a sword strapped to her back.

"You and Vega are telepathic. Fascinating," she hummed, sounding sincerely interested. "Tell her I said hello, would you?" Marlena fluttered her fingers in a delicate wave and pushed herself off the wall.

Bridger said nothing, glaring while fantasizing about all the ways he should be able to kill her.

"Cat got your—" She held her finger up, chuckling to herself. "Sorry, *Kitten* got your tongue?" Marlena acted as if she might choke on the nickname. "You betray me and then have nothing to say for yourself?" Faking a sigh, she took another step towards Bridger. "At least I let you dig your own grave years ago. When the time comes, I'll bury you in here with the people you let die."

"Do you like hearing yourself speak? Is that it?" His tone held no humor—this wasn't the normal joking, ready-to-get-under-Marlena's-skin type of question Bridger was usually a fan of.

Marlena's eye twitched at his response, forcing Bridger's mouth to tick into a small smile.

"Bridger, De—"

The sound of Vega's voice flooded Bridger's body with relief. *"Marlena's here,"* he cut her off.

"Get out of there," she pleaded. The desperation in her voice almost made him listen, but he wouldn't run from Marlena. Never again.

"She can't hurt me. I need a minute," he told Vega.

"I take it you didn't like my handiwork?" Marlena faked a deep pout. "I told Meyer to handle this for me, but apparently he's too busy dealing with defectors fleeing Fortis." She eyed him. "You've caused quite the uproar."

More soldiers were coming, meaning Marlena's numbers continued to drop.

"When will you stop killing people?" Bridger spat.

"Never." She smiled a real fucking smile—one he remembered seeing her do when they were young, when she might have actually been happy. "I will continue to wipe this world clean of the people who defy me."

"What happens when you have no one left to kill?" he questioned.

Marlena's lips puckered, and she looked to the ceiling. As if she had to contemplate at all... "I guess I'll have to find a new world to destroy."

Halo stayed behind Bridger, which is exactly where he wanted him—as far from Marlena as he could be.

"You should know by now I won't stop until all of you are dead." Marlena shrugged. "It's a shame you chose to join them, Bridger. After everything you've worked for." She motioned to the hall they stood in. "You're just going to give it all up for Vega."

"Death doesn't scare me, and neither do you," he told her honestly.

A laugh bubbled from the pit of Marlena's stomach. "Of course not, but you're weak enough to let the death of others affect you. I'll make sure it's you who watches them die before I give you the satisfaction of following them to the underworld."

"I'll see you down there," he preened with a rotten smile.

Marlena took a step back and looked around at the blood-splattered walls, inhaling the smell of death more noticeable by the minute. "Your betrayal caught me off guard, I'll admit. But what doesn't surprise me is that you are here... leaving the others to fend for themselves against my newest curse."

Bridger hid his confusion, digging in deeper to throw her off. "They do say practice makes perfect, and from what I've seen, you need it. I don't think you're as strong a cursemaker as you'd like to think." He faked a wince, as if he'd told a good friend he hated the outfit they wore.

"I was young and acted on a whim." It wasn't often anyone heard Marlena admit to being wrong. "I hadn't expected Vega to retaliate with a summoning of her own. That was a mistake I'll have to live with for the rest of my immortal life." Marlena disappeared and reappeared with a knife to Bridger's throat. He didn't move. "I didn't make a mistake with the curse on Demuto."

Halo flinched forward, readying to draw the dagger at his side.

"Don't fucking move, Halo," Bridger warned, deciding not to take any chances by throwing a shield around him. It kept him in and Marlena out.

The blade bit into his skin, blood trickling down his neck in a warm stream. "Blood oaths aren't curses."

Marlena leaned in close to Bridger's ear, speaking loud enough for only him to hear. "Let me let you in on a little secret... The shifters didn't take a blood oath. That was just the lie I told them." She leaned back, meeting his eyes. "I repurposed the power of the curse on Demuto, using the blood of the Fera line to extend its reach to every descendent of the goddess Diana. Vega stole my power to shift, and that's okay, because every single shifter is now mine to control. Whenever and however I want."

"Vega, get out of there. It's a trap," Bridger blurted.

"Wh-what?" she stuttered. *"We can't leave y—"*

There was no time for Vega to argue. Bridger interrupted her again. *"Marlena is coming, Vega! She is coming and she lied about the blood oath. It's a curse. She cursed the shifters. Get. Out. Of. There!"*

Marlena dropped the dagger from Bridger's throat. "Halo, it's not too late to come with me, my sweet boy. It'd be a shame to lose a power like yours." Her eyes twinkled with promise. "I'll give you everything you've ever dreamed of and more." Marlena held out her hand for him to take.

Halo recoiled. "I'd rather die."

Bridger breathed a sigh of relief. He'd been right about Halo—there was good in him.

"That can be arranged," Marlena said before taking a step and disappearing, slipping through the cracks of Tolevarre. Once the rising puff of smoke was gone, the carnage she'd left behind was the only proof she'd been there at all.

37

EVERYTHING ALWAYS HAPPENED TOO FAST.

Bridger was telling Vega to run, but she couldn't. Everyone was stunned into stillness, staring at the face of a girl, now a woman, they never expected to see again.

"Hi, Khort." Tears streamed down her face, her jaw quivering.

Silence followed her greeting, everyone waiting for Khort to breathe. To move. To speak. To *anything*.

Vega scanned the group, and they all shared the same bewildered look.

"Delori..." Khort whispered her name like a breath.

Delori was alive.

And she had daughters.

Silence fell again. The breeze even paused its rustling through the trees.

"*Delori is alive.*" She'd been trying to tell Bridger before, but everything was happening stacked on top of each other.

Marlena killed all of Vincere.

She cursed the shifters.

"*What?*" Bridger's shock amplified her own.

He knew Delori from before... and then he'd been with the rebels when her last correspondence arrived.

Delori started to reach her hand across the space like she could touch Khort from a distance, but her hand fell, and she hesitated. She looked so much like Olenor, their mother—it felt like Vega had stepped into the past. "It's okay," she reassured, giving him the opportunity to make the first move.

That freed Khort from his trance. He stumbled forward and collided with his sister seconds later. She folded into his hug, engulfed by Khort's desperate embrace.

"She's the leader of Demuto." Vega finally remembered to respond to Bridger.

Khort believed his only sibling had taken her own life fifty-one years ago... and now here she was. *Alive.*

"Halo's here. I'll be there soon." The bond went cold as Bridger slipped out of her mind.

"H-how? Why? You're alive." Khort sounded like he'd been woken up from a deep sleep and forced to have a full conversation.

"I know. I'm sorry. I have so much to tell you, so much to explain, but I did what I needed to do. I did what *you* would have done if Demuto needed you." Delori pulled away and flashed a smile to Vega and Arlet. "Quick." She crooked two fingers at them.

Arlet didn't hesitate a single second, tears rolling down both their cheeks.

Vega stepped up next, wrapping Delori tight. They were close to the same height, Vega's mouth resting near her ear during their hug. "I'm proud of you."

Someone had to tell her.

"Thank you." Delori squeezed her tighter, pulling back to look Vega in the eyes. "I'm so happy you're here."

Vega held her tears back, shoving her heart behind a wall. Marlena would be here any minute. She had to keep her head on straight. "Me too." The words tasted like the lie they were.

"You've met Octavia. My eldest," Delori said, wiping at her tear-stained cheeks. "And this is Nora," she added, motioning to the younger sister sticking close to Octavia's side. "My youngest daughter. Your nieces." Delori looked back to Khort, reaching out to touch his cheek. "Gods, you're handsome. Haven't changed a bit except for this beard." She pulled at the end gently. "I'm not sure how much time we're going to get for me to explain, so let me start by telling you how much I love you. How much I've missed you." Delori patted his cheek and let her hand fall to her side. "When I sent my last message, I was nine months pregnant. I had Octavia three days later."

Khort lost a breath, shut his eyes, and wagged his head slowly. "Del."

"Dad was dead. We'd just lost Mom. I knew if I told you I was pregnant, if I continued to let you believe I was alive, you would have eventually done something stupid—like get yourself trapped in Demuto with me."

Khort narrowed his eyes. "You shouldn't have been alone. I should have—"

Delori interrupted. "You were meant to be right where you've been this entire time. The rebellion needed you." Delori rested her hand on Khort's forearm. "And I wasn't alone. I had the girls' father. I was the last Fera in Demuto. I had to put the pieces together and hold them there, with or without glue, whether I wanted to or not."

Vega knew their time was running out. She felt the wind picking up, the rush of it through her fingers awakening Death. It roared, the sound echoing up the abyss and rattling the shield Vega was trying to hold in place.

Her focus was pulled in too many directions.

Bridger.

Delori.

The shield.

Death clawed closer and closer.

"I really hate to be the bearer of bad news..." Everyone unwillingly dragged their eyes away from Khort and Delori. "But I think our time is up. Marlena wiped out every soldier in Vincere. Bridger found them already dead." Arlet's hand shot to her mouth, and she gasped. "It's not a blood oath. Marlena curs—"

The air beside her chilled, and every person who'd arrived with Vega unsheathed their weapons. Leo's flame whipped around above their heads with the wind Marlena rode in on.

Vega couldn't hold Death back anymore. It tore through her shields and slammed to the front of her mind. Her vision blurred black around the edges, and Death bared its teeth while her finger tips turned inky with its power releasing back inside Vega's bloodstream.

She shivered involuntarily.

Message received.

We have a job to do.

"You two really can talk to each other." Marlena tucked a strand of hair behind her ear, awestruck.

Vega faced Marlena. "Makes it kind of hard to lie about what you're doing, doesn't it?" she asked, catching Octavia ducking into the woods with her sister in tow.

"When have I ever lied about what I'm doing, Vega?" Marlena cocked her head like a striking snake. "I may have withheld the truth, but I've never once outwardly lied. We're not bringing up the past again, are we?"

Vega didn't move. "All you've done my entire life is erase the things that matter most. Of course it's time to bring up the past."

Death slid up her arms, darkening the visible veins. Her electricity skittered, chasing it back down as if to tell it to wait.

Vega wasn't ready.

She stared at her sister for the first time in what felt like forever, fully taking Marlena in. Against the black of the fight suit she wore, her perfectly straight blonde hair and the crystal blue eyes they shared popped. She'd been graced with an ethereal beauty anyone could fall for. The realization made Vega's chest tighten into a dull ache.

Not because her looks had been wasted, but because her sister could have been anyone she wanted, and she'd chosen *this*.

Vega was no longer blind to the part she played. There was so much she could have done to help her sister—so many red flags she overlooked because it had been normalized in their lives. Vega had spent too many nights thankful she wasn't the eldest child instead of fighting for what she knew was right.

Blaming herself wasn't going to get Vega anywhere, but there would always be a piece of her who wished she could go back and say something—to save Marlena from herself.

"You were a child." She'd thought the words were her own until the sensation of Bridger inside her mind told her otherwise. She hadn't even known she'd been sharing down the bond.

"How much of the past are you willing to bring up?" Marlena asked, her gaze tracking over Vega's shoulder to Arlet.

Vega stepped to the right, blocking Marlena's view. "Never enough to bring her into it." Her words took on a feral growl.

"Ah, she's finally spilled about how she fell in love with the villain, huh?" Marlena gloated, glowing with a radiant fake smile.

Vega took the attention off Arlet. "Tell the shifters what you've done." If she wanted to say she wasn't a liar, then it was time she told the truth upfront, not *withhold* it until she felt necessary.

"Straight to the point, I see." Marlena strode away from Vega, eyes landing on Delori and Khort.

Khort looked like he was still trying to thaw his mind from the shock of Delori, a step behind everyone else.

"Tell them what you've done," Vega urged harder this time.

"I taught Delori not to trust the first person to offer help... especially not the person who cursed her land to begin with." Marlena let out a *tsk* sound. "I'll admit I never cared enough to see who was keeping the people of Demuto in line. I can say it was a pleasant surprise to see Delori's face when I arrived." She jumped spaces, ending up beside Delori.

Khort put himself in between his sister and Marlena, growling like the wild dragon he was seconds from becoming. His pupils turned into those of a reptile, steam puffing through his nose. "You'll lose an arm if you lay a single finger on her."

Marlena smiled at Khort, batting her long lashes. "Would you have killed Ivelle had you known Delori was alive?" she asked, showing for a split second that Ivelle's death had hit something deep inside her.

Smoke billowed out Khort's mouth as he spoke. "I would have ripped her to shreds sooner had I known it would hurt whatever's left of your heart."

Marlena's smile turned haunted. "You can't hurt something someone doesn't have." The ground rumbled with her words, screams from behind Demuto's border echoing through the sky. "You want to know what I've done to the shifters?" Marlena asked, locking eyes with Vega. "I'll do you one better. I'll show you."

38

MARLENA NEVER MOVED, DIDN'T EVEN FUCKING BLINK. A scream shrill enough to break glass ripped from Delori's chest, startling everyone.

By the time Vega had a chance to turn around, Delori's red wings were shooting from her shoulder blades. People jumped out of the way, giving Delori enough room to shift without crushing them.

Within a breath, Delori was no longer the small redhead she'd been. In her place was a crimson dragon, somewhere in between Khort's and Avi's sizes. She stumbled on her legs, tripping over herself. Her wings rose, muscles flexing in a long overdue stretch.

Delori found her footing quickly. Her serpentine neck reared back, a piercing roar rattled Vega's eardrums. She lowered her head, eyeing the length of what would become their battlefield. Steam shot through her closed jaw, slipping through the spaces in her giant teeth.

Vega pulled from the damp air around Lake Vehemens to conjure up a quick storm. She'd never needed the spark from a storm to control her lightning; her electric current was alive somewhere deep inside her. Some rain would make the battlefield more difficult, bringing a slippery edge to the fight, and it would give Vega the upper hand with more control—putting more power in her hands.

As if I need any more...

Vega was no longer the lost twenty-year-old she'd been when this started.

People martyred her, seeing Vega as the hero... but heroes didn't really want the villain to die, did they? They wanted a happy ending where the villain changed—became a trusting individual who understood everything they'd done was wrong and learned from it.

Heroes wanted the villain to get redemption.

Vega wanted Marlena to die, and above all else, she wanted her to suffer—to feel every ounce of pain she'd caused the people who'd once loved her.

The Marlena Vega had loved was dead, and she didn't know when it was she'd actually lost her, couldn't go back to the exact moment she'd watched the real Marlena fade away completely. And for that, Vega would hold a shred of responsibility for the rest of her life. *For eternity.*

Marlena could have been saved.

But it was too late for that now.

Death clicked inside her head, sounding like an alien hiding in the shadows of a dragon.

Vega understood without words. *Where's Marlena?*

They lost sight of her in the commotion, but Vega knew she was around... Death could feel her.

Lightning bluer than the coldest ice cracked from the sky and scorched the ground in four points, shaping the clearing of trees in a rectangular box. Vega's electricity followed a direct path to her, hitting every corner, singeing the ground in its wake until it crawled up her legs and into her palms.

Avi's battle cry was unmistakable as she appeared out of thin air across the horizon, dipping down into the tree line with her bottom claws set to strike.

Screams of shifters as they were ripped apart faded behind the sound of Vega's growing thunderstorm.

Rain started to sprinkle from the clouds, giving everyone a fair warning of what was to come.

Khort stood nose to nose with Delori in her new form—a fire-breathing dragon who didn't have the same kind look in her eyes she'd had when she stared at her brother moments ago.

It wasn't the mother of two daughters or the leader of a territory that had been left to die. It was a starved dragon who'd been locked away without food for half a century.

Delori clacked her jaw together in warning, saliva dripping from the teeth longer than Khort's human leg. Khort didn't back away, his lips moving frantically. Vega couldn't hear him, but she didn't need to, knowing he was begging Delori to listen—to *see* him.

Delori stalked closer, and a screech from above might have saved Khort's pretty face from mutilation.

Avi grabbed Delori by the nape of her muscular neck, fighting to thrust her into the sky. Arlet's brown dragon was massive, but she still didn't touch the size of a dragon shifter.

Delori twisted out of her clutch, her loud jaws snapping at the spike on Avi's tail.

Khort bellowed, finally shifting into his dragon. Vega dodged his wings as he took off towards the morning sunrise, chasing after Avi and Delori so fast he was nothing but a black blur streaking across the sky.

"Behind you!" Bridger warned.

Poised for a fight, Vega spun with her bonded dagger in hand, coming face to face with the biggest grizzly bear she'd ever seen.

A shredded piece of Octavia's cloak wrapped around his neck from where she'd tied it for him by the fire. Poe had been forced back into his shifter form, losing whatever sanity he might have been holding onto.

"*Where the fuck are you, Dimico?*" Vega growled as she ducked Poe's first strike. Claws whizzed by her face, slicing through the air.

More shifters crawled out of Demuto, and Vega knew she could end them all with a single strike of lightning. Vega didn't see herself as the hero anymore, but that didn't mean she wanted to kill innocent shifters acting against their will.

What would it do to Khort if they killed the people he'd just gotten back?

"Here." Bridger's voice wasn't inside her head this time.

When Vega turned around, dodging another swipe of Poe's eight-inch claws, her breath caught in her throat.

There he was.

The commander of Tolevarre.

He was dressed in his classic black battle suit, the Dimico family's gold insignia, a shield with swords, over his heart. The wind from Vega's storm blew his hair out of place, bringing attention to the sharp line of his clenched jaw. His bonded sword twinkled like starlight as he brought it down—a blow meant to strike through Poe.

"No!" Vega summoned a gust of wind, his sword piercing the grassy terrain instead.

Poe barred his razor-edged teeth, the vacant look in his eyes the same as the one Delori had worn.

"They aren't in control of themselves," Vega warned. "We can't kill them!"

Death warmed her insides, as if to say, *I disagree*.

Bridger locked them in a shield a second before Poe charged. "Listen, I respect you and your sweet heart, but this is a real war now, Vega." He grabbed her cheeks in his calloused hands, the chilled metal from the pommel of his sword bringing her back to reality. "What are you fighting for?" His dark eyes bored into hers with an intensity she hadn't felt in this life or any of the others she'd had without him.

Death didn't reach for Bridger like it did anyone else. It rubbed against the inside of Vega's mind like it longed for his touch too.

"For a future worth living." The words fell from her lips before she could think of an answer.

"Then you have to be willing to kill for it. You don't win wars by letting everyone live." Bridger dropped his shield, and Vega watched as he drove his sword through Poe's chest. His body collapsed to the slick grass, returning to his human form.

Vega stared up at the sky, able to see clearly through her storm despite the intensifying rain. Lightning the same color as her own sputtered through the clouds.

Marlena was nowhere in sight, but the shifters kept coming, slinking out from the depths of a territory that'd been lost inside itself for too long. They didn't act on their own volition—they were now owned and operated by the same woman who'd left them to their own devices, punishing them for decisions out of their control.

"How many people from the caves are here with you?" Bridger asked, killing another shifter coming after them with a loose swing of his sword.

"Khort, Arlet, Leo, Octavia, and three of your soldiers," Vega answered quickly.

He took stock of the battlefield Vega boxed in. "Clear the battlefield. Get every single one of our people out of your markers."

Leo swung his axe at two approaching wolves, bouncing back as the smaller of the two lunged for him.

Arlet had a confused panther running in circles, fighting an opponent who wasn't there, while she undoubtedly debated on taking its life.

Vega's storm opened to a torrential downpour, drenching everything in a matter of seconds. Lightning crackled across the sky, splintering like broken glass.

This was Death's battlefield, and it wouldn't be satisfied until it got what it wanted.

"You." The word sounded like an exhaled breath, her fingertips going black from Death's touch.

I won't be satisfied until I get what I want. Death reminded Vega who she was—who *they* were.

What *did* she want? The question echoed in her mind like someone else asked it.

Death. It wasn't only Vega's voice who answered.

"No." She glanced up at Bridger, water dripping off the sharp but beautiful angles of his face. "Marlena's here. I'm not leaving."

"Where would you go anyway?" Marlena asked, appearing out of thin air. It was likely she'd been standing there the whole time. Blood ran down her face, smearing from the rain.

She looked every bit of the villain she'd made herself.

"The caves?" Marlena asked, eyes sharp as glass. "What makes you think they'll be safe for much longer?"

No, no, no.

"Halo took Octavia's sister back to the caves," Bridger said with worry evident in his tone.

Vega was so sick of being easy fucking pickings, feeling like she was always one step behind whatever Marlena was doing no matter how far ahead she might actually be. "What more do you want, Marlena?" she asked, hoping to get a real answer for once. "What more could you possibly want?"

Marlena pulled a couple daggers out of their sheaths across her chest, twirling them through her fingers. "I want what I have since the very beginning. To be the only god our world has to worship. I want the bonded"—she sneered at their donned title—"dead."

How ironic they wanted something similar.

Vega let Death creep up her arms, leaving the cavern of her mind and releasing itself into her bloodstream. It pumped through her heart with an out of time beat, catching Vega off guard when it stopped beating altogether.

An explosion of undiluted death ruptured in her chest, resetting her heart and putting what felt like blinders on Vega's focus.

One goal. She had one goal.

"Then kill me," Vega challenged, letting her wind reach out like an extension of her hand, snatching one of Marlena's daggers. It snapped back to Vega's open palm.

She could feel Bridger's slow inhales, could sense his eyes on her arms littered with what looked like black lightning tattooed on her skin. He took a shaky breath when Vega took a step closer to Marlena.

Her sister didn't budge as Vega reached out with the tip of the dagger, but the snarl on her lips grew when she trailed the knife featherlightly down Marlena's face where Vega's scar was.

She didn't press hard enough to break skin, only traced the exact lines Marlena had marked across her own eye and upper cheek. "Want to know a little secret, sister?" Vega palmed the dagger, quickly striking Marlena in the side. Taking her by surprise, she leaned in to where only Marlena would hear her over the roaring storm Vega kept alive above.

Marlena's face distorted in pain, but she didn't scream.

"You can't kill what's already dead." Vega pulled the dagger from Marlena's side, blood dripping slowly as the wound already began to heal itself.

It wasn't the knife wound that made Marlena lose a breath.

Without any more of a warning than her words, Vega dropped a cyclone from the sky.

It tore through the clearing, staying within the marked ground Vega had planned out before she'd realized why. It sucked up the wolves threatening to tear into Leo's throat, freeing him up for the next beast on his heels.

Khort and Delori flew overhead. Delori's jaws snapped around Khort's tail, spraying the field with fresh blood and a chest-rattling bellow of pain.

Green flames erupted from Marlena's palms. "What did you do?" Vega had expected Marlena to call her a liar, not question the reason behind her admission.

"Go. Get everyone out of here," Vega told Bridger, never taking her eyes off Marlena.

"I'm not leaving you." The strike of his sword through another shifter's chest was the period to his sentence.

"Bridger, I can handle this! I can't handle losing another person I care about. Get Leo, get your soldiers, and get back to the caves." Vega left no room for arguing, shutting their door to get her point across.

Vega snatched her tornado back inside the swirling clouds above to give Bridger a clear shot to Leo.

He hesitated, visibly fighting against what he wanted and what he knew he needed to do. Vega knew where Bridger needed to be right now. He seemed to understand she was exactly where she needed to be too. "Be careful," he begged before sprinting across the wet battlefield, leaving the Caelum sisters by themselves.

Vega continued their conversation smoothly, never missing a beat between the one happening inside her head with Bridger.

"I made a deal, and all it cost me was your soul and the gods inside you." Vega wasn't going to give Marlena any details worth knowing. What she planned to do with her wasn't one of the details she planned to keep secret. Vega wanted Marlena to know exactly what was in store for her. "I wasn't going to let the curse take one more fucking thing from me. No matter the cost." Lightning struck behind Vega, the electrical buzz fizzling out along the wet grass. "I wanted what I bartered for the night of my own summoning." Vega's smile was saccharine. "To avenge our people. To kill my sister."

"You don't have what it takes." Marlena laughed.

Vega wiggled her brows and her fingers, reaching out for Marlena's hand. "Bet on it?"

Marlena put more space between them, focusing on Vega's dark veins like they would jump out and bite her. "If I cut your hand off, would it regrow?" Flames licked at Marlena's feet. "If you touch me again, I'll take them both to see what happens."

Vega continued to offer Marlena her hand, lightning sizzling from her fingertips. "Take it. Let's find out." She couldn't see Death's shadow inside her mind anymore. It was no longer lying in wait. It was in her blood... and it was hungry.

Marlena pulled a dagger out with fast fingers and lunged.

Their parents had taught them the basics of hand-to-hand combat growing up. Their school in Aeris had battle skills, but no one took it seriously unless they hoped to join the military one day.

Vega dodged Marlena's attempt to connect with her side and continued to circle her. "I guess the handshake before a match is out."

It wasn't until Bridger came along that Marlena decided to push Vega and the others to spend extra time mastering the skill.

If only Vega knew then what she knew now.

Regardless of the motive, without the encouragement from Marlena, she never would have become the threat she was today.

Vega knew a good warrior was more than just physical strength. They had to be able to keep their wits about them the entire fight. From beginning to the very end.

For now, Vega forgot everything else—giving herself one target, one goal: get a hand on Marlena. Feed Death.

A happy chuff of approval echoed inside Vega's mind.

She tore the world away and stepped onto the mat with her sister. Marlena knew Vega's weaknesses, but so did Vega. She knew the second she let someone get in her head, it was over.

So she wouldn't let that happen.

Disconnect. Get lost in the moment. Leave it all on the mat. Have fun.

She took all the advice Bridger had ever given her and mixed it with the version of herself she'd become—the last version she'd ever be.

Vega dodged another blow, jumping back to avoid Marlena's blade. Marlena disappeared, but Vega could still sense when she got close.

Death trembled with longing whenever Marlena was near.

Lightning cracked across the sky, and all Vega had to do was blink to pull the energy to her. A piece of lightning fell from the clouds, absorbing into her body like a sponge. By the time she'd opened her eyes, Vega had already wielded the current at Marlena.

The bolt slammed into the center of her chest, her body twitching from the high voltage. She shimmered with a sheer blue electric current, until it slowly started to shift to green. Marlena's eyes rolled back from inside her head and landed on Vega.

What. The. Fuck.

Death pulsed through her veins again, its claws grabbing at Vega's lightning to yank it back inside like it was protecting her from Marlena's mimic.

Marlena recovered quickly, bouncing green lightning from palm to palm. "You know, I don't play with this enough. I really should, shouldn't I? Since you've gotten so good with it."

The terrain under their boots had become saturated and slick with mud. "Aw, did you just compliment me?" she mocked. "I'd say I'd teach you all about it, but I think I want to be the only lightning-wielder again."

Before Marlena had time to react, Vega pulled her bonded dagger from the waistband of her pants, the material clinging to her wet body, and flung it directly at Marlena's heart.

It stuck.

And for the briefest of moments, Vega hoped maybe, *just maybe*, this would be the end. That somehow it could be that easy.

It was foolish to believe, but Vega hadn't expected it to have zero effect on Marlena. They couldn't die, but that didn't mean they couldn't feel. Getting stabbed through the heart should still cause pain!

I would know.

A figure Vega knew well slinked out of the brush behind Marlena, camouflaging herself completely with the backdrop of the open field.

Vega knew Arlet's tricks, knew where to look to catch a flicker of her power fading at the edges. Arlet's ability must have fixed its weaknesses without the curse to keep it contained, because there were no flaws.

Arlet was truly invisible.

Vega blinked, and the field she'd been standing in changed. They were no longer surrounded by late winter blooms and the colors of rising dawn. Vega and Marlena were the only two in the middle of a rotten field, everything the color of tar and soot. Appearing beside Vega were two identical copies of herself. When she twisted to look at them, they turned too, like she was looking into a mirror.

Vega lifted her hand, and her twins followed.

Fucking creepy.

Anyone who had ever claimed Arlet wasn't frightening should consider themselves lucky to have not fallen victim to the visions she could make people believe were real. Arlet hid herself from view, tucking inside whatever crevice of her mind she could.

When the three Vegas turned to face Marlena, the real Vega snickered, and the sound echoed from their mouths too. "Let's play a game," she said, lips pulling into a slow smile. "You find the real Vega, and I'll let you keep your lightning," Vega cooed. "For now."

39

Noneᴀ ᴏf ᴛʜɪs ɪs ʀᴇᴀʟ. Nᴏɴᴇ ᴏf ᴛʜɪs ɪs ʀᴇᴀʟ. Nᴏɴᴇ ᴏf ᴛʜɪs ɪs *real*.

Marlena repeated the words to herself as the gods chattered in the background.

She was beginning to question if Vega's soulless black eyes and spidering veins were part of the illusion too.

Arlet.

"Get out of my fucking head!" she screamed, spinning in circles as she caught one of the Vegas in the side of her head with a green fireball. "You fucking *bitch!*"

It hardly faltered, continuing toward her.

"She's not in your head," one of the mirrored said, her voice echoing an unnatural hiss.

"But they are, aren't they?" Arlet's voice... *Where is she?*

Arlet knew about the gods. Marlena had let her inside her head for only a moment, and now she knew what was going on in there.

"A mistake. A mistake."

"You're a mistake."

329

She didn't know where the voices were coming from. It was too loud.

"Can't fight your own battles, Vega? Have to bring your friends into everything you do?" Marlena spat, her voice cracking at the end.

This time it was actually Vega's voice. "You had to bring the gods to help you because you had no friends. I don't see a difference." The real Vega appeared like she had an affinity for invisibility... but Marlena knew better.

This was all Arlet—forcing an image that wasn't actually there.

If Marlena were still the complimenting type, she'd tell Arlet what a magnificent power she was. But she wasn't, and she could never be that version of herself again.

She'd given her up for this. For *power*.

"The difference is it makes me stronger." Marlena threw a dagger, the blade nicking Vega's cheek. "You rely on them. Use them as a crutch. You've never had it in you to beat me fair and square."

A gust of wind swelled from behind, like Jupiter himself watched her back at the same time she took hold of the fire burning in her core. Tendrils of her emerald flames crawled over the ground, turning to steam as the rain from Vega's storm fell in fat, heavy drops.

"You're wrong, sister." The voice came from directly behind Marlena, the staccato rhythm giving away the fake's identity.

Spinning with her leg, Marlena kicked through the illusion's calf, but since it was nothing more than a mirage, it dwindled away for a breath and reappeared before the next.

Lightning lit the fake landscape around her. Skulls without eyes stared up from the ground, skin stuck to their hollowed cheeks. The snap of crunching bones under her boots sounded so real. *How* was Arlet doing this?

The unknown faces slowly started to morph into the dead Marlena wished she couldn't recognize. Her parents, Lucius... Ivelle.

The sounds of battle from people Marlena could no longer see echoed in the distance, but all she could focus on was the screech of her own voice inside her head. The scream of a girl she'd locked away.

Ivelle might have been the last person Marlena truly cared about.

The distraction lasted only a few seconds, but that was all it took—one moment of hesitation, and Vega got her hand around Marlena's wrist.

Panic flared—an emotion she hadn't felt in years. The heat of her flames roared, warming her skin to the touch. It had always been the first to jump to Marlena's defense.

The emerald glow of her favorite power bubbled, but it never made it to the surface.

The fluttering in the pit of her stomach quickly changed to a pain Marlena knew wasn't her sister's electricity. She was stuck in the middle where nothing but Vega's power lived, unable to fight her off.

Marlena had been thrown inside the dungeons of her mind and left to rot while whatever power Vega now possessed ripped her apart like a reaper.

It was the same way she'd felt when Vega stole Diana from her.

"What has she become?" one of the gods screeched as Marlena's body burned like a fire she'd never felt before.

Not even when she'd been given Vulcan's power during her summoning.

The realization of what Vega was doing slammed into Marlena like a pack of rabid dogs, shredding her to bits.

My fire.

She tried to fight, tried to scream, but nothing happened—nothing worked.

Marlena was powerless.

She'd given up everything she had for this... to be this.

All for the sister she cursed to become her undoing.

Marlena tried with everything she had to pull away, to regain some type of control, but nothing she or the gods did could stop Vega from draining what was left of the god of fire.

When Vega finally let go, silence fell around them.

Marlena's eyes widened, her sister's face mirroring her level of shock. Much to Marlena's dismay, Vega rebounded quickly, and what she did as the cherry on top sent a blinding hot ball of rage through Marlena's entire body.

It wasn't the heat of her fire, no. *My fire is gone...* and it illuminated in Vega's hands, burning as bright blue as their eyes—as bright blue as Vega's lightning.

Her sister had stolen yet another piece of what Marlena deserved.

The illusion of death and Vega's mirrored image faltered, flickering until the battlefield returned.

"Give it back." The growl from Marlena's chest wasn't a voice of just her own—it was a mix of all the ones left inside her head.

She'd summoned twelve.

Ten remained.

"Give me my fire!" Marlena pounced, slicing out with the daggers she had left, jumping between the folds of Tolevarre to get there faster.

Vega tucked, rolling on the sodden ground. When she popped up behind Marlena, the fire she'd stolen raged up her arms until it fizzled to nothing but smoke. "I didn't even want your fire." She laughed. Vega fucking *laughed* in Marlena's face. Her fury grew into something unrecognizable. "I was aiming for your lightning." Vega snapped both fingers, and the blue flames returned. "Oops."

Marlena saw red, picturing her sister's blood coating their realm. She couldn't lose what she'd fought so hard to have, so hard to keep.

Control.

Power.

"If you put your hands on Vega, she can take more." The

statement inside made Marlena halt, digging her boots into the ground.

Arlet appeared beside Vega, her eyes widening with fear—she looked like the twenty-year-old girl Marlena remembered seeing before she walked out of her parent's home—the day she had finally had enough of their abuse and fought back.

"Vega." Arlet's voice shook like it had then too.

Vega blinked, and the fire was gone. She fixed her gaze on Marlena, and for the first time in all her sister's lives, Marlena was terrified of who she'd become.

"What are you?" Marlena murmured.

"Death." Her eyes weren't solid black anymore, maybe they never had been... but darkness sank down her arms, traveling through her veins until it disappeared at her fingertips.

A shriek had everyone covering their ears as Arlet's brown dragon dipped to the ground and snagged both Vega and Arlet into her front talons and took off into the sky, disappearing behind the storm clouds slowly dissipating without Vega feeding them.

The field was littered with scorch marks, a mess of trees and limbs from Vega's tornado, and the dead bodies of shifters.

Delori crashed to the ground, landing on all fours with a roar that shook the trees. The deep red of her scales matched the blood dripping from her teeth. She lowered her head to Marlena, blowing a puff of air through her nose.

Marlena's hair whipped behind her back. "To Aeris," she said with a raspy voice, laced with the heaviness of defeat.

Delori's eyes exposed the hatred the woman inside the beast felt towards Marlena, but her cursed blood wouldn't allow her to deny the command. She would try to rip Marlena to shreds if her body let her, but Delori and the shifters were at Marlena's mercy now—hers to control.

She had offered Delori the deal of a lifetime. The curse on

Demuto would be lifted and her people freed from its clutches, and all she had to do was fight on Marlena's side of the war.

Simple.

Except Marlena wouldn't give Delori, or anyone else for that matter, the chance to betray her again. The youngest Fera never would have remained loyal... Not on her own.

This was Marlena's insurance, her way of guaranteeing Delori couldn't break a promise. Blood oaths were only deadly to the ones who broke them. The Fera's were heroes, always stoic with a need for adoration. Delori would have let herself die if it meant saving the shifters.

A blood curse as simple as the one Marlena had done was only breakable by the creator or the cursed, and something told her Delori had two extremely important reasons she wouldn't go looking for a way to break it.

Delori's wings sent a torrent of wind downward. Twigs and dirt flew, pelting Marlena until she stepped through the in-between and within seconds, she stood outside a door she'd almost been denied access to. How different would things be if Lucius had sent Marlena away? Or worse, if he would have told her parents what their eldest daughter, future leader of Amora and Aeris, had proposed...

Marlena didn't wait to be invited inside like she'd once done, and the guards didn't try to stop her. In fact, they took one look at Marlena, drenched from head to toe, mud and blood smearing her skin, and they moved at supersonic speed to get out of her way.

Marlena filtered the air through her fingers, sending a burst of wind crashing through the double doors.

The sudden intrusion made Katrin's eyes almost bulge out of her head. The blunt raven bob she always wore was styled straight and tight to the edge of her jaw, her sharp jawline nearly identical to her son's. She looked dressed for a funeral—colorless and muted. "Marlena." She shot up from her chair, gripping the edge of the desk.

Marlena caught a glimpse of herself in the mirror behind Katrin's desk.

She looked like she had when this all began. When she went from territory to territory, killing anyone who tried to flee or had chosen to take a stance against her. A time when the gods were loud and encouraging, whispering about all the magnificent things she could do.

They were staying quiet, hiding in the corners of Marlena's mind. Too afraid to come out of the shadows in fear Vega would be waiting when they did.

"Find Meyer. Tell him to assemble the army for full departure." Marlena braided her wet hair, her fingers working quickly to secure the battleworn strands around her head in a coronet. "It's time to clear them out of Vates." She tucked a few loose strands in place.

The war she'd been keeping at bay was here... and it was going to be worse than anything their people had ever seen or studied.

Katrin trembled, stammering through the first few words. "Meyer defected. He's gone, and so is half the army."

40

Avi dropped Vega and Arlet gently outside the cave, her landing making the ground palpitate. She skidded to a stop and whipped around, snapping her jaw at Vega.

She definitely felt steam on the last one. Vega jumped back, a crack of lightning striking inches from Arlet's dragon as a warning.

Death didn't react.

Vega understood now. She was Death, the very personification of it, but the shadow inside her wasn't a mirage she'd created—this wasn't like the fire-breathing dragon looming over her.

The shadow wasn't an extension of her power. It *was* her power. The shadow was death... a living entity inside her, acting out Death's darkest desires.

I am Death.

But Death was just a name without the ability to use it. The two couldn't exist in this way without one another.

They were one.

Vega felt a weight lift off her mind, a soundless sigh of relief flooding her senses.

She had finally figured it out...

It was quiet, empty while Death's shadow did whatever happened in the deepest part of Vega's mind after dragging a god into the pit with it.

Vega spun around to Arlet, ready to find out what her dragon was so angry about, when the look on her best friend's face needed no explanation.

Her dragon was pissed because Arlet was pissed.

Vega held her hands out, palms facing Arlet like Vega was dealing with an angry street dog. That didn't stop this rabid canine... Arlet shoved Vega's shoulders, sending her stumbling back a few steps.

"What was that about, huh?" Arlet asked, going in again for another shove.

Bridger intercepted before she could get a third in, putting himself in between the two... and a giant dragon. "Hey, hey. What's going on?"

Khort grabbed Arlet by the wrist, pulling her back as she continued to charge towards Vega. "Arlet, stop."

Vega let Bridger back her up a few more paces, staring around his bulky frame when the reality of Arlet's mood hit her.

"Tell them, Vega. Tell them what you told Marlena." Arlet flung Khort's grip off, standing in front of her dragon.

Avi swayed her head, locking in on Vega.

Bridger's arms fell from Vega's biceps where he'd held her in place.

"What does it mean?" Arlet yelled. "Why did you tell her you're Death?" She sobbed the last part.

"What is she talking about?" Bridger asked, his dark brows knitted.

Her heart raced, but she said loud enough for the three of them to hear, "Because I am."

"What?" Khort gasped.

Vega sighed, her head drooping down like she'd been caught

with her hand in the cookie jar. She'd hidden this from them for as long as she could. Vega hadn't planned on keeping it from them forever... just long enough to get ahead. She had wanted it to be too late for anyone to try and change her mind.

There's no going back. Her fate might not be fair, but it rarely ever was. Vega wouldn't have wished this on herself, and if she had the choice she would certainly pick another option.

But it was too late. She'd already made the deal.

There was no way to avoid telling them, knowing what she had to do going forward.

"What did you give him?" Bridger asked only her this time.

Chills shot down her back.

He knew.

Vega wondered when he'd put the pieces together. *"I'm so sorry, Bridger."* She truly was. For everything that had already happened and for all that would. *"I don't think any of you are going to like this,"* she told him before stepping around and locking eyes with Arlet.

"When Marlena cursed me to die, the curse promised my soul to the underworld." Vega fought against the headache starting to build behind her eyes.

Vulcan didn't go easily. He fought the entire way down.

But Death fought harder.

"When I was floating somewhere between Earth and Tolevarre, he spoke to me." She still hadn't found it inside herself to say his name... "He told me I couldn't escape destiny." Vega looked at Bridger, biting the inside of her lip to stop it from trembling. "The sister destined to die." Vega knew who she'd made the deal with, but saying his name would make it too real.

Vega felt Bridger inside her mind. She watched understanding click for him way before the others.

"I knew I only had two options. I was going to the underworld and taking you all with me, or I was going to barter my life for yours." Vega could see the absolute heartache flash across Bridger's face. She hadn't needed to see it though—not when she could feel it in the way her own chest tightened. "He wanted the gods. I wanted to make sure you three lived, to make sure the people of Tolevarre lived. I wanted Marlena dead. This was how we all got what we asked for that night..." She inhaled a shaky breath.

Vega's voice didn't quiver. She made sure to sound as confident in her choice as she was the moment she made it. "He didn't just give me a power. He made me his property. He gave me what I always wanted."

She didn't want to leave them... but she would to ensure they got to see the world they'd been fighting for. Her life for theirs.

It was an easy trade.

"Gods can't be killed," Arlet said without much confidence.

"I'm not killing them. I'm taking the gods from Marlena, killing her, and then delivering their souls to the underworld." Since taking the first god, Vega had been lying alone at night, fighting sleep, afraid to slip back into the pit with Diana. It didn't happen every night—but it always happened when Vega let her guard down.

It gave her plenty of time to ponder, to ask questions she somehow eventually knew the answer to.

"You. *You're* a god," her best friend choked out, doing what she could to control her tears. "You can't die."

Everyone's emotions roared to the surface, and Vega had a hard time ignoring them.

She let her eyes sweep over the three people she'd always loved more than anyone else in the entire universe. "I did the moment I traded my soul to become Death."

She hadn't realized Death, in its shadow dragon form, sat at the edge of her internal pit, watching her with its hollow sockets made of moving darkness. It was bigger than it had been before dragging Vulcan to the bottom.

It curled up at Vega's feet, a new, unmistakable warmth creeping up from her toes in a dangerous rush.

"The euphoria I felt taking Marlena's fire..." Tears threatened to spill, burning her eyes. Vega blinked them away, refusing to show the others how terrified she really was.

"You took her fire?" Bridger asked, the same ice-cold fear she felt slithering down their bond from him.

A low growl vibrated the room inside her head, rattling the door to Bridger's mind. Her fear slowly faded away, skittering like a scared animal under the eyes of a watchful predator.

Vega extended a steady hand to the swirling shadows of Death. It nuzzled its head into her open palm, and on the outside, the veins at her wrist turned black.

"*Vega.*" Bridger's voice bounced off the walls of her mind and echoed down to the pit, where she could feel the newest god taking space inside her.

Death lifted its head and looked in the direction of Bridger's voice coming through the open door.

Vega returned herself to the real world, slipping out of her mind and leaving Death to nap with its tail curled around the abyss and one leg hanging off the edge.

"I wanted to keep it," Vega admitted out loud. "It felt so good. The strength, seeing the panic in her eyes as I took something she loved." She wiped her dirty sleeve across the sweat building on her forehead as the morning sun broke the horizon. "I know I shouldn't have wanted it, but I did."

Bridger stared at her with a look she couldn't place. Fear? Sorrow? Dread? Whatever it was, he'd kept the way it made him feel to himself this time.

"Denying the gods and their powers is going to get harder if it's anything like the fire that burned through me today." Vega took a pause to regain her thoughts. "But there's no other choice." Thankfully, no one was around. It was only the bonded and Avi.

"No." Arlet shook her head, her curls bouncing off her shoulders. "No, this isn't right. This isn't fair! I won't accept this."

Vega frowned. "It's already been done... There's nothing we can do to reverse it."

Khort did what he did best when he got nervous. He paced.

Arlet was still mad. Vega could feel it—they all could. "I refuse, fucking *refuse*, to let us get this far to lose you in the end." Her best friend's tenacity would always be Vega's favorite thing about her... but when did that stubbornness turn to not being able to let go?

If this was the way to rid their world of Marlena, would they really choose to save Vega over every single other life in Tolevarre?

Bridger had proven he would choose Tolevarre over her—it couldn't be that hard to get the others on board.

Bridger was too quiet, but Vega felt him on the other side of her open door as if he could see through into the room with her sleeping shadow of death.

"A deal is a deal. We can't change it. I would trade my life for your happy endings a hundred more times if I had to." Apparently willing to add more fuel to the fire of everyone's anger, she took a deep breath. "I'm going to have to try and break the bond." Vega had once believed there were certain things that couldn't happen—but that wasn't the case anymore. Nothing was impossible. "Our bond ties our lives together."

It wasn't *what* she was taking... It was *who*.

"It's not just the powers I'm taking from Marlena. I'm taking the gods, their lives, their souls." There was a short pause where everyone was afraid to breathe. "I can feel everyone's." It was clear she didn't mean powers... Vega realized she could when she'd laid her hands on Jak while breaking up the fight. He'd seemed to know something wasn't right either. "If I tried, I could probably snap whatev—"

"No." Bridger clipped, speaking what Vega knew would be a unanimous vote. "Absolutely fucking not."

"For once, I agree with him," Khort said, jerking his thumb towards Bridger.

Avi clacked, a chuffing sound only Arlet and Khort could understand. Even in his human form, Khort nodded, agreeing with whatever the dragon had said.

"She's right. We don't know what we'd lose if the bond was broken." Arlet had already lost so much. Vega didn't want her to lose any more.

Which was why the bond had to be broken.

"Let's remember why we started this in the first place." Vega raised her scarred brow. "To defeat Marlena and set our people free. No matter how that looks."

Vega knew this wasn't the last she'd hear of this—not even close.

"I'm sorry I didn't tell you the whole truth." She wasn't sorry about what she'd done, though. "I didn't want anyone to waste time on trying to find a way out of this because there isn't one." She held her arm out, wrist facing towards the sky. "It's too late anyway."

Vega didn't need to speak the words, all she had to do was think them and Death would hear. *You answer to me. Not him. We belong to no one.*

In her mind she watched the shadow shifter flare its wings and lower its head, slowly sinking into a bow. "*My Goddess of Death.*" Vega's title was the first it had spoken with a clearer voice. There was still an unnatural strain, but it was fading, and Death's tone sounded oddly feminine.

Death entered her bloodstream, and the dragon in her mind disappeared, becoming one with Vega. Her veins turned black, creeping up her inner arm like lightning of the underworld.

Vega's cheeks heated from the swell of death inside her body. She shivered, sending it back down her wrist until it disappeared at her fingertips.

Bridger's Adam's apple bobbed as he fought to control the wrath growing inside him. He took a deep breath and ran a hand through his tousled hair. "We'll find another way." His dark eyes bore into hers. "*I'll find another way.*"

Arlet and Khort nodded their agreements, and Avi settled some, slowly lowering herself into a crouch.

"For now we move forward like nothing's changed," Vega said, knowing there was absolutely no other option.

"But this changes everything," Arlet said, holding back the tears Vega knew were threatening to spill over again. She knew her best friend—which meant she knew she wouldn't give up. "I won't pretend it doesn't so you feel better about the choice you made."

"Oh, c'mon. Like you all wouldn't have done the exact same thing if you were in her shoes." Every one of them spun to face Octavia. "And that's coming from someone who doesn't even know you that well."

How long had she been standing there?

Octavia could read their facial expressions almost instantly, like the group had been displaying the same question in subtitles over their heads. "My bonded animal is a fox. I find myself in a lot of places I shouldn't be. It's how I got that awful nickname," she said with an eye roll. She leaned against the cave's rock wall and crossed her leg over the other. "I've been keeping a low profile for over fifty years."

Fifty years. Delori has a daughter who is over fifty years old. The people she loved had missed out on so much of the life they should have lived, all because of a sister who had to take her anger and hurt out on others... instead of learning to deal with it like the rest of the world.

"This conversation doesn't concern you, nor does it require your input," Arlet snapped.

Octavia bit her bottom lip and fought a smile. "I like you, Videri. You've got something scary about you." She wagged her finger at Arlet before Tilie scurried out from the distant woods.

"Where do you think you're going?" Khort asked like some lifelong authoritarian.

Octavia paused, giving Khort a sideways glance. "Um, one. Chill. Two, to get the children out of Demuto."

Khort scoffed. "No, you're definitely not going alone. Delori wouldn't want—"

Octavia interrupted. "With all due respect, you have no fucking clue what my mother would want."

Khort's jaw dropped, and Bridger's lips pulled at the corners. Arlet stared at her like she was trying to solve a puzzle.

"To no fault of your own, you've missed out on the woman she is today, and you don't get to tell me what she would want of me. I know what she'd want." Octavia pushed forward, Tilie weaving through her legs as she walked. "What she would want is for me to go get the shifter children who have been stuck in the confines of a single territory their whole lives and take them somewhere safe."

She nodded towards the cave. "Which isn't here..."

The sound of footsteps echoed from the cave, and Octavia's younger sister came barreling out with Halo slinking behind her, sticking close to the shadows and out of Khort's direct line of vision.

"I'm coming with you!" Nora proclaimed, throwing a small bag over her shoulder.

Octavia shook her head. "Negative. You're staying here."

"But—"

She didn't let her finish. "No. You're not trained. You're not ready. Stay with them." She nodded to the bonded.

Avi took off into the sky, alerting Arlet of movement to the south. "We need to get out of the open. Better yet, we need to get out of the caves. We're not safe here. We've never been safe here." She turned to Bridger. "Is Vincere still an option?"

A muscle ticked in his tight jaw, a movement Vega knew she had been the only one to see. "It needs to be cleared out. Marlena killed everyone who stayed behind."

Arlet closed her eyes and shook her head, silently mourning the people they'd lost.

"I'll go." Halo stepped forward, the bags under his eyes a clear indicator the boy hadn't been sleeping worth a shit—not even behind the safe walls of Vincere. "I'll take Nora, make sure she's safe." He stole a glance at her and Octavia, then looked back to Bridger.

"Thank you." Octavia gave him a soft smile and kissed her sister on the cheek. "Be good. Be *nice*."

"Leave your boots on." Nora didn't let tears spill over, but they glistened in her eyes.

A part of Vega hurt at the memory of what she and her sister had once been.

"And don't sleep with my back to the road." Octavia winked at Nora. "I know." She looked at Vega and Bridger. "Marlena doesn't know we exist. My mom would like to keep it that way. I'll get to Vincere as quickly and safely as I possibly can. I'll have Tilie send a message if we run into anyone who can deliver one."

She waited for them both to nod, understanding what targets they would be if Marlena did, before slipping into the Vates forest and disappearing with Tilie by her side.

When she was gone, it was back to business. "You can't clear all the bodies by yourself, Halo." Bridger hadn't mentioned how many had died, but if they needed more than a few people to clear the dead, it must be a big number.

"You should go with them," Vega told him.

"I'm staying with you" was his quick response. Out loud. For everyone to know his stance.

"I'll go." Leo came forward.

Fuck, how long had *he* been standing there? Vega was losing it. She needed sleep.

"It's been a long time since I've stepped foot in Ardor. I'm sure my fire would love the heat." He smiled, glowing at the prospect of going home.

"I can help," Nora offered.

Bridger and Halo both answered at the same time. "No."

Oh, it was bad *bad then.*

"While we get the dead to a burn pile, you can get everyone on the road. It'll take a while with the elderly." Leo made a good point.

"Khort and I could stay back if you two need to go," Arlet offered.

"Okay," Bridger responded. Accepting for them both. "Halo, take Nora and Leo first. Go straight to my study. Do not let her see anything. Give Leo a quick tour and let him get started."

Nora almost argued, but she saw the look on Bridger's face and thought twice. It didn't take a genius to recognize the haunted stare Bridger wore as a way to process what he'd seen at Vincere.

Halo wasted no time grabbing Nora's hand gently. The way his eyes fluttered down to her gaze made Vega's heart melt. "Try keeping your eyes closed this time. It might help with the nausea."

"He likes her." Vega could hear the smile in her voice.

Bridger stared, watching as Halo extended his other hand to Leo.

"This is gonna fucking suck, isn't it?" he asked, hovering his hand over Halo's.

"Yes," Halo deadpanned. "Don't let go," he warned like he always did.

"Or what?" Leo swallowed hard.

"He better be careful who he tells." Bridger glanced to Khort, staring menacingly at Nora's hand in Halo's.

"I don't know. You'll get stuck in the in-between, maybe. But most likely you'll die." Halo barely had the last word out when he snatched Leo's hand in his and whisked them away to Vincere.

Leo's gasp echoed even after he was gone.

Arlet immediately turned to face Vega. "I'm not sorry for almost kicking your ass... and I hope you know our conversation from earlier isn't over."

Vega nodded. "I figured."

"I won't let you kill yourself for us." Arlet scurried toward the cave.

Khort watched her go and then turned his attention to Bridger and Vega. "Hurt her again, Dimico, and I'll find a way to kill you myself."

Before either made it inside the cave, Halo was back.

Alone.

"What?" Bridger asked, rushing towards Halo with an outstretched arm.

Vega followed, unsure of what she was about to get herself into.

"Meyer's at Vincere."

41

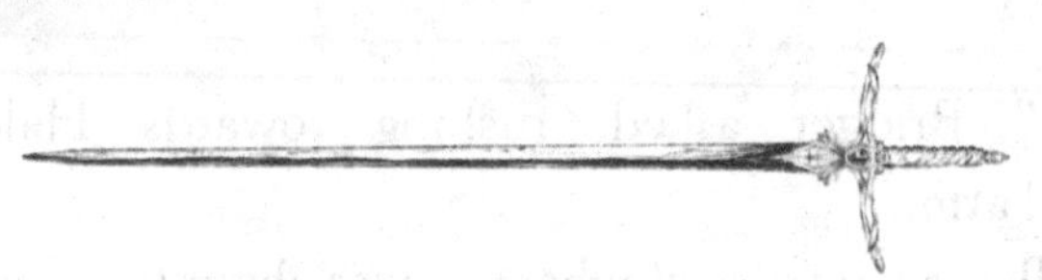

Bridger had learned to travel with Halo like the power was his own. "You really do get used to it," he told Vega, who was bent over with her hands on her knees. The look on her face spoke loud and clear—no words needed anywhere.

Shut the fuck up.

Halo dropped them outside the entrance of Vincere. A fire roared on the western corner of the training land.

When the wind changed directions and the smell of the fire whipped their way, Bridger and Vega both froze.

"He's burning bodies." Vega said what they were both thinking.

"No fucking way." Bridger and Vega looked at each other with the same confused expression. "Did he...?" Bridger's question trailed off.

"You gonna stand and watch or help me clean up our dead and send their souls to the afterlife?" Meyer asked, coming up from behind. His dark skin glistened with sweat, and blood stained his clothing from the fresher bodies.

The gates to the main entrance of the underground barracks opened, and a line of soldiers filed out. They all carried the dead.

"We decided we'd rather die fighting for our own lives than fighting for hers." *He did.* Meyer defected and followed Bridger.

Bridger closed the distance between himself and Meyer, pulling him into a big hug.

"Better late than never, huh?" Meyer asked, the question muffled from their embrace.

Meyer had and always would be Bridger's brother. Neither of them had any real siblings, but Bridger had never believed it was blood that made you family. "Thank you."

"I would have been back sooner... but more and more soldiers kept coming forward about wanting to leave when I got to Fortis." Meyer looked over his shoulder. "I couldn't leave them."

Bridger would never, had never, second-guessed his decision in making Meyer his general.

Without another word, everyone but Nora went to work clearing the bodies from the bunker.

Halo went from room to room, marking ones that needed extensive cleaning. Soldiers went through and wiped any trace of blood away, erasing Bridger's failures.

He'd locked himself away in his head, focusing only on setting the souls of his soldiers free.

They deserved a rightful burning, if nothing else could be given.

The body count was up to 894 soldiers... and they were still finding more.

It took a few more hours to burn the rest of their dead, condemning their souls to whatever afterlife was awaiting.

"Nora's sleeping," Vega told Bridger. She'd gone to check on her once the bodies had been cleared.

"Good." He'd been short with Vega since arriving. Bridger wasn't used to letting people see his darkest parts... and having Vega inside his head when he felt seconds away from losing himself in knowing what she'd done, that was going to be the darkest anyone had seen Bridger yet.

It was bad the first time Bridger lost Vega, and he'd just gotten her back.

Bridger wouldn't survive a second loss.

No. I will not fucking lose her. He wouldn't let himself entertain the possibility, choosing to concentrate on what really mattered—finding a way to change Vega's fate.

"What do you need?" The question made him stop and pause.

He didn't respond for a moment. He glanced down at himself, covered in dried blood, dirt, sand, and gods knew what else. It was all a mixture from battle and from cleaning up the dead. *"A shower."* Bridger's stomach rumbled. *"And food."* He looked up to find Meyer standing by the pyre, staring into the flame he'd started himself. *"Stay in my office. I'll come to you. Let me check in with Meyer."*

Vega tugged him into her mind, letting him see her feet kicked up on his desk, her freshly washed hands not matching the rest of her body skimming through paperwork that had been strewn across his desk. *"Take your time. I'm studying."*

Studying. Snooping. Same thing, right?

Halo had gone back to the caves to let everyone know it was safe to travel, staying behind in case a message needed to get to Bridger or Vega.

The rest of the soldiers who'd come with Meyer were cleaning up last minute things and settling in for the night. The day had quickly disappeared as the cool night air slipped over Ardor. It was a welcome break from the blistering heat they'd worked in all day.

Bridger approached Meyer, and neither said anything for a moment, simply sending up private prayers to gods they all now knew weren't there to listen anymore.

"So, should I start praying to you then or would you prefer I worship Vega instead?"

Meyer was grinning like a fool when Bridger glanced his way. "Ha-ha. You're sooo funny." Bridger glowered, folding his arms across his chest. "You can start referring to me as *the* god of wrath if you'd like."

"I hate that." Meyer sneered, and they both laughed like they weren't watching the bodies of their soldiers burn.

"How about we leave the praying to the acolytes? We're better off strategizing, prioritizing, and scheming instead," Bridger said as he watched an ember flutter down and land on his filthy shirt.

"You've got a plan then," Meyer stated.

Bridger quickly and quietly brought his shield up around his mind and blocked out anyone from peeking, simultaneously throwing one around himself and Meyer.

"Oh, you've definitely got something up your sleeve." Meyer rubbed his hands together in excitement.

"How much do you remember about what we learned of the underworld when we were in school?" Bridger's attention shifted to focus solely on Meyer. He had to do this quickly in order to hide from Vega.

He'd gladly keep secrets if it was to protect Vega from herself. He didn't care what promises he'd made before finding out exactly what Vega had done. She'd gone behind their backs and sacrificed herself for the greater good—in true hero fashion... but Bridger wasn't a fucking hero, and he didn't mind getting his hands dirty to save the girl he loved.

Loved? Past tense? Love? Fuck.

Bridger told Romulus to deliver a message, and he intended on upholding his threat. If Pluto wanted Vega, he'd have to go through him to get her.

Meyer raised his brow, crossing his arms too. On the outside it looked like the commander and his general having a chat. On the inside, the start of a scheme Bridger would soon cling to was about to be set free.

"Not enough to speak on it. I was too busy flirting with our tutor to pay attention to what she was saying." Meyer smiled, his eyes glazing over like he could see a picture of the girl in his mind.

Bridger, on the other hand, hadn't even known there'd been a tutor who taught the lesson. He'd been too busy training beside his father to remember much of those days. "I'd like you to find a personal interest in it. Or at least find someone who does and make sure they understand it's to be kept a secret."

Meyer snapped out of his goofy mood and scrunched his brows as his eyes raked Bridger's body. He did this when he felt he needed to read someone's seriousness.

Bridger had watched him do it all their lives.

"Pertaining to what?" Meyer asked when he'd finished his scan.

"Anything and everything you can find. I want to know it all." Out of all the bloodlines in Tolevarre, Bridger's family would probably know the most about what came after death—and he knew next to nothing. "There's not much about the history of our realm I don't know, but I can't remember learning much about the underworld. Only it's where we go when we die." Bridger let the sound shield fall abruptly, signaling the end of the conversation.

Meyer watched as Bridger backed away. "I might have a few people who'd be willing to trade information for protection."

Bridger dipped his head. "Keep me updated." He began to let his personal shields down.

"Hey, Bridger," Meyer called, making him pause. "Marlena's got us outnumbered after her massacre... Add in the shifters and we're in an unfortunate situation."

Bridger sighed, fully letting the shield around his mind down... and Vega wasn't waiting on the other side for him, ready to claw his eyes out.

"For now." He hated to admit it. "We need to make a statement. A public one. Tolevarre needs to know there's another option." More territories would follow. Not everyone was as loyal to Marlena as meets the eye.

Keeping their head down when the vast majority of the realm was doing the same thing was safer—after Vega took Marlena's fire, Bridger wasn't sure anyone in Tolevarre was safe.

Recruiting regular civilians would do nothing but add to the death toll, but death was unavoidable, especially in war—especially when Death walked among them.

Meyer raised a brow and cocked his head. "I heard there's a fire-wielder among the rebels who escaped the mines. How liberating would it be for him to save them?"

Bridger cracked a smile. "I like the way you think." He took a few steps backwards, ready to see Vega. "Let's talk more tomorrow. Get some sleep."

The mines were a great place to start, and it would send the type of message the people of Tolevarre needed to see.

Everyone was done playing by Marlena's rules.

42

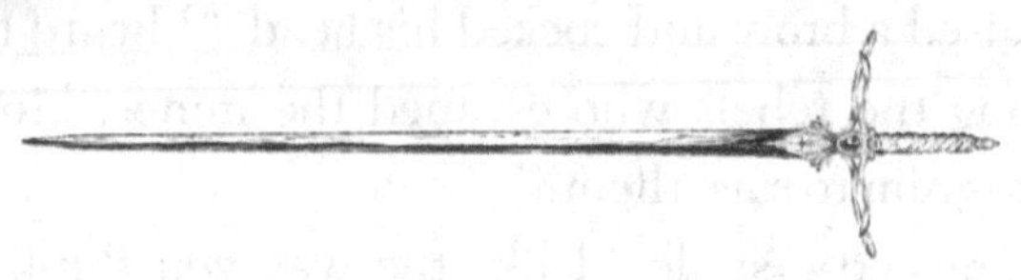

Nora slept soundly on the black velvet couch in Bridger's office; the sound of her shallow breathing mixing with the fire Vega must have started with a zap of lightning. The flame was as blue as the eyes staring at Bridger from the chair at his desk.

Vega had her bare feet tucked underneath her legs in a criss-cross, elbows resting on the desk with her chin resting in her palms.

"You really made yourself comfortable, didn't you?" he asked. Bridger's smile felt heavy as it slid across his lips.

"This chair is really great." She bounced up and down a couple times, and maybe in her mind she thought it was showing the spring of the entirely too expensive chair, but after the long day Bridger had had, he couldn't stop picturing her riding his—

"How many women have you fucked in this chair?" she asked.

Bridger choked on air. Had she known what he was thinking? The timing of that question was almost too perfect. "Vega." He growled, but she was up with her hand over his mouth in a second.

"Shhhh. Nora is sleeping." She gave him a playful look, her scarred eyebrow rising as high as it could go. Vega reached down and

grabbed her socks. She slipped them on and then stepped into her battered boots.

He held the door open for her. *"I think it's time we get you a new pair of those."* There was no telling which life she'd been holding onto those since.

She paused, looking back at Nora. *"I like these boots."* Nora was curled on her side with the blanket pulled up to her chin. *"What happens when she wakes up alone?"* Vega's eyes twinkled with what Bridger knew was worry.

Nora was close to Halo's age, give or take a year, and Vega had been right—the boy was smitten.

If only Bridger knew now what he'd known at twenty when he was just a young man in love with a girl... He would have killed Marlena before she had the chance to ruin everyone's lives.

"I'll send a guard to stand outside the door and bring her to you when she wakes. Come on." Bridger let the door click shut quietly, leading them towards the end of the long hall where an elevator sat.

"You're an expert at changing the subject," Vega admitted, keeping pace beside him.

"Vega, we are not talking about my sex life." He shook his head, pushing the Up button on the panel.

"Why not?" He felt her nerves spike.

"Because I can feel how uncomfortable it's making you." The door opened and Bridger stepped inside, turning around to face Vega, who hadn't stepped through the open doors.

"It's not the sex life that's making me nervous. I've had plenty of it in the forty years we haven't been together."

Wrath bubbled in his stomach like it always did at the thought of someone else's hands on Vega, but he bit it back, pressing it into the pit of his stomach so Vega wouldn't catch the shift.

He had no right to feel this way—Bridger knew that, but self-awareness didn't magically make it go away.

"It's because I really don't like elevators," she admitted from the other side as the doors started to close.

Bridger stuck his arm out, sending the doors sliding back. "Since when?"

"Since I got stuck in one, had a panic attack where I blacked out, and learned the super hot dude I'd seen in dreams name was Bridger."

Bridger reached out and pulled her in, guiding her into his chest as he leaned against the wall. "I'd love to hear more about this super hot dude..." Vega slid her arms around his torso and rested her cheek against his chest, causing Bridger to pause. He placed his chin on top of her head, reaching across to hit the button for his floor. "But I'd rather you tell me something real instead," he finished.

"New or old?" she asked, not picking her head up as the elevator started its smooth descent.

"Whatever you're willing to share." He kissed the top of her head and pulled her in tight. It didn't matter they both probably smelled like actual death or were crusted with blood... It mattered that they were getting this moment together—a tiny moment of peace they both deserved.

He felt her take a breath. "When I stabbed you after our kiss..." She peeked up at him with one eye. When she saw no reaction other than a raised brow from Bridger, she continued. "I told myself the kiss was nothing more than a momentary distraction, and in the moment it had been... but then it opened up these feelings. Feelings I hadn't really had the chance to move through." Vega rested her chin on his chest, meeting his gaze.

Bridger pushed back the hair sticking to her forehead, not saying a word. He didn't want to distract her.

"Feelings I called myself crazy for having about you."

Keep going. Fuck, he wanted to hear her say what he knew she was thinking.

"I hated you, hated that you'd left me, or at least hated the way losing you made *me* feel... but you hated me too, right?" Her face didn't look sad or hurt. The warmth was still in her eyes.

"I never hated you. I hated myself for the person I became without you around, and then eventually I hated myself so much I couldn't look in the mirror and accept who I was. So I put up shields, shields I wouldn't have if it weren't for you, ironically." He smirked down at her. Vega's disheveled clothing and hair brought him back to a place and time before the curse had ripped their lives to shreds. "I disconnected myself from the person I'd become and felt only what I allowed myself." He'd known then he would regret it for the rest of his life, but leaving her was the only option at that point. "I let myself remember the bad moments, never the good. I had to make you into the villain of my story... like I was in yours... It was better than the pain of losing you."

The bell dinged, but when the elevator doors opened, neither moved.

"I had to lose you too. Over and over again, just like you lost me. Every time I got my memories back, I had to be reminded that the man I used to love, still loved in some lives, didn't want me anymore," she said, her voice close to a whisper. "I can't go through it again. Please, don't make me go through it again."

The elevator door closed. "Let me make myself clear. I never stopped wanting *you*. I won't make the same mistake twice." Bridger trailed his thumb over Vega's bottom lip. "It's always been you, baby. I just lost myself there for a little bit... but you found me again."

"I'll always find you." Vega closed her eyes and nuzzled her cheek into Bridger's open palm. "In this life and all those that follow." When her eyes opened, her lashes fluttered over her dirty cheeks. "I knew you were in there somewhere."

The door to the elevator opened, and a stunned soldier stood on the other side. "Oh... Commander," the woman stuttered. "I'm s-sorry."

Vega smiled mischievously as she untangled herself from

Bridger. "Handsy one, he is." She winked at the soldier and sauntered off the elevator.

Bridger squeezed by the girl. "Carry on." He didn't wait to see if the level three soldier actually got on the elevator or not because he was too busy catching up to Vega, who walked down the hall as if she'd been here a million times.

They walked side by side, passing a few bedroom doors as they continued to the end of the hall where it branched off into a T. At both ends were bathrooms with showers and changing rooms.

"Lost?" Bridger asked, his crooked smirk pulling at the side visible to Vega. He didn't wait to hear her response. "Bathrooms on both ends of the hall." He pointed to them and then nodded behind him where they'd come from. "My room is at the other end." A room he would really love to get Vega in right about now.

Instead of waiting for Bridger to lead, Vega stomped down the hall in the opposite direction. "You could have stopped me."

Bridger watched her for a second, chuckling to himself. The voice in his head told him he didn't deserve a second chance with Vega, but the part of him that believed he'd suffered enough let himself, if only for the time being, believe this was the light at the end of his tunnel. "You seemed to know where you were going. I didn't want to interrupt."

Except, there couldn't be a light at the end of the tunnel. Not when Vega's soul belonged to the underworld—belonged to Pluto.

I'll find a way to save her.

There were a thousand different ways he could say he was sorry, a million ways he could beg Vega to forgive him, but none of those would mean anything if she wasn't going to make it to the end to see his promises through.

Vega slowed when she got to the end of the hall. Bridger slipped around her and opened the door at the very end, letting her slip inside before he closed it behind them. It automatically locked, the light flicking on at Bridger's presence.

Nothing had changed. It looked exactly as it had when he'd left. The plush mattress on the boring metal frame in the corner of the room was made with pillows piled high.

He watched Vega scan the place, running her fingers over the dresser as she looked at the blandness of the room. Compared to the decadent office he spent most his time in, Bridger's bedroom held almost no personality.

He let Vega wander. When she got to the desk, she thumbed through the pages of whatever report he'd left out, then opened a drawer.

She'd find nothing more than a couple pens, a pad of paper, and a corkscrew to open the bottles of wine he left stored on the shelf above his desk.

Vega turned around, leaning against the desk. She crossed one foot over the other. "I have to tell you something before we do... whatever it is that's about to happen between us."

Bridger raised a brow. "Okay." There was no telling where this was about to go.

"I kissed Khort in my last life. The night before you took me from the witch's cottage in Fraus." Vega said it so nonchalantly he instantly understood there was nothing to worry about. The heat of anger still sizzled, threatening to spark at any second.

"Lucky him. I hope it was everything he dreamed it would be," Bridger managed to respond with theatrical enthusiasm.

"And then I tried to fuck him."

Well, that did it.

The wrath inside Bridger's body turned to molten lava and melted his rationale.

Vega cocked her head, watching Bridger like a hawk ready for its next meal. "It was before I'd gotten my memories back, but I still *wanted* it, wanted him."

Khort had been the better choice for Vega, and everyone knew it —except Bridger. There had never been a second where he considered leaving because he felt like he was the wrong choice for the only girl he'd ever loved.

His motives behind leaving had never had anything to do with Khort fucking Fera.

Bridger was the bad boy. The commander's son who had been known to fly through the ladies lined up at his door. Everyone assumed whoever he'd end up with wouldn't be for love, but for power. It was what his parents had intended the night they'd introduced their son to the Caelum sisters. Except he'd fallen for the wrong sister. Immediately.

Khort was the kind, strong, chivalrous shifter who could promise Vega a life of fun party planning and cute kids with a house in the woods.

"And I still chose you. Despite what everyone expected of me."

Fuck, had he said those things down the bond?

The anger clouding his judgement could be blamed for that.

Vega stepped forward, and Bridger didn't dare move. "I wanted him because he looked at me like I was the center of the entire universe, like I could fix everything that was broken. Like maybe *I* wasn't broken..."

Bridger was afraid his teeth would break with how hard he clenched his jaw.

"But do you know what he sees when he looks at me?" Vega asked, slipping her hand into his. She pulled his wrist with the scar up to her eye level, inspecting the brand they all wore.

Bridger didn't have the answer to her question, and even if he did, Vega wasn't looking for one—not from him.

"He sees the girl he used to know. The kids we were before this started. He sees a version of me I can never be again." Vega grazed a single finger over the raised line of their bond. "You stopped seeing that version of me the second I died. You treated me like the person I was becoming, not the person I'd been. How could anyone blame you for not loving the person I turned into when I wasn't who I'd been when you fell in love with me?" Her sad smile made Bridger want to barf. "I don't blame you."

Bridger's fury started to dissipate, but it was replaced by something else. A hum traveling up his arm from Vega's touch.

"You saw my weaknesses, the cracks in my soul." Their eyes met, and Bridger reached out with the hand he kept suspended for her to inspect and cupped her cheek. Vega wrapped her hand around his branded wrist. "You showed me that sometimes loving someone isn't enough to save them. Your love couldn't have saved me from this. I was the only one who could save me from this." Vega stretched up on her tippy toes, placing a soft kiss on Bridger's lips. "Khort would have pretended to love any version of me because it was what he was told he wanted." Another light kiss on his lips. "You knew what was most important to me even when I couldn't. It's never been my life I wanted to protect. It was theirs. The people of Tolevarre. The people we care about. They deserve a happy ending even if I can't get one."

Bridger was ready to argue when he felt a rush of pain slam against the bond. His gasp turned into a hiss of air as his eyes fell to Vega's hand wrapped around his wrist.

The brand was black, inked the same color as Vega's veins.

Bridger snatched his hand back, the color disappearing as soon as her touch was gone. "What the fuck was that?" She'd distracted him long enough to slip between his shields unnoticed. "Did you just...?" His question trailed off because he already knew the answer.

"I'm sorry. I just wanted to see if I could feel it." Vega didn't look remorseful. "I can. I can also feel how strong you are when you're angry."

Irritation flooded Bridger's senses, but he knew it would be misplaced if he took it out on Vega. She was doing what any of them would do if they were in her position.

What other choice had she been given? Her soul was already his—all she'd done was get what she wanted out of it.

He slowly slid a shield around his bond, letting Vega feel the grating door close. "I didn't get you back just to lose you." Bridger closed the distance between them, his index finger pressing underneath Vega's chin, forcing her gaze to meet his. "Don't you ever fucking do that again."

Vega nodded.

"Say it." Bridger gripped her chin delicately, holding her head in place.

"I won't," she whispered, her eyes telling Bridger all he needed to know.

She would.

Which meant he had to keep shields up. He couldn't let her slip through again like that. He wouldn't let her be the one to break their bond. "You're lying, and I know it."

Vega sighed, taking a step back. "I know this is going to be hard for everyone... But it's already done. We can't change this ending."

"You gave up fifty-five years of your life to a curse. You're not giving the rest of it away." Gods, why did this woman have to be so fucking stubborn?

I take back everything I said about loving her sassy-ass attitude.

"You don't get to tell me what I can do with my life," Vega bit back.

"It's not just your life, Vega! It's mine too. It's Khort's. It's *Arlet's*." He couldn't help the natural rise in his voice's volume.

"Not if I break the bond." Vega reached for him again, but Bridger pulled back.

He wanted to touch her. *Fuck.* He wanted to so badly, but he knew he'd let this go for another time if he gave into the craving... and if they were starting over, it wouldn't be on shaky feet. "What if you break the bond and it takes Arlet's powers? Her dragon? What if it takes Khort's enhanced warrior abilities?" He slipped inside her mind. *"What if it takes this?"*

"This is going to come to an end eventually..."

Her words felt like a punch to the gut. Bridger inhaled a sharp breath at the same time a knock at the door interrupted their conversation. He closed his eyes, flexing his hands a few times before reopening them.

"Commander?" Halo's voice was muffled on the other side.

Bridger used the small amount of wind he could control to swing the door open, knowing it was another piece of Vega he'd been given access to after the summoning—because of their bond.

Halo stepped inside and froze when he caught the tension in the room. "Oh, sorry. Should I come back?" He took a couple steps backwards, looking like a child sneaking out after snooping on his parents. "I'll come back."

"What do you need, Halo?" Bridger asked, glancing over his shoulder.

"The others are arriving in five minutes." He stood awkwardly, more than likely waiting for Bridger to shoo him away.

"Thank you. Let them know I'll meet them at the gates." Bridger turned back to Vega, and he didn't have to look to know Halo left. The smell of his smoke lingered in the room after he was gone.

"Shower. I'll get them settled." Bridger walked past Vega, pushing the door to his small bathroom open.

"I'll go with you," Vega said, following him in.

He reached inside and adjusted the temperature of the stand-up shower to exactly what he knew Vega would like—scalding hot with a side of third degree burns. "Vega, please. Will you not fight me on this one thing today?" Bridger turned around to see the softening of her eyes.

Vega sighed, her shoulders sinking with the breath. "Fine."

Bridger forced a smile. *"Thank you."* He caressed the bond with his words and watched the chill travel up Vega's spine.

"Are you sure you don't want to stay and join me? I bet Halo can handle the tour just fine." Her fingers traveled to the end of her shirt and pulled the battle torn garment over her head.

Bridger drank in the sight of her while she kicked her boots off and slipped out of her pants. *Good gods, this woman could break me right now.*

If she told him this had all been a scheme, her big revenge plan to break his heart, Bridger would happily shatter into a million pieces for her.

He stepped forward now that she was in nothing but her underwear, running a hand over the soft skin of her curves and pulling her flush against him while the steam from the shower filled the room and fogged the mirror. "As amazing as that sounds, I'm not going to earn your friends' trust again by ignoring them to fuck you senseless in my shower."

Bridger moved his hands from her sides to the braids holding the hair out of her face. He gently worked the ties from the ends, placing them on the counter to his right. Bridger's fingers returned to the braids, delicately unbinding Vega's hair. "And even though you were finally truthful with me, I'm still not even sure *you* trust me." He rubbed the spots on either side of her scalp where the braids had held tightly, watching Vega's eyes flutter closed.

He leaned in and placed a sweet kiss on her lips while she wasn't expecting it. "Make yourself at home," he said as her eyes opened. "I'll bring Arlet to get you once I've given the tour. I have a room down the hall for you both." And Khort too, but he was sick of hearing his name out loud when the feel of Vega's lips was still on his.

Before Bridger lost his fight to leave, he ran a hand over Vega's cheek and exited the bathroom, closing her in and fleeing from his own room.

The elevator doors had begun to close when Vega's words came as a whisper in his mind. *"I do trust you..."*

DING. The doors closed.

"And you've never been the villain in my story."

43

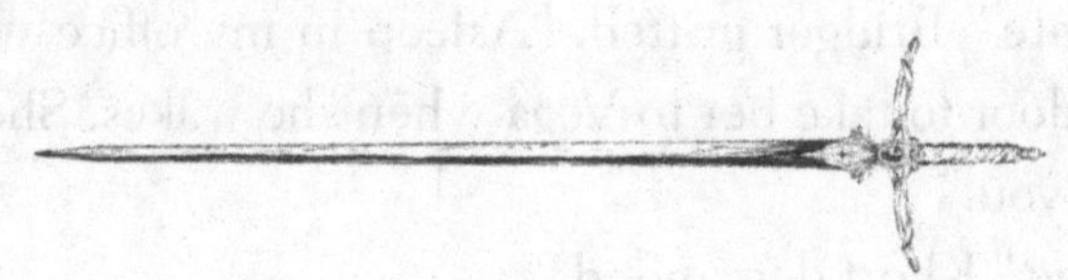

"WHERE'S NORA?" KHORT ASKED THE SECOND BRIDGER approached the opening gates of Vincere. "Has Octavia made it yet?"

"Hello to you too." Bridger forced a smile. "Glad you all made it in one piece."

Khort rolled his eyes so hard Bridger could *feel* it.

Mmm, nope, hate that.

Bridger wouldn't mind losing the bond to Khort and Arlet...

"We aren't friends, and I don't even want to be here." Khort glanced at Arlet, who looked as exhausted as Bridger knew they all were.

"Where else would you like to be, Khort? In the caves with no protection from Marlena's next attack?" Bridger asked, eyebrows drawing in with seriousness.

"Doesn't seem Marlena had any issues slaughtering your soldiers behind the very walls you're claiming will protect us," Khort fired back.

Bridger pulled out his dagger, ready to slit the lizard's throat for bringing up his soldiers' deaths.

"Bridger." Arlet intervened in time to save Khort from a blade through his eye socket.

A few tense moments passed while Bridger fought against the need to watch Khort bleed out.

"Is Nora safe?" Arlet asked, bringing the conversation back to where it needed to be. "Has Octavia sent word?"

"She's safe," Bridger gritted. "Asleep in my office with a guard outside the door to take her to Vega when she wakes. She'll be given a room near you."

"With me," Khort demanded.

His possessive nature was getting worse with age. "As you wish." He shrugged, realizing he didn't give a shit where Khort's niece stayed as long as she was out of Bridger's way. "I haven't heard anything from Octavia. Your dragon might be of good use if you're looking to expedite that." Bridger wasn't going to waste his time babysitting the Fera family. He had other things to worry about. Which was exactly why he'd left Vega naked in his shower to come up here in the first place. "Vega is the one I'm worried about."

Without hesitation, Arlet nodded. "Me too."

Khort had nothing to say, to Bridger's surprise. "Why don't you follow me? We have a lot to talk about."

Leo was put in charge of getting the rebels from the cave settled into rooms and fed while Bridger took Arlet and Khort to the control room—specifically because of the built-in power block sealing the room from the use of abilities outside his close staff, and the shields in place to keep people out who didn't have clearance.

"A place where we can't access our powers but you can doesn't seem fair," Khort pointed out while standing on the other side of the door.

"I'd be happy to do it somewhere else," Bridger said, eyes bouncing back and forth between Arlet and Khort. He'd already let Vega know everyone had made it safely, hoping her first warm shower since Earth was keeping her distracted.

"Good." Khort nodded with a smug smile like he'd won.

Bridger slid behind Khort's shields with such ease he almost felt bad... *Almost.* The shifter inside Khort flared to life, showing Bridger what life looked like through the eyes of a dragon.

"Get the fuck out of my head, Dimico." He growled octaves lower than his normal voice.

"Make me," Bridger taunted, leaning his body against the frame of the control room's door. He watched his body move under his control from the eyes of someone else. It was pretty cool, Bridger had to admit.

Khort had nothing to grasp on to because he didn't know what he was looking for, but Bridger could feel him fumbling around inside, trying.

"You can't keep me out, which means you can't keep Vega out." He slipped back into his own head. "And she's a sneaky little goddess if you're not paying attention. So, unless you can prove you've perfected your shields in the next ten seconds, then I'm going to insist you follow me in." He stepped to the side, watching Arlet inspect him from head to toe like she'd be able to see if he was planning an attack. "Your dragon form wouldn't fit in the room anyway, and I'd love to keep the control room intact. Again, unless you have another way to allow access to the entire camera system placed throughout Tolevarre's cities, then trusting me is kind of your only option." Bridger shrugged his shoulders. "You don't have to like me, but accepting I'm actually on the same side as you again will make things easier... and it might just save Vega."

Arlet stepped through without a word to Bridger. "Put your pride aside, Khort. We're at war with two sisters now. One who wants to kill us and the other who might already be dead."

Khort took a deep breath and joined Arlet and Bridger inside the room.

Bridger shut the door. "It's going to lock because the place is built to work alongside my powers as an added layer of protection. Don't freak out," he said as the sound of the lock slid into place.

Arlet looked around in awe at the screens staring back at her, flickering light onto her face as they rotated cameras every so often. "This is the place you dreamed of building, isn't it?" she asked as she walked down the first row of screens with seating and chairs underneath for those trusted individuals who were Bridger's security team.

Most of them were dead now...

"I spared no expense." Bridger waved his hand over a small scanner in the center of the room, and his credentials popped up on every screen, giving full access to the entire system. "I worked with the smartest mechanics and makers in Littera. This place is designed to withstand the war we've just started."

"The war began fifty-five years ago," Khort countered.

Bridger shook his head. "No, it didn't. Marlena wasn't scared then. Those battles were nothing more than her asserting her dominance and reminding people to stay in line." Bridger pulled up cameras to the city of Stella, where soldiers who hadn't left with Meyer patrolled the streets. The citizens kept their heads down and shuffled to and from where they needed to be with a sense of urgency that had Arlet fixated. "We need a safe place for those wanting to flee. Vates, Imber, Solum, and Demuto have been diminished to nothing and offer us the same. I'd like to see Fortis burned to the ground." Not all of its people, but his mother included. "Fraus needs no explanation. Pax, Oro, and Littera have nothing to offer other than their people. Leaving this the best and obviously"— he motioned to the control room—"the smartest location to set up base."

"Is Zetta Ignis of no worry to you?" Arlet asked about Meyer's mother, peeling her attention away from the screens. "This is her territory, after all."

"This is Marlena's territory. As is the rest of Tolevarre. It would take nothing to storm Zetta's home and take Ardor for ourselves. I can almost guarantee she would leave peacefully without a fight. Especially if we free the people Zetta allowed Marlena to use as slaves in the northern mines to produce energy for her overconsumption in Aeris. They'd be happy to tear Zetta to pieces if she tried to fight back."

Khort scoffed. "And you think Meyer's going to let you do that?"

Bridger snapped his head towards him. "Meyer is my second, and he's made his choice. He knows he's going against his parents by standing beside me. It will come as no surprise to them when he shows up at their door to commandeer the territory I've claimed half of already." Bridger flipped camera views, pulling up the city around the Ignises' home in Ustilo.

The place was surrounded with angry citizens. "Ah, would you look at that?" He zoomed in with his fingers on the main screen, the others following behind. "The foundation is already crumbling." The people of Tolevarre were finally ready to fight back against their oppressor. "Now, let's talk about Vega before she tracks us down and kicks our asses for conspiring behind her back."

Khort had barely moved from his place at the door. "We shouldn't hide things from her."

"Vega's been hiding things from us since before she left for Earth to break her curse, and she hasn't stopped since she got back either." Bridger would play by her rules only if she followed them too. "As of about thirty minutes ago, I've decided that I'm happy to hide whatever I need after Vega snuck behind my nearly impenetrable shields and started poking around at whatever power binds the four of us together." Bridger backed up to the counter and lifted himself into a seated position on the edge in hopes it would get Khort to relax. He was seconds from pacing. Bridger would have to snap his neck and see how long it took for the ichor inside to fix the break if he started that right now.

"She *what?*" Arlet barked.

Khort stumbled forward, finally leaving the entryway. "She can do that?"

"Apparently, which means she's going to do it to you two as well. Especially if she thinks you don't know she's capable of it." Bridger didn't have to explain Vega to them. They knew exactly who she was.

"You think she'll break the bond the second she gets the chance?" Khort asked.

Bridger shook his head. "No, but I also don't think me calling her out on it is going to stop her from trying."

"Gods, Vega." Khort sighed.

"She's done exactly what she promised she would. We can't be too surprised," Bridger added. "This started because she wanted to kill her sister—to save our people."

Hesitantly, Bridger told them everything he knew about Death, giving them an insight on the Dimico family's lore and what he suspected it meant for Vega.

They were missing something. Bridger knew it. "I just can't stop thinking about the things Romulus said, about the tie Vega's had to death since the night of our summoning."

Arlet shook her head, staring at a spot on the floor like it might spring a head and jump out at her. "Isn't the whole point of her breaking the curse so she doesn't die anymore?" She looked up, waiting for Bridger to have an answer to a question he knew nothing about.

He shrugged again. "We can go back and forth questioning technicalities all night, but that's not going to get us anywhere. The fact is, Vega sold her soul. Her curse has nothing to do with what happens to her now. Immortal or not, a soul can still be bartered, and there are worse things in life than death..." Bridger slid off the counter, his boots hitting the ground with a soft thud.

The room was quiet, nothing but the high-pitched hiss of electronics filling the silence.

"I'm assuming you have a plan." Khort was the first to speak. "Or we wouldn't be here."

Bridger's crooked smile pulled at his lips. "I'm the commander of Tolevarre. I always have a plan."

Arlet rolled her eyes. One of Khort's twitched.

"How much do you know about Pluto?" Bridger asked.

"You mean, the god of the underworld?" Arlet asked with confusion fusing her brows to the middle of her forehead.

Bridger nodded. "That's the one."

"Do not let her get her hands on you for too long. I'm not telling you to avoid her, but don't give her the opportunity to browse around if you can avoid it," Bridger mentioned before the elevator rolled to a stop and the doors opened.

Standing there was a freshly washed Vega dressed in the oversized black sweater and lounge pants Bridger had delivered while she showered. Her hair was still unbound and damp, only starting to dry at her roots.

Arlet threw herself through the doors and into Vega's open arms. "Hi! Ugh, you smell so good." She pulled out of the hug quickly, playing it off like she was looking down at her dingy clothes. "Bridger promised warm showers. It's the only reason I followed around on his long, boring tour." Arlet spoke the last part out of the side of her mouth like she was trying to keep a secret.

He stepped beside Arlet, exiting the elevator after Khort. "Hilarious." He didn't laugh.

Khort scanned the hallway. "Has Nora come to you yet?"

He'd known his nieces for less than twenty-four hours and he was already overbearing and annoying. "She's showering. I was headed to find someone who could find her some clean clothes."

"I'll send some down. Let me show you to your rooms." Bridger nodded to the end of the hall.

"They're small, and we conserve most of the energy for the common areas of Vincere, so don't expect luxury," Bridger said over his shoulder.

"Better than a cave," Arlet mumbled as Bridger opened the first door and then reached for the other directly across the hall.

"Two bunks in each. Bathrooms are at the end of the hall. If you'd like to keep your current clothes, feel free to use the laundry facilities on the bottom floor. Otherwise, I'll have some clean ones brought down with Nora's for now." Bridger knew he was missing a lot, but they could figure the rest out tomorrow.

Everyone was exhausted, their bond piling it on extra heavy.

Khort nodded and slipped into the room on the right, leaving Bridger alone with Arlet and Vega.

"Thanks, Bridger," Arlet said, before telling Vega, "I love you, and I wanna make sure you're okay, but it's been over a month since I've had a warm shower, and I don't think I can wait another minute." She scurried off towards the bathrooms.

"Did you eat?" Bridger asked now that they were alone.

"Yes," Vega answered. "I also looked through all your drawers, under your bed, inside your closet. I found nothing of interest, which was boring, and before I could track you all down, Nora showed up." She stepped into Bridger's personal space but didn't reach out for him. "Have *you* eaten?"

"I will," he told her.

"Okay" was all she said in response, but then the buzz of her voice on the inside lit a warm fire in Bridger's gut. *"I'm afraid to touch you again."*

Bridger looked at her like she had two heads. "Why?"

"Because of earlier," Vega replied softly.

"You mean when you expertly slipped behind my shields like you've been doing it all your life?"

She nodded once.

Bridger grabbed her by the back of the neck and pulled her into his chest while he wrapped the other around her in a hug. "I'm a little impressed by it, but I'll shut you out for good if you ever pull that shit on me again."

He wasn't kidding either. If anything, he'd at least keep her locked out until he found another way to handle this.

Vega laughed. "Fine. I'll just practice on the others instead."

"Vega." Bridger pulled from the hug and saw the honest smile on her lips.

"I'm sure you mentioned it while you gave your little tour, didn't you?" she asked, getting the answer she needed by whatever she saw on Bridger's face. Vega shrugged. "They'll drop their guard eventually."

"You're exhausting." Bridger sighed. "Can I at least trust that you'll get some sleep tonight? I'd hate to have to sleep at the foot of your bed instead of in my own on the first night back."

"Surprised you didn't suggest I join you in your—"

"Hey Vega, d—" Khort popped his head out of his room, stopping when he saw Vega wasn't alone. "Oh, uh, never mind." He started to retreat when Bridger waved him back out.

"I was just leaving. I have some things to finish up before I call it a night." Bridger took a step away, locking his hands behind his back. "I'll see to it you have everything you need for now. I'll send for you all in the morning. I think we're long overdue for a training session." Bridger dipped his head at Khort and caught Vega's longing gaze. "Goodnight."

Bridger was halfway down the hall when Vega reached down the bond to him. *"Sleep well."*

How the *fuck* was he supposed to *sleep well* knowing Vega was just down the hall from him, ready and willing to jump into bed and keep him up all night long?

It took everything in him not to invite her to his room, but Bridger didn't want her to think his feelings came purely from a sexual place. He cared about her well-being over everything else... or he'd suddenly started to again.

"You too," he said back as he stepped into his room and the door locked behind him.

44

"*The sister.*"

Two voices hissed beside Vega's head—no, *in*—echoing inside darkness she had never experienced before. She reached for her lightning, hoping to illuminate the blackness Vega felt she might suffocate in.

She pushed, and pushed, and pushed, pulling against the thread of power deep inside, but no matter what she did, her lightning never came.

"*Use us,*" the first voice begged.

"*You wanted the flames,*" the other cooed.

Fumbling around, Vega felt her surroundings. Inches from her fingertips was a wall that felt like it was made of stacked rocks.

"*You can't escape us,*" voice one hissed.

"*We are a part of you now,*" the other said slowly, hauntingly.

Vega ignored the panic rising from the pit of her stomach, swallowing as she continued to fight whatever kept her powers at bay. The air around her felt thin and stagnant, and she was unable to get the wind to stir through her fingertips like she should.

Vega ran her hands across the rock wall, using it to guide her.

"Where do you think you're going?" The voice sounded like it'd come from behind her this time, but Vega couldn't tell if it was the first or second voice anymore—not with the sound of her heart pounding in her ears.

She picked up her pace, going around, around, around. Vega skidded to a halt when she realized her feet stayed pointed to the right. "I'm walking in fucking circles," she said out loud.

She was in a dark, circular... pit.

Death. She couldn't feel it either. She couldn't dip into her head and pull the shadow out.

There was no inside here, wherever here was.

It was just Vega.

Alone.

"Never alone. We're with you."

Vega panicked, overestimating how much room she had, and slammed into the other side of the wall. The crunch of her nose made Vega yelp in pain. She didn't need to see to know she was bleeding. Her hands shot up, cupping a palm to catch the pooling blood. The taste of iron filled her mouth as it dripped between her lips and down her throat.

"Oh dear. Let us see what you've done to yourself."

"Use my fire."

The warmth of the flames she'd used on the battlefield with Marlena heated her palms. Vega's hand shot down from her face, the blood from her nose dripping down her chin. She balled them up tightly, pushing back against the urge to feel that heat again. "Fuck off!"

Vega slid her hands down her body, searching herself for the daggers strapped to her thigh... but they weren't there. She patted frantically, as if she could have missed them.

"That's not very nice, Vega." The way the voice said her name made another wave of fear slam into her stomach.

"Who are you?" she screamed, her voice echoing above her head. Vega craned her neck back, expecting to see something, *anything,* but there was nothing but darkness there too.

"You know who we are," they said at the same time.

"You could know us better if you let us in."

"Yes, let us in. We can defeat him if we join together. We can save you."

Vega threw her arms out beside her, one hand scraping up the side of the rock as she tried to determine how large the space was. "Defeat who?" Her hands didn't touch from side to side without leaning. "Save me from who?"

"The one who bonded you."

Remus? What does Remus have to do with any of this?

Six feet. The round room wasn't a foot wider than Vega's full height. The room felt like it was closing in on her.

The voices snickered, and Vega knew they were laughing at the words she hadn't said out loud. *"Remus."*

"Remus never made it here."

"How?" she screamed, turning in circles like one of them would show their face.

"We are inside you. We know all your thoughts." They spoke at the same time in two different vocal patterns and pitches. *"We know everything about you, Goddess of Death."*

Vega heard the roar of Death above her then, claws scraping across what sounded like stone. Pebbles rained down, pattering against the floor but never making contact with Vega.

Vega. Vega. Vega. Vega. Vega.

She shook her head, trying to clear the echo of her name. "Wait..." Vega felt like she was drifting, being forced out by some unknown source. "Why would we need to save my soul from who bonded me?"

Her name came again from somewhere else, down a pathway she knew. "Bridger," she gasped.

"Use us and we'll tell you..."

Vega.

Vega.

Vega!

Vision flooded back at the same time Vega's electric current snapped on. Bridger's dark eyes and worry-stricken face came into view, but it was too late to stop what happened next.

The fear consumed her, and Vega's lightning was always there to jump to her defense. Even Death was slower to react.

It nuzzled against her mind, helping bring her back to this new reality. One where she was fitting pieces of a puzzle together she thought had been completed years ago.

Bridger managed to break away from the hold Vega had on his left forearm, but not without a jolt of lightning zapping him like he'd stuck his finger in a light socket... only ten times worse, probably. He whacked his head on the top bunk Arlet had been sleeping in, hissing as his hand shot to rub the spot he'd hit.

Vega felt like she couldn't get enough air in her lungs, and fuck, why was she so *hot?* Gripping the blanket, Vega slipped her legs out and froze when she saw the blood staining her sheets.

"Your nose was bleeding. You're okay." She felt the mattress sink beside her as Bridger lowered himself back down, reaching for her face.

His voice was muffled by the ringing in her ears.

He turned her head in his hands, inspecting every inch before he moved down to her neck and then her arms. Bridger paused at the knuckles on her right hand. "You must have scraped your hand on something when you were thrashing."

"What... what happened?" Vega finally spoke, her voice cracking from how dry her throat was.

Khort appeared with a cup of water. Vega snatched it while mouthing, *Thank you,* and downed it in only a few gulps. It sated her thirst, but it did nothing to cool the heat of her body.

"You tell us." Arlet crouched down to her knees by the edge of the bed. "We were the ones you woke up with your screaming."

"Screaming?" Vega asked, trying to remember what had made her—*Oh shit*. Vega couldn't see it, but she knew she'd gone pale by Bridger's reaction.

The gods...

She shuddered at the memory of their eerie voices... But it was what the gods *hadn't* said that sat heaviest on her.

Vega swallowed the saliva pooling in her mouth from the nausea rolling her stomach like an angry sea. Everyone stared at her, waiting.

They all looked like they had no idea what to say.

Everyone was too quiet, making Vega's nerves skyrocket.

Bridger finally let his hands drop from her body after he'd inspected every visible inch.

Lie.

Vega forced a laugh, and even to her own ears, it sounded forced. She cleared her throat. "I had a nightmare." Wiping the back of her hand over her nose, Vega smeared sticky blood across her cheek.

Death rose from its curled-up position, flaring its nostrils like it smelled her lie. It had been trying to get to her, clawing its way through layers and layers of a shield Vega hadn't placed.

"A nightmare? Vega, you've been screaming for ten minutes. We've been trying to wake you for *ten minutes*." The fear in Arlet's voice made Vega's heart ache.

She didn't need more worries.

Fake it.

Vega kept up the obviously fake laugh. "Weird." She scooted to the edge of the bed, swaying from a dizzying rush of adrenaline. She swatted Bridger's hand away. "I'm fine." She looked him in the eyes and realized she couldn't feel him.

Her shields were locked.

Shit.

Vega flung them open, and Bridger flooded her senses. *"Fine? You expect me to believe you're fine?"*

Khort stayed quiet, a somber and exhausted set of eyes meeting hers.

"I've had nightmares since some of my very first lives. It's nothing new." But this one was... This one wasn't a nightmare at all. Real nightmares she woke from.

"Not like that." Arlet pointed at the bed where Vega's blood stained the sheets and blanket.

"I..." Vega started, biting her lip and shrugging. "I don't know what to tell you. I had to have hit something, maybe hit myself in the face." She glanced down at the black clothes, thankful for the dark color hiding the bloodstains she knew she was covered in. "Speaking of, I can see how horrible I look."

Sliding behind Arlet's and Khort's open shields was too easy. Vega saw herself through her best friends' eyes, rotating between the two. "I should clean myself up."

Vega slipped out of their heads and back into hers, fleeing the room. She walked as quickly as she could without sprinting to the bathrooms at the end of the hall.

The door hit the wall behind it as she crashed inside, beelining for the sinks. Vega's face was covered in blood, most of it drying and crusting around the edges of her hair.

Vega snatched her ring off and slapped it on the counter. Blood smeared her hands, and when she turned them over, it was obvious it had pooled in her palms—as if she'd really been inside her head with the gods and everything that had happened was real.

You've had enough time. How had Vega missed the clues?

Death bared its teeth at the pit, a tar-like black liquid dripping from its fangs. Vega slipped out when she heard an unintelligible whisper echo up.

The scrape across her knuckles stung when she turned on the faucet and ran them under cold water.

Vega leaned down and splashed her face, cupping her hands to repeat the motion. She groaned at the soreness of her nose when she applied too much pressure.

It wasn't broken, but it had to have come close from the amount of pain still lingering.

A suffocating stillness gripped the room as a shield bubbled around her, and Vega knew who'd be behind her when she stood up straight, pink water stained with blood dripping onto the counter.

Bridger's onyx eyes were fixed on hers in the mirror, the tick of his jaw catching the fluorescent lighting. "You can lie to them, Vega." Gods, his voice was deep. Deeper than usual from sleep and... anger? "I'll gladly lie to them for you if that's what you want, but you won't lie to me." He reached out and gripped her shoulder rougher than she'd expected, twisting her around and slamming the small of her back against the counter.

Vega gasped as Bridger caged her in, his hands gripping the counter edge behind her. "I didn't lie. I had a nightmare." She thought if she kept saying it out loud, she'd convince herself too and she wouldn't be afraid to go back to sleep.

She wouldn't be afraid to face what the voices had said... what they'd made her realize.

Your soul was mine before you begged for the power to kill her. It was right in front of her face.

"I know what nightmares look like. I've had plenty. That wasn't a nightmare."

Vega stood as still as she could, glancing down at the bulging veins of Bridger's forearms and his bare chest's steady rise and fall from the deep breaths he took.

"Why are you half naked?" she asked, her eyes dragging slowly back to his after she noticed he was in nothing but a loose fit pair of black sleep pants.

Bridger cocked his head, his mood not dulling. Everything about him was rigid—every muscle in his body tight with an anger Vega knew he was fighting to keep control over. "Because I woke up to the sound of you screaming down the bond, begging someone to let you out. I woke up because Death came and got me."

Vega went numb.

Death stilled inside her, worried she'd be mad.

"It came to you?" Vega exhaled.

"Yes. It slipped through our open door and snatched me from my sleep. So excuse me for forgetting to completely suit up." Bridger leaned in, getting inches from her face. "Now, tell me what the fuck that was before I drag Death out and demand answers."

Death perked at its name on Bridger's lips again. Its wings shivered, fluttering overhead in a flitted stretch before it sauntered and rubbed its shadowed body against the doorframe to Bridger.

It didn't have scales like a dragon or fur like a cat, but its actions were becoming more feline as time grew.

Vega closed her eyes, took a breath, and told him everything she could remember. From the way everything felt, to hearing Death screeching from above like she was stuck in her mind's pit.

"It's the gods I took from Marlena. Diana and Vulcan." Fear made Vega go cold at what they'd told Vega without saying anything at all. "They told me if I used their powers, we could defeat him. We could save my soul from the one who bonded me."

Death roared down to the pit again, rattling Vega's mind. She blinked away the fuzz of its shared outrage with Bridger. "I begged for the power to bind us, to kill her. I asked for Marlena's death." Her voice was so small, so scared. "And I was saved... unable to be killed by the death curse already placed on me. He didn't bind you all to me. It was the other way around." Her body went cold. "He bound my life to the three of you so I wouldn't die, in hopes I'd find a way to kill my sister and send the dead gods to the underworld with her..." Vega knew the second it clicked for Bridger. She could almost see the image he had inside his head.

Vega, Bridger, Arlet, and Khort around a fire. Their bloody

hands linked together. Willing to do whatever it took to save their world from Marlena.

She'd never found anything about Remus or his curse... because Remus never made it to Tolevarre.

"Bridger," Vega whispered. Her voice quivered. "I don't think it was Remus we summoned."

Only the sound of their shaky breaths filled the space between them. Vega was too afraid to say another word.

"Me neither..." Bridger whispered.

Vega felt her eyes glaze over, losing herself inside her mind. She'd been so young, so desperate to keep everyone safe from her sister. Vega hadn't known what she was doing—she wasn't the sister who'd spent years researching.

"Look at me," Bridger said softly.

Vega hauled her head up, finding Bridger already staring at her. "We can't change anything from before. Whatever happened... we move forward."

She had no idea what to say, at a complete loss for words. Why did things have to be so fucking complicated all the time?

"They can't control you if you don't let them." He stared at her pointedly. "Keep fighting." His eyes trailed over her face, and he sighed, reaching around her.

Vega turned her head to see him flipping the faucet on behind her and dunking a washcloth under its running water.

After wringing the cloth, Bridger brought it to her face and gently wiped around her hairline, cleaning the blood Vega hadn't gotten before he interrupted. When he was done with her face, he moved down her neck and then to her chest, half exposed by the too-big sweater draping off her shoulder. "Lift your arms," he told her, putting the damp cloth on the counter. He gripped her by the hips, gently placing her on the edge next to the sink, and then slipped his hands under the hem of her sweater. Bridger slid her out of the top and cleaned the dry blood marks that had dripped down her bare chest.

Vega leaned back on her arms, giving Bridger access to the stains sliding past her navel. He was laser focused on cleaning every streak off her skin.

Her nipples perked when the warm rag brushed against the peak of her breasts. She closed her eyes and rested her head against the mirror, the brush of her down hair across her collarbone sending shivers down her spine.

Vega concentrated on the sound of Bridger's calm breaths, the sureness of his touch. This was the gentleness she remembered—the man Bridger had been when it was just the two of them. The obsessive need to please, the desperation to be seen for who he was and not what he was supposed to be.

He dragged the cloth up the slope of Vega's neck. The air had cooled the once warm fabric, and though the temperature of her body wasn't as heated as it had been when she'd woken from the void, the nearness of Bridger and his delicate touch kept it elevated.

Chill bumps raced across Vega's skin.

"Bridger," she hummed, her eyes fluttering open to see him sitting on a short stool he must have pulled out from under the sink, placing kisses on her thighs, his hands gripping tightly at her hips.

"Yes, Kitten?" he asked, his voice scratching something inside her brain.

"Kiss m—"

Bridger's lips were on hers before the demand was even out of her mouth. He consumed her, kissing her like he'd truly been worried Vega wouldn't wake.

The strokes of his tongue, the ravenous hunger Vega could feel down the bond was too much. She lost herself in him, in the feel of rough hands sliding up her shirtless sides, the tangle of his hand at the back of her head where the hair met her neck.

Vega wanted Bridger. Her body *needed* him... but not like this.

She was on overdrive and couldn't get her emotions under control. Vega turned her head, breaking their kiss. Bridger trailed down her neck, biting intently on the places he knew would drive Vega wild.

And they did. She gasped, rolling her body against his mouth. *"Bridger, I..."*

He felt the urgency in her tone, his lips leaving her skin to search the meaning behind whatever look she wore.

"What do you need?" he asked, releasing his hold from the back of her head. "Tell me and I'll do it." So much hunger burned behind his dark eyes.

Vega rested her arms on his shoulders and looked up at him when he stood to his full height, stepping between her spread legs on the counter. "I want you." She put her hand on his chest. "But not like this. Not with my head like this."

His grip on her hips loosened, his hunger settling to understanding, and he smiled a small, sweet smile just for her.

The left side of his lip pulled slightly higher than the other, and the tiniest dimple formed. Vega leaned up and placed a kiss over it, her hands holding Bridger's exposed hips.

Bridger moved, and Vega saw him reach for her blood-soaked black sweater. "Put this on. I know the perfect distraction." Bridger stepped back, adjusted himself—which Vega would have been a fool not to notice—and held his hand out for her to take.

Vega threw the sweater over her head, grabbed Bridger's hand, and felt the shield he'd been holding around them fall as they stepped through the doorway back into the hall.

Before they turned the corner, Vega paused. "I don't want them to know about..." Her voice trailed off.

"It can be our little secret for now," Bridger promised. "We'll tell them when we're sure."

Vega was sure... She nodded her head anyway, happy to avoid it until she couldn't anymore.

Arlet and Khort stood outside the open door of Khort's room, Nora peeking out as they approached. Vega let his hand go and flexed her fingers while Bridger spoke.

"Assuming none of you are going back to sleep, we should probably utilize all the free time we have to train."

"I'm awake," Khort said, staring down at Vega like she was lost at sea. He longed for a person who no longer existed, and it was written on every worry line etched across his face.

Arlet nodded. "Nora could use some hand-to-hand training too."

Khort opened his mouth to object, but Nora spoke for herself. "Tav has taught me some. Since I haven't manifested yet, we've kept most of my training to a minimum." She pushed her dark curls behind one ear.

"At this point, everyone needs to be trained to fight. Being weak and underestimating the battles to come are how you get killed." Bridger nodded towards the elevator at the end of the hall. "I have the perfect opponent for her."

Twenty minutes later, everyone was suited up in fresh, brand-new training gear, and they stood in the middle of the most insane gym Vega had ever seen in her life.

This was it. This was Bridger's dream.

Everything he'd told Vega he wanted to do when his father finally stepped down.

She looked around in awe at the well-lit, multi-level facility circling in a big dome. On the top floor was something similar to what Vega would have seen on Earth with all the complicated equipment regular people had to Google how to use before going in, hoping they wouldn't embarrass themselves.

The middle level had a track where soldiers jogged or sprinted, more cardio equipment in the center.

While the bottom floor, which was the biggest, was covered in training rings of different sizes. The largest ring sat in the center, a cylinder with a barely visible shield around it.

Halo yawned, rubbing the sleep from his eyes. "Commander, no disrespect, but what was I dragged out of bed for again?"

"Because you're a string bean and I've seen ten-year-olds fight better than you," he blurted, coming to stand next to Vega.

Arlet filled her cheeks with a puff of air and slapped her hand over her mouth.

Vega side-eyed her, rolling her lips between her teeth and biting down to hide the laugh threatening to spill out.

"Noted." Halo blushed, crossing his arms and doing what he could to make himself small, slinking behind everyone.

"Warm up and meet me at the center mat in ten minutes." Bridger glanced at Vega, brushing his fingers against hers as he walked away.

45

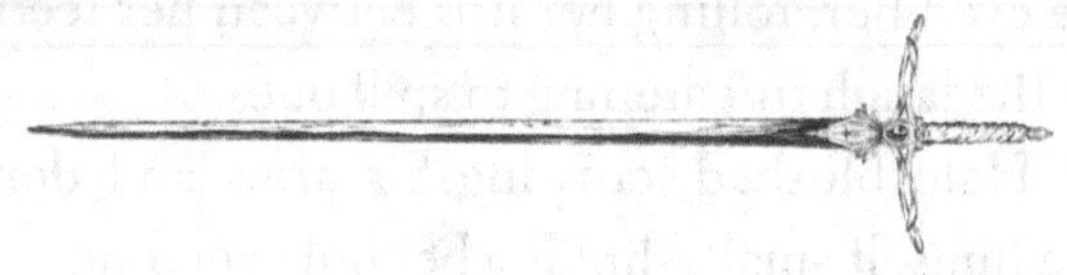

MEYER STOOD LEANING AGAINST THE RING, LOOKING BORED, tapping three times against the glass-like forcefield when Bridger stepped up beside him.

The soldiers stopped their sparring, sweat pouring down their faces from the heat they'd created with their fire. One's hands went to his knees as he fought to catch his breath. The other had long honey-colored hair pulled into a tight ponytail with waves flowing down her back. Her deep olive skin glowed from the ember of fire flickering out in her hand, and she was the last person Bridger had ever expected to see on this side of the war.

Her eyes were fixed directly on Bridger, and a smile that spelled trouble brightened her face.

"Go cool down and finish with a five-mile jog," Meyer ordered, watching the two head for the exit when he dropped the shield.

"You didn't tell me Helena came." Bridger kept his voice neutral.

"You didn't ask, and I didn't find it necessary. She's a great asset to the war. It's not my fault you fu—"

"Commander," her voice purred from behind the two men.

Bridger spun around and gazed down at her. She was tall, but still short enough she had to tip her chin to meet his eyes. "Helena."

Full transparency. Bridger hadn't slept with anyone for the first ten years after he'd left Vega—there was too much else he'd needed to do, too many feelings he had to overcome and lock away.

After that, the only pleasure he let himself feel was that from meaningless sex. No attachments. No feelings. Raw, unfiltered sex.

Helena had been that quite a few times over the last couple years. And apparently, she hadn't heard the news...

Before anyone had the chance to speak again, *the news* and her friends arrived.

"Why is she looking at you like a midnight snack?" Her words were almost playful, a hint of the darkness from earlier still evident in her tone. *"I mean, I get it, but—"* Vega cut herself off when the group settled in around them and Helena's blazing stare settled on her. *"Ohhhh. Y'all fucked."*

Bridger coughed, covering his mouth with his fist, thankful Arlet stepped forward to introduce herself to Helena and the young man she'd been sparring. "Hi, I'm Arlet."

It took the attention off him for at least a few seconds while the rest exchanged pleasantries, including Vega.

She shook Helena's hand last. "Vega" was all she said with a smile proving she didn't care.

"Wow," Helena mused. "The infamous sister." Her eyes flicked to Bridger and then back to Vega. "It's crazy how similar they look. Don't you think, Commander?"

He'd kill her if she thought she could step in between what he and Vega were working to rebuild. "*I think* the general told you to go for a jog." Bridger turned away from Helena, focusing on Vega and Arlet. "You two first." He nodded towards the ring the others had just come out of.

Arlet winked at Vega, pulling her hair up into a messy bun. "Ready to have some fun?"

Vega's smile grew as she slipped her arm around Arlet's shoulders. "Let's see what you've learned while I've been gone," she said, popping a kiss on Arlet's cheek.

Bridger felt his heart constrict in his chest, watching Vega with her best friend. She'd already given too much of her life. She deserved a chance to experience what was stolen from her.

When the girls slid into the ring, Bridger stepped up to where Meyer had been standing and leaned over. "We all know I'm a huge fan of hand-to-hand and that it's the foundation of every good warrior, but there's nothing more deadly than a warrior who can perfect both their ability and the art of fighting at the same time." He raised a brow. "Which is exactly what this ring allows you to do."

Vega checked over daggers sheathed at her thigh while Arlet pulled out her swallow—the bonded double-edged sword she'd had for nearly fifty years—from behind her back.

"The use of your powers inside the forcefield will not kill your opponent, but weapons will. Unless you're us." He smiled deviously. Bridger waved his hand over the controls, and the shield traveled from the floor up until it caged Vega and Arlet in. His voice echoed through a speaker. "We need to learn to use our bond to our advantage on the battlefield. Drop those shields and see through each other's eyes. Learn to anticipate each other's next move."

Arlet and Vega nodded, reaching out to shake hands like every good match should start. Instead of shaking hands, though, they did what they'd always done. They wiggled the tips of their fingers against each other's.

"Begin." Bridger's voice boomed, and the girls wasted no time getting started.

Clouds formed from nothing, water droplets immediately peppering the forcefield like a window on a rainy day. Vega's storm clouds swirled, but a cyclone didn't form. Blue lightning scattered across the clouds, jumping down to Vega's hands before crawling up her arms.

Death stayed put.

Bridger would never forget the feel of it creeping into his mind, dragging him out of a dreamless sleep to the sound of Vega screaming down the bond.

Then the cylinder shield transformed before everyone's eyes, earning gasps from those who had taken a moment away from their training to watch a couple of Tolevarre's new gods spar.

No longer was the ring a fighting mat. It had turned into exactly what Arlet wanted it to be. The fucking *sky*.

It was as if the girls walked through the clouds of Vega's power.

Arlet ducked in time to avoid a lightning strike to the chest but took her eyes off Vega for a split second, not watching the backside of the electricity channel waiting to be recalled by Vega in the cloud Arlet rolled through.

Arlet's cry of pain couldn't be heard through the shield, but the bulging veins in her neck were proof enough Vega had landed the first blow.

"I thought you said powers wouldn't hurt us inside the ring, Dimico," Khort growled, grabbing him by the shoulder.

Bridger glanced down at Khort's hand, sneering at his touch. "No, I said they couldn't *kill* you. I never said anything about the pain."

Meyer gripped Khort by the wrist and seared a handprint where he'd wrapped his hand. "Hands off, you giant gecko."

Khort hissed and rounded his fist, ready to strike Meyer.

Bridger sighed, turning his back to the ring where Vega and Arlet continued to fight. Without missing a beat, Bridger caught Khort's fist in his hand. "Would you two like to step on a mat?" He wouldn't let Khort pull his hand back, holding tight. "That's the only place we fight now." He made sure to look them both in the eyes. "We don't have to like each other, but we do have to fight on the same team." He let Khort's hand go. "Learn to get along."

He turned back to the fight in time for Vega to take a fist to the jaw. He cringed at the blood spilling from her busted lip.

"I don't take orders from you, Bridger," Khort grumbled, turning away to focus on the fight too.

Rolling his eyes, Bridger elbowed Meyer in the side when he snickered. "Enough."

Meyer cleared his throat and went serious. The three of them watched Vega and Arlet continue, Arlet changing the vision everyone saw to something much darker. Billowing night swirled inside, stealing the ability to see inside the ring, and for the briefest of seconds, Bridger felt the sheer panic shoot down the bond to him before a crack of her lightning lit the entire shield up in a blue glow. The crack that followed shook the gym.

The dark. He didn't need her to tell him it took her back to the place she'd been stuck inside her head.

"Did you get the chance to talk to anyone?" Bridger asked, pushing his shield to block the three of them from wandering ears.

Khort's head snapped to Bridger immediately, and Meyer eyed Bridger like he was nuts, peeking around to glare at Khort suspiciously.

"He knows. So does Arlet." Bridger shrugged. "You wanna be the one to deal with the backlash from Vega if I find the information I need?"

Meyer didn't have to respond for Bridger to know the answer would be a resounding no. "You're serious about this." Meyer hadn't phrased it as a question.

"Dead."

Sighing, Meyer looked ahead at the ring, where it seemed Arlet might have the upper hand for the moment. "My contact can be here in four days."

Bridger almost questioned who he'd reached out to, but Khort interrupted.

"And what about Ardor?" Khort added.

Meyer's brows pinched together. "What about Ardor?" he asked with a much different inflection.

Khort raised both brows, realizing what he'd done. A smile slid across his lips. "Oops."

"Meyer, you know we have to take Ardor, right?" Bridger asked, diving into the conversation he'd planned to have with him later in the day when they'd decide what to do about the people in the mines. *Thanks, Khort.*

"Why would we need to overthrow Ardor? My parents—my mother won't bother us here." Meyer leaned against the control board to the ring beside him.

"We can't share a territory with the enemy," Khort interjected.

Bridger wasn't sure Khort had ever thought before speaking a day in his life.

"They're my parents... not the enemy." Meyer seethed, his finger tips glowing.

"Hmm, I'm sorry. I must have confused them for the people who plotted with Marlena behind everyone's back." Khort looked like he was ready to spit on Meyer's grave. "Oh, wait."

"You assho—" Meyer raced towards Khort with fire burning behind his eyes. Bridger grabbed him by the collar of his suit and yanked him back.

Meyer was a big dude, and if Bridger weren't who he was, Meyer would be stronger than him by a lot... but he wasn't, and Bridger hadn't had to use much effort to stop him in his tracks. "You two are giving me fucking *hives*," Bridger groaned, using the words Vega had said to him back on Earth while he stepped in between them.

A crack exploded inside the ring, and this time the fight was over. Vega landed what would have been the killing blow. Arlet's mirage faded away, revealing Vega pressing one of the tips of Arlet's swallow over her heart.

Vega twisted the handle and held it outstretched for Arlet to take as she helped her best friend up.

Bridger made sure neither Meyer nor Khort were going to jump at each other the second he moved out of the way and hit the button to bring the shield down. It fell like someone had popped a bubble.

"You bitch!" Arlet said with a laugh, wiping the water from Vega's storm out of her eyes. "How did you do that?"

Vega threw her head back, laughing like that was the most fun she'd had in years. "I can see through your mirage when I'm in your head." Vega hugged Arlet, pulling her back to inspect her for injuries.

Bridger let them have their moment, but he didn't miss the way Khort watched every move Vega made—the way his eyes longed for her to look his way.

"Meyer, we need Ardor. All of Ardor. We have to claim something Marlena can't have. A place to set up the rebellion, to house the people who flee. A place for the people in the mines to recover. If your parents are going to stay with Marlena, they can go be with her in Aeris."

Through an almost locked jaw, Meyer said, "I get it when you say it like that, but when Scales over here starts talking, nothing but a bunch of bullshit spews out."

"Getting along for fifteen minutes was too hard?" Arlet asked, her hands resting on her hips as the girls approached, soaked from head to toe like they'd survived a tornado. Vega pushed her wet hair off her forehead, raising a brow at Bridger.

The shield Bridger had slid around himself, Khort, and Meyer extended to let Vega and Arlet in, but no one else. The rest of the room was silent around them, despite the training facility buzzing with early morning activity.

"*Toddlers. Everyone keeps acting like toddlers.*" He grumbled his annoyance.

Vega smiled softly, rolling her eyes. She was healing quickly, her split lip barely swollen.

"Fine. We take Ardor," Meyer agreed with a grumble, crossing his arms over his chest.

"Do you think the people in the mines are going to be on our side just because we set them free?" Khort asked, actually bringing up a great point. "No offense, but I can imagine you're not one of their favorites."

Bridger had sentenced a few people to the fates of the mines...

It was either that or death—some would call his decision merciful.

"I think with the right person there to lead them, they'll remember who the real enemy is," Bridger answered, having already thought this through.

"Leo." Khort caught on quickly.

"Leo," he agreed. "A person for them to follow. The one who escaped back to save them."

Everyone needs a martyr.

Bridger had learned a lot about what people wanted and what they needed over the course of his time as commander of Tolevarre. People wanted something to fight for and to believe in... no matter what side of the line they lay on.

People believed Marlena would keep them safe. So they stayed.

Others saw through her facade and got out as fast as they could because they believed in a different type of world.

But the one thing above all else was that the people of Tolevarre wanted to feel seen, to know they weren't forgotten.

The people, the criminals, deemed so by Marlena, who were locked away to mine coal to fuel Tolevarre's richest and most powerful, were going to fight—Bridger had to make sure they were fighting for the right side, not becoming another problem they had to fix.

"We need bodies in this war." Bridger held a hand out, stopping Khort from arguing what he knew he was going to: *These are people, not bodies!* "And their lives are no less important than all the others we are going to lose. The people in the mines are some of the strongest fire-wielders and metallurgists ever. We don't want to have them as a separate enemy, but leading an army isn't easy, Khort. You have to make decisions based on the overall likelihood you're going to win. You have to make decisions based on the fact people are going to die and you can't control who it's going to be or when." Bridger didn't feel fear when it came to leading armies. He knew what happened in wars. His entire existence was based around leading people into them... but there was one life he was set on saving over all others—and it went against everything he'd been bred to believe. *I will save her.* "You have to stop thinking you can save everyone, or you'll lose the war."

Vega said nothing, but he could read the look on her face, knew why her lips were pulled to the side in a tiny smile. She was proud of him.

The calculated monster he'd had to become didn't scare her.

"You all understand that, right?" His gaze grazed over the group of people standing around. "We can't control fate. We can't control who we lose."

Meyer included—Bridger couldn't ensure he'd live... Meyer knew too, but he was still standing by Bridger, ready to fight against the entire sanctum he'd been taught to defend.

"Understood," Khort said, not looking happy about it.

Bridger could feel he *got it*, at the very least.

"We need to act fast. Marlena has probably already thought of the mines at this point. Look how quickly she snatched the shifters up, swooping in to play savior one minute, only to betray them the next." Vega added.

Marlena could curse another set of people, forcing them to follow against their will. Knowing Vega could take the gods and their powers from Marlena made it hard to argue against using them.

Bridger was more concerned with what holding the gods inside for too long would do to Vega. If it was this bad at two... Bridger couldn't imagine what was in store as that number grew.

Vega deserved a chance to enjoy the world she fought for.

And Bridger was set on making that happen.

With the piece of knowledge he'd obtained this morning in the bathroom with Vega, he might have an upper hand he hadn't expected to have.

"Tomorrow. We waste no time. Get our groups ready, strategize, and we move out early morning." He scanned the circle one last time. "Anyone opposed?" He waited for Khort, because if it was going to be anyone, it'd surely be him.

To Bridger's surprise, he said nothing, only shook his head. "Good. Now, back to this morning's agenda. Train... and then we tell Leo." Bridger let the shield down, and the rattle of weights, echoing voices, and sounds of the facility returned.

"Okay, so who's next?" Vega asked, raising that scarred brow of hers. She wiggled both at Meyer, always ready to toy with him.

Bridger chuckled, the rumble deep in his throat. "Me."

Sparring with Vega was like returning to a dance he hadn't done in years. Sure, they'd battled and spent plenty of time trying to kill each other over the course of the last forty years, but it was different stepping into a ring with someone when the outcome wasn't the other's death—when it was to test how well they knew each other's strengths and weaknesses, Vega and Bridger excelled.

"*Hi,*" Vega purred, rolling her shoulders as they settled on opposite sides of the mat.

"*Hello, Kitten. Are you ready to play?*" he responded, cracking his neck with the cock of his head to each side.

The shield locked into place, making the outside world disappear.

It was just Vega and Bridger... and he was ready to see how much she'd paid attention. He extended his hand, and Vega took it, never breaking eye contact.

She let Death come to play, nibbling at his fingers like a playful pet.

Clouds rolled around them, forming like they had with Arlet. The vapor clung to Bridger like a cloak, making him feel wet all over.

"Born ready." She let go of his hand.

For every strike Bridger threw, Vega blocked. It went blow for blow for a while, both of them taunting the other with a move they'd already seen coming.

What turned the tides for Bridger's win, though, was his new ability to wield Vega's electricity as a weapon... to be able to force her lightning into a sword.

Though she'd seen it happen a few times before, Bridger using it against her threw her off, and he was able to land what would have been a killing blow. He swung the electric sword over his wrist and held it out, the tip hovering over Vega's heart. "You know better than to let a surprise throw you off." Bridger scolded lightly, letting go of her power. The lightning traveled back down his leg and slithered across the floor until it found Vega, disappearing inside her.

"If you fight every battle with one of those, I think you'll shock people to death and won't even need to draw blood." Vega shook her head with a light chuckle.

The rest of the day flew by.

Bridger had Khort and Arlet pinned next in under three minutes. They'd never been able to read Bridger like Vega had, but the best thing that had come out of today was the bonded learning they could also wield Vega's power.

When in shifter form, Khort could pull bolts of lightning from the sky like his own fire and Arlet could manipulate them to strike where she wanted.

They were all truly connected.

Everyone's mood lifted after training, seemingly moving on from the terror of their morning. But it was still at the forefront of Bridger's mind while he went about his day...

While he'd technically deserted his official title as commander of Tolevarre, he knew things needed to be documented for years to come. When people looked back on this part of Tolevarre's history, Bridger knew how important it would be for them to have firsthand accounts of every detail transpiring during these times.

He mulled over a leather bound book unrelated to what he'd spent most of the day doing, telling himself the light research was to give his mind a break.

Bridger took notes in the margins, not worried about marking the book up for others in the future. It would never leave his desk, and the information felt engraved inside his brain after the last few nights of reading.

Bridger had more than one plan, more than one theory brewing in the back of his mind.

He'd left the training facility as soon as their session was done, moving throughout his day with Meyer and the soldiers from his side who would make the best leaders.

Unfortunately, Helena was one of them... She'd already proven it through her years of service.

While they all were now fighting for the same outcome, it was silly to think there wouldn't be division. They might technically all be rebels in the eyes of Marlena and her followers, but each side still had their trusted leaders.

Bridger and Khort were opposite sides of the same coin.

A knock at his door stopped him from flipping the page. His empty dinner plate sat beside him on his desk, an untouched glass of his favorite dark liquor sitting on a coaster.

"Okay, I knocked because I was trying to be polite, but you were taking too long to answer." Vega opened the door, waltzing in wearing a fresh set of sleep clothes free of this morning's blood. "So. Hi." She stopped in the middle of the room, looking more beautiful than the day he'd met her.

"Hey, baby," Bridger responded, transfixed on the girl he'd fallen in love with almost fifty-eight years ago.

Seventeen-year-old Vega was a knockout. She was always dressed in the best clothes and styled like the eye of a storm. The eighteen-year-old who'd finally given the dangerous warrior a chance beyond friendship would always be a personal favorite of his. The twenty-year-old who'd led a summoning and bonded his soul to hers and two others had changed his life forever. But the seventy-five-year-old goddess standing in the middle of his room in a pair of loose black pants and an oversized sweater with a scar proving the passage of time?

That was the woman Bridger found himself wanting to know.

Not the girl she'd been.

Bridger wanted to get his forever with her. He wanted to spend the rest of their eternal lives getting to know all the versions of themselves they were going to become.

Which only reminded him Vega still wasn't his to keep. Her soul belonged to someone else...

"Why are you looking at me like that?" she asked, pulling at the sleeves of her sweater nervously.

Bridger smiled lazily. "Like what?"

"Like you're planning your goodbye."

He stood, crossing the room. "There will not be another goodbye." The words tasted like a lie coming out of his mouth. "I was just thinking about how beautiful you are, how fucking incredible you are. About how lucky I am." Bridger couldn't help himself. Vega was like a magnet, and he couldn't fight the pull.

His hand slid up the shoulder exposed by her sweater and over the side of her neck until he held the back of her head.

She stared up at him. "Lucky?" she asked, batting her big blue eyes that always made him get a little lost.

"Because you're giving me a second chance to love you the way I should have in the first." He rubbed his thumb over her bottom lip. "And you've already forgiven me for not warning you about Helena," he said, hoping it was actually true.

Vega chuckled. "Bridger, I don't give two fucks about Helena or anyone else you've fucked over the last forty years, for that matter. We weren't together, and I, unfortunately, have been sleeping with others far longer than you, I'm afraid." Her hands wrapped around his torso, pulling their bodies together.

Heat built up in Bridger's core, the need to remind her what she'd been missing tearing through him. It wasn't Vega's fault she'd been with other men while simultaneously still being in a relationship with him a realm away—but the reminder still hurt sometimes.

"A second chance..." she said softly. "That's what you want?"

Thankfully, Vega pulled him out of his spiral with her question. "If you'll let me have it." His eyes flicked back to hers, searching for the answer because the anticipation was going to eat him the fuck up if she didn't hurry.

She puckered her cute lips and looked at the ceiling. Vega really made it seem she was thinking hard, but the playfulness in her eyes gave her away.

"I dunno." She drew the answer out, sighing. "I promised Arlet I'd make you grovel, and you haven't begged yet, so..." Vega shrugged sadly. "I'm gonna have to sleep on it."

Then the brat stepped back, out of his hold and headed for the door. Vega took slow, calculated steps, giving Bridger enough time to figure out his next move.

He stayed planted, watching Vega stalk for the door. Her hand landed on the knob, and she looked back before twisting it. Apprehension settled in her gaze, but she pushed the door open anyway.

She'd leave out of principle. He knew it, but he didn't plan on letting her leave his room tonight. Bridger was playing her game for the fun of it.

"Have a good night, Bridger."

He let her take one more step before striking.

Bridger grabbed Vega by the wrist. "Oh, I plan to."

46

Twisting around, Bridger pulled Vega into a kiss, lighting every fiber of her being on fire.

She had no idea if the door closed, had no idea if it locked... all she knew was Bridger was kissing her like she was the oxygen he needed.

You're the air I breathe—my life. The words Bridger spoke to her the night of the summoning, the night their lives changed forever had more meaning now than they ever had.

Death slipped into the pit, giving Vega the privacy it knew she wanted.

She reached her hands down to the hem of Bridger's black T-shirt and tugged it up his body until he got the hint. She wanted him shirtless... Now.

He didn't protest, and Vega knew, *fucking knew,* if he was letting her have control now, he'd be taking it from her later.

In the bedroom was about the only place Vega was willing to give up without a fight. She didn't care. Whatever needed to happen for her to get her hands on his skin. The zap of their touch had warmth spreading between Vega's thighs. It was her favorite buzz, a drug she could never get enough of—a high not even her own electricity could touch.

Death might be the only thing that had ever come close to making Vega feel as alive as Bridger did.

That should scare her, make her skin crawl with disgust, but it didn't. Death had settled in, finding its home inside her quicker than Vega could have anticipated.

Their lips were apart for no longer than a few seconds. As soon as Bridger pulled his shirt over his head and tossed it to the corner, his tongue slid across her bottom lip and her body reacted without her brain needing to.

Bridger slipped his tongue through her parted lips, kissing her slowly, taking his time moving her to his bed.

He kissed her like they had all the time in the world... like there weren't only ten gods standing between her and whatever happened when her job here was done.

The backs of Vega's legs touched the plush bed Bridger had fawned over while in the caves.

If Vega had limited time, the least she could do now was enjoy what bit of sanity she had left. She sighed against his lips, sitting down and wrapping her legs around his waist.

Much to Vega's dismay, Bridger grabbed her by the ankles and pried free from her hold. She whimpered as his lips slid down her jaw, to her neck, and then settled on her collarbone. "Slow. Let me go slow. Let me show you how badly I want you. How sorry I am."

Every kiss formed another set of chills ravaging Vega's body. Her head rolled back, giving Bridger all the space he needed to pepper her neck and chest with his soft kisses.

He dropped to his knees by the bed and pressed his palms together, resting his elbows between her legs while closing the dark eyes Vega couldn't believe she'd been able to forget.

His nose rested on the tips of his fingers, the light curls of his freshly washed hair sweeping over his forehead. "Goddess of Death, my bonded soul."

"What are you doing?" Vega asked, looking down her nose with a brow raised in confusion.

Bridger opened one eye, peering up at her. "Shhh, I'm praying. Don't interrupt." He closed his eye and continued on. "I come to you tonight, begging for your forgiveness."

Holy shit... he's praying... to me.

"I sit at your feet, ready to devote my life to you, to remind you of the eternal tie my life has to yours."

Vega's heart bloomed to life at his prayer, rushing blood directly to her head. It should have made her dizzy, but it actually did the opposite. It grounded her, becoming a reminder of the god she was... the gods they all were.

"I summon your heart, your mind, your body, and our souls."

Vega floated, like the stars miles above in the sky called to them, and they could soar away into oblivion together.

"Vega Caelum, I am yours from now until the end of time. Let me prove my loyalty tonight and every other night. Forever. I live for you."

Her heart answered, contracting in her chest when his eyes fluttered open. She searched and searched and searched, looking for any sign of deceit... but none came. Vega reached out her hand and pressed it against Bridger's cheek.

He nuzzled into her touch like he'd been longing for it, placing a kiss to the center of her palm.

Vega wasn't sure if she was breathing. *"From now until the end of time."*

A thread of something she couldn't place slipped around her heart, pulling tight.

Out of his pocket, Bridger pulled the ring she'd been wearing every day since Arlet returned it to her. She'd taken it off while washing up this morning, completely forgetting to grab it off the counter.

Taking her hand in his, Bridger kissed the finger it belonged on before sliding it back in place. "Everything I do, everything I *will* do, is for you. I plan to spend the rest of our immortal lives reminding you exactly how much you deserve to be worshipped."

"What if my life isn't meant to be eternal?" she whispered, afraid to ruin the moment.

Bridger didn't hesitate to answer, dragging his hands up her thighs. "Then I'll find a way to go with you. There's not a realm in existence I want to be in without you there beside me."

The three words she'd been fighting over in her mind seemed to get lost when she tried to choke them out. She bit her lip and grabbed Bridger by his bicep with one hand. "Come here." She guided him up, sliding back to the center of the massive bed as Bridger crawled his way over her body.

"I know you feel it too," he whispered, pressing a soft kiss to her lips. "But you can say it when you're ready." Another sweet kiss, this time on her jaw. "I, on the other hand, don't plan on letting another day go by where you don't know how undeniably, irrevocably fucking gone I am for you." Bridger raised her shirt up to underneath her breasts, exposing her stomach to the cool air. He trailed kisses down her body as she propped herself up on her elbows, watching him work his way down her torso. "I love you."

Electricity exploded inside, and Vega let out a moan of pleasure. Nothing but his words had her ready to topple over the edge and sink into the sweet bliss of his touch.

Another kiss, another confession. "I love you."

"*Bridger,*" she moaned inside, because words felt too hard right now.

"I was so fucking stupid." The vibration of his words against her skin sent goosebumps dancing across her body. "I'm going to make sure you know just how sorry I am."

His fingers slid into the waistband of her pants, pulling them down until she was bare in front of him. The hunger on his face was the same she'd seen on the table in Vates... the same she'd seen in a coat closet in Fortis fifty-six years ago. "Gods, *fucking gods*, Vega. I'm so in love with you."

Vega watched him lick his lips, spreading her open with one hand to get a look at how absolutely drenched she was for him already.

He ran his thumb over Vega's clit, and her hips lurched forward, fighting for friction. "Baby, *please*."

Bridger's eyes snapped to hers, and a look she could only describe as feral washed over him. Every muscle in his body tightened, his jaw flexing from the force of his bite.

Vega had never called Bridger anything other than his name, be it his first or last. Bridger had never seemed like a nickname kind of person, but boy, *oh fucking boy*, had Vega been wrong!

"I'm going to make you come so hard you'll wish you never called me that." The gravel in his voice had Vega panting, readying herself for him as he lowered between her spread legs, flattened his tongue, and ran it from her entrance to the mound of nerves he eagerly sucked between his lips.

Vega gripped the sheets like they'd keep her body from writhing in pleasure. "Oh fuck." She looked down at him with hooded eyes, watching as he devoured her and slid two fingers inside.

Her mouth watered at the thought of him in her mouth, craving the taste. In her daze, Vega must have said so down the bond, because Bridger chuckled, the vibration against her clit making her hips buck. *"Not tonight, my beautiful girl. Tonight I worship you."*

Vega stifled her moan, biting her bottom lip until she tasted the familiar tang of blood.

Stars exploded across her vision as he flicked his tongue over her in a slow, languid motion, and his fingers massaged the soft spot inside her. *"Don't hold back. Let me hear you. No one else can."*

Vega plopped back, a hand shooting to her hips where one of Bridger's arms looped through her leg, holding her down. She couldn't sit still while having him between her legs—ever. Her nails dug into his wrist. "Shit," she moaned as Bridger loosened his grip only enough to let Vega roll her hips against his tongue.

He said he was going to take his time, but Vega's body hadn't gotten the memo. She shattered under his mouth, her body releasing the hold on her sanity.

It had taken him seconds to get Vega to come after all the verbal worshipping and praise he'd given. Her body quivered, abdomen flexing tight as she rode out the hardest and quickest orgasm of her entire life.

She couldn't form a coherent thought and barely recognized her own voice when she cried out Bridger's name.

Vega had been with other men—the curse forcing her into relationships she never would have sought out. In some of them, she'd been happy, at least for a moment until something traumatic happened and ruined whatever semblance of peace Vega had found in that life.

But no one, not a single one of the men placed into her life by her curse, had ever made Vega feel the way Bridger had... *The way he does*.

Not emotionally or physically.

Vega had loved him since the night they met, even before they'd been bonded. Bridger had always been her person, and when he'd left, she lost a piece of herself. One she had to learn to live without—but now she didn't have to.

She could let herself love him again.

I can let myself be loved.

She'd spent so many years being mad, reacting out of anger and heartbreak. She hadn't gotten the opportunity to heal from not only what she went through in Tolevarre but Earth too.

She might not ever get the chance to now... Those thoughts

weren't going to ruin this moment for her, so she banished them to the pit with Death, clearing her mind of anything but Bridger.

Vega sat up on her elbows again, watching Bridger in no hurry to remove himself from between her legs. If she let him, he would happily give her another.

Vega tangled one hand in the hair at the top of Bridger's head, moaning as he stuck another finger inside. "*Oh.*" Her eyes rolled back at the wave of pleasure it sent through her.

"*Mmm, you're so fucking pretty when you come for me.*" His voice introduced a new type of need pulsing through Vega's body.

"I need you. Gods, Bridger." She panted, coming down from the high of one orgasm and the rise of another. She moved her hand to the back of his head and leaned forward, slipping it under his jaw to pull his mouth away from her.

He looked up at her, a dazed smile pulling at the corners of his lips while he ran his tongue over her sensitive clit one more time. "I could stay here all night." He kissed up to her navel, pulling his fingers out.

Vega felt empty, but that feeling was soon replaced with the chills of his kisses coming back up her torso. Bridger pushed Vega's sweater up, a happy grumble rising from his chest when he found Vega without a bra. One hand cupped her breast, fingers applying pressure to the nipple already pebbled tight from her orgasm. His tongue slid over the other, mouth warm as he took it between his lips.

Vega pulled her sweater over her head, pressing into Bridger's mouth as she arched her back. He nipped at her nipple, sending shockwaves to her clit.

He let it go with a pop and sat back on his knees, his hands exploring every inch of her naked body—even slipping back between her spread legs to rub against her clit *so fucking slowly* while he watched Vega writhe in pleasure.

Vega's lips parted, letting out a breathy moan. She couldn't help but stare at him, his muscles flexing with each breath he took. The veins in his arms bulged so deliciously, she got lost watching his hand pleasure her. If she wasn't careful, she might actually start drooling.

Bridger's body was chiseled better than any Roman statue depiction... and so was the bulge pushing against the thin material of his lounge pants—she could confirm they hadn't gotten the size of those right on Earth.

Her body and mind were still trying to recover from her last orgasm. Why did he always do this to her?

Always. *Always.* Bridger had always turned her into absolute mush. She could act as tough and badass as she wanted, talk all the shit she could, but the second he put his hands on her, she was putty —moldable by his hands only.

He added more pressure to Vega's clit, bringing her back to life. She reached forward and untied the drawstring of his pants.

Bridger wrapped one hand around Vega's wrists, pinning them in place. He stared down at her with dark eyes and sharp features, looking like a fallen god.

Vega leaned in more, taking his grip with her as she rubbed a palm over his hard cock through his pants.

Bridger twitched, driving his hips into her touch with a groan of approval.

Vega bit her lip and pressed harder, her fingers gripping what they could with his pants in the way.

"Let me get you ready," she purred. Vega pulled one leg over the other, twisting to one side. With her hands trapped together in his, she was still completely at his mercy.

Bridger had the perfect view of her ass in this position, all pooched out and on display for him. She watched his eyes flick down to get a peek, his free hand giving it a rough squeeze. For a second, Vega thought he might flip her over and fuck her senseless, but he surprised her by letting go of her wrists.

She moved slowly, twisting to get on her knees. He was drunk off the sight of her, taking in every movement of her body. "Let me remind you what this pretty little mouth can do." His eyes fell to her lips as if he, too, remembered what he'd said to her before locking her up in Aeris—what had he been picturing her mouth doing then? She smiled, placing a kiss to his sharp jawline. She slid her hands down his bare chest, feeling his muscles tense the lower she went. "I want to taste how excited you are to fuck me again," Vega whispered against his neck as she kissed her way down his chest.

"Vega," he groaned as she freed his massive dick from his pants and fitted boxers at the same time.

Sure, she'd seen it the night they'd fucked in the car... but the shadows hadn't given her the view she had now. It bobbed against his lower abdomen, reaching much higher than anything else she'd ever seen in any of her lives. "Sit back."

"What happened to making me beg?" he asked but did what she told him to, propping himself up with a couple pillows behind his back.

Vega stripped him, throwing what was left of their clothes to the floor. "I'll have you begging some more here in a second," she said with a devilish smile, sinking down to drag her tongue up the length of his shaft while holding eye contact—knowing damn well what it would do to him.

Bridger hissed a breath, reaching around Vega's ass perched in the air while she sank her lips around the head of his cock. She moaned around him when Bridger's fingers slipped in her pussy from behind.

Vega's mouth watered, drenching him as she sank down as far as she could go. He hit the back of her throat before she was even close to taking him all in. Her eyes watered, and she gagged around him, making him groan and his eyes roll to the back of his head.

Vega was rewarded with his fingers hitting so deep she shivered.

She pulled her mouth off, using her hand to stroke him while she fell into a moan that shook her body, breath catching in her throat.

"I love hearing you choke on my cock, gods damn it, Vega." Bridger grabbed her by the chin with his free hand, running his thumb over Vega's bottom lip.

She nipped his finger, squeezing her grip tighter, unable to wrap one hand all the way around his girth. She pulled out of Bridger's grasp and sank back down, swirling her tongue around his head. She rotated her hand at the base, stroking what she couldn't fit inside her mouth. Vega took him all the way to the back of her throat again and again until she gagged.

Bridger's hips jolted, moaning so sweetly Vega wondered why men didn't do it more often. It was literal music to her ears, knowing she was the reason Bridger made those sounds.

The next shift in his hand was to sink a third finger inside her, filling her so tightly she had to come up for air. "Holy fuck," she gasped, her nails digging into his upper thigh. Her walls clenched around his fingers, shattering at the very moment he unexpectedly pushed her onto her back, twisting her hips and legs to one side.

Bridger fingered her to the end of her orgasm and gave her no time to recover before he slipped himself inside her with one smooth thrust. He gripped her ass, pushing her leg forward to sink in *so fucking deep.* "Gods, you're so tight." His free hand reached down to push Vega's hair out of her face. "Fuck, baby." Bridger shivered and pulled almost all the way out before sinking back in slowly, angling himself where he'd hit exactly where Vega needed every single time.

She was going to sink into the euphoria and never come up for air. Vega couldn't form words, couldn't see past the blinding desire she had to fall into oblivion where only she and Bridger existed.

Time meant nothing to Vega as she lost all sense of herself and what the world around her was doing. All she wanted was this moment with Bridger—where they could act like nothing beyond this room mattered.

Bridger groaned, leaning down to claim her lips in a kiss, yanking her from the depths of her pleasure only to throw her down again when he grabbed her by the throat and came inside her.

His abs quivered as he filled Vega up, every pump of his cock noticeable with its snug fit inside her. The hand around her throat had moved to her pelvis, pressing down gently to feel the movement of him inside her.

Bridger backed out to the tip, slowly pushing inside a few more times. His eyes were fixed on where they connected, and the sexiest, slowest, smile spread across Bridger's wet lips. He slid his tongue over the edges of his top teeth and lowered himself between Vega's legs again.

The stamina of a god was easily rejuvenated, and before long, Bridger was fucking them into round two.

All night, they let themselves forget there was a world outside who needed them. They allowed themselves to get lost in what it felt like to just be.

When Vega finally came to from the sex-drunken haze, her head rested on Bridger's chest and his heart beat in time with hers as he twirled a piece of her hair around his finger.

The sheets were lazily draped across his hips, covering only half of Vega's legs. She was too hot to crawl under fully with him yet.

They stayed silent for a long while before Bridger went to grab them water. "Thank you," she said when he handed her a glass, looking up at him from the bed where he stood over her and downed his water in three gulps.

Vega took a long sip and placed what was left on the bedside table in case they needed it later.

"It was just water." Bridger chuckled, abandoning his empty glass on the nightstand. He leaned down to press a quick kiss to Vega's lips before slipping back into bed beside her.

She yawned, cuddling into his side. "Not for the water. Thank you for fucking my ever-loving brains out and not being afraid to choke me until I black out."

The last thing Vega heard before she fell asleep was the sound of Bridger's deep laugh.

It repaired the final broken piece of her heart.

47

THE SCALDING HOT SHOWER DID NOTHING TO NUMB VEGA FROM the memory of the voices in her head.

The electric current inside her body buzzed, making her skin so hot the water practically matched the temperature of her blood.

She hadn't dreamed last night—or fallen into the pit of her mind. She'd been able to stay on the outside, for the most part.

Death helped keep the whispering voices at bay, guarding Vega's mind while she tried to rest.

Eventually, the gods slowly dragged her out of the depths of sleep with their chatter. She could hear them calling to her, longing for Vega to join them again.

They told her they just wanted to talk—they knew a way to save her from her destiny.

When awake, Vega could hold her shields, blocking the place they lived from existing, but when she slept, they could sneak their way to the top, luring her down with them.

Death could stop them, but Death couldn't stop Vega. Sometimes, the voices of the gods got too strong, and she tumbled to the depths of her own mind.

Bridger eventually joined her, and they stayed in the shower until the water ran cold.

Leaving the bathroom, Vega expected to be met with the chill accompanying Vincere. The desert surrounding them could be unbearable at certain times of the year, but with how far down into the core of their realm they were, the heat couldn't reach them.

If Vega closed her eyes, she could almost convince herself she was in Castra. A sharp pang of sadness washed over her for the home they'd lost. She knew deep down it wouldn't have been a big enough facility to house as many people as they had now, but that didn't mean it hurt any less when hundreds of innocents lost their lives.

Vega was surprised to be met with a toasty warm bedroom, heat pouring from a small space heater roaring in the corner.

It wasn't electric like the ones she'd become accustomed to on Earth—it was the good old-fashioned Tolevarrian kind with a live flame in the belly. The glow of the fire flickered against the tempered glass, casting shadows across Bridger's room.

She smiled. Their clothing still strewn across the floor, and a couple empty glasses littered the nightstand. The room was small, but bigger than the others Vega had seen by at least double.

Perks of being commander? A room double the size of a walk-in closet with the tiniest bathroom she'd ever seen. The bed was pushed against the wall, but Vega would admit: it was the most comfortable fucking bed she'd ever slept in.

All this time, Vega had pictured Bridger living it up, lapping up the luxuries of being commander of Tolevarre... when really, he was using whatever he had to put back into the army with new training facilities and state-of-the-art equipment.

Wait a second.

She turned around to find Bridger leaning against the bathroom doorframe with his towel wrapped loosely around his hips. He brushed his teeth, looking as relaxed as he would if this were just any other day and not the day they claimed Ardor and infiltrated the mines.

"When did you start building Vincere?" Vega asked, holding her towel tight with one arm.

Instead of talking around a toothbrush with a mouth full of toothpaste, he replied down the bond. *"Thirty-nine years ago."*

A year after he left. "Why didn't you put the upgrades into Atrox?"

"Did you forget I burned the Dimico Manor to the ground after Marlena killed you in your second life? I couldn't really live there."

His answers weren't what Vega was getting at. "You could have easily rebuilt or moved into the commander's wing of Atrox's fort. Much easier than building all this."

He returned to the bathroom, finished brushing his teeth, and came back out. Vega stole a glance at the deliciously low towel once more but quickly reminded herself she had a point to her questions.

"I didn't want to live in Fortis anymore... especially not in Atrox with my mother after she became praefectus," he answered plainly.

Vega knew there was more to it than that.

"But by building Vincere, you separated the military into two. Why?" She wanted to hear him say the words without having to coax them out.

"Where are you getting at with this? Ask me what you want to know." Bridger opened the armoire in the corner, grabbing two black battle suits. He tossed one at Vega, who caught it with her free hand.

"Did you build Vincere in hopes that one day you'd need a base away from Marlena?" she asked.

"Yes," he responded immediately. "One of the biggest issues with the start of our rebellion was how fucking unprepared we were. I knew if something else were to happen, whether it be because of you or not, when I turned on Marlena, because I knew I would one day, I needed a place to go, a place to be prepared to fight from."

He was calculated, always thinking about what needed to come next. It was why the beginning stages of the rebellion were hard for him—there was no way to prepare for anything.

"I watched her ruin families for fun, starve entire villages because one person messed up... and I couldn't do anything to stop it, but if they got to me, to Vincere, I could save them. This isn't just a place for people to train and hide from Marlena. It's the only home some have ever had." Bridger walked to her, resting his hand on the small of her back to pull them together. He tucked Vega's hair behind her ear. "You ready for today?"

Vega nodded. "As ready as I'll ever be." She was still trying to figure out how to cope with everything. How do you prepare for the inevitable?

Death stirred, stretching awake with a yawn. Its nails dug into the edges of the pit, knocking a few loose rocks down into the abyss.

The sound of them hitting the bottom never came, as if they floated inside the darkness forever.

They dressed quickly, ready to meet the others for today's briefing. Vega ran her hands down what was no doubt the nicest suit she'd ever worn. When she turned in the dim lighting of Bridger's room, she caught the black lightning bolts traveling up her sides.

She traced the stitching with delicate fingers, smiling absently while Bridger pulled what looked like every weapon he owned out of a hidden safe in his wall. "When did you have this made?" Vega asked, watching Bridger approach behind her in the mirror, sliding his bonded sword into the scabbard on his back.

"Before I went to Earth. I figured you'd like one that paid homage to the original." The one Bridger had made for her when they first started training—thanks to Marlena. The same one Arlet and Khort had tried to mimic for her in her last life.

Vega strapped her own daggers to her legs, hoping she didn't have to use any today. There was still hope this wouldn't turn into a battle scene—that they could take Ardor peacefully... but when had they ever gotten that lucky?

Marlena would show. She was going to be wherever Vega was, especially after she'd taken her fire.

"I love it," she said, meeting his eyes in the mirror. "The new boots are comfy too, I guess," Vega added with a playful eye roll and pucker of her lips.

Vincere was booming with activity as soon as they stepped into the halls. Everyone seemed to be in good spirits despite the day ahead—Arlet and Khort included.

They ran into them waiting for the elevator, and Arlet threw an arm over Vega's shoulder. "I knew our time as roomies wouldn't last long," she whispered into Vega's ear. "Did you make him beg?"

Death didn't react to the touch of Arlet like it did to Bridger, but it did perk up like it remembered it should be curious about the bond.

Before Vega would let it reach out and grab at anything, she pulled away and gave Arlet a look that said, *Really?* Now wasn't the time for this conversation or for snooping.

The people of Tolevarre had advantages their human ancestors would have killed for, making her whispers basically pointless. Bridger fought a smile as the elevator door opened, and Khort pretended to be really interested in a spot on the wall.

Vega's stomach dropped as they stepped inside the tiny elevator, and it wasn't because of the elevator this time. Vega knew she was breaking a part of Khort all over again by choosing Bridger... for a second time. She had to talk to him about it but reminded herself to take one thing at a time.

Her relationship status took the back burner on the list of things to do today. The most important thing was getting everyone out of the mines safely, followed by not starting a full-on battle in Ustilo.

The second the elevator doors shut, the tension was too thick to ignore. Vega felt like she might break out into a nervous sweat if she let the thick tension grow.

They couldn't go into today with a divide. This conversation couldn't wait—not when the lives of their people depended on them working as a unit.

Vega slapped the Emergency Stop button and spun around, standing in front of the closed doors. *So much for not making a thing out of this today...*

"Bridger and I are back together." She spit out the words like they were fire threatening to scorch her. Vega didn't focus on the open doorway connecting to Bridger's mind. She pushed the love she felt for her lifelong best friends and hurled it down the hallways of her mind at them. They might not be able to talk to her like Bridger, but they could feel her... "And I can live with you both questioning why I would ever do that, but I can't bear to live without my best friends. My *family*." Her eyes jumped between Arlet and Khort.

Khort's features softened, giving Vega the courage to keep going.

"I'll never be able to thank you both enough for everything you've given up for me. Words cannot express how lucky I am to have you two, but we all made a decision the night of the summoning." Vega didn't let her mind settle too long on the words she'd chosen that night, or the things she'd asked for. It would only lead her down a road she couldn't afford to go right now. She had to keep her head on straight. She couldn't change the past.

"Regardless of what's happened since, we're in this together. The four of us. No more blocking each other out." She shot a look at Bridger, who'd been using his powers to ignore the bond for nearly forty years. "No more jealousy." Vega's gaze moved to Khort, who had his arms crossed, looking down his nose at her. "I love you, Khort, but I've never been the girl for you, with or without Bridger in the picture. I hate that you've spent all your life wishing I could be. I'm sorry for the role I've played, and for giving you hope in my last life that something could ever come of us, but I have a feeling you know it wouldn't work." Before she could see the hurt in his eyes, Vega turned to Arlet. "And you..."

What could Vega even say to Arlet? To the girl who'd saved her life more times than she could count.

"I don't know what I did in life to deserve a friend like you," Vega finally said. "You're my sister in every way that matters. You're brilliant, fierce, and deserve so much more than this life has given you." Vega refused to cry, refused to make this a goodbye. There had already been too many. "The next time you fall in love, I want to know all about it. I want to celebrate with you." Part of Vega had this sinking feeling, this surety in her gut she wouldn't live long enough to see it, but the other part still prayed she was wrong... that she'd live to see her best friends happy again. "Okay?"

Death sat by the pit, head hanging down like it, too, worried about her fate—their fate. *Our fate.* It chattered, teeth clacking in agreement.

Arlet nodded, a sad smile pulling at the corner of her lips. "I love you," she said, snatching Vega into a hug she hadn't known she needed.

Vega breathed in Arlet's honey scent, closing her eyes to lose herself in a different time. When she pulled away, Arlet had tears to wipe off her cheeks.

Khort reached for Vega next and wrapped her in a hug. "Please don't hate me," she said against his chest.

"I could never," he whispered against the top of her head.

She took a deep breath, stepped out of Khort's arms, and turned to Bridger. "Okay, I think we're ready now."

Bridger reached out and caressed her cheek, rubbing his thumb against her soft skin. He didn't say anything, because he didn't need to. Vega knew what he'd say.

I love you.

48

OCTAVIA HAD FINALLY SENT WORD THAT SHE'D BE ARRIVING tonight, under the cover of nightfall, with forty-two children from Demuto. Arlet was the first to know since the message had been relayed to Avi by a bird Tilie sent.

Everyone was eager to return and get the young shifters comfortable and settled.

But there was still a war of wits happening. They still had to free the mines and remind Marlena she wasn't the only player in motion on this map now.

Meyer, Leo, Helena, Halo, and a girl with leg muscles the size of tree trunks waited outside the door when they arrived.

"Alright, let's make this quick. I'd like to have this done so we can all be back before Octavia." Bridger leaned against the back of his desk chair, the desk lighting up like a screen at his proximity.

Vega was still in awe at some of the technology Bridger had. There was a time long ago where Tolevarre didn't have modern technology, but no one alive today could remember that. What Bridger had here in Vincere reminded Vega of something straight out of a futuristic dream.

Live footage from the cameras in both the mines and Ustilo appeared.

"We'll have three groups. Leo and Helena at the mines, another with me and Meyer at his parents' home, and one here with Yara to protect the people staying behind in case of an attack. Halo will jump between locations as needed." Bridger leaned down to zoom in on the mine entrance with the pinch of his fingers. "Leo and Helena, you'll need to take out the guards. Don't give them time to sweet talk you. They'll say anything to save themselves." He swiped over to the camera in Ustilo's square. "Meyer, you'll need to get control of the city. Let them know Ardor is now home to the revolution."

The room hummed with a new current of energy when Bridger didn't call them a rebellion anymore. Rebellions were only a resistance. Revolutions were an overtaking. He spoke of their cause like they'd already won.

"They can stay and join us or leave peacefully and keep their lives. Death is the only other option. I'll deal with your parents." Bridger turned his attention to Khort. "Where do you want to be?"

Death's purr vibrated Vega's chest the same way a dragon's deep bellow would when Bridger spoke about it.

Khort raised a brow. "You're letting me choose?"

"Yes, Fera, I'm letting you choose," he fired back quickly, his annoyance pulsing through their bodies. "Where do you think you'll be the most useful?" Bridger followed up his question with a brow raise of his own.

Khort stared for a few seconds, trying to read Bridger's intentions. Vega knew he'd never be able to. "The mines. It's got great airspace in case of an attack, and if need be, I can withstand the heat inside them out of my dragon form," Khort answered confidently.

Bridger nodded, his way of silently agreeing. He turned his head farther to the right until his eyes landed on Arlet.

He didn't have to ask before she blurted her answer. "I'll stay behind and keep watch. Avi's got the skies, and I can communicate with Khort through her. If something happens here, I can create a big enough distraction until help arrives." As if giving a reminder of her powers to the ones in the room who weren't familiar with what she could do, Arlet cupped her hands together and let the image of Vincere form inside them. A wave washed over the gates, sending the foundation of all that was visible of the underground facility crashing to pieces. It washed away, slowly dissipating with Arlet's mirage.

People stared where the image had once been until Arlet dropped her hands back down to her sides.

The room was silent until Bridger spoke again. "And where do you belong, my love?"

Vega looked away from everyone when their attention shifted from Arlet to her, locking eyes with Bridger, who had been staring at her for a lot longer than she realized. His gaze turned her molten. "With you," she responded with conviction.

He hid his full smile, slipping behind the commander's mask he wore too well. "Is that where you're most useful?" he asked like he'd asked Khort.

"Yes," she answered back.

"Why?"

Vega lowered her eyebrows. *"Why the third degree?"*

"Answer the question," he urged.

Vega sighed, slightly annoyed, but answered anyway. "Because wherever I go, Marlena will follow. I'm public enemy number one again after Demuto." Did everyone in the room know what she meant by that? "I can't be at the mines, or it'll draw attention while we're evacuating. Staying here not only does the same thing, but it's also a complete waste of my powers and abilities. If a fight breaks out, it's going to be in the city. I'm *most useful,*" she sneered, "wherever the biggest threat is."

"Exactly. I just wanted to make sure the rest of the room

understood you weren't making this choice to follow where I go." He twisted back around and eyed the faces at the table. "Any questions? Complaints?"

Everyone shook their heads.

"Good. Let's get this over with."

"Oh no, I'm not riding with you two," Meyer gruffed. "I'll ride up front."

Bridger snagged Meyer by the shoulder and led him into the cab of the military vehicle. "Yes, you are. Don't be ridiculous. I can keep my hands to myself." He patted Meyer on the back as he dipped into the backseat. Bridger held his hand out for Vega like they were loading up for a ball and not a battle. She placed hers in his delicately, winking at him. "I got enough last night to hold me over. I think," he said under his breath, giving Vega a quick tap on the ass as she slid inside.

"Nope, no. That's it. I'm outta here." Meyer tried to scoot for the door, but Vega pushed him by the shoulders, sending him flopping back to the cushioned bench.

"Relax, will you?" Vega sat on the opposite side of the cab, facing Meyer and crossing one leg over the other. "It's been too long since we've spent any time together. I'd love to talk about how you froze instead of holding up your end of the bargain *you* came looking for."

Meyer slumped further into his seat, putting his arm on the rest by the window, and propped his head in his hand.

Bridger plopped down beside him and stared at Vega with a lopsided smile. "If I sit too close I won't be able to keep my hands off you." He teased.

"Was I supposed to kill you in front of everyone? Why

wouldn't Scales or Spooky help you?" Meyer's lips pressed into a tight line, ignoring the comment Bridger made to get further under his skin.

He did not just nickname Arlet "Spooky."

As retaliation, she shot him a devious smile. "Bridger told me about the night he ditched you to come and track me down in Demuto. Is that why you don't like me? Cause I stole your boyfriend?" Vega picked at her fingernails. The black nail polish she was known for had chipped off weeks ago, and who had time for a manicure these days? She honestly felt naked without it.

Death read her thoughts, and the very tips of her nails began to fade to black.

Vega hid her hands in the crevice of her crossed legs, trying to stay present in the argument she'd just started instead of drawing attention to whatever the fuck that was.

"Okay, okay, that's enough." Bridger pointed at Meyer to sit back down. He'd hopped up, ready to strangle his best friend for saying anything. "If I have to be nice to your friends, you have to be nice to mine," he said, trying to hold back his laughter.

Vega quickly glanced down to see her nails were black, as if painted by Death, but didn't hesitate long enough for anyone to notice before crossing her arms over her chest, frowning. "Good thing you only have one."

Meyer let out a snort, letting Vega know the spat was over.

They approached a town where parents sat on rickety chairs under their covered porches, already hiding from the early morning sun, watching their kids run out to the convoy as it drove by. Most of them waved, smiling ear to ear, while a few of the younger ones stared in amazement.

The further they got into town, the more obvious it became how little those here had. Their homes were crumbling in on them, holes in roofs being patched with whatever the family could scrounge up. Ripped up pieces of tarp, dried clay, scrap metal.

Kids ran around without shoes, and their animals were skinnier than Vega could stand to see.

"Does this not make the two of you sick?" Her eyes burned with the threat of angry tears. "People are living like this"—she pointed out the window no one could see into—"and we're all sleeping in cush beds with absolutely no worry as to where our next meal is coming from." Sure, Vega had worried about that and more in most of her lives, but only because a curse had made it that way.

A little boy sat on an overturned bucket, picking at a single slice of bread. He stared at it, ripping off a small corner before feeding the rest to the chickens pecking around his feet.

"Stop the vehicle," she croaked. Bridger opened his mouth to say something, but Vega didn't want to hear it. "I said stop the fucking vehicle!" Static had the hairs on their arms standing. She was seconds from turning the cab into a plasma globe.

Meyer slapped the hidden window between them and the driver. "Pull over."

Vega flipped the bench seat she'd sat on forward, tearing through the compartments until she found what she knew would be stored inside.

Vega was out before they came to a slow stop, her arms full with rations of dried food.

People watched from their porches, tugging their children by the collars of their shirts to keep them from running out to greet Vega.

She approached the boy on the bucket, his chickens running away, clucking unhappily while retreating. "Hi," Vega said, sinking down to one knee in front of him. "I'm Vega. What's your name?"

He didn't speak, his big green eyes scanning her.

"I have something for you." After dropping the pile of meals by her down knee, Vega took two and offered them to him.

He kept his hands tucked against his chest, apprehension building.

Vega nodded to the packs in her hand. "It's food. For you and whoever you want to share with." She pointed to the pile in front of her. "All of this."

He slowly reached out and took them, studying the exterior. One second he was looking at the package of food that read Red Meat and Potatoes, the next he stood on the bucket, startling Vega as he yelled for the whole neighborhood to hear. "Hey, guys! Vega's got food!"

The sound of excited children filled the street, followed by the echo of footsteps running towards her. Vega turned, greeted by a young girl wearing tattered clothing barely holding on by threads, her arms outstretched.

Before long, kids and parents alike surrounded Vega, taking what she had to give. It didn't take long to run out, but they had five vehicles in their convoy—hopefully stocked with food too. "Stay here. I'll go get some more," Vega told a young mother with a toddler on her hip and another on the way. Soon, if the size of her stomach was any indication.

Vega hadn't seen Solum since Saturnalia, but it was clear by the state of this town, there was likely nothing left of the farmland that used to feed their entire realm. People were only able to survive off what they had or could grow on their own.

Vega cleared through a small crowd of children, their laughter bringing smiles to the faces of their families. She paused halfway to her destination, a smile of her own forming at Bridger talking to the driver of the lead vehicle. He was too far away to hear, but Vega knew what he was doing.

Meyer was already passing out packs of food to the forming line in front of him. The kids were elated to meet Meyer Ignis, the original bloodline of Ardor. He gave the kids warm smiles, passing out high fives like candy.

Behind Meyer's mask, she could see the pain in his stare. It killed him to see the people of his territory like this.

Vega could feel someone staring, but she didn't have to worry about who it was. She found him instantly, eyes locking on the ones he already had fixed on her. *"Our realm hasn't been the same without you."*

Vega only hoped they could carry on without her if—*when*—the time came for her to leave again... She might already be as close to death or dead as she could be, but that didn't mean her soul was safe.

After handing out all the dried food they had, they got back on the road. Vega waved at everyone standing on the street even though they couldn't see her. She rested her hand against the glass when they reached the edge of town, finally letting it fall when they were back in the vast and lonely desert.

Thankfully, they stayed on the outskirts of the rest of the feeder towns. Whether that was intentionally done by the lead driver or not, Vega was thankful for the route. If she had to pass through another starving town with nothing to offer, she might break.

Bridger and Meyer discussed the plan for when they arrived in Ustilo. Vega listened, putting her two cents in when necessary but mostly stayed quiet for the remainder of their travels.

"We enter together. Meyer, you show your face, let your parents know you're safe and not being held against your will, and then leave to handle the citizens," Bridger reminded. "Who I'm going to assume will be on high alert the second they realize we're here."

Meyer nodded, watching the city roll into view with a solemn expression he did his best to hide. This was where Meyer grew up— the place he'd called home his entire life.

Vega knew it wasn't easy to feel like you no longer belonged.

The deeper they got into the city, the more worried Vega became. The streets were empty, and everything was too quiet. "Where is everyone?" she asked as Death rose on alert, dissipating from its dragon form into the shadows cast around her mind.

If Ardor was quiet, there might as well be a red flag waving high in the sky.

Bridger and Meyer shared a look, dread sinking to the pit of Vega's stomach.

"I don't think we're making it out of here without bloodshed," Bridger said, his tone taut.

There were no guards outside the Ignises' home like there should be. The grounds were silent, and the people of Ardor who were protesting the injustice brought upon by Marlena's latest impositions were nowhere to be found.

When they exited the vehicle, Bridger closed the door and placed his hand on the small of Vega's back. "Plan's changed. Stay together. No one leaves my shield."

Vega nodded while Meyer held his fist out in front of Bridger, who returned it with a quick bump of his own before giving orders to the rest of the group.

Meyer extended the same to Vega. She glanced at his hand and then at his small but genuine smile before returning the fist bump. "Welcome to the A Team, Sparks."

49

"Sɪᴛ."

Marlena snapped her fingers and pointed to the chair beside her.

"Let them have Ardor, Marlena. We don't have the people to put up a fight for it right now."

Marlena stared at Zetta, her fingernails digging into the wooden arm of one of the chairs she'd dragged into the center of the room—the same room she'd killed Vega in for the very first time.

What a full circle moment.

Miklov, Zetta's husband and a very strong fire-wielder, sat to her left, and an empty chair where Zetta should be sitting was to her right.

"I don't give a shit about Ardor. Vega stole something from me, and I want it back. Now sit before I break your legs and make you." Marlena had been reeling since Vega took her fire, but she had to stay calm—had to keep her head on straight.

Have to keep my people in line.

The gods had been unhappy with her after losing Diana, but when Vega snatched Vulcan from them, they'd become nearly unbearable.

"Get him back."

"You're making us look bad."

"We chose you."

Zetta slowly sank to her chair, unable to relax.

Ardor had been sucked dry by its own people, taking more than they should have when Marlena's rule began. There was nothing left here for Marlena to fight over. If the rebels wanted the tattered fucking mess, fine. She'd let them have it… but Vega couldn't have her fire.

If Vega wanted to give the people of Tolevarre a safe place to live before Marlena found a way to eradicate them from existence, then Vega would give her what she wanted.

Consequences. They were one of Marlena's favorite currencies to deal in.

The door swung open on a gust of wind that wasn't Marlena's, and in strolled her dear baby sister with Bridger and Meyer in tow. "You're so predictable," Vega snapped.

"Meyer," Zetta gasped. She stood, moving across the room to her son. She slammed into the shield Marlena knew was there, encompassing the three of them inside Bridger's protective circle.

Marlena sighed, pulling at her wind like a rope. It wrapped itself around Zetta's ankles and slammed her face-first onto the hard floor. The sound of her nose breaking and teeth shattering filled the space, followed by Meyer lunging to help.

Bridger didn't let the shield go, trapping him from getting to his mother.

"I told her to sit." Marlena pulled back on the tendrils of her wind and dragged an unconscious Zetta across the floor, blood smearing her path. "Didn't I, Miklov?" she asked, raising a brow.

He nodded, a bead of sweat forming across his brow.

"Speak," she commanded, treating the people who'd once been her allies like dogs.

Her allies had only been a stepping stone. Once she met the gods, she no longer needed anyone else.

"Yes, you told her to sit." Miklov's throat bobbed with a swallowed sob.

"What else did I say to her?" she asked, leaning towards him in the chair, twirling a piece of her bright blonde hair playfully.

"That you'd break her legs if she didn't." His dark skin blanched, eyes fixed straight ahead at the wall on the other end of the room.

Marlena smiled at him before standing. "So, I guess I was nicer than I could have been, than I *should* have been." She walked to the edge of the shield and looked Vega in the eyes. "That's good news for you. It means I'm in a good mood, and I'm feeling generous."

Vega took a step towards her, putting them inches apart, the shield the only thing keeping Marlena from ripping Vega's heart out. Too bad Marlena was way up here, and Vega way down there—her sister had to tilt her head back to meet her gaze. "It's over, Marlena. Ardor is ours. We're freeing the people in the mines as we speak. Leave before anyone has to die."

Marlena chuckled. "Did you think that'd work? Really, honestly. Did you?" She asked. "I don't care who dies. I don't care what you've become. You will never be able to intimidate me."

The way Vega's lips curled into a slow smile sent the gods inside Marlena spiraling. "Liar."

"Get away from her."

"She will take us."

"Let her."

"I always wanted the sister."

Jealousy shook the home underneath Marlena's feet. The gods scattered, leaving her alone in her head. *Never alone.* Marlena hadn't had a mind to herself in fifty-five years. "I'm here to make a deal with you."

"Whatever it is, we decline," Bridger said.

Marlena's attention flipped to him, his dark stare locked on her. Losing Bridger had been a blow Marlena hadn't seen coming—but she should have—until it was too late.

She'd been played... and Marlena would make him pay for it.

"You haven't even listened to what it is I want." Marlena objected, placing her hand on the shield Bridger hadn't let falter. Mars thundered inside her, his power calling to the piece of Marlena who controlled him.

Meyer couldn't stop staring at his mother.

"I don't give a fuck what you want," Bridger growled, masked anger simmering behind his eyes.

Marlena sighed, circling them as her fingers grazed the outside of the shield. "Bridger... we were so good together. What happened?" Marlena feigned the emotion she knew others would feel if they'd been abandoned, her face falling in mock sadness. "You say you don't want what it is I have to offer you, but you should know me better than that by now." She stopped circling after inspecting the shield fully, finding no holes to slip through—she hadn't expected to find any, but she'd checked anyway, using it as a way to taunt them. "If I don't get what I want, I'll just take it instead. I'm giving you the chance to walk away with no lives lost on your end this one time."

A muscle ticked in Vega's cheek. Hook set.

"Haven't enough people died because of your little rebellion, Vega? How many more will you sentence to death because you don't know when to quit?" Marlena asked.

"You're not getting them back," Vega stated, staring at Marlena with their matching eyes. "They're mine... and they seem super content to stay."

Green lightning buzzed dan Marlena's hands, readying like her fire used to. "Are you willing to take whatever consequence I deem appropriate because you won't give back what doesn't belong to you?"

Vega fell back beside Bridger. "I don't answer to you, Marlena." She gushed with a laugh. "*We* don't answer to you."

They really were a beautiful couple—they always had been, but their union was the start of Marlena's demise, a reminder of the person she'd once been and the one she'd never gotten to be.

"It was worth a shot." Marlena shrugged, gracefully walking towards Zetta's motionless body.

"No," she heard Meyer say with a sharp breath. "No. Stop her. Vega, stop her."

Meyer Ignis, the boy who followed all his life because he'd never had the fucking guts to make a single decision on his own. The boy whose parents loved him more than anything but chose power over the safety of their child.

Meyer Ignis, the man whose life hung over a sword... saved by the only friend he'd ever had.

Bridger had traded Vega's life and love for his only friend once. Would he do it again?

"Last chance, Vega. Give me my fire back, and you can have Ardor and all the useless fucking vermin in it." She looked over her shoulder at her sister, who had her eyes on Bridger.

He shook his head side to side, just once.

"Father! Do something! Save her!" Meyer threw himself against the shield, banging against it like an animal locked in a glass cage.

Miklov didn't move, and it wasn't because Marlena trapped him. He didn't move because he was a coward—he always had been.

A tear slid down his cheek, eyes meeting his son's with a ghost-like expression. "I can't," he whispered.

"Bridger, let me out! Let me out!" Meyer begged.

Marlena lifted Zetta without touching her, thrusting her into the air. With the soar of her natural power, Marlena closed her eyes and took a slow, steady inhale, focusing on the rapid breaths of the people in the room.

Vega's control of the wind had never allowed Marlena to slip inside her lungs. Wind-wielders knew when someone was manipulating the air around them.

Miklov's breaths came out quick, panting, scared.

Zetta's inhales sounded wet and shallow.

Bridger's were as steady as ever, calm.

Meyer's breathing was heavy and panicked as he continued to pound on the shield Bridger never let falter.

Marlena couldn't physically slip behind his shield, but she could control the air inside it.

Meyer's screaming stopped and was quickly replaced with the sound of labored breathing, the struggle to pull air into lungs desperately needing it. Soon it would turn to choking on nothing...

Marlena opened her eyes, keeping Zetta's limp body extended above her head as a dagger zipped out of the holster on her leg, digging into Miklov's throat with enough force to draw blood.

Marlena did this all without lifting a single finger, without calling to any powers that weren't her own. She had been strong before the gods, able to do more with the powers she was born with than almost all who shared her ability.

This display was a reminder of who Marlena was even if Vega stripped her of every single god.

Vega grabbed Bridger's arm, and a jolt of pain mangled his features for no longer than a single breath—long enough for him to falter and drop his shield.

Long enough to fall victim to the trap Marlena had set for them. She laughed, pulling the veil of her invisibility around herself and crossing the room. "You say I'm predictable, dear sister, but you just made the mistake I knew you'd make if I threatened the loved ones of the people you care about."

Meyer's face turned ashen the longer he fought for air.

Vega spun in circles, her eyes following the sound of Marlena's voice. "Bridger, shield Meyer!"

"That won't help you when I'm already inside his lungs." She cackled, moving around the room too quickly to pinpoint her exact location.

Meyer fell to his knees, clawing at his throat while gasping like a fish who'd been thrown to land.

"Fine! Fine! I'll give it back! You can have your fire back! You can have it, just don't kill Meyer!" Vega screamed, positioning herself in the middle of the room, hands outstretched on either side. "Here."

"*Yes*," multiple voices hissed in her ears at the same time. "*Go.*"

Marlena breathed happily, a sigh of relief washing over her body. She let one slip of air back into Meyer's lungs—keeping him barely conscious until Vega held up her end of the bargain.

She cleared the room, keeping her invisibility locked in place until she was ready. Her hand hovered over Vega's. "I'll kill him if you cross me."

Vega shivered at the words spoken over her shoulder and nodded.

Bridger's head snapped back and forth between his best friend and the girl he loved. "Vega," he whispered. "No."

"Get him out," she responded, and before Marlena could move, Vega grabbed her by the arm like she'd sensed her closeness the entire time.

White-hot pain seared through Marlena's veins, slowly turning to emerald green. For a second, Marlena felt the heat of what she thought was her fire. She could hear the voice of Vulcan like a child's whisper in the night... but quickly, *too quickly*, it turned—and now it was too late to pull away.

Marlena screamed, but the sound got lodged in her throat. Frantically, she tried to fight against Vega, losing like she had the other times.

Zetta crashed to the floor, cracking the tiles she landed on. The dagger at Miklov's throat followed with a clatter, and he went crawling to his wife in the center of the room. Bridger got Meyer up on his feet, hauling him out of the room.

Pain continued to erupt through Marlena, her eyes dragging across her body slowly coming back into view.

The first thing she noticed was her black veins, just like Vega's... only moving in opposite directions.

Vega's traveled inwards, sucking the power out of Marlena. Marlena's traveled out... leaving her.

No. No. *NO!*

You fucking IDIOT! Why? Why did you trust her?!

Marlena couldn't tell the difference between the voices in her head and her own, not when Vega sucked one of her original abilities out like it didn't even affect her.

Marlena stood frozen, unable to move until Vega stumbled back, fighting to keep standing.

It does affect her.

Their eyes met, both breathing sharp and labored. "I promised to send you to the underworld where you belong... Who knew I'd be your escort too?" Vega disappeared like Marlena once had.

Marlena's anger caused delirium, her vision turning red, nothing but the sound of her own scream echoing in her mind.

Vega thought she'd won, but she hadn't... *She won't.*

No one took from Marlena fucking Caelum and got away with it.

She took a step through time, folding Tolevarre into a clean, crisp piece of paper, and stepped out on the other side. Right where she wanted to be.

Bridger helped Meyer down the stairs of his childhood home, the color finally coming back to his face.

She took one last step, crossing the hundreds of feet between them in less than a second.

By the time they noticed Marlena, it was too late.

One moment she was leaning into Bridger's ear, whispering the words she knew would haunt him forever. "I hope Vega was worth it." The next, she stood behind Meyer, blood dripping down her arm with his still beating heart clutched in the palm of her hand. "She did this."

50

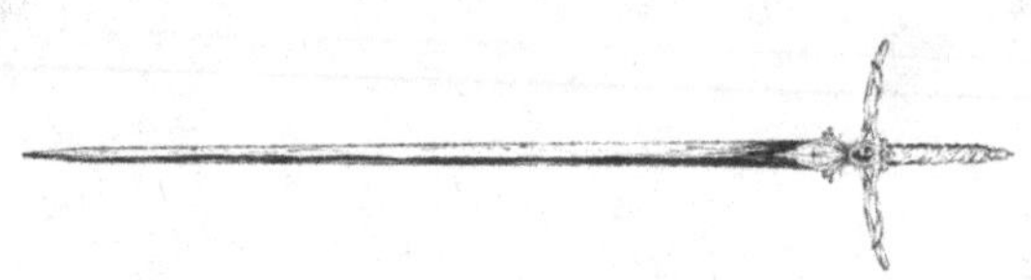

Bridger caught Meyer's lifeless body before it hit the ground.

I'm holding Meyer's dead body. I'm crouched on the steps of my best friend's childhood home, holding his lifeless body. My best friend is dead. My brother is dead. Meyer is dead.

One second he was there.

And now he's not.

Blood from the hand-sized hole in Meyer's chest leaked all over Bridger, pooling around his knees. His jaw hung open, his golden eyes fixed on the hot Ardor sun high in the sky. That should hurt his eyes, but it didn't because... *Meyer is dead.*

Bridger couldn't block out the pain he felt with a shield if he tried. He looked up from his position on the ground, expecting to see Marlena hovering over with a sinister smile, but instead he watched Vega appear at the top of the steps out of thin air.

She'd taken another.

Her jaw hung open... like Meyer's. Tears welled in her eyes... but not Meyer's. *He's dead.* He'd never feel anything ever again.

"No."

The whisper of her voice inside his head brought his senses back. The iron smell of Meyer's blood, the warmth of it soaking his suit, the moisture of his cheeks from the tears he hadn't felt falling.

He hadn't even noticed his vision was blurry.

Vega sprinted down the stairs and skidded to a stop on her knees.

"The blood." Bridger babbled his first words, worried about Vega staining her skin with the ichor of his best friend on the steps of his family's home.

"My best friend is dead."

"I know, baby, I know. I'm so sorry." Vega grabbed both sides of Bridger's cheeks, forcing him to meet her eyes.

Bridger hadn't meant to say that to her. He'd meant to say it to himself, but it was so fuzzy—the pathway to his own mind and hers. He couldn't tell which way to go.

Waning in and out, Bridger barely felt the brush of cold empathy against the open door of his mind.

The stroke of Death was hard to miss.

He looked down at Meyer's lifeless body, Vega's hands falling from his face. Bridger pulled an arm out from underneath Meyer's knees, resting him on the warm ground below, using his free hand to close his eyelids and mouth.

If it weren't for the blood splatter across his cheek, it would look like he was sleeping.

Footsteps echoed from behind. Bridger drew his sword without thinking, spinning to meet the tip of the black blade to the throat of his assailant.

Except it wasn't an assailant... It was Halo—who looked like he might pass out from the combination of the sword at his jugular and the very dead Meyer resting in Bridger's arms.

"Oh my gods," Halo gasped, jumping from the tip of Bridger's blade to behind Vega where he probably felt safest. "No, no. What... what happened?"

Meyer is dead.

"Marlena," Vega croaked. "It was my fault." Her voice shook. "I should have listened. I shouldn't have—."

"No," Bridger rumbled. "Not your fault." He couldn't figure out how to speak in full sentences yet, but at least he wasn't crying anymore.

Or maybe he was.

Oh, how did my sword get on the ground? Had he dropped it?

His eyes wandered, finding Vega still sitting across from him, her own face streaked with tears.

"His parents?" Bridger asked.

"Gone," Vega whispered.

Bridger didn't know if that meant dead or fled, but he didn't want to know either way. "We need to burn him."

"Of course," Vega said, reaching out to wipe the tears off Bridger's face.

Apparently, he *was* still crying.

"We can take him anywhere you want to go," Halo added.

"Here. He'd want to be burned here. At home."

So, that was what they did. They burned him at home in the town square where all the bodies of the Ingises before him had been burned.

The people of Ustilo slowly came out of their homes, no longer needing to hide from Marlena's potential attack. She was gone for now, tending to her wounds.

People brought flowers from inside their homes or their small backyard gardens. Some brought trinkets—metal fire pins for shirts, wooden figurines of Vulcan—the god of Ardor.

Everyone who had yet to flee the city came to pay their respects, dipping their heads at Bridger in silent respect. He could barely look them in the eyes.

Vega stood by his side the entire time, her thumb rubbing circles on the back of his hand. She thanked every person before they walked away.

They'd found allies in Ardor, and all it had taken was for Marlena to kill the son of their once-beloved original family.

Halo jumped to the mines to tell everyone the news of Meyer's passing, returning with word from Khort that they'd successfully evacuated the mines and were headed back to Vincere with the survivors.

When Halo returned, he had Leo in tow. With a few other soldiers, they began going door to door, giving people the option to stay or go.

For every one who left, fifteen stayed. Ardor had been sick of Marlena's reign for much longer than anyone could have imagined.

They stayed until the fire went out and Meyer's body was nothing but ash. The sun started to dip behind the mountains in the far-off distance, and people had stopped coming by almost an hour ago.

It was just Vega and Bridger, her head leaning against his arm as they sat on a bench, staring at what was left of Bridger's best friend and brother.

Bridger took a deep breath and stood, disconnecting himself from Vega. She didn't follow, but he could feel her eyes on him as he approached the pyre. He sank to his knees, not caring what soot or ash he got on himself.

He closed his eyes, imagining Meyer beside him. "I promise to make her pay for what she did." Bridger sat there until the sun sank below the mountains and the sky shone bright with the most beautiful sunset.

Orange and red illuminated the city, taking the day his best friend died with it. He stayed quiet until the sky had gone dark. "Goodbye, brother."

Bridger pushed himself off the ground, trudging back to Vega on legs that felt too weak to carry him much longer.

She stood when he towered over her on the bench. "Let's get you home."

Home.

Home was wherever Vega was.

Bridger didn't have anything left inside today, so all he did was nod his head.

Halo whisked them away, and they landed outside Bridger's bedroom in Vincere.

Wasting no time, Bridger opened the door. He didn't care he was covered in blood, soot... none of it. He collapsed on his bed without undressing or taking his boots off.

Through the crack in the open door, Vega gave Halo a tight hug, brushing the bright blond hair from his eyes. "Get some sleep. You did well today."

Before Bridger was drawn into the depths of sleep, he heard the shuddering sob of a boy who wanted nothing more than to belong. "I should have been there. I could have saved him."

Bridger free-fell into sleep before he could tell Halo it wasn't his fault... *It was mine.*

When he slept this time, it wasn't dreamless. At least these dreams weren't meant for torture like the others—it was a montage of Bridger and Meyer, of the best friend he'd lost.

"Ow, ow, ow!" Meyer cried, holding his limp arm against his chest.

Bridger tried to inspect the break, but Meyer wouldn't let him too close. "I told you it wasn't worth it. She didn't even look at you."

Summer Laudo was the prettiest girl in Oro, with her long black hair and charcoal eyes. She was visiting her cousins in Fortis during a break from school. Meyer crushed on her all summer, and instead of going over to talk to her like a normal thirteen-year-old boy would, he decided to try to do a backflip off the tallest tree in the city park.

He didn't have enough momentum and landed on his face, his arm getting caught up in the wreckage. It hung at an unusual angle.

When Bridger visited him in the Atrox med-ward later, Summer sat in a chair beside his bed.

Meyer winked at him when Summer wasn't looking.

Bridger chuckled and let his best friend pretend to still be in pain for the sake of a pretty girl's attention.

They were thirteen and fourteen and had just started to realize girls were pretty.

But then they were fourteen and fifteen... and Meyer was no longer in the med-ward bed. He was in the middle of a ring, facing off the biggest dude of his year.

Bridger was already ahead of everyone in his class and spent most of his time training at the army's facilities—he was determined to be the youngest person to complete level ten training, and he was so close he could taste it.

Today he got the night off while his father had meetings outside Fortis. A night off to mingle with kids his own age, and of course it had to be at an unsanctioned fight ring.

If their parents found out...

The crowd gasped at Meyer taking a knee to the chin. Bridger gripped his fists at his sides. "Watch his left foot!" he called to his best friend. He led whatever move he was about to make with it, giving a piece of intel to his opponent if they knew where to watch.

Meyer grew up sparring with Bridger, learning everything he could from the future commander of Tolevarre, but he still lacked some of the obvious skills it took to be on Bridger's level.

If anyone believed Meyer could take this big, burly Fortis-born down, it was Bridger.

Meyer honed in on the bit of shared information, and within two minutes had him pinned.

Cheers came from crowd at Meyer's win. Bridger reached over the ring and popped his fist against Meyer's like they always did. "Nice pacing, but you should have seen that knee move coming from a mile away."

Meyer wiped his brow with his shirt, throwing it over his shoulder as he exited the ring. "Yeah, yeah, I still won."

Bridger chuckled. "Could have left without a bruised chin though."

"Who's next?" someone called from the other side of the room.

A man Bridger had never seen before stepped forward, raising his hand. "Me!" And then before they could leave, the stranger turned and pointed at Bridger. "And I challenge him!"

The crowd went silent as Bridger looked from the tip of the man's finger to his eyes. "Me?" he asked, with a raised brow and the puff of a laugh.

"Yes, you. Or is the commander's son afraid to get his ass kicked?"

Okay, so this man was not only cocky, but stupid.

Bridger rolled his eyes, a smile pulling at the corner of his lips. "I'd like to see you try."

That was the first night Bridger's father set him up, allowing his son to be jumped by four grown men for the sake of "teaching his son to multitask in a fight."

It would become the start of a new grueling training regimen.

And then Bridger and Meyer weren't fourteen and fifteen... They were eighteen and nineteen.

"I'm going to marry that girl," Bridger said as they strolled down the steps of the Aeris estate.

"You met her seven hours ago." Meyer scoffed, slipping into the vehicle taking them back to Fortis.

"So?" Bridger asked, following in behind him.

"Plus, that is *not* the sister your father was introducing you to." Meyer reached under the seat and pulled out a flask, tipping his head back to take a swig.

"My father can manage every single part of my life, but I'll be damned if I let him tell me who I'm allowed to fu—"

"Okay, I get the point," Meyer said, tossing the flask at Bridger. "Rumor has it she's been promised to the dragons."

A cocky smile slid over Bridger's lips before he took a long pull of the too warm liquor. "I didn't see her eyeing the Fera boy all night."

"He's probably already been there, done that," Meyer said with a shrug of his shoulders.

Bridger chucked the flask at Meyer in warning. "Don't talk about her like that."

Meyer fumbled to catch it, eventually getting a good grip before he started to laugh. "Ohhhh, you're fucked."

He joined in his laughter because Meyer had been right.

Bridger was fucked from the moment he met Vega. The second their eyes met, he knew his destiny would be whatever aligned him with her.

He was doomed the day Vega stole his heart.

Bridger continued to dream of the life he'd lived with Meyer by his side, remembering everything there was to know about the best friend Bridger could have ever had.

51

Vega watched as Bridger's chest rose and fell in a steady rhythm. Night had come and gone, and by the clock on the wall, Vega knew the sun had already risen and Vincere would be a buzz of movement outside the bedroom walls.

Unable to sleep, Vega crawled over Bridger, who didn't budge when the mattress shifted. She slid into her boots and closed the bedroom door behind her quietly. When she turned around, she nearly bumped into one of Bridger's soldiers.

"Gods, I'm sorry," she sputtered, glancing over her shoulder. "If you're here for Bridger, he's still sleeping."

The young boy with copper hair shook his head. "No, ma'am."

Well, *that* made her feel old. She held in her comment, reminding herself it was how the people in Bridger's army were taught to show respect to the leaders above them.

"I came for you. Octavia Fera has arrived and asked to talk to you, Khort, and Arlet."

Octavia had sent word late last night that a few of the kids had fallen ill and she'd chosen to let them rest at a safe house until the sun came up.

Vega took the stairs to Bridger's office two at a time, skipping the elevator altogether.

She thrust the door open, colliding with Khort, who circled his niece like a hawk, checking her for any visible injuries. "Are you alright? How are the kids?" He barely noticed Vega had run into him. "Have you heard anything about Delori?"

Tilie curled up by the fireplace, paying no mind to the conversation unfolding.

"I'm fine. The kids are fine. They came down with a flu of some sort. Rest will do them good," she said, nodding. "Marlena locked Aeris down. No one can get in or out. I haven't heard anything from a single shifter."

Arlet leaned against Bridger's desk. "Then how do you know about Aeris?" Vega noticed the way she dragged her eyes up Octavia's dark clothing.

"The shifters are gone, not the Solum-born with bonded animals," she said, motioning to Tilie snoozing by the fire. "I still have contact with Tolevarre's animals."

Vega hadn't spent much time around anyone with the ability to bond an animal. It didn't allow them to communicate with all animals, but they didn't need to when their bonded could do it for them.

"Khort, stop. I'm good." She held her hand out and stopped the manic circling. Octavia glanced at Arlet, her eyes pleading for help.

"Seriously, you need to chill." Arlet reached out and grabbed his wrist, forcing him away from Octavia, who sighed a breath of relief.

"What happened in Ardor?" Octavia asked, worry creasing her forehead.

"Marlena killed General Ignis... Bridger's best friend," Arlet told her, a moment of silence following.

"The animals whispered of Marlena's meltdown when she returned to Aeris... What did you take this time?" Octavia asked quietly.

Her best friends' attention snapped to her. She'd left that part out when filling the two in about what happened leading up to Meyer's death.

"Vega," Arlet said with a shaky breath. "Who?"

"Sorry." Octavia winced.

Vega bit the inside of her lip, drawing out the inevitable. "Venus." The goddess of Amora and of love and beauty.

Arlet went pale.

Khort dropped to the couch behind him.

The room stayed quiet for what felt like an eternity until Arlet broke the silence. "Her original ability is gone?"

"One of them, yes." Vega nodded. She still had her wind...

It was why Marlena retaliated in the way she had—that and because Vega hadn't given her fire back.

Vega hadn't known if she'd even be able to do it when she told Marlena she'd give it back. It was clear the second she touched her the fire wasn't going anywhere—and not because Vega didn't try... but because Vulcan didn't want to.

Death hadn't been happy at the thought of dragging his soul up from the bottom of the pit either.

"Gods damn it." Khort sighed, slumping back against the plush couch and running a hand through his untied shoulder-length hair.

"Did you get any sleep last night?" Arlet asked. "Or are you afraid of the nightmares?" The second question wasn't asked like she wanted to know the answer. Arlet asked like she was testing if Vega would lie to her again. "You think just because we don't get to be inside your head like Bridger, we don't know when you're lying?"

Arlet knew her too well, and so did Khort.

"For all we know, it could have just been a one-time thing." Vega decided to dig herself deeper into the hole she'd jumped in, certainly not ready to reveal all the details she was hiding. "After all, Marlena's favorite power would be the loudest if I were to guess." But that was all it was... a guess.

"And you think the one she perfected at nine won't be worse?" Arlet asked, although no one needed to answer.

Vega knew by her tone she was growing more agitated with Vega and her shenanigans with every passing second. "What other option do I have?" she asked, throwing her hands up and letting them fall back to her sides, smacking her thighs. "I didn't trade my soul for nothing, and I'm done apologizing for it." Vega looked her best friends in the eyes and took a deep breath. "Enough, please. This isn't about saving me. Not anymore. You did that already. You made sure I was here to fulfill this fucked-up destiny. It's about saving our world now. I'm a small price to pay..."

The door to the office swung open, and a blur of dark curls whizzed by. Nora threw herself into Octavia's arms, who held her tightly.

Vega's heart constricted in her chest, and she had to look away. She stared into the fire until Octavia spoke again. "Fortis is next to lock down, followed by Fraus. The people of each territory were told to run while they still could."

Things were about to get so much worse.

"You should get in touch with Quinley, Khort. It's not safe for her to be out anymore," Vega said, reaching for the door handle. "We need to prepare for an influx of arrivals into Vincere and Ardor."

"Where are you going?" Arlet asked, taking a step towards Vega.

"I just need to get some fresh air. Clear my head a little. Don't worry... I'm not going to run away and face Marlena alone." Not yet anyway.

She left the room, passing by a group stumbling down the hall with a bottle of liquor being passed amongst them.

People were celebrating their win at the mines yesterday—time of day no longer mattered when no one was guaranteed to survive the night. People were learning to celebrate now, not save it for later.

While the rebel side of their army celebrated, Bridger's soldiers mourned the loss of their beloved general.

It was easy to tell the groups apart when Vega passed them in the halls or when she walked through the large common area.

The rebels chatted, laughed, and for the first time in Vega had no idea how long, they looked happy.

Bridger's soldiers were somber, drinking alone or in small groups looking as sad as the rest.

The tightening feeling in her chest intensified, turning out to be Death wrapping around her like a warm blanket when a soldier with red-rimmed eyes looked up from her glass of amber liquid.

Something about Vega startled her, and she backed her chair away as Vega passed.

She glanced down to see the veins in her arms clouded with a murky black hue.

Stop that. Vega no longer had to speak the words inside her mind to be heard.

Death grumbled and slowly disappeared.

Vega made it to the top just in time, inhaling a breath of Ardor's hot and dry air to calm her racing heart. She found a tree to sit under, overlooking the outdoor training arena where a group sparred.

Tucking herself into the shadows, Vega rested her head on the trunk of a tall palm tree, its fronds creating the perfect shady spot for her to be alone.

Death seemed to have gotten the hint too, snaking out of her mind and hiding in the pit where Vega could truly get a moment's peace.

With her eyes closed, Vega felt the call of sleep, despite the sun being high in the sky. She barely slept the night before last, spending most of her time wrapped up in Bridger, completely oblivious to what the coming hours would have in store.

Last night, she didn't sleep at all.

The rustle of the tree above her head acted as the soundtrack to a white-noise machine, begging her to let sleep take over. When she felt herself dozing off, whispers of the voices somewhere inside jarred her awake... and not a moment too soon.

A dragon-shaped shadow shot overhead, and for one second, Vega thought Death was outside of her body... until it scurried from the pit and poked its head out.

A tug Vega would know anywhere announced Arlet's arrival. When she appeared, it seemed she came bearing gifts.

Arlet wiggled a bottle of wine in front of Vega. "Do the thing."

Vega smiled, her eyes heavy from nearly falling asleep.

She didn't have to focus hard on popping the cork from the bottle these days. It was as easy as breathing. When she finished, she handed the bottle back to Arlet, who took a swig.

They'd never needed glasses.

Vega took a long drink and wiped her lips with the back of her hand.

"You okay?" Arlet asked, sitting down next to Vega on the ground.

"I don't know," Vega answered honestly.

The copse of trees shook, swaying as Avi settled her head as close as she could to Arlet's leg without crushing her. "She's been a little clingy lately since she's living in the caves alone now."

Avi chuffed a puff of steam at them on a long, tired-sounding breath.

The girls sat in silence for a while, passing the bottle back and forth as the sun slowly moved across the sky.

"Can I ask you something?" Vega looked over at Arlet, arms wrapped around her legs, giving herself a chin rest.

Arlet bobbed her head. "Anything."

Vega didn't know how else to ask this question without it sounding harsh. "Did you actually love Marlena or was it because you were lonely?" It sounded worse coming out, but luckily Arlet hadn't taken offense.

"I loved her," Arlet whispered, her focus on her hands, picking at the hem of her shirt. "But I was also very lonely. You had Bridger, Khort was avoiding you, and Marlena was looking for someone to make her feel something." She glanced at Vega, and a sadness she'd only seen from Arlet twice crossed her face.

When her family left her behind... and the Saturnalia before Marlena's induction.

Oh my gods. Vega had seen it—had been right there during the break-up. Vega hated herself for being so fucking selfish then, for not paying closer attention to the people she claimed to love more than anything.

Arlet's confession felt like a supersonic boom, blowing Vega to tiny pieces. "I'm sorry, Arlet."

"I have never resented you for not being around. Not once. You were in love. I was *happy* for you. I'm happy for you..." Arlet unfolded herself and grabbed Vega's hand. "We've both got to stop apologizing for her. She had a shitty life, yeah, me too. I was born without powers and was completely useless, so much so my family ran and left me behind to be someone else's problem. I made the right decision when I broke up with her." She let go of Vega's hand. "It would have been worse trying to get away after she'd summoned the gods. We both know I wouldn't have actually been able to stop her—even if I had known."

She felt sorry for anyone who had never experienced the type of friendship she had with Arlet—for anyone who would never know the love of true girlhood.

Vega took the last sip of wine and put the empty bottle to the side.

Silence swept over them as they sat side by side, backs against the palm tree. They stayed there for nearly an hour, never saying a word, just enjoying the breeze grazing through the oasis of trees.

"Is Bridger still sleeping?" Arlet asked, breaking the silence.

Vega didn't have to reach down the bond to know. "Yes." It was nearing the twenty-four-hour mark.

"He okay?" Arlet asked quietly.

"No, he lost his best friend," she replied, unable to keep her emotions in check. Her heart was absolutely crushed from what she'd been the cause of.

Meyer's death was Vega's fault—she'd gambled and lost.

She wouldn't be surprised if Bridger woke up, realized it, and immediately turned on her again...

Vega might if she'd lost Arlet.

"It's my biggest fear," Arlet whispered, closing her eyes as she rested the back of her head against the tree. "I spent fifty-five years of my life working to get you back, and now that I have you, I still might lose you."

"I hope you don't have to." And she did... but she couldn't make any promises.

She hadn't let herself break down, to feel everything all at once. Vega knew it was coming, but it wasn't time yet. Not when Bridger needed her to be strong—not when Tolevarre's peaceful fate rode on her back.

She could cry for the life she was being robbed of later.

Vega would never be able to repay Arlet and Khort for all they'd done. The only way that made sense was to make sure they lived to see the world they'd been fighting for.

"I have to be the one to fix this," Vega said, sounding sad despite her best efforts. "I'm the one who begged for her death. I'm the one who brought this upon us." She was the one who summoned—Death hissed, stopping his name from crossing Vega's mind.

"We," Arlet whispered. "We did this."

Vega. Bridger. Arlet. Khort.

Her family, and the only people Vega would face the gates of hell for...

Vega rested her head on Arlet's shoulder, who in turn rested her head against hers and slipped her hand in Vega's. She'd been up since yesterday morning. The sun setting mixed with the calmness from the wine, and she knew she wasn't going to be able to fight off sleep for much longer.

Vega yawned, the sun finally dipping behind the mountains in the distance. They'd lost track of time, and even Avi had drifted to sleep, twitching noticeably because of her size.

With her hand in Arlet's and her shields down, Vega woke Death. It had crept out of the darkness to lounge around the edge, but now, it skipped its usual stretch and slipped through the cracks of Vega's mind to become one with her.

Vega watched as Death traveled down her arm and slowly wrapped around the brand of their wrists.

The bottle of wine they'd shared was all Vega needed to get Arlet relaxed enough for her to poke around like she'd done with Bridger. Her mistake with him was how hyperaware he always was about everything—every sense, every movement.

Vega didn't push Death in quickly, only seeping enough of her power to feel the heartbeat of their bond thrumming along with the beat of her own.

She could tell the difference between Arlet's power, her life, and her soul. There was a familiar darkness around their bond. She'd felt it with Bridger too... had known Death would know how to find it.

As if it was made from the same place Death came from...

Vega called Death back, slowly releasing it inside her mind, where it would eventually stretch out for a nap as Vega and Arlet stayed until the sun was gone.

She couldn't feel guilty for slipping behind Arlet's shields. Vega had to remind herself of the power she was given and what the motivations behind obtaining it had been.

When they went back underground, Vega gave Arlet a hug at the door to her room. The sound of Khort's soft snoring made Vega smile when Arlet opened the door and sighed. "Octavia and Nora might have to share a bed, cause I'm about to go sleep with them instead," she grumbled before slipping inside the room.

Vega was still shocked Khort hadn't demanded to sleep on the floor of his niece's bedroom instead of moving into the open bunk under Arlet now that it was clear Vega wouldn't be returning as a roommate.

Gods, nieces.

Delori was alive.

Meyer wasn't.

Vega and Bridger were back together.

So much had changed and still so much had to.

It's not over.

Bridger was sound asleep when Vega crawled into bed next to him after changing and brushing her teeth. She didn't care that he was covered in blood or smelled of the fire they'd lit to carry Meyer's body to the afterlife. Vega wrapped her arms around his back anyway, keeping him close as she did what she could to fight off sleep.

She lost the fight within minutes, drifting into the blackness of her mind.

It was quiet for a while—peaceful.

Until it wasn't.

Vega startled awake... or at least she'd thought she had, but she wasn't where she was supposed to be. She wasn't in bed next to Bridger.

It was black again. Darkness so deep Vega could feel it in her bones.

"We can see you," a voice Vega instantly recognized crooned.

"All of you," the newest of the voices said.

"Do you want to see us?"

"The fire can help you."

"Or maybe you should disappear."

This time she couldn't hear Death clawing to get to her. She could feel it. The vibration of its irritation rattled her chest.

Vega fought away the fear this time, forcing herself to get off the cold, damp floor and stand tall. "What do you want from me?" she asked, slowly turning in a tight circle despite not being able to see anything.

"*We want you to use us. We need you to save us.*"

"Save you?" Vega practically spit the question at them.

"*Do not let him get us,*" the loudest voice said.

"*It will be over for every god if he does,*" one agreed.

"Who?" she asked, trying to stay calm. Vega called for her lightning, but it wasn't there, and neither were her storms. On the outside of her natural power, she felt the pull of the gods she'd taken from Marlena.

Vulcan—fire.

Diana—shifter.

Venus—invisibility.

Those were the only powers she could feel.

"*You know who.*"

"*Save us. Save you.*"

The feel of a hand on her shoulder made her heart rate spike. "Don't fucking touch me." Another slid down her spine. "Get your hands off me!"

The panic rose, and when it hit, Vega couldn't escape. No matter what she told herself or how she tried to calm herself down, the fear was there to stay.

"*Say my name, Vega.*"

It was a different voice this time. It was his voice now. It was—

"*Tell me who I am. Tell me who saved you.*"

Vega had never been so scared in her entire life, not in any of her lives.

"*Tell me who you belong to.*"

What have I done?

52

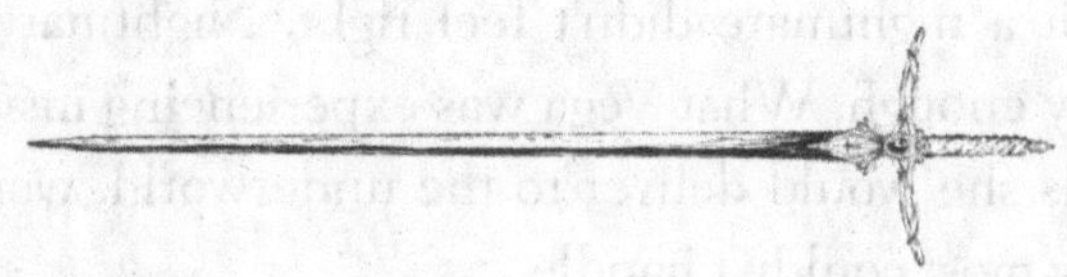

HE'D WOKEN TO THE SMELL OF SMOKE, FOLLOWED BY THE LOUD beep of a fire alarm, but that wasn't what'd pulled him out of his coma-like sleep.

It was Death's claws, dragging him from the depths of his own mind. Bridger nearly broke his neck tripping out of bed to extinguish the small fire glowing in the corner of the room.

Panting, Bridger stomped the fire out. When it was nothing but smoke, he turned around, expecting to see Vega staring at him...

But she wasn't. Her body convulsed instead.

She was stuck inside herself again, but this time she wasn't screaming out for help down their bond.

"It's me. You're okay." Bridger slid a shield over his skin, not wanting to get electrocuted twice this week.

"You're okay," he repeated over and over until Vega came to.

Her eyes opened, and she sank into his chest, her body limp as she concentrated on breathing.

Bridger wrapped her in his arms, pulling her onto his lap seconds before the door shuddered under Khort's terror.

"What's happening, Dimico?" he yelled.

Bridger allowed his power to unlock the door, and Khort and Arlet clamored in, freshly woken from sleep.

Arlet stared blankly. Khort looked around the room, noting the still smoking spot in the corner.

"What happened?" he asked.

"Nightmare," Vega said through chattering teeth.

Calling it a nightmare didn't feel right. Nightmare wasn't big enough, scary enough. What Vega was experiencing inside her head with the gods she would deliver to the underworld, was something Bridger knew most couldn't handle.

Fuck. Fuck! FUCK!

On the inside, Bridger was flipping tables and shredding Vincere to the ground, but on the outside, he barely blinked, keeping Vega against his chest until she signaled to let go.

She clung to him like her life depended on it.

His best friend was dead, and the girl he loved was on her way to losing control—on her way to becoming someone none of them would recognize again.

But this time it would be so much fucking worse.

"I-I ne-nee—" Vega stuttered.

"Get out," he told the others, scooping Vega up as he stood.

"What's happening to her, Bridger?" Khort reached for Bridger's shoulder, but he never made contact.

With nothing but the power of his shields, Bridger shoved Khort across the room and pinned him against the wall. "I said get out!" He hurried to the bathroom and reached into the shower to turn the hot water on, but then looked over his shoulder. "Later."

He slammed the bathroom door in their faces.

Fully clothed, he stepped Vega into the shower.

Somehow, they continued to end up in the shower together... It was mainly used by Bridger as a well-known tactic to calm her down —or bring her back to reality when she needed it.

"Bri-dg-g-er." She shivered against his chest. "I-I'm f-f-fi-ine."

"No, you're freezing." He held her under the water, desperate to warm her up.

"So h-hot inside."

The fire.

The fucking fire.

"You used the fire," he said, his voice sounding like a ghost. The flame that burned in the corner had been blue.

In his waking panic, the color hadn't registered until now.

Just like the one in his office had been the day they arrived to Vincere. He'd thought she used her lightning to spark a flame...

"N-no." A chill ran through her, racking her body against Bridger's hold.

"Yes, you did." He sighed, noticing the pink water around his feet from the blood washing clean of his uniform.

Meyer's blood.

It took everything inside him to concentrate on what Vega was saying, his mind drifting to the memory of Meyer's heart being ripped from his chest.

He couldn't stop thinking, *I won't let it be her blood next.*

"You lit a fire in your sleep." Bridger finally snapped back into himself.

They were quiet for a while, Vega mulling over the information he'd dropped. She finally stopped shivering. "I think you can put me down now."

He examined her quickly and tipped his arms forward, letting her step out of his hold. She staggered a bit but reached out for Bridger to steady herself.

"I didn't mean to. I kept pushing them away... I never..." She switched from speaking out loud to finishing the sentence inside. *"I never reached for it."* Vega glanced up at him with a fear he'd never seen from her before.

It nearly ripped his heart out.

Bridger leaned down to kiss her temple as she slid back into his arms. "It's okay. You're gonna be okay." He was going to make sure of it. He'd already left his mark on her in this world.

He grabbed her hand with the ring and kissed each finger, lingering over the sparkling jewel a moment longer than the others.

They stripped off their clothes and showered. Bridger stayed quiet, listening to Vega talk about what she'd seen this time.

"He was there this time." The words struck him through the chest, making the water feel like icicles as it peppered his skin. "He told me to say his name... to remember who'd saved me. Who *owns* me..."

Bridger felt like he was floating. "Don't." He paused, making sure Vega understood how serious he was. "Not yet." Bridger couldn't fucking lose Vega. He wouldn't let anyone take her from him again.

No matter who or what they were.

After helping Vega wash and condition her hair, Bridger gave her a soft kiss, caressing her cheek before leaning in for one more. "Finish up. I have a few things I need to get done today."

"Bridger, are you—"

He cut her off, knowing what she was about to ask. "No, baby. No. I'm not, but I will be." He rubbed his thumb over her bottom lip and retreated. *"We will be."*

He hoped she would go back to sleep or at least try to relax, but Bridger knew her better than that.

She'd avoid sleep for as long as she could.

In a fresh uniform, Bridger ripped the commander's cape off and threw it in the waste bin by his desk. He hadn't wanted to wear the stupid thing in the first place—but he had for the sake of looking the part.

Bridger was so fucking sick of pretending.

The door to Khort and Arlet's room opened before Bridger had the chance to knock. "My office. Now."

"Bridger, what you're saying is insane." Arlet shook her head.

Khort hadn't said anything, only looked through the information Bridger pulled up from the digital archives.

Bridger hadn't expected the detailed documents when he looked into Meyer's files. There was so much he'd gathered in only a few days' time.

"Yes, it is... but I don't think it's impossible." Bridger crossed his arms, leaning back in his office chair.

Bridger told them everything. About the gods inside Vega and about what they were saying. About Death coming to wake him... twice. He'd made a promise not to lie to Vega anymore, they all had, but if the lie somehow saved her soul, Bridger would gladly take her wrath and whatever consequence came with it.

"I..." Arlet let her words fall. "Vega wouldn't like this."

"You know what I don't like? Vega convincing herself to believe any of us would want to live in a world where she doesn't exist." Bridger fiddled with the pen in his hand, spinning it between his fingers like he would a dagger. "I've lived in a world without her. I'm not keen on returning to one."

"Why are you telling us?" Khort asked.

"I know you'll take care of Vega if I don't make it." To the point. It was the only way Bridger could be about this. "And because someone has to lead the army while I'm gone..." It should have been Meyer.

But Khort would do right by Tolevarre, and it was Bridger's duty to ensure their realm was handed down to someone who would protect it like he did.

A knock on the door had them staring at one another in silence until the door opened and Halo slipped in. "Commander, you have visitors. They said Meyer sent for them."

Had it already been four days? Bridger had almost forgotten.

Halo stepped to the side, and an acolyte dressed in an emerald-green robe followed him in. Her inky-black hair and obsidian eyes found Bridger's.

Her smile was soft as she pulled the hood from her head, bowing as a way of respect... and not because Bridger was the commander. "Bridger Dimico. I wondered when you were going to come asking about this."

Meyer had reached out to the girl who'd devoted herself to the gods instead of a man—instead of him.

Summer Laudo.

Meyer, you fucking genius.

The would-have-been heir to Oro's Curia seat if it weren't for Marlena—the strongest light-wielder left and the only person Bridger would ever consider trusting with something of this magnitude.

"I'm sorry to hear about Meyer's death. He made it, in case you were wondering."

53

Going back to sleep hadn't been an option, not after she'd gotten out of the shower to find the burn mark she'd left on the floor.

Vega had used the fire in her sleep... and she hadn't known it.

She took a right hook to the jaw, and her vision scattered with stars.

Leo winced, charging towards her with hands outstretched. "I'm so sorry, oh my gods."

Vega had begged him to spar with her, specifically in the fancy ring where they could use their powers. Leo had hesitated, finally giving in when she promised to warm up with him in the sparring mat first.

She was desperate to see what someone else using fire near her would feel like.

Would she crave it?

Why didn't she feel the need to reach for the shifting power when she was around Khort? Or the invisibility when someone from Amora was around?

Why was Vulcan the loudest?

Death was agitated, pacing in a giant circle inside her mind, disagreeing with Vega's attempt to test this out.

Vega couldn't get out of her head, couldn't get herself to focus on what she was doing.

Meyer's death.

The anticipation of feeling someone else's fire.

Hearing *him* again...

Vega rubbed her jaw, flexing it open and closed. "Fuck." She held her hand out, stopping Leo. "It's fine. I'm fine."

"I don't want to do this anymore," he said with a sigh.

"Why? Because you hit me? I've been hit harder." Vega tried to reassure him.

He squinted his eyes, mouth opening a few seconds before he said anything. "I don't know what I hate worse. Hitting you and knowing Bridger might kill me if he finds out or the fact that you told me I hit like a wimp."

Oh, now he's worried about Bridger killing him?

Vega rolled her eyes, the pain in her jaw almost gone completely. "I didn't say that, and Bridger won't get mad. We're training."

"Uh-huh, sure." Leo went to grab his things, but Vega blocked him from his bag in the corner. "What are you doing?"

"What are *you* doing?" she retorted.

"We're done for the day." He stared at her with serious eyes, the crimson flecks in them catching Vega's attention as they usually did.

"No, we aren't. You're going in the big ring with me," Vega told him, pointing across the room, where a few people from the mines trained. "Leo, please." She stuck out her bottom lip, slouching her shoulders.

"Not gonna work, Princess," he responded with a sly grin and a boop to the nose. Vega swatted his hand away. "I bet you can con one of them into fighting you. I'm sure they'd love to land a blow to Marlena's sister."

Even the mention of her name made Vega pause, reeling her back into her mind with all its questions.

Another that kept popping up was, *Is this what Marlena feels? The power?*

Death growled, its shadows melting from the dragon form, reaching for Vega.

Her lightning sprang to life, zapping it back in shape. It bared its teeth, snapping.

I have to know. It wasn't Death who wanted others' powers. How much control did the gods have over her?

Vega huffed a breath, grumbling as he walked away. With Leo gone, she slipped out of the current ring and made her way to the group of freed miners waiting for their turn on the big mat.

A blonde girl who couldn't have been more than sixteen or seventeen turned, eyes lighting with excitement when they landed on Vega.

Vega waved politely at the group, introducing herself as she always did. "How are you all settling in?" Really, she did hope they were feeling at home here in Vincere, but her current motivations weren't for the sake of being welcoming.

The young girl with the bouncy blonde bob answered. "This place is insane. I've never seen anything like it in my life." Her hair fluttered over her cheek as she looked at the people around her.

Most of them were fire-wielders. Vega knew without having to ask. She could *feel* it. That should be enough to answer her question... but it wasn't.

"We can't thank you enough for—"

Vega shook her head with a polite smile. "Please, don't thank me. I wish I could apologize for what my sister put you all through, but it won't change anything." She had spent too much time apologizing for Marlena. Vega couldn't do it any longer.

The girl, to Vega's surprise, laughed. "I mean, I burned down my community viewing center... I knew what would happen to me even before doing it."

"You were fourteen, Ro. The mines weren't a place for children," Helena said, making her presence known as she walked up from behind Vega.

Ro shrugged her shoulders. "I took a stance, and Marlena didn't like it. You're lucky she didn't come after you as punishment."

Vega noticed the resemblance then. Their flawless dark-olive skin, the slight uptilt in their noses. If they weren't sisters, they had to be related closely somewhere else in their lineage.

"I was untouchable in my position," Helena said with a smile.

What she meant by that, Vega didn't care.

"I got lucky. I was the youngest there, and people felt bad. It wasn't all that awful... for me, at least." Ro smiled at Vega, like she was trying to impress her.

Helena changed the subject without warning. "Leo mentioned you're looking for a fire-wielder who isn't afraid of Bridger's backlash." Vega wasn't a jealous person, per se, but the way she purred his name made her consider letting Death have some fun with her.

"Don't let her get to you." It was the first time they'd spoken since he'd left the bathroom this morning.

Vega could feel his presence in the room but couldn't see him from where she stood. "I guess you could say that," Vega told her. "I suppose that's you, huh?"

Helena pulled her hair into a tight high pony. "If you're up for a challenge, yes."

Bridger's breathy laugh rose the hair on her arms as he approached from behind. "I wouldn't be so cocky."

Vega might have been gone for fifty-five years, but she wasn't without her memories anymore. It was like riding a bike, coming back to her powers and skills. Her body wasn't a weak little thing anymore—no, this version of her was deadlier than any of the others combined.

Even though Death had been scolded, it still flicked its tail of shadows in wait.

Vega had learned one thing since they'd returned to Tolevarre. Death would protect her like nothing else ever had, not even herself.

"God or not, you can still be outsmarted in combat." Helena crossed her arms and popped her hip.

Ro spoke through the side of her mouth. "Helena." She drew out her name, eyes nervously bouncing between her and Vega.

"You're not wrong." Vega wasn't scared of Helena—no, she was too afraid of herself these days to worry about anyone else.

Bridger gently grabbed Vega by the forearm before she could head for the ring. "She'll be there in five minutes."

Vega looked down at his hand first and then met his eyes. He looked exhausted despite sleeping for over an entire day. He pulled her to the side, still within eavesdropping distance of the group.

A sound shield wrapped around them, to no one's surprise. "Is everything okay?" Vega asked, eyebrows knitting together.

"Yeah." He pulled her against him. The sound shield didn't hide them from view, allowing the entire room to see this moment. Though most were trying to make it look like they weren't watching...

Seeing Bridger and Vega back together was probably something no one had ever expected to see. Fuck, it was something Vega had never expected to see.

She breathed in his familiar scent, letting it calm her racing heart as he slipped his arms around her. "I've got to head to the mines for a bit, look around and see if I can find a list of names for who was there. The paperwork Khort brought back only accounts for half the bodies we brought in." Bridger ran his hands up and down her arms, like he was soothing her—or maybe it was himself he was trying to comfort? "I just wanted to say goodbye before I left."

Vega tilted her head back, his hand moving up the length of her body to settle on the back of her neck. "I can come with you." She hummed at his soft touch.

"No." Bridger's hand slid from the back of her neck to cup her cheek, his thumb tracing the outline of her chin. "Go kick Helena's ass and show everyone what happens when they underestimate you."

"You'll be back tonight?" she asked, a sense of worry creeping into her chest.

"Before you know it," he replied, leaning in and kissing her like it was the last one they'd ever have. Bridger didn't hold back. He didn't care about the eyes on them. His kiss made Vega weak in the knees.

When he pulled away, Vega was almost gasping for air. Had she forgotten to breathe?

Even Death purred, the sound too clicky to be feline.

"I love you." He placed a small kiss on the tip of her nose and let her go, stepping away as he let the sound shield fall.

Something's not right. Her gut twisted, and Death stilled.

Vega usually regretted it when she didn't follow her intuition, but she reminded herself Bridger had just lost his best friend. The fact he was out of bed and trying to go about his normal life this soon after was a feat Vega wasn't sure she'd be able to do if she'd lost Arlet.

"I'll be back as soon as I can, okay?"

Vega nodded, watching him go. Halo stepped out of the shadows, unfolding his arms as his frosty-green eyes met hers.

"You coming or what, Caelum?" Helena called, waiting for her in the ring.

Halo followed Bridger out of the training center, disappearing behind the closing doors.

With Bridger out of sight, Vega turned and reached for the doorway between their minds. It was open.

That settled Vega enough for her to ground her powers and step into the ring, rolling her shoulders and wiggling her fingers. Her lightning hissed to life in her hands, ready to play.

Someone from the outside hit the button, and the shield traveled from the floor to the ceiling, locking into place.

Helena's bright orange flame sparked to life, fire creeping from the palm of her hand. She reached out for a handshake, fire sliding to her wrist. Her perfectly straight teeth made her smile sparkle, but Vega knew better than to trust a friendly mask.

Death turned the tips of Vega's fingers black as she reached out, her lightning copying Helena's flames, wrapping around her wrist too.

Helena's cocky confidence fell when her eyes flicked to Vega's fingertips. It only took a half-second for Helena to look back up, but everything had changed in her stare.

Vega grabbed her hand before she could pull away, only letting Death nip at her palm as a warning.

Helena jumped back, snatching her hand from Vega's. She flicked her wrist like a match, sending her flame back to her palm.

Vega answered with her wind, sending Helena tumbling. She was back on her feet in seconds, wrapped up in the clouds Vega pulled from thin air.

The ring fed abilities, allowing everyone an equal opportunity.

Vega couldn't see Helena through the fluffy vapor of her clouds, but she could *feel* her. It should have been because her clouds parted around Helena's body, making space for her as she passed through.

But that wasn't why Vega could feel her.

A warmth so unlike the electricity she was used to spiked somewhere inside her mind.

A fireball flew past Vega's head, inches from colliding directly with her face. A buzz of need grazed the side of her cheek as it whizzed by.

Seconds. That was how long it took for Vega to realize her body craved the new power she was suppressing.

She could have stopped the fight right away. Sent down a torrent of rain to drown out Helena's power.

Fire-wielders were strong, and some of them, like Meyer and Leo, could still work with their flames in most storms... but Vega could create more than what most storms were capable of.

If she wanted to asphyxiate Helena's power, she could. Something—*someone* in her wanted more.

The rush in her head almost completely drowned out Death's voiceless begging for her to stop.

Helena stepped through the clouds, making them glow with orange. Another flame flew past Vega's head, but she noticed the way Helena's eyes gave away her next move.

She looks where she's going to strike.

Watching where her eyes landed, a bolt of her lightning struck Helena, making her screech with pain. Her body seized, and by the time she hit the floor, she was already coming to, an animalistic snarl rupturing in her chest as she picked herself up.

"Fuck you," she growled, throwing another ball of flames as she hurtled herself towards Vega.

Vega unsheathed the dagger strapped at her thigh, slicing a line down the side of Helena's training suit, her only intention to make the surface cut sting for a second.

"I thought you were going to give me a challenge?" Vega tapped over her mouth as she fake yawned, flipping the dagger in her other hand before returning it to its sheath. Her thunder rumbled the shield, vibrating like glass in the wake of a storm.

Vega wanted to get her hands on Helena—to see if the god inside her would react.

She intentionally slowed her reaction time, letting Helena believe she'd let her guard down. Vega rolled into a somersault, reaching out at the right time and wrapping her fingers around Helena's ankle.

Heat soared up her arm and through her chest.

Helena's scream pierced Vega's ears.

Death roared so loud she was sure everyone outside her head could hear it too.

The gods hissed, pouring through her mental shields like feral beasts. Vega had to pry her hand off Helena's leg, but that didn't stop them.

Their wails kept coming, kept getting louder.

"Stop him."

"Stop him."

"STOP HIM!"

Vega cried out in pain, her screams echoing inside the ring's enclosure and her head. Her lonely, empty head.

Death was gone, a sliver of shadow disappearing behind Bridger's now closed door.

Stop who?

She shrieked again, barely noticing the shield of the training ring fall. Helena fought through pain of her own, on her hands and knees, panting for air.

People flooded around, but no one came too close to Vega, all checking on Helena instead.

They were afraid—they were afraid of Vega.

"Stop him."

"Stop who?!" Vega shouted out loud, drowning in pain.

Where are you? Vega reached for Death. She felt hollow and alone for the first time since returning home.

The people inside the ring stared, and Ro helped Helena to her feet.

Helena's voice sounded raw. "Someone find Khort or Arlet." She choked. "Now!"

Vega had no idea how long passed before Khort was beside her, hands on her cheeks as he tried to search her face for an answer. "What happened?"

Vega couldn't focus over the screeching in her head.

"Your bonded soul."

"Stop him!"

"Bridger," she said on a breath. "Where's Bridger?" She reached for him, but the doorway was closed. Sealed off completely with no chance of sneaking through.

Khort paused for too long. "What?"

His hesitation was the answer Vega needed. He knew.

Vega had known something was wrong... just five, ten minutes ago—*fuck*, how much time had passed?

She grabbed Khort by the collar of his shirt, shaking him wildly. "Where the fuck is Bridger?"

He didn't answer, sending Vega into an all-out frenzy. "Khort, please. Please! Where is he? What is he doing?"

She begged for Bridger to open the door, pulling at the handle with all she had.

Not being able to lean on Death, to have it there beside her in a moment like this—oh gods, Vega hated it.

"We'll never make it in time to stop him," Khort finally answered.

"To stop him from what?" she screeched, her world coming to a tumbling halt when she realized what Khort meant.

He couldn't. *He wouldn't.*

No. Oh no. *"Bridger, no! Stop!"* But he couldn't hear her, no matter how loudly she screamed.

54

Marlena gripped her head, falling off her office chair onto the floor.

"Stop him!"

"Find him!"

"He cannot go through with it!"

The voices in her head—the gods—screamed, their panicked cries sending a roll of nausea through Marlena's stomach.

"Who?" she asked through gritted teeth, swallowing down bile.

This had never happened before.

Marlena couldn't grasp on to any of her powers, couldn't quiet the screams and pure fear raging inside her head. It wasn't her fear she was feeling, she finally realized.

It was the gods'.

What would scare the gods so badly?

"Stop him!"

"Stop him!"

Marlena hissed, stumbling at the pain shooting through her mind.

"Stop who?!" she screamed, her throat sore.

"*Him. Him. Him.*"

Marlena had no idea what they were saying, but she couldn't push them away, couldn't get her mind to be her own again.

"*The mines.*"

"*He'll answer the summon in the mines.*"

"*It's as close as you can get to his throne.*"

"Who is summoning? What... summoning?" She had a hard time finding words.

Marlena crawled, trying to use her power to travel—to take herself right to the mines to find out for herself, but the pain kept her pinned to the floor, sinking its teeth in.

"*He wants us. He'll take us. All of us!*"

"What does that even fucking mean?!" Marlena screeched in a mix of pain and anger.

"*Go to him. Stop him!*"

Marlena couldn't tell the voices apart.

55

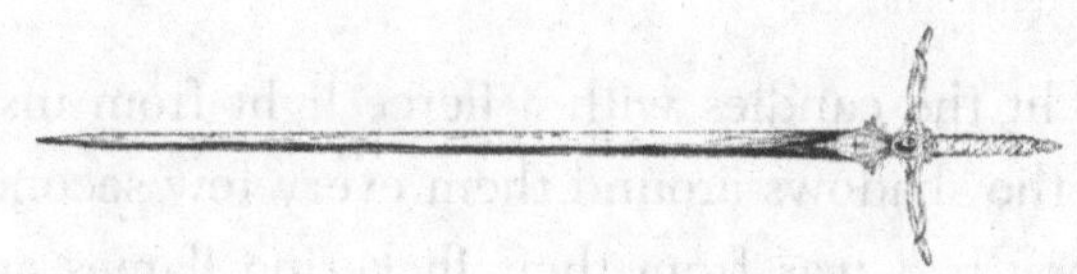

"Do you trust me?" Halo, with his pale-green eyes and ice-blond hair, was the second person Bridger had asked that question to in less than a month.

There was only a second of hesitation. "With my life."

Bridger swallowed hard, pushing what was left of the nerves as Summer set up the black candles around them. "When I tell you to jump, you jump, okay?"

He expected Halo to ask him why. But he didn't. He simply nodded, keeping his eyes locked on Bridger's. "Okay."

The leather book he'd spent the last few days studying had information he wasn't sure anyone else had ever seen—it went into detail about how gods bound themselves together as one, through acts of love or by other means. It answered questions Bridger hadn't even known he had.

Summer might have a plan, but so did he.

I will not die. Bridger would not damn the others for his decision.

He'd let the god of the underworld take him on one condition. He'd damn himself for all eternity *on one condition.*

Vega lives.

The heat of the mines had sweat rolling down everyone's brows and cheeks. This was as close as they could get to hell itself. Plenty of lives had been lost here, making it a graveyard in its own right.

Death surrounded them.

Bridger could *feel* it slithering through the cracks of his closed door.

Summer lit the candles with a fierce light from inside herself, illuminating the shadows around them every few seconds until the only light they had was from their flickering flames and the dull sconces lining the walls.

The shadows seemed to melt back into their places, making themselves at home where they belonged.

Summer had brought a young acolyte to assist her, and she approached Bridger, careful not to cross the candle's circle. She extended her hand to the edge, holding a worn-out booklet. "Some prayers in case you need them."

Bridger looked at the page she had open.

"Are you ready?" Summer asked, glancing at Bridger and then to Halo, her eyes asking what she didn't need to say out loud.

"We don't have a portal, but we have the next best thing to bridge the gap between our world and his." Bridger spoke loud enough for Halo to hear, giving him the opportunity to change his mind.

He said nothing, peeking over Bridger's shoulder at the book in the acolyte's hands.

Everyone in Halo's life had failed him. His parents. His peers. The people who were supposed to look out for him had never given a shit.

Fraus-born, but his heart was pure. He wanted to belong somewhere.

Bridger wouldn't fail him. He would give him a place to belong.

"Do you know Latin?" he asked, glancing back at Halo, who looked up from the open page.

"Not a lick," Halo responded with his goofy smile.

Bridger declined to take the old prayers from the acolyte. "I won't be needing it then."

The young girl butted in. "I really do suggest—"

"I'm a Dimico, the original bloodline of Mars. I've known the death prayers since before I could wield a sword." He felt a shiver of something slide down his spine, a purr of a shadow caressing his mind.

It was murky, but the feeling was unmistakable.

"You're ready." This time, it wasn't a question. Summer took a step back and turned to the acolyte with the doe eyes. "It's time for you to take shelter. No matter what you may hear, you stay away until I come for you." Summer knew the nature of the god they were about to call on—she might be the only one to ever exist in this realm who did. "Remember, the shadows are not your friends. Find light."

The girl scampered away, finding a well-lit area to hide. Once out of sight and they could no longer hear her footsteps, Summer inhaled a breath and sank to her knees. She feathered her hand over the hot earth, digging her nails into the dirt.

A shadow slithered from the newly made mark in the ground. It chased the light on her fingertips, slithering through her fingers until her whole palm was a mix of glimmer and shadows. It was mesmerizing to witness.

Bridger followed the line of shadows shooting from beside Summer, encircling around him and Halo. They settled against the ground, locking into place when they connected with the candles and light Summer used to set the wick ablaze.

The familiar shadow in his mind recognized the ones slithering around his feet like serpents.

Eyes closed, hands digging into the hardpacked dirt again,

Summer's face fell forward, her umbra-like hair blanketing around her as a shield when she began to speak in what might have been the most fluent Latin Bridger had ever heard.

"Divine Pluto, King of The Underworld, God of the Dead, I call to you, I do you reverence. I ask that you might answer Bridger, a new god of Tolevarre, our god of wrath's call. May you know the sincerity of my request from the soul I have given to you, my soul you own. Hear his plea, accept him into your world, let him walk through your gates."

A rumble Bridger knew like the thunder of his own anger shook the ground below.

"He's here," Summer gasped, shadows weaving through her now splayed palms.

Bridger's breath rattled in his chest as he closed his eyes and inhaled. The power pulling at him from the ground, sliding up his legs with little tendrils of shadows, was intoxicating.

Oh gods. The need to make that power his almost made him drop to his knees like Summer.

"Her. Not him." The voice was feminine and jagged, echoing inside his mind. He knew the voice, even though it had never talked to him before.

He understood. *I get on my knees for no one but the goddess of death.* Bridger forced his eyes open, letting loose a shaky breath.

Honesty hadn't gotten Bridger here—lies and deceit had. He'd painted pretty pictures, forcing those around him to believe he only wanted to travel to the underworld. He hadn't needed the book of death prayers... because Bridger wouldn't pray for death.

Death was already with him, and he'd bound himself to her, to Vega, to Death, with a ring and a prayer.

To save Vega, Bridger had to do more. He had to *become* more.

"A challenge for my throne?" A deep voice beat down the door to his mind, leaving it open and accessible to all who could enter.

Gods, how had he not realized who'd spoken to him inside the portal to Earth immediately? It was unmistakable.

With the door removed from its hinges, Vega's pleas echoed down to him—*She knows.*

"No!" Bridger bellowed out loud, slamming a shield up, pulling from the power he felt below him.

The shadow in his mind took form, wrapping around his mental shield and closing it tightly. Death kept Vega out.

It protected her.

"She is who you fight for, but she belongs to me." Pluto's voice was as smooth as the shadows swarming Bridger. *"She's belonged to me for a very long time."* His whisper made Death roar. *"And so have the rest of you, Bridger Dimico. Bonded. By the god of the dead. Until she traded her soul for yours. She saved you this time."*

"Where's Remus?" Bridger growled, reaching for his bonded dagger.

"Dead. Since the day he crossed me. Like you're about to be, God of Wrath." Shadows shot out of the room, searching for who Bridger already knew was here. *"I see Death is there with you already, the little traitor. Watch that one. She bites."*

The blare of Death's growl felt like his own wrath pouring through his body.

Bridger flung his dagger out of the circle, severing the band of shadows not linked to the ones of Death. *"They are not part of this. None of them. I challenge alone."*

From the end of the long tunnel, Vega came into view, sweat making her face glisten. She eyed the shadows around her feet, a tendril of lightning flickering to life in her hand.

Bridger could have sworn he heard the shadows sigh as they mixed with the lightning trickling from her fingertips.

Death vibrated with happiness inside his mind, sending a message to Vega.

"No," she whispered. The look in her eyes almost made Bridger pause—but it was too late to turn back.

Arlet and Khort came barreling after Vega. She'd beaten them by almost half a minute, running with everything she had, pushing to whatever limit she could get to in her mind.

To stop him.

Vega took her first step towards him, and with a power he'd never known, Bridger brought a dome of shadows up from the ground, snatching them from Vega's lightning to seal himself and Halo inside a shield of darkness.

The shadows fell, letting what little light they had in, but the shield held strong.

Vega stood outside, her open palms resting against the new forcefield. "Bridger," she choked, tears streaming down her cheeks one after the other after the other. "What have you done?"

"I'm finding a way to save you." Bridger took a step forward, the shadow-made shield separating their hands from touching when he rested his on the other side. "You belong to no one, Vega Caelum."

"I know what you want if you win, but what do I get if you lose?" Pluto rumbled back. *"I've already promised your soul remains safe, but if it's you who barters... Who am I to decline?"*

Every power inside Bridger intensified. *"An eternity of service from the strongest warrior our kind has ever seen. Stronger than Mars ever was. Imagine the realms we could conquer."*

"No, no. Don't," Vega pleaded. Arlet put her hand on Vega's shoulder, offering her comfort. Vega shoved Arlet off, throwing her into Khort.

Bridger eyed Arlet and Khort. "Focus on the war. Don't let her come after me."

Summer rose from the ground, spots from her knees in the dirt staining her cloak. She made an attempt to approach Vega, to explain.

Vega didn't let her get close. Her lightning pushed everyone away like an electric bubble, closing her into a shield of her own.

Pluto finally responded. *"I need a soul. As payment for crossing into the underworld."*

"Look at me, Bridger. Look at me," Vega sobbed.

If he did, he knew what he'd see. Vega's heartbreak.

It took everything inside him to drag his gaze down to hers. Vega's eyes were bluer than he'd ever seen them, glowing like her lightning against the shadows interlocking with the electric shield.

"You can't leave me. You can't. You said no more goodbyes." Her sobs hurt him, physically twisting his heart into a knot.

"I have to, baby," he whispered, feeling her heart shatter along with his words. His hand fell from the shield.

"Why hide in the underworld when I have an offering who'd let us go anywhere?" Bridger asked down the newest bond crowding his head.

Death reached for Halo, sliding around Bridger's thigh, and pouring off his boot. Its shiver of approval electrified Bridger's senses like a zap from Vega's own touch.

"It is done," Summer murmured, drawing Vega's attention for only a second. "He accepts."

"You," a voice growled before coming into full view. Marlena, with fresh blood stains dripping from her ears, stepped out of a cloud of smoke.

She charged Vega, no, charged *him*.

Marlena never made it, getting wrapped up in a vision of Arlet's making—no, no, it wasn't Arlet's power. It was the shadows.

Everything blended together. The murkiness in his head clouded all the details.

"You don't know what you're doing, Bridger! You'll damn us all!" Marlena screamed, getting turned around inside the maze of shadows keeping her from getting to anyone.

"I just got you back. You can't leave me." Vega let out another sob. "I *need* you. I love you."

Her words pulled the thread around Bridger's heart, locking it in place.

I love you.

"You said it," he marveled.

Death slipped through her electric field, sliding along Vega's cheek like the caress of Bridger's hand.

Vega's mouth parted with a gasp.

He'd wanted to do it, wanted to reach through and touch her beautiful face one more time. *Just in case.*

Instead, Death acted as an extension of his wishes.

"Tell me something real." Vega fell to her knees, losing to the quivering muscles in her legs. "Don't leave me with nothing." She knew it was over—knew Bridger wasn't going to change his mind.

Pluto's shadows tugged at Bridger's ankles, beckoning him down. *"It is time,"* he summoned.

Bridger crouched down, his boots grinding against the dirt and stones. The shadows lifted her chin delicately, raising her gaze to his. "I will never stop fighting for you. Not in this life or any that follow. My love for you is stronger than any darkness this realm can create. Me and you, forever." They were the same words he'd spoken to her the day he'd given her the ring shimmering on her finger. "Not even the underworld can keep me from you."

Bridger stood, staring down at Vega, whose tears started to turn into sniffles of acceptance. "You're needed here. Do what you set out to do, and don't lose sight of it. I'll be back for you, my Goddess of Death."

It was his promise.

He would save Vega.

Emerald lightning flashed, traveling across an unseen current. Its crack of power shifted the ground underneath them, debris from the mine's ceiling raining down.

Vega sat on her knees, eyes void of the happiness he'd seen returning in pieces. In its place, black, soulless eyes stared up at him.

Vega's veins pumped Death into her bloodstream, inking her with what looked like black lightning spidering up her arms.

Bridger took a step back, centering himself in the middle of the circle out of necessity and pure shock.

Death had touched Bridger... but it belonged to Vega. Its presence no longer lingered inside his mind.

Bridger looked over his shoulder, checking on Halo.

He stared, eyes wide with fear, frantic for an answer. "I'm your sacrifice." It wasn't a question, so Bridger said nothing and watched as the shadows traveled up Halo's shoulder and whispered a confirmation into his ear.

Bridger turned back in time to catch Summer's laugh, the sound too happy for what was unfolding. "Will I have a new god to worship? Or will I fight beside you when he takes over every world?"

No one heard her question, not over the sound of Marlena's fizzling electricity traveling towards Vega, no longer trapped.

Bridger opened his mouth to warn her, but Pluto's shadows shot down his throat, filling his lungs with the taste of the dead. It seeped through his insides, into his bloodstream, tying itself to his soul.

Vega's lightning consumed Marlena's, mixing from her bright blue to turquoise before making its way back to Vega in her natural color.

The gut-wrenching scream ripping from Marlena's chest got caught in her throat as Vega rose from the ground.

My Vega.

If she can rise from the ashes of her curse, I can face the embers of the underworld for her.

"*Come to me,*" the voice of his future called.

The shadows returned his dagger, placing it inside his right hand with the exact placement he would have chosen for himself.

These shadows were not Death... They were something else entirely.

Vega's tearstained face transformed as she ripped another god from Marlena without laying a finger on her. She sank deeper into the depths of her internal hell, sacrificing another piece of herself.

There was no more time to waste. He lifted his arm and spun around. "Jump."

Bridger's dagger sank into Halo's heart at the same time they became one with the shadows.

- graphic descriptions of killing
- death & gore
- manipulation & torture
- mentions of sexual abuse (off page, vague without details)
- physical abuse from a spouse (not the MMC)
- imprisonment
- mention of off page drug use, smoking marijuana on page
- panic attacks
- mentions of suicide

If there is a theme you are looking to avoid and it is not listed, or you think I should add one to this list, please reach out on my website and myself or someone from my team will respond as quickly as possible!

Acknowledgments

It'll always take a village to get these books from brain to page. This is my village in a short n' sweet way.

Josh, for loving me when it's hard to do it myself.

Mom, for everything.

Mollie & Kristen, for the sisterhood we have. Oh, and thanks for being funny enough to use our jokes in mine and Mol's books. Is someone keeping track?

Jen, for hyping me up when I was ready to delete the whole manuscript.

SBP, for being my reason to leave the house.

My Alpha & Beta teams, Tay H., Kristen O., Jen B., Haley C., Kait G. This book wouldn't be what it is without your early eyes.

Katie Wolf, my editor. Thank you for pushing me to be a better writer and storyteller.

Maria Spada, for yet another cover we can all drool over.

And as always, I save the best for last. My readers. Because if it weren't for you, my stories would be nothing but a dream inside my head.

ABOUT THE AUTHOR

Dany is an adult romantasy author currently living in southwest Michigan with her husband and four fur babies. Revenge of the Forgotten was her debut, introducing the world to Tolevarre and the bonded. Whenever she's not stuck in a fictional world, she enjoys traveling, diving into books that make her cry, and belting songs anywhere she goes like it's her own concert. She's known for her mid-scene cliffhangers and emotional twists with a side of comedy to lighten the blow.

INSTAGRAM: @DANYCROOKSAUTHOR
WEBSITE: WWW.DANYCROOKS.COM

Also by Dany Crooks